MW01383680

If a Tree Falls

A Love Song Comes True

Kathleen Kifer

Dedication

To the members of the Lewiston Writers Group
for unwavering support and guidance

and

To Norah for editing, nurturing and believing in me

TABLE OF CONTENTS

Chapter 1
Behind the Window

Late July, 1985

It was time. Time to take the first step into a new life. It wasn't her choice, but circumstances had scoffed at her carefully made choices and knocked them off the table, scattering her plans like so much junk mail. That had happened six long, painful months ago. It was time to find a new plan to fill her empty future, even if it meant taking a chance at something she'd never thought she would do.

Amanda Morgan braked her white Mustang convertible and checked the address that was spelled out on the mailbox: *Sixteen Meadowlark Lane.* As the woman on the phone had directed, she found herself in front of a charming, two-story white cottage with black shutters marked "Carriage House". It had been easy to locate, eliminating the first concern about her job interview, but as she turned off the road and drove slowly up the long driveway toward the sprawling, Victorian style house, she was seized with an acute case of the jitters.

Why are you so nervous? she scolded herself. In the past, as a secretary, she'd been more confident applying for much more difficult and demanding positions than that of "babysitter". So what was the problem now?

The problem, she admitted as she made a final appraisal of herself in the rearview mirror, was that in her brief twenty-six years, she'd never done anything but office work. And as much as she loved children and had often babysat for neighbors, what exactly did you do with a child *all day*? If he became troublesome, you certainly couldn't file him away somewhere – even if you wanted to. Yet, she had firmly decided, it was time to step away from the stagnant familiarities of her secretarial career and try something new. And while she'd told herself this was strictly about the challenge, somewhere inside she knew she needed to get moving and renew her purpose in life before this frightening sense of defeat became too big to overcome.

She turned onto the small, paved apron near the large front porch and pulled off her sunglasses, fluffing her long auburn hair over her shoulders and surveying her face in the mirror with critical, large green eyes. Was her carefully applied make-up too much? Over several months of unemployment, she'd grown accustomed to wearing little, if any, and her hair hadn't seen a perm or trim in ages. In fact, she'd spent an hour just debating what to wear. While she'd never been prone to indecision, the unexpected, painful end to a promising engagement earlier this year had set her world upside down.

Her career goals – even her financial goals had changed when there was suddenly no one to share them with. So she'd quit a decent-paying but unfulfilling secretarial job a few months ago to allow herself some time to take a breath and figure out her next move. She'd decided to explore new possibilities, however scary, and this was her first opportunity.

Her time away from the work force had done nothing for her fashion sense, but she'd finally chosen a pale green scoop-necked blouse, a white wrap-around skirt and matching white sandals, hoping the total look would be one of simplicity and neatness – just the thing an employer would be seeking in a potential babysitter.

With a resolute sigh, she picked up the folded newspaper section she'd brought with her and re-read the ad once more, still trying to place herself between the lines: "Wanted: Responsible live-in babysitter for six-year-old boy. Weekends and holidays off. Light housekeeping and cooking. Room, board plus $300.00/wk. Occasional overtime."

It almost sounded idyllic, especially now, as she glanced around at the lovely house and peaceful, green surroundings. But could she really picture herself spending her days dusting, vacuuming, washing dishes and making peanut butter sandwiches? What if this kid was a brat who hated peanut butter sandwiches and didn't want a babysitter anyway? There was only one way to find out, now that she'd made it this far.

Drawing a breath to calm her fluttering stomach, she climbed out of the car and hastily straightened her skirt. Then taking her purse from the seat she closed the car door, the bang no doubt announcing her arrival. The stateliness of the house could have been intimidating but on the phone, the voice of the woman who lived here had been kind and welcoming. "I can't wait to meet you," she'd said. It had given Amanda the encouragement she needed to see this through.

With a toss of her hair she turned just in time to glimpse a curtain falling back into place in an upstairs window and as she started toward the house, she sensed she was still being watched. Was it curiosity or suspicion? She decided it was both, with a possible undercurrent of hostility. Whatever it was, it sent a prickle up the back of her neck. Accompanied only by the clicking of her heels on the stone path, Amanda walked toward the porch. As she went up the steps she swallowed the sudden dryness in her throat and tried to convince herself that it was only her imagination working overtime and this secret scrutiny had been nothing more than a harmless peek, a normal act for any little boy expecting a prospective babysitter.

Before she could knock, she jumped as the front door opened and her first reaction was surprise at finding nothing at eye-level.

"Are you the lady?" a small voice inquired from somewhere in the area of her waist.

She looked down at a pale, slender little boy with curly blond hair and large, shining blue eyes. It passed through her mind that he was not the least out of breath, in fact hadn't even had the time it would have taken to run downstairs to answer the door. So who had been looking out that window?

"Well, I *am* a lady," Amanda quipped, deciding to test her skill at playing along. "What lady were you expecting?"

He grinned, obviously pleased at her reaction. "The babysitter lady!" he replied with mock impatience.

"Well, that could be me, I suppose."

"Dylan, for heaven's sake, let Miss Morgan in!" a woman's laughing voice called from another room.

"It's the babysitter lady, Grandma!" he yelled over his shoulder.

"I know, dear! Now let her in!"

Dylan smiled back up at Amanda. "Wanna come in?" he asked as though he'd just thought of it himself.

"Why, thank you. That would be nice."

He studied her with a child's unabashed curiosity as she stepped in and closed the door.

She found herself in a quaintly furnished entrance hall with a carpeted stairway in front of her. There was a large kitchen to her right and a spacious living room to her left.

The boy sized her up a moment more, then ran off yelling, "Grandma, she's here!"

"I'm on the sunporch!" the woman called out. "To the left of the living room!"

Amanda could hear the low din of a television set in the direction of the voice. She made her way across the living room, briefly glimpsing its most noticeable features; a fireplace on the outside wall with a carved wooden mantle and brass utensils; colonial sofa and matching chairs and to the right at the far end of the room a dining area with table, chairs and a china cabinet that looked out onto the back yard through a set of French doors. The entire room was done in warm shades of dusty rose and muted shades of brown and gold and the cozy, relaxed feeling it evoked in Amanda immediately told her more about the owner's taste and personality.

Another pair of French doors opened onto a bright, airy sunporch with floor-to-ceiling multi-paned windows, where she found the older woman seated with Dylan on her lap. A set of knitting needles, mid-project, lay on the small table in front of her and a soap opera was on the portable television across the room.

"Honey, please turn off the TV for Grandma," the woman said.

Dylan grabbed up the remote with both hands from a shelf beneath the table and eagerly clicked it off.

"Hello, Amanda. I'm Helen Sterner." Mrs. Sterner smiled and held out her hand. "You don't remember me, do you?"

"Helen Sterner..." Amanda gazed into the increasingly familiar blue eyes. "Oh my goodness! Mrs. Sterner, the Assistant Librarian! Now I remember you!" It wasn't until Amanda took her hand and found her soft fingers slightly gnarled that she also noticed the older woman was seated in a wheelchair.

"It's Helen, my dear, and the fact that you remember me may be good or bad," she laughed. "It was quite a few years ago, Amanda. I believe you were only sixteen."

"Yes! I volunteered for the children's summer vacation program at the Library for two years, and you were in charge of it."

"Actually, *you* were. I was very impressed with the way you organized and looked after the children. You were very good with them and you were a pleasure to know. I'd just moved here and you made me feel welcome."

"That's right – we went to lunch together a few times." Amanda was immediately reminded of how Helen's kindness and attention had made her feel special at a time when she needed it most.

"I can't tell you how happy I was to receive your application for this job, Amanda. Please sit down. We have so much to talk about."

"So you knew it was me all along," Amanda said as she sat in one of the wicker chairs across from Helen. "But I had no idea who I was responding to. The ad just said to send resumes to 'Babysitter', care of this address."

"Yes. I received it in this morning's mail and couldn't wait to see you. I dreaded having to interview and try to evaluate a group of strangers for such an important job, but I already know how responsible and trustworthy you are. Of course, you've already met Dylan."

Amanda suddenly realized that the little boy on Helen's lap hadn't taken his eyes off of her since she'd arrived. "Well, he didn't officially introduce himself, but I had a hunch who he was."

Dylan smiled knowingly at his grandmother, then giggled and buried his face into her blouse as she affectionately mussed his curls. "You're my boy, aren't you?" She patted his leg. "Why don't you go outside and play awhile so Amanda and I can talk?"

Dylan let out a sigh of exasperation. "But what can I do, Grandma?"

"What do you mean, what can you do? You can ride your bicycle and have a fine time!"

"But Daddy told me I can't ride my bicycle until he says it's okay again!"

Helen frowned. "For heaven's sake, why not?"

Dylan held up his arm and pointed to a small scab on his elbow.

"Oh, really, Dylan! That happened two days ago and it was just a little scratch! Besides, how can you learn to ride better if you stay off of your bicycle?"

Dylan's face brightened with new hope then clouded with wariness. "Are you sure Daddy won't get mad?"

"I'll talk to him and I'm sure it'll be all right. Now you run along!"

"Thanks, Grandma!" He smacked a wet kiss on her cheek and took off between the French doors.

Helen chuckled softly and shook her head. "Do you think you could handle someone with that much energy?"

"He's beautiful," Amanda said, "and I can tell he's a bright little boy. You must be very proud of him."

"He's the sunshine in my day," Helen admitted wistfully. "The only sunshine, I'm afraid." She straightened in her chair. "But that's neither here nor there," she concluded, obviously anxious to get on with the interview.

"Are you raising your grandson alone?" Amanda couldn't help asking.

Helen cleared her throat and paused as if to choose her words. "Well, in a way. You see, Dylan and his father have been living with me for the past several months —"

"Oh, and your son works?"

Helen hesitated again, then replied slowly, "No, not at this point. My son – Mark – is recovering from an injury he suffered in a car crash about a year ago. He nearly lost his leg and he's also had a great deal of difficulty adjusting emotionally to – what happened." She gazed out the window in melancholy reflection as she quietly added, "My daughter-in-law was killed in that accident."

"Oh, Helen, I'm so sorry."

"Thank you, but it's best you know some of the facts right from the beginning. It may help you to understand how much I need someone to care for Dylan. I kept hoping that as Mark recovered from his injury, he would re-connect with Dylan and put his son's needs above his own. When I could see that wasn't happening, I insisted they move in with me, at least until Mark –" Helen paused and shook her head. "Well, at this point, even though my son is around the house, he really isn't any more capable of seeing to Dylan's needs than I am."

It was apparent that Helen had not exaggerated on the phone when she'd mentioned her arthritis as one of the reasons she was seeking a live-in babysitter. Amanda remembered that Helen had been in obvious pain at times when she'd worked at the Library, and she eyed the pile of knitting on the table with new respect. But it was plain to see by her firm handshake and direct look that Helen was not the type to let her handicap get the best of her.

"The needlework is mostly therapy, my dear," she smiled when she saw Amanda looking at it again. "I'm really not that good at it. And don't be fooled by the wheelchair, either. I can still stand on my own two feet if I have to. I just can't do it for very long anymore, so I spend most of my time 'wheeling and dealing', so to speak."

Amanda joined her in an appreciative laugh, grateful for being made to feel so at home. It was Helen's strength that had won Amanda's admiration years ago and the way she handled her worsening handicap now, awed her even more. The past ten years had left Helen more frail but had done nothing to weaken her spirit. She was still beautiful with her high cheekbones and long, graceful neck that held her head at a regal angle. Her blonde hair had turned a striking silver that accented her snapping, blue eyes. She still dressed with sophisticated flair, wearing a powder-blue blouse and long, dark blue skirt, taking the time to tie a colorful scarf around her shoulders and accent it with earrings. Amanda recalled hoping, as a teenager, that she could be as lovely as Helen at her age.

"I didn't mean to ask too many questions, Helen."

"It's perfectly all right. It was only natural for you to be curious and I hope what I've just told you will suffice." Those same blue eyes were suddenly all business as they turned to Amanda. "That's why I need a certain kind of person to care for Dylan, and with what I already know about you, I think you could be that person."

Amanda smiled but shifted uneasily in her chair, unsure of how to respond. It sounded as though Helen was willing to hire her right then, but she already had more questions than answers as to what this job was really about.

"Now then, the conditions of the job are exactly as the ad stated," Helen continued. "For the remaining few weeks of the summer, your hours would be from noon to seven-thirty

14

in the evening – that's Dylan's bedtime. He and I can manage his breakfast, but I'd want you to give him lunch, fix the evening meal and see that he's bathed and into bed on time."

Amanda nodded, trying to see herself performing those duties.

"Dylan will be starting first grade in a few weeks, and that's the main reason for my wanting to hire a babysitter now, so you'll have time to get to know one another. Come September, I'd need you to get him up, get his breakfast and drive him to school. You could plan the rest of your day as you wished until you picked him up in the afternoon. Then you'd see to his needs again until bedtime. Of course at Dylan's age, he doesn't require constant supervision, so that's where the light housekeeping would come in – just a little dusting, vacuuming and laundry, and I'd like you to pick up some groceries every so often." Helen sighed and added, "I'm afraid I haven't been able to keep a steady housekeeper here..."

There was a moment in which Amanda wondered, but was afraid to ask, why?

"Which reminds me –" Helen reached into the pocket of her skirt and produced a key. "You must have a look at the living quarters. It's the apartment above the carriage house, and it's furnished. I've had some live-in help from time to time, but it's been empty for awhile. I've just had the telephone reconnected and I had the place painted and some new carpeting put in. It's simple, but I think you'd like it, Amanda. Of course," she added with an appealing arch of her eyebrow, "you'd be welcome to fix it up to your own liking."

Amanda couldn't suppress another smile. Helen's sales pitch had been sweet and hopeful, not the least bit manipulative. It was a welcome relief from the serious tone the conversation had taken. "I'm flattered that you feel I'm right for the job, Helen," she said, "but all I have on my resume is secretarial work, and –"

Helen raised a finger. "Ah, but I already know you love children."

"Well, I do, but –"

"Amanda, anyone can physically care for a child; bathe him, clothe him, fix his meals. But as I've indicated to you, I'm looking for something more for Dylan and I see that in you. I consider myself a pretty good judge of character. I will admit, though," she added as she busied herself with smoothing her skirt, "it baffles me somewhat as to why a girl your age would want to give up a well established secretarial position for less money and possibly a good deal more aggravation..." Helen's sentence lingered between them and Amanda was again aware of those inescapable eyes.

"I guess it *would* seem baffling," she said. "It's just that I'm at a point in my life where I need a change."

"My goodness, and at only twenty-six years old, how did you know you needed a change already?"

Amanda looked at her hands. "It was my situation. I'd been at the same company for five years and I didn't mind it, but my main reason for working hard and trying to win promotions was because I was engaged and I wanted to help out financially after my fiancé and I were married."

"Sounds like past tense," Helen murmured.

"It is. The engagement was broken several months ago."

16

"I'm so sorry." Helen leaned forward and touched her hand.

"Please don't be. Believe me, it was the best thing, under the circumstances." And circumstances there were, but Amanda didn't want to burden Helen with them now, especially at their first meeting. "Anyway," she continued, "after my plans changed, I realized there was really nothing to keep me at that job and I felt a need to take some time and get back in touch with myself and see what I wanted to do. After all," she added with a little shrug, "my life *is* back in my own hands."

"That's the stuff!" Helen beamed. "I admire your spunk! That's another reason I think you'd be good for Dylan. He's a lonely little boy and I think someone like you could draw him out and undo some of the damage –" Helen caught herself as her voice took on a bitter edge. "Well, I just think you're right for the job."

Amanda's forehead wrinkled as she tried to phrase a nagging question.

"Is something the matter?"

She cleared her throat. "Well, I can't help wondering why your son isn't taking part in the interview, if I'm to be caring for his child." Again she sensed an uneasiness in Helen.

"My son is not thinking clearly enough right now to know what's best for Dylan. As I told you, he's going through a difficult period in his life and quite frankly, he's thinking a lot more about himself than anyone else. So the fact is, we simply must have someone here to care for Dylan. At barely six years old, he's quite a handful at times. His father isn't up to giving him the attention he demands, and you can certainly see that I'm not, either."

Amanda nodded but her question still seemed disturbingly unanswered. "I can't help feeling that your son might not approve of your hiring a babysitter for Dylan at all," she admitted.

"You're very perceptive, Amanda. No one puts anything over on you very easily. I like that in a person. I think it would be an asset in caring for Dylan, and perhaps in other ways too." Helen paused thoughtfully, then flashed her eyes back at Amanda. "In answer to your remark – no. My son is not in favor of my hiring anyone, but until he's willing to be more of a father, it's something that must be done."

"But I don't want to be in the middle of a feud –"

"Please don't give it another thought. The truth is, you'll be lucky if you see my son at all. He stays in his room upstairs most of the time and wants nothing to do with anyone – which, I hope, further illustrates to you the need to have someone here for Dylan."

Amanda nodded, even though Helen's answers only added to her concerns.

"Now you go on, and have a look at the apartment. I know you'll like it."

Deciding she could use the opportunity to think, Amanda accepted the key and set out for the apartment. She was halfway across the living room when she heard a series of odd, hollow thumps and paused to look around in curiosity. Tracing the sounds to the stairway, she glanced up in time to see a pair of trousered legs and a wooden cane as they disappeared from view onto the second floor. She stood listening and the thumping took on an eerie effect as it faded slowly down a hall and ended abruptly with the closing of a door.

Amanda remained motionless, wondering whether she should be frightened or angry. But one thing she was sure of was that Mark Sterner had taken part in her job interview, after all.

***

The apartment was just as charming inside as it looked from the outside and Amanda could tell it was an authentic, converted carriage house. When she'd passed it on her arrival, she'd noticed curtains at the second-story windows and had wondered if it might be the living quarters for the new babysitter.

Although the rooms were small, the multi-paned windows were large, letting in all possible light and giving the place an open, airy feeling. The furnishings were simple but comfortable and the tiny kitchen had an apartment-size stove and refrigerator, perfect for one person. Amanda fell in love with the place, despite the undeniable feeling that she might be wise never to occupy it.

After about a ten-minute appraisal she let herself out, locked the door and descended the black, wrought-iron steps to the yard.

"Hey babysitter lady!"

She looked in the direction of the excited little voice and saw Dylan riding toward her on his bicycle. Holding her breath as he reached up to wave and the bicycle swayed precariously, she was relieved when he got it back under control and stopped in front of her.

"Did you see me?" He was out of breath.

"Yes, I thought that was an amazing recovery."

He looked perplexed. "A what?"

"Never mind."

"I meant, did ya see me riding? I did the whole driveway five times!" He held up his hand, fingers spread, to prove his point. "And I never fell off once!"

"Fantastic!" Amanda tried to match his enthusiasm. "But you didn't really think you'd fall, did you?"

He gazed at her, then broke into a bashful grin and shook his head. "Uh-uh."

Amanda couldn't resist stroking his blond curls. His hair was baby-soft and warm from the sun. "And you can call me Amanda."

"But you're gonna be my babysitter lady too, right?"

"Well, I'm not sure just yet."

The brightness seemed to leave Dylan's face. "Why not?"

Searching for words, Amanda gazed thoughtfully across the large yard, but was distracted by something in a second floor window of the house. Without moving her head she squinted in the bright sunlight and distinctly saw the rigid silhouette of a man, slightly back from the window, but obviously facing it.

Biting her lip, she took her sunglasses from on top of her head and drew them back over her eyes. "Well, there are some things I have to think about." Head down, she started back toward the house.

"Like what?" Dylan persisted, half hobbling, half riding beside her.

"Just – some grown-up things, that's all." Amanda forced herself to look at the ground, not wanting to know whether the man in the window was still there.

"Well, what do you think of it?" Helen wanted to know when Amanda reappeared with Dylan at her side.

"It's lovely." She handed the key back.

"Grandma, can I show Manda *our* house now?" Dylan asked eagerly.

Amanda began, "Oh, no – I don't think –"

"Well I think that's a fine idea! You'll have to know where everything is, anyway, Amanda."

"Okay, Grandma! I'll show her everything!"

And before Amanda had a chance to dread the thought of seeing absolutely "everything", Dylan was dragging her through the dining area she'd already seen and through an archway into the large, cozy kitchen with oak wainscoting and wallpaper borders, color coordinated appliances and plenty of counter space. There was an inviting oak breakfast nook with high-back benches in front of a plant-festooned picture window that overlooked the front porch and yard with its graceful, old shade trees. The room was bright and cheerful, and Amanda could almost imagine spending time here, preparing meals and helping Dylan with his schoolwork.

Then, jibber-jabbering all the way, Dylan eagerly showed her the pantry and bathroom off the kitchen as well as "Grandma's room", a small but comfortable den with a love seat, matching chairs and single bed in the corner, which Helen had apparently taken over as her bedroom when the stairs to the second floor had become too much of a struggle.

"Now I can show you the bestest part! My own bedroom!" Dylan continued as they left the kitchen and he pulled her back toward the stairway.

Amanda had to resist the overwhelming urge to shrink back. She hated to spoil Dylan's obvious pleasure at playing host, but given the unnerving series of events since she'd arrived, she had the distinct feeling she would be entering enemy territory on the second floor.

When they reached the upstairs hallway, Amanda blinked warily from side to side as Dylan led her to his bedroom to the left at the end of the hall. There she was treated to a series of enthusiastic demonstrations of various toys and games and after awhile she found herself relaxing enough to comment and ask questions as he proudly showed off his favorite things.

After about fifteen minutes and much gentle reminding from Amanda that she would have to be leaving soon, Dylan finally agreed to finish the tour. He showed her a full bath to the right of his room and pointed out "Daddy's room" just beyond that to the left. Judging from the spacing of the doors, Amanda assumed that Dylan's father occupied the master bedroom and although it looked like any other room with its door closed, it seemed every bit as forbidding as she'd expected. There was another spacious bedroom across from that one, which had probably been Helen's.

"Now there's just one more room," Dylan said as he led her to the opposite end of the hall and they stopped in front of another closed door. From Amanda's calculations, it appeared to be the large room above the garage. "No one can

22

ever look in here, Manda, 'cause this is a secret room. Daddy told me only he can go in here."

Amanda eyed the door with more apprehension than curiosity. "Well, thank you, Dylan – that was a great tour." She took his hand and turned to go.

"Wait!" Dylan urged in a half-whisper. "It's always locked, but I like to check it sometimes."

Amanda's uneasiness returned. "If it's a secret, Dylan, that means it's for no one to see."

But Dylan had already broken away and was stealthily trying the doorknob with practiced skill. "No one'll know – I promise –"

"What are you doing, Dylan?"

The voice from behind them broke the silence so suddenly that Dylan and Amanda grabbed onto one another as they jumped.

A tall, slender man with the cane she'd seen earlier, moved down the hall toward them from the direction of his now-open bedroom door.

"Daddy, I wasn't doing anything," Dylan whined as though he knew exactly how much trouble he was in. "I was just showing Manda –"

"What have we said about that door, Dylan?" the man asked in an overly patient tone as he reached them. "There's nothing in there that concerns you – or anyone else." He turned his unnerving gaze toward Amanda.

"You – must be Mark Sterner," she got out in as steady a voice as she could manage. "I'm Amanda Morgan."

The man stood stiffly, regarding her with cool detachment. She immediately recognized the posture and demeanor of the figure she'd seen in the window. His hair was curly, like Dylan's, but surprisingly dark for the father of such a fair-haired child. It was long and full but neatly kept, along with his close-cropped, full beard. His blue eyes had the potential to be as appealing as Dylan's, but instead they had a dullness in them, sparked only by the resentment with which they now regarded Amanda.

"I know who you are and why you're here," he said in the same patronizing tone he had used on Dylan. "And if my mother's foolish enough to hire you, you'll stick to your job description. Is that understood?"

Amanda felt a rush of adrenaline that ignited her fear into a flash of anger at his attempt to intimidate her. "I haven't accepted the job yet, but from what I've seen so far, Dylan has enough needs to keep anyone occupied." She saw him tense slightly and was glad he felt the intended sting of her remark.

"One of my son's needs is supervision, Miss Morgan, and now that I've seen you in action, I can see you're somewhat lacking in that area."

Amanda's mouth opened but before she could respond, he turned to Dylan. "Don't let me catch you around this door again. Understood?"

Dylan nodded vigorously. "I promise I won't do it again, Daddy."

As Mark Sterner headed back to his room, he moved slowly and with an effort that was obviously painful as he favored his left leg with the help of his cane. Although Amanda wished she'd had a quick answer, she was immobilized as she watched him. When he reached his door

24

he looked back at her over his shoulder. "And as for your career plans, Miss Morgan, I suggest you apply for a position more suited to the qualifications you have – now that we know which ones you don't have."

Amanda's face reddened before he stepped into his room and closed the door.

"I didn't mean to get us into trouble, Manda," Dylan murmured as she hurried him back toward the stairs.

"Just forget it, Dylan. There's nothing special in there anyway, I'm sure."

"Yes there *is*!" Dylan insisted loudly. "Grandma says there's things in there that used to belong to my mommy and –"

"Shhh!" Amanda glanced nervously behind her, afraid that Mark could hear them. "I said forget it, Dylan, okay?"

"Okay. But Daddy's got the key in a drawer beside his bed. I've seen it in there." He was careful to keep his voice as low as hers. "And someday when I'm bigger and not so scared, I'm gonna get it and unlock that door!"

When they reached the living room again, Dylan wandered out the front door, head down, hands in pockets and Amanda stood looking after him until Helen called out, "How do you like the house, Amanda?"

As she reached the sunporch, she hoped the after-shock of what she'd just been through didn't show on her face. "It's very nice," she said.

"Then you'll take the job?"

"Could I think about it? I mean, taking a new job is a big commitment any time, but picking up and moving as well..."

25

"I have a plan," Helen said. "Why don't you take a few days just to come and stay with Dylan for a few hours and see how you get along. I'll pay you for the time you spend here, and if you feel it isn't for you, nothing will have been lost, and I'll just look for someone else."

"Oh, Helen, I couldn't let you do that."

"I'm only doing it because I know you'll find Dylan so irresistible, you'll take the job anyway."

Helen laughed and Amanda forced herself to join in, already certain there was no chance of her finding Helen's son to be anywhere near as irresistible as her grandson.

"Come tomorrow morning – say, around ten o'clock. We'll do that for the next few days and you can take the weekend to think about it and let me know next Monday what you decide."

"That's very kind of you." More than anything, Amanda knew she needed to get away and try to evaluate the situation objectively. "I'll see you tomorrow, then," she said.

Dylan was sitting on the front step when she went outside. He jumped up and walked with her to her car. "Did you think yet?"

"About what?"

"You said you had to think about grown-up things and then maybe you could be my babysitter lady. So did you?"

Amanda smiled. "A little bit, Dylan. I have more thinking to do, but I'll be back tomorrow."

"You will?"

"Of course I will. Your grandmother's letting me come for the next few days so I can decide."

"Oh, you mean to see if you like me?" he asked in a dubious tone as they reached the car.

She wished she'd put it differently. "No." She reached out and touched the side of his face. "I already like you very much."

He looked up at her with wistful eyes and she was taken by how blue they were. "I'm sorry I was bad, Manda."

"What do you mean?"

"When I tried to look in Daddy's room and he yelled at us. I won't do it again. Honest!" Dylan's expression held a plea for forgiveness.

"It's okay," she assured him as she got into the car. "I don't think either of us will ever do *that* again."

When she closed the door he stood on tip-toe and leaned against it looking at her, chin-on-arms. "If you say no to Grandma, I won't be mad, Manda. But I hope you don't, 'cause I wouldn't like any other babysitter lady as much as you."

Deeply touched, Amanda turned to smile at him when something caught her eye over his shoulder. It was the same curtain, pulled back in the same window as when she'd arrived. It was *him* again– only now he had a face.

"I have to go, Dylan." She hurriedly started the engine. "I'll see you tomorrow." She backed up, turned and headed down the driveway slowly, watching in her rear view mirror as Dylan stood waving, then picked up his bicycle and teetered around in a circle, his small, lonely figure shrinking until she turned onto the road. As she lost sight of him and drove away, the irony of his situation became poignantly clear. Dylan needed a babysitter because of his father, but it was for the very same reason that he might never have one.

Chapter 2
Shades of Howard Hughes

Through the upstairs window he watched the small convertible until it turned out of the driveway, blended into flashes of white car and flowing auburn hair through the foliage along the road, then vanished.

He supposed she was lovely. He never really looked at people anymore – least of all, women. But she was only a girl, barely into her twenties by the look of her. She should be easy to discourage. And after the expression of shock and uncertainty his behavior had invoked in her this afternoon, he doubted she would be back.

Oh, there had been a moment when he'd thought she might try to put up a fight. He'd seen the indignance in her eyes, the flush of outrage in her cheeks. But she'd been unsure of how far she should go. That was good.

A rueful smile flitted across his lips. He hoped that any wounds his insults had inflicted would heal soon. He sensed she had a great deal to offer – but at another job, somewhere else.

He looked at the little boy who straddled his bicycle, still gazing at the end of the driveway, and he knew his mother was right. The boy needed someone to care for him, someone like a mother; the mother he'd taken from him.

Letting the curtain drop he straightened, wincing at the ever-stabbing pain in his leg as he moved across Dylan's room with the help of his cane. Crossing the hall, he went into his own room and closed the door. There he paused in front of the mirror and forced himself, as he did so many times each day, to gaze into the gentle, smiling face of the woman in the photograph on the dressing table.

She'd been the kind of wife men dreamed of, and had only wanted what he'd wanted. She'd spent all of her time and energy supporting his career and making his life as pleasant as possible, until the end when she'd had nothing left to give – had in fact, accused him of ruining her life before she'd been taken so suddenly, leaving him with nothing but the gnawing guilt that he was responsible for what happened – the same guilt he felt every time he looked at their son.

Even so, there could be no live-in babysitter for Dylan. It would be far too risky. He'd tried to convince his mother of that, but it was as if she'd lost her sense of urgency for his situation. Enough time had passed that she believed things could be better now – had even suggested that he dare admit his lie.

But he knew he could never afford to have anyone else around, especially not someone as young and appealing as this girl. She was far too sharp and perceptive. She would notice things, eventually put things together. Worse yet, she'd known his mother before and was obviously preapproved for the job. And his mother, given the opportunity to form an even closer relationship with someone she already knew, might be tempted to confide the truth.

The man in the mirror looked back at him through expressionless eyes. He had always believed that when physical death came, the spirit left the body and lived on. It had never occurred to him that the spirit could die first.

***

Amanda was fixing herself a light supper that evening when there was a knock at her apartment door.

"It's Tom!" a familiar voice announced from the hall.

"Hi! I haven't seen you in a couple of days!" she welcomed him as she let him in.

"You sound like you missed me! Mmmm–" Tom sniffed the onion and green pepper frying in the pan on the stove. "Something smells good."

Amanda rolled her eyes with a knowing smile. "It's Chinese fried rice, if you'd like some."

"Thought you'd never ask!" He eagerly peeled off his jacket.

She laughed and shook her head. In the few months since she'd quit her job and had been around the apartment building more, she'd gotten to know Tom Fredericks, who lived down the hall. Attractive and in his late twenties, Tom was an accountant with a reputable firm in the area. Amanda had found him to be an easy-going, good-natured friend. Tom was a great conversationalist and they'd shared many an evening at the movies or weekend afternoons just enjoying each other's company without any romantic pressure, much to her relief.

There were shared confidences, too. Tom knew the story of how Amanda's fiancé, Brad, had claimed he wanted to marry her regardless of the fact she could never give him children. It was something she'd known since adolescence, when an operation to remove a tumor had cost her the ability to ever conceive. She'd spent several difficult years adjusting to that reality before meeting and falling in love with Brad, and looking forward to adopting children to complete their family.

But in spite of her honesty from the start of their relationship and regardless of his assurances to Amanda that he'd fully accepted their situation, Brad confessed just weeks before their wedding that he couldn't go through with it. He couldn't let go of his all-important dream of having his own children. Brad's leaving her had caused Amanda so much pain that she wondered if she could ever dare to love and trust a man again.

Tom seemed to understand. He, too, had been hurt by love in the past. Between his empathy for her situation as well as his casual manner and warm sense of humor, he seemed the perfect companion for her at this time.

Amanda watched him pick up the evening newspaper and begin to read it as he seated his tall, robust frame on one of her snack bar stools. He was striking with his athletic build and clean-shaven look and Amanda never failed to notice the envious stares of other girls whenever she was out with him.

He had a smooth, handsome face with a strong jaw line and friendly brown eyes. His hair was a sandy brown and always meticulously groomed and styled and Amanda sometimes wondered why, despite all of his too-good-to-be-true attributes, she didn't feel a stronger attraction.

"Hey, what's all that stuff?" he asked when he glimpsed the stacks of tape cassettes and old records Amanda had been sorting on her living room floor. "Looks like you're moving or something."

"I thought it wouldn't hurt to get organized, in case I do." Amanda broke the eggs over the rice and vegetables in the pan.

"Why? What's up?"

"Remember that live-in babysitting job I applied for?"

"You're kidding! You mean you got it?"

"It's mine if I want it."

"Amanda, that's fantastic! Congratulations!"

Catching his enthusiasm as they ate dinner, she told Tom all about Helen Sterner's phone call, the surprise that she already knew her and how well the interview had gone.

"So this woman's raising her grandson?" Tom's question naturally followed. "No wonder she needs a babysitter. What happened to the kid's parents, anyway?"

"Dylan's father is recovering from a car accident that killed his mother."

Reaching for the cookie plate, Tom paused to look at her. "Geez. That's pretty heavy. So where's the father? In the hospital?"

"No, he's living there – with Helen and Dylan," Amanda said as matter-of-factly as possible. She sipped her coffee as he stopped chewing to look at her again.

"No kidding. So what's he like?"

Amanda shrugged. "Oh, it's hard to tell. I only saw him for a minute, and Helen says he prefers to keep to himself." Somehow, she couldn't bring herself to tell the truth – that she knew exactly what Mark Sterner was like and that he clearly did not want her to babysit his son, much less ever come back.

"Sounds like shades of Howard Hughes."

Amanda cast him a light shrug as they shared a laugh.

"So you'll work a few days, see if you like it, and maybe move in by the end of the month?"

"That's it. One furnished apartment to another. All I'll have is my clothes and personal belongings. The move would be the easy part. Deciding if I'm right for the job is what's hard."

"Well from the way you talked about Dylan awhile ago, I can tell you really like him."

Amanda sighed. "Given a little more time, I'm afraid I could love him like my own."

"And you like Helen."

"Oh, very much. I'd love to work for her again."

"And Howard Hughes keeps to himself, right?"

"Right." Amanda cast him a sideways glance.

"So if you got along with Dylan and his grandmother, and it looks like you would, it could be a great job. It sounds like the change you've been looking for. But I'm glad you're trying it out for a few days before you pick up and move."

"Me too," Amanda agreed.

"And if you do take the job," Tom put his hand over hers on the table, "Dylan will be one lucky little boy. I can vouch for that."

Amanda smiled as she felt the color rise to her cheeks. Even in their platonic relationship an occasional tender moment arose, and it was then she could tell Tom was beginning to care for her more and more.

With a final squeeze of her hand, he stood up. "Great supper."

"Make yourself comfortable while I clear the table." Amanda picked up the dishes.

He wandered into the living room and began browsing through her scattered record collection. "It sure brings back memories, seeing all these old album covers," he murmured as he sifted through them. "Look at all these classics! I'll bet they're worth a lot of money now – the Beach Boys, the Rolling Stones... Marshall Stewart? You've still got his records after all this time?"

"Of course I do." Amanda joined him on the floor. "Even though all of his work is on tape now, I'll never part with his records. I still play them just for sentimental value. He was my favorite, and not only that!" Amanda lifted one of the album covers so Tom could take a closer look.

"Get out! You have an autographed Marshall Stewart album?"

"Well, I wouldn't have if it weren't for my best friend shoving me to the front of the line after one of his concerts. She was too scared, so she had me take my album and hers to get them signed." Amanda still savored the memory of standing in front of her idol, so nervous and shy that she could only stare at his slender hands as he held each album and scrawled his name. She would never forget the tingle through her entire body, even though she was barely able to look into his face as he handed them back to her and thanked her for coming to hear him play.

Tom shook his head as he gazed at the photograph of the smiling young man with the long, tousled blond curls on the faded album cover. "How long has he been gone now?"

"Ten years." Amanda sighed and hugged her knees against her. "I still remember the day of the announcement as if it were yesterday."

"Yeah, that was awful," Tom agreed. "Word spread so fast – all the kids in school were talking about it the minute somebody heard the news on the radio. I guess he'd been missing for a few days before his manager said anything. Man, he just vanished."

"He walked off the stage after a concert in Toronto and he and his wife were never seen again. Not knowing what really happened was the toughest thing for his fans to accept. I know it was for me. I was sixteen years old and my hero was suddenly gone. When he couldn't be found, my world was shattered."

"And he was just a young guy, too."

"Twenty-six. Funny how that seemed like such a mature age to me then. Now I know he was barely an adult." Amanda paused thoughtfully. "I loved his music and lyrics. Somehow he always knew what people were going through and knew how to speak to their souls. His music was such a comfort when I was fourteen and my parents were divorcing. He inspired all of his fans that way. I couldn't wait for the next album to come out. That was the worst part, besides never knowing what happened to him – longing for more of his music."

"Didn't they finally declare him and his wife legally dead?"

"Yes. I remember the memorials that were held for him. Nobody wanted it to be true, but I guess the world needed to move on."

"Too sad." Tom glanced at his watch. "Almost eight o'clock." He got to his feet. "I've got to run. I promised the boss I'd go over some figures tonight for a meeting tomorrow."

"Okay." Amanda reluctantly let him take her hand as he helped her up. "As long as it's just numerical figures you'll be going over," she couldn't resist teasing him.

He turned to her with a look of surprise, then drew her toward him. "Why, Amanda Morgan, I do believe you just sounded like a girlfriend."

"I know – where did that come from?"

He drew her closer. "Well, maybe we should talk about that when we have more time." His voice had softened and his gaze moved over her with a flicker of deepening appreciation.

As she looked back at him, it was as if they were seeing each other from a new perspective. A warm wave of anticipation teased her senses as his lips took hers softly, gently, his arms wrapping her in a tender embrace. She slipped her arms around his neck and found herself instinctively responding, eagerly returning his kiss and sensing his desire for more. When she drew back slightly, he gave up the kiss but still held her close.

"I'd say it's about time – wouldn't you?" he asked quietly.

"I guess it is."

"How about a cookout on the balcony at my place tomorrow night?"

"I'd like that."

"Make it around six. And you can tell me all about your first day on the job."

"Sounds good."

As though unable to resist, he leaned toward her once more, his lips briefly touching hers before he turned to go.

When Amanda had let him out, she leaned against the door. In the space of a moment, their relationship had taken on an entirely new dimension. Although kissing Tom had happened naturally and she'd done nothing to discourage it, she was left with the uneasy feeling that it could complicate things. So far, they'd enjoyed an unassuming, no-strings-attached friendship and it had given her the space and time she needed while she was still getting over Brad. She wasn't sure if she could ever cope with another serious relationship, especially so soon after her loss.

The word "loss" lingered in her mind, evoking a vague picture of Mark Sterner. All she could remember was his dark hair and empty eyes, but she distinctly recalled the feeling she'd been left with once she'd gotten over the shock of their first encounter. Despite his clever put-down and cool manner, he seemed to be a man filled with loss.

And for the first time since Helen had told her about the accident that killed Mark Sterner's wife, Amanda imagined what a horrible ordeal it must have been and how devastating the lingering effects must be. As much as she still didn't know about him, she had no doubt he was a tormented man.

As he watched the credits at the end of the evening news on the TV in his room, it occurred to him that Dylan hadn't been in to say goodnight. In fact, he hadn't seen his son at all since that afternoon.

Helen and Dylan always had dinner together around five o'clock. Occasionally he joined them, but just as often he went down later and made something to bring upstairs. Sitting at a dinner table with his mother every night had turned out to be nothing more than an invitation for an argument and he didn't want to subject Dylan to any more tension than there already was. He would allow that most of what his mother picked at him about was true and she did it out of frustration, but it only made things worse. Glancing at the clock he noticed it was after seven-thirty and he still hadn't heard Dylan come upstairs or get ready for bed.

He lifted his cane from against the side of his chair and struggled, getting up slowly, grunting with the effort it took to get his leg working again. It was his own fault, for sitting in the same position for so long. Regardless, he never missed the evening news and always watched the entire hour. He read at least two newspapers a day, as well.

Even though he was no longer a participant in the activities of the world, he felt a responsibility to keep up with day-to-day events. It seemed the only way he had of establishing what was real and what was not.

As he moved across the room, he muttered and cursed with the pain of each step. Penance – that was what this was, every minute of every day with no let-up. Better that he'd died in the accident and had done with it. Instead, he seemed condemned to forever feeling like a piece of unfinished business.

He went into the hall and glanced each way. The bathroom door stood open, the light out. He turned and made his way to Dylan's bedroom door. It was partially closed and when he reached it he nudged it open enough to peer into the darkness. "Hey, Scoot," he called softly. It was a nickname he'd had for Dylan since he was a toddler, one of the few remaining signs of fondness he seemed able to show his son anymore.

There was a rustling of sheets. "Oh, hi, Daddy," a sleepy voice replied.

He reached in and flipped the light switch on the wall. The small lamp on the dresser came on, softly illuminating the room and Dylan sat up in the bed, rubbing his eyes as he clutched the toy puppy he always slept with.

"I'm sorry I woke you up, but why didn't you come to say goodnight?" he asked, surprised at the disappointment in his own voice.

Dylan shrugged slightly. "I thought maybe you didn't want to see me."

There was a sudden ache in his throat as he made his way over to the bed. "What're you talking about?" He mussed Dylan's hair, then clumsily arranged the covers. "We always say goodnight and you give me a kiss before you go to bed. What was wrong with tonight?"

Dylan shrugged again, blinking back tears. "I thought maybe you were still mad at me."

"I was angry this afternoon because you knew better than that," he said quietly. "But I'm not anymore because you promised you wouldn't do it again, remember?"

Dylan nodded, then thought a moment. "So that means you're not still mad at Manda?"

"Who?"

"Manda – you know, the babysitter lady."

He sighed. "I wasn't mad at her."

"Then why'd you yell at her, too?"

"I didn't yell. I was upset, that's all, Dylan. We have rules here and everyone has to follow them."

"Well, I just got an idea, Daddy."

"What?"

Dylan cupped his chin in his hand. "All you hafta do is tell Manda all the rules so she won't do anything wrong and she can stay, okay?"

He felt his jaw tighten and gave some thought to what he was about to say, as he moved around the bed to adjust the window blinds. "You never know, Scoot, this Amanda's probably looking other places for a job, too. She might find something else and decide not to come here, after all." *Any smart person would*, he thought.

"But she told me she'd be back tomorrow!"

The note of panic in his son's voice confirmed his worst fear – Dylan had taken to the girl immediately. If she did have the nerve to come back, he would have to take more drastic measures to discourage her. He couldn't let his son get too attached to someone who would only have to go away again. Dylan was still trying to make sense of his mother's absence. His child didn't need another trauma of that kind, and he didn't need any outsiders under his roof.

"All right, we'll see. Just settle down and go to sleep."

Dylan lay back down, but his eyes were wide with a child's fervent hope. "If we're both real good and don't make anymore trouble, can she stay?"

"We'll see. C'mere, you." He bent over, returned Dylan's quick, wet kiss and gave the covers one last tuck. "Now go to sleep and don't worry." As he crossed the room and reached for the light switch, he paused to look back.

"We won't let her go, Dogby," Dylan murmured to the stuffed puppy in his arms before he rolled over, obviously secure in his resolve to do whatever it took to ensure that his babysitter could stay.

And he, with all his complicated, grown-up reasons, was determined to do whatever it took to drive her away.

**

When Amanda arrived at the Sterners' the next morning, Dylan was sitting on the front step in the already-hot sunshine. As she drove in and parked, he jumped up and ran to meet her, then threw his arms around her as she got out of the car.

"You came back!" he shrieked.

"Of course I came back." She crouched and returned his embrace. "I told you I would, didn't I?"

"Yeah, but Daddy said you might not!" he explained breathlessly. "He said you might get another job and *never* come back!"

"Oh, he did, did he?" Amanda stood and they started up the walk hand-in-hand.

The presence. It was just overhead, coming from the same window as yesterday. The disapproval filled the air, coming at her like darts. She hadn't slept well last night because of what had happened with Mark Sterner the day before. It had even taken precedence over her confused feelings for Tom, because she knew she would have to make her decision about this job within the next week.

How ironic that Dylan would be so relieved to see her return, she thought, when she'd come very close to phoning Helen and thanking her for the opportunity before declining the job offer. But she'd decided that Dylan was the real issue here. She could not just give up and walk away if there was a chance she could make a difference in his life. She'd even tried to convince herself that miracles happened and as unlikely as it seemed, there was always the possibility that Dylan's father might come around.

"Believe me, there was no living in this house until you got here today, Amanda," Helen chuckled as they greeted each other. "Dylan had this stubborn notion in his head that you might not come!"

"I wonder where he got *that* idea?" Amanda made no effort to hide her sarcasm.

"Well, we're all very glad you're here. I was going to make a point of introducing you to Mark today, but he told me the two of you met yesterday." She paused, nodding slightly as she searched Amanda's face for a reaction.

"Oh yes, we've met."

"Well, I hope he was pleasant and well-mannered."

None of the above, Amanda thought with a smile.

Dylan tapped his grandmother's shoulder and whispered in her ear. Amanda was thankful for the diversion.

"Dylan has something he wants to ask you," Helen said. "I've told him the decision is up to you because it's fiercely hot outside." She winked at her grandson.

"We got a swimmin' pool a couple blocks away at the park!" Dylan announced as though he'd been bursting with the news. "I never got to go there yet, but Grandma says I can go if you take me – pleeease! I even made us peanut butter sandwiches we could take 'cause we could be there a really long time."

Amanda laughed at his careful planning and presentation. "Well, if Grandma says it's all right, then it's all right with me. I could use some time in the sunshine, myself."

*****

The pool was to open at eleven o'clock, but ten-thirty found Amanda and Dylan the first ones there, watching the maintenance man as he skimmed the leaves and debris off the top of the water. Dylan was enjoying it so much that Amanda wondered if he would be able to stand the thrill of actually going in. She was glad she'd remembered to bring her camera, hoping to capture some of his enthusiasm on film. She was beginning to realize how uneventful and isolated Dylan's life must be, and how many childhood pleasures he was probably missing.

Although her first encounter with Mark Sterner had left her unsettled, Amanda was amazed at how quickly Dylan had seemed to forget the incident and get on with the business of having fun. As he struck up a conversation with the maintenance man, she marveled at the amount of interest and fascination he had for everything around him. He was such a bright, inquisitive child that she found it hard to believe he could be the son of such a miserable man. Dylan seemed determined to enjoy life, despite his father's apparent determination not to.

As she watched him, she tried to remember what it was like to be his age and live in the moment. He seemed to accept his father's brusque manner, but what choice did he have? Yet despite how unaccustomed she was to such treatment, she'd decided not to tell Helen what had happened yesterday – at least not until she had it in perspective.

Dylan was one of the first few children to get into the pool when it opened, and by eleven-thirty, it was full of splashing, screaming youngsters and surrounded by watchful mothers who sat along the side benches or stood in small groups.

Amanda sensed the air of confidentiality which always seemed to accompany a gathering of housewives as they chatted among themselves. She tried not to feel out of place as she wandered around the pool, camera at the ready, snapping an occasional shot of Dylan as he flailed his arms and called out to her to watch his antics. The fact was, she had nothing in common with these women. She wasn't a housewife or a mother and had no idea what they were talking about.

"I haven't seen you here before. Are you new in the neighborhood?"

The woman standing beside Amanda was probably about thirty and had short brown hair and a slightly chubby figure, which was carefully tucked into a pair of designer jeans. She had a round, pretty face and a genuine smile, which won Amanda immediately. "I'm Angie Wilson."

"Nice to meet you." Amanda reached out to shake hands. "I'm Amanda Morgan."

Angie looked perplexed, then cheerfully accepted Amanda's hand.

Realizing the awkwardness of the situation, Amanda smiled. "Pardon my business-like approach, but I left a secretarial job just a few months ago and I guess I'm still using my office etiquette."

"Well, you must have been a very good secretary." Angie was obviously impressed. "Where did you work?"

"Ketter's Printing in Hartford."

"Oh yeah. That's a pretty big company. So you're between jobs. Do you live around here?"

"No – at least not yet, anyway."

"Oh. You mean you just brought your kids here to try out the pool?"

"Well, not exactly that either. I brought Dylan Sterner here today, but I'm just a friend of the family."

"You're kidding!" Angie whipped off her sunglasses and squinted toward the pool. "Dylan Sterner? Where?"

"Over there." Amanda pointed him out. "The little guy with the blond hair. Why?"

"Well I just can't believe it!" Angie craned her neck for a better look. "Isn't he cute!" she remarked as though she'd always wondered what he looked like. "Do you know I've never actually seen that child and he only lives a few blocks away from us? I don't think any of the other mothers have, either."

46

"Why not?" Amanda asked.

"Well you tell me. You're the family friend."

When Amanda didn't respond, Angie continued, "Why, it's unheard of, seeing Dylan Sterner out of his yard! What's the occasion, anyway?"

"Occasion?"

"Sure. Everyone knows he never leaves the property, and none of the other kids are allowed in, either. It's all because of that crazy father of his, from what I've heard." Suddenly Angie stopped and covered her mouth sheepishly. "I'm sorry, Amanda. You just told me you were a friend of the family, and here I am, saying nasty things –"

"Actually, I'm a friend of Helen and Dylan," Amanda said. "I hardly know Mark Sterner."

"Then maybe you don't know what's been going on, but believe me, it wasn't always this way. Mrs. Sterner lived alone in that house for years and she's a lovely person."

"That much I know."

"Mrs. Sterner never minded having the kids around. She even used to invite them in for cookies or fruit once in awhile after school. Everybody in the neighborhood liked her and I think anyone would have done just about anything for her. But a few months ago her son and grandson moved in." Angie shrugged. "Nobody even knew she had a son until then. But who would want to tell anyone you had a miserable son like that anyway?"

Amanda smiled and shook her head, keeping her eyes on Dylan and trying not to appear as eager as she was to hear the rest of the story.

"Anyway, from the time they moved in, everything changed – almost overnight, it seemed. Now they all keep to themselves – even Mrs. Sterner who was so outgoing. I've never seen her son, but the kids say he walks with a cane and he's mean. When Dylan first moved in, my Conner and a few of his friends went over to say hello and see if he wanted to play baseball, and Dylan's father came to the door and yelled at them to stay out of his yard and not come back. When did it get to be 'his' yard, anyway?" Angie sniffed indignantly. "All us moms thought that was a terrible thing to do to a bunch of kids who were just trying to be friendly, don't you think?"

"I certainly do." Amanda said, reminded of her own humiliation at Mark's hands.

"That's why I'm so surprised to see Dylan here today. From what I've heard, his father never lets him out of his sight. I hope he's finally softening up and letting his kid live in the real world!"

Amanda was suddenly seized with the awful possibility that Mark might not know about this trip to the pool and that she may have become an unwitting ploy in Helen's strategy to launch Dylan on a more normal way of life.

"There's one thing I don't get," Angie said, pushing her sunglasses back up the bridge of her nose. "You said you didn't live here yet. Are you planning on moving here?"

"I'm still trying to decide," Amanda said. And while Angie listened with obvious fascination, she explained about applying for the job with the Sterners and Helen's offer of a few days' trial period before she committed herself to moving in.

"Living-in at the Sterners'?" Angie gazed at Amanda with a skeptical tilt of her head. "You mean being in the same house with that grouch twenty-four hours a day? I don't think I'd have any decision to make. Are you really sure of what you'd be getting into? I mean, Dylan looks like a darling boy, but..."

"I'd be in the apartment over the carriage house," Amanda said, "so I'd have some privacy – and distance."

Angie shook her head. "Not enough distance for me." She shot Amanda a calculating look. "You're not married, are you?"

"No." Amanda detected the slight change in Angie's expression.

"Well... maybe it wouldn't be so bad," Angie said with a quirk of her lips. "You never know, it might even get interesting." She glanced at her watch. "Oh, shoot! Conner's got a twelve-thirty dentist appointment and I'll probably never get him pried out of the pool in time! It was really nice meeting you, Amanda. Will you be here again tomorrow?"

Amanda glanced over to where Dylan was still bouncing and splashing in the water. "If Jacques Cousteau, Jr. has any say in the matter, I probably will."

Angie laughed. "Great! Maybe I'll see you then."

Amanda watched as Angie ordered a protesting, roly-poly youngster out of the pool, helped him dry off and cajoled him toward the shower room. As she looked back to where Dylan was still playing with several other boys, she became more concerned with the realization that Mark probably had not approved this outing, much less knew about it.

She sat on a bench and waved to Dylan as he continued to show off. She couldn't resist snapping a few more shots, knowing Helen would love the pictures. No matter how much fun the other children seemed to be having, none matched Dylan's exuberance. He shone among the others like a little beacon. Or maybe she was already prejudiced. What she'd said to Tom the night before was true; given enough time, she could love him like her own.

Helen had said Dylan would be starting the first grade in September. Wherever he'd come from, he must have gone to kindergarten. How had his father kept him isolated then, and how could he hope to do the same now? But the most troubling question was, why did Mark feel he needed to keep his son and himself away from the rest of the world?

Chapter 3
"Miss" Morgan and "Mr." Sterner

It was nearly one o'clock before Amanda could coax Dylan out of the pool, and even then he protested between chattering teeth.

"Your grandma will be worried about you," Amanda urged.

"But we didn't get time to eat our sandwiches!" Dylan reminded her, stalling for time.

"We'll eat them as soon as we get home," Amanda promised as she helped him dry off.

"Okay, then we better hurry, Manda!"

She laughed at how quickly he could transfer all his energy from one direction to an entirely new one and, suddenly starving, he rushed Amanda home.

When they reached the house and entered the front hall, laughing and out of breath, they stopped short at the sight of Mark waiting in the living room. It appeared he'd been there for some time as he struggled up from the couch, eyeing them with stern disapproval. Amanda desperately looked for Helen and the hope of a swift rescue, but she wasn't around.

"We went to the pool, Daddy!" Dylan was still too excited to realize he could be in trouble. "We had lots of fun and Manda's takin' me tomorrow, too – right, Manda?" He sent her up a pleading look.

She gently tried to hush him.

"I'm learning to float! You should come tomorrow and watch me –"

"Go on upstairs and change your clothes, Dylan," Mark interrupted in a low voice.

Amanda grabbed Dylan's hand. "Come on. I'll help you!" she cheerfully announced as they started upstairs.

"No, Miss Morgan. I want you here."

The words ran down her spine like icicles and she reluctantly let go of Dylan's hand. As she watched him run the rest of the way up, she would have given anything to go with him. Instead, she turned and forced herself back down the few steps to where Mark stood waiting. His posture was the same as yesterday when she'd met him; erect and tense, cane clutched in front of him as he sized her up.

"I'd prefer it if you called me Amanda," she got out in a steady voice.

"What's the camera for?"

She glanced down at the Nikon, which was still on the strap around her neck. "Well, it's generally used for taking pictures." She looked back at him, daring to let a hint of a smile play at the corners of her lips before she saw his jaw tighten.

"I know what it's used for.   What've you been photographing?"

"Your son. In case you haven't noticed, he's a beautiful child and I wanted some pictures of him –"

"What for?"

"I didn't know I needed a reason. I just happen to enjoy taking pictures. The last I checked, that's not a crime."

"No, but taking my son anywhere without my permission could be."

Amanda felt her mouth drop open.

"So I see you failed to take my advice, Miss Morgan."

"I would still prefer Amanda, and what advice was that, *Mr. Sterner*?"

She could tell the unfavorable emphasis on his name had irritated him before he continued, "If I remember correctly, I told you this was not the job for you."

Amanda folded her arms, suddenly fuming at his second attempt to intimidate her. "So that's what you were hinting at yesterday?"

His knuckles whitened around his cane. "This is not a game, Miss Morgan."

"No, it's not. So why are you playing with me?"

"I'm not playing with you. I'm dismissing you – right now."

Amanda folded her arms tighter. He would not get away with this, not without Helen there to hear it. "I don't think it's possible for you to let me go, since I haven't taken the job yet. Your mother would like me to spend some time with Dylan this week before I make my final decision –"

"And that's another thing I want to talk to you about, Miss Morgan."

"Yes, *Mr. Sterner*?"

The look of utter frustration her taunting reply aroused in him told her that, with a little practice, she might be able to handle him, after all.

"I don't want you taking Dylan back to the pool. Had I known about it, I never would've allowed it."

"Then thank goodness you didn't know about it, because he had a wonderful time – or don't you like the idea of your son enjoying himself?"

"That's not true and I'll thank you to keep your observations to yourself –"

"Then why on earth would you have a problem with Dylan going back to the pool?"

"It's none of your business!"

In the momentary silence that hung between them, she felt her cheeks burning with the desire to tell him off. Instead she said calmly, "I'll continue to follow your mother's wishes, since she's the one who wants to hire me."

He gazed at her as if trying to break her nerve before she tossed her hair and added, "To be perfectly honest, I couldn't respect anyone as my employer who felt he had to lurk on the stairway during my interview, rather than meeting me face-to-face."

She jumped as the butt of his cane slammed the floor and he began to move toward her. She could not remember when anyone had aggravated her into wanting to be so spiteful, and she suddenly regretted allowing him to bring it out of her.

"All right," he said as he reached her, "we're face-to-face now."

As she stared at the front of his shirt, inches away, she began to regret most of what she'd said. Deciding not to put it off any longer, she slowly looked up to brave the hostile glare she was sure would be waiting for her. Instead, she was surprised to find his blue eyes curiously exploring her face, as though seeing her for the first time.

She realized that it *was* the first time they'd taken a good look at each other. And as she took closer notice of his features she had to admit that in this unguarded moment, without the scornful expression that seemed so characteristic of him, his face was younger than she'd expected and had the potential to be quite appealing, at least what she could see of it under his heavy beard.

As though his curiosity wasn't fully satisfied, his gaze softened slightly, sweeping down the curve of her neck and – she was almost certain – across the soft folds of her yellow knit top. She wanted to be offended but found herself fascinated by the undeniable flicker of admiration in his eyes.

Suddenly he was all business again. "Let's get one thing straight," he warned in a low, even voice. "In spite of what you might think or what you might have heard from my mother, I'm in charge here. Dylan is my son. And I will not tolerate any interference – especially in my own house."

"And I will not tolerate any intimidation from you." Amanda's anger was back. "Maybe I shouldn't have said what I did earlier, but you've been very unkind to me and I've done nothing to deserve it."

He quickly looked away. "I'm sorry if I've seemed unreasonable," he said in a weary tone. He sighed and she noticed the resigned shake of his head. "But Dylan is not to go back to the pool. He's to stay in this yard at all times."

"Fine. But *you'll* have to tell him that, because I won't. I'm here to see to Dylan's needs, not to deprive him of them."

"Well, I see you're back! And did you and Dylan have a good time at the pool?" Helen asked cheerfully as she guided her wheelchair through the kitchen doorway into the living room.

"Helen!" Amanda wanted to throw her arms around her. "I was wondering where you were!"

"Oh, I was watching my soap operas in my room, and sometimes I get so wrapped up in them I forget all about the time. Well, you two finish your conversation. Don't let me interrupt!" There was a hint of delight in her voice at having found them engaged in what she perceived to be a friendly chat.

"I think we're finished," Amanda hastily replied. "Weren't we, Mark?" She cast him a look of mock innocence.

He stood in silence, obviously still smoldering at her last remark and now the use of his first name. Despite the show she made of staring boldly back at him, the look in his eyes sent a flush of heat through her entire body.

"Yes, we're finished. For now." His tone carried the unmistakable promise that there would be a next time.

***

Amanda swirled the wine in her goblet and gazed into its dark, ruby depths.

"Amanda? Amanda!" Tom's impatient voice suddenly broke through.

"Oh, I'm sorry." She straightened and looked up to meet his perplexed frown. "I'm sorry – what is it you were saying?"

They were seated on the couch in his living room as the sizzle and aroma of steaks on the grill wafted through the balcony door on the evening breeze.

"Which time? I don't think you've heard a word I've said since you got here. What's bothering you tonight?"

"Nothing really..."

Tom sighed and set his wine glass on the coffee table. "Well, if nothing's bothering you, then I'd hate to think it's the company."

"No – not at all!" Amanda put her hand on his arm as he turned to look at her. "It isn't you. I guess I was just thinking about the Sterners."

Tom's impatient expression melted into concern. "Amanda, if you have as many doubts about this job as I think you have, maybe you should just forget it and look for something a little less complicated. I know you well enough by now to see that you haven't been yourself tonight. If it's this hard for you to decide –"

"But I have. I'm taking the job." Hearing her decision out loud made it final.

"You are?" Tom eyed her with a mixture of admiration and uncertainty. "What made up your mind?"

Amanda gazed into her glass and smiled. "Well, for one thing, I've met Howard Hughes."

"Oh, yeah?" Tom settled back and draped his arm over the couch behind her. "So what's he like?"

"Pretty miserable."

"And that made you decide to take the job?"

"Well, sort of. You see, I found out today that I can handle him. And if I can handle him, I can handle the job."

"Why – is he that tough to get along with?"

Amanda thoughtfully traced the lip of her glass with her finger. "Not as tough as he'd like."

"So his bark's worse than his bite?"

"Something like that." Amanda set her glass down. "Anyway, I'm going to let Helen know tomorrow and I'll see about moving next weekend."

Tom reached out and stroked her hair. "If you're really sure this is the right thing for you, I'll help you move, but have you considered what you'll do if this kid's father doesn't come around and you're stuck there?"

"I want to take care of Dylan." Amanda searched his face, then blinked back a couple of unexpected tears. "I want to do that more than anything else. I may never have a child of my own, but this child has lost his mother and I know in my heart that he's come into my life for a reason. I'm willing to take on any difficulties that come with it."

Tom touched the side of her face. "Okay, you've convinced me," he said softly. He gazed at a lock of her hair between his fingers. "So now I have to help you move away from me. I must be crazy to go along with this, but I want to see you happy. And you'd better believe I'll miss having you here – especially now. All I've got to say is, this Dylan must be a pretty special little guy. I haven't even met the kid yet and I'm jealous." He shook his head. "I should've known you'd wait till you were moving to get romantic on me."

"I won't be that far away," she reminded him. But as she took another sip of her wine, she sensed that her move to the Sterners' would take her much farther away than either of them could anticipate.

***

When Amanda arrived the following morning, she was anxious to share the news with Helen and Dylan that she was definitely taking the job. She knocked at the front door but when there was no answer, she let herself in.

"Helen?" she called out from the entrance hall. She crossed the living room, checked the sunporch, then headed for the kitchen. Dylan was kneeling on the bench of the breakfast nook, still in his pajamas and wolfing down a huge piece of chocolate layer cake. He was so absorbed in every bite that he didn't notice Amanda in the doorway.

She smiled at the way he brandished his fork and concentrated out the window, his cheeks puffed with such gargantuan mouthfuls that he was barely able to chew.

"Good morning," she said.

He jumped, dropping his fork, and pasted on a smile that did nothing to hide his guilt. "Hi, Manda!" He slowly lowered himself to a sitting position and tried to look nonchalant. "Want some breakfast?"

"Is that what it is?" She walked over for a closer inspection of the half-eaten cake. "Who got it for you?"

"Nobody. I got it myself."

Amanda saw the uncovered cake plate on the kitchen counter. The chair, which was pulled up beside it and the

59

trail of brown crumbs across the floor to where Dylan sat, told the rest of the story. "Where's your grandma?"

"In her room, gettin' dressed." He picked up the fork again. "Sure you don't want any breakfast, Manda?" he added before popping another mouthful.

"I'm sure," she said, taking the fork from between his sticky fingers, "and I'm also sure this is not your breakfast."

"Then whose is it?"

"I don't know, but you're having eggs."

"Eggs? Yuck!" he exclaimed as she took the plate from him. "I never eat eggs for breakfast!"

"Well, now's a good time to start." She opened the drawer of the stove and found a frying pan.

"But Manda!" He clambered from the bench to stand in front of her. "I'm already full!"

"You're never too full for eggs, Dylan. They're good for you," she said as she opened the refrigerator door.

"But I don't want any!"

His protest had turned into a whine, which surprised but didn't deter her. She dropped a pat of butter into the heating pan. "I was only going to fix you one egg, but if you keep complaining, we can make it two."

"Oh, yuck!" He stamped his feet. "I thought you were gonna be a *nice* babysitter lady!"

"What's the problem in here?" The unexpected sound of Mark's voice silenced them as they turned to find him standing in the doorway. Amanda noticed his demeanor hadn't changed since their last encounter and she wondered how he managed to make her feel no older than Dylan.

60

"Daddy, Manda threw my cake away and she says I hafta have eggs for breakfast!" Dylan was quick to tattle.

Amanda swallowed the urge to defend herself and returned her attention to the pan where the butter had begun to burn. If Mark was going to chastise her in front of Dylan for interfering, she would rather get it over with. After all, it was "his" house and "his" son, as he had emphatically pointed out to her the day before.

***

From where he watched as she worked at the stove, head down, he was surprised that she didn't turn around to confront him. Whether it was out of respect for his authority, or disrespect for the very fact that he was standing there, he couldn't be sure. But it appeared that she was content to leave the outcome of this situation totally up to him.

He looked at his son, who was still awaiting the verdict, and it was hard not to smile. Dylan's pajama bottoms were twisted and the tell-tale chocolate around his mouth made his obstinate expression even more comical. "Go get yourself dressed, Scoot, and when you come back, your eggs will be ready."

Dylan frowned and opened his mouth but his father frowned back and sternly nodded in the direction of the door. Without another word, the little boy trooped from the room.

For several moments, he stood and studied the girl who still had not looked up. Maybe she was afraid to, but from what he'd seen of her, that hardly seemed possible. Most likely, she was leaving the next move to him. Maybe it was her way of dealing with the difficulty she expected from him.

As he made his way toward the coffee maker on the counter beside her, he allowed himself to notice her firm, lithe figure in her blue jeans and pullover top. Her graceful, erect posture emanated strength and confidence, yet there was no hint of vanity in the way she handled herself.

He leaned his cane against the counter and when he reached for the coffee pot and stood beside her filling his cup, he sensed the sudden tension in her but she still wouldn't look at him. Replacing the pot he took a sip and cast her a sideways glance. She was more petite and delicate-looking than her sometimes feisty attitude implied. And now, probably due to his nearness, there was a wary set to her profile as she busied herself with flipping and scraping the eggs.

"Thank you," she said.

"For what?"

"For backing me up."

He took another sip from his cup, determined to use the opportunity to his advantage. "I wasn't 'backing you up.'" He made her terminology sound silly. "Dylan doesn't get away with eating cake for breakfast any time, and eggs are better for him."

She sagged slightly but didn't respond.

"As a matter of fact," he added, allowing a smirk into his voice," I had no idea you were qualified to be a nutritional consultant as well. Couldn't you get paid more for that somewhere else?"

The spatula clattered loudly as Amanda dropped it, set the frying pan aside and turned to him. "It really doesn't matter, because I've decided to take this job and I'm staying."

Her voice faltered slightly as she realized how close he was standing, but there was no mistaking the defiance in her green eyes, and no amount of cold staring from him was going to change that.

He set his cup down and turned, leaning back against the counter, arms folded. "Well, Amanda, you've proven that you're a very bold, determined girl, even though I've made it clear I don't want or need you here."

Amanda angrily wiped her hands on a towel and tossed it onto the counter. "This has nothing to do with you. I don't care how you feel about me, I'm only here for Dylan. I'll be more than happy to stay out of your way, if you stay out of mine, but as long as I'm here, Dylan will get the care and attention he deserves."

He folded his arms a little tighter and fixed his gaze across the room. *You can't let her win this battle*, he told himself. *Say something!* But nothing came.

"And by the way, I'm not a 'girl', I'm a twenty-six-year-old woman."

When he looked, her face was upturned. His gaze was unintentionally drawn to the triumphant twitch of her lips and, without warning, he was seized with the urge to grab her and crush the insolence from them with his own mouth. If that wasn't unnerving enough, her fearlessness disarmed him with the possibility that she'd caught onto his act.

He straightened and grasped his cane. "I can see that you're a woman, Amanda," he said quietly. "But right now you're being a very foolish one." He dared to look into her eyes. "Staying here will be a mistake, and you've been warned for the last time."

He made his way across the kitchen as Dylan bounded back through the doorway in shorts, tee shirt and sneakers, already over his pout. "Okay, Manda, maybe some eggs won't be so bad!"

"You never know, once you've tried them, you may find you like them very much." Amanda's babysitter tone had returned as though she'd put their argument behind her.

She was so young and sure of herself, he thought as he labored up the stairs toward his room. He wondered if she'd ever experienced the helplessness of fighting something she could never conquer.

Chapter 4
Marshall Stewart's Incurable Fan

By the time Amanda announced her decision to accept the job, Dylan had decided he did like eggs and was as delighted as Helen to officially have his own "babysitter lady for sure." Neither of them mentioned another trip to the pool that day or any day after that and Amanda could tell Mark had won that battle.

Amanda divided the next few days between looking after Dylan, packing her belongings and dealing with a nervous stomach. There were moments when she feared she'd made her decision too impulsively and wondered if she'd been influenced by her determination to not let Mark Sterner drive her away. Mark's warning at the end of their latest confrontation had been softly spoken, almost regretful, with no attempt to bully or frighten her away, as before. There was something more going on with him at a much deeper level than the grief of losing his wife and the pain of his accident. He was holding something in and he was alone with it. She began to wonder if her constant presence really could cause problems for him in ways she could never understand. Yet everything else about her decision felt wonderfully natural.

Much to her relief she did not encounter Mark again the rest of the week. She knew it didn't mean he wasn't observing her, but once she was able to relax somewhat and settle into her new duties, she put that concern aside. She knew she would love working for Helen and taking care of Dylan and their beautiful home, and that was what mattered most.

Once she had officially taken the job, Amanda began her summer hours of noon to eight. She arrived each day in time to make Dylan's lunch, tidy up the kitchen, check with Helen for any small household chores that needed to be done and familiarize herself more with the large house, including the vast basement and laundry room. She found it fascinating that the basement door was built into the kitchen side of the main staircase and it was like entering a hidden, other world.

Down there was a comfortable family room with a fireplace that had a well-worn sofa and a couple of equally worn recliners along with a large, older model TV; probable castaways from upstairs that were still useful. It was obvious this area hadn't been used in a long time and Amanda realized that Helen was no longer able to get up and down the stairs and it was probably too much bother for Mark.

Beyond the family room was a separate room in the corner where she found the washer and dryer, a storage closet for laundry items and cleaning supplies and an ironing board. A partition ran down the center of the basement and on the other side was typical basement fare: dusty boxes, old paint cans and a corner workbench with cobwebs across it.

As Amanda went about her business, Dylan was often at her side, full of questions and chatter and always seeking a hug or some special show of attention from her. It was as if they had bonded from the moment they met and she knew this would be the most worthwhile aspect of her job. Helen was aware of the growing affection between them and commended Amanda on the good it was doing Dylan.

That Thursday and Friday, Amanda made dinner and both nights were filled with light-hearted conversation and much praise for her cooking. Helen said she would leave the menus mostly up to Amanda, but there was no doubt that Dylan would voice his preferences. The three of them ate at the cozy breakfast nook at the picture window and it seemed strange to Amanda to know Mark was somewhere in the house but not taking part in the family meal. She knew it must be by choice because Helen and Dylan never mentioned it as though they were resigned to the arrangement, but Amanda decided that one of her goals would be to find a way to get Mark to join his son at the dinner table each night.

On the last night in her apartment, Amanda lay in bed, amazed at how her life had changed since she was hired the Monday before. By Saturday morning when she and Tom packed both their cars with the first load of her clothing and belongings, she couldn't wait to move into her new place and had no misgivings about her decision. Although it would require another couple of trips to get everything moved, the fifteen miles each way posed no problem and even the dark, drizzly weather didn't dampen her spirits. She was excited about moving ahead with her life and leaving behind the heartache of the past year, and she was eager to show Tom her new apartment and introduce him to Helen and Dylan. She was sure Mark would stay out of sight and was not concerned about him, at least for today.

"This is really some place," Tom remarked as they headed back across the yard after a brief visit at the house. "Mrs. Sterner's really glad you're moving in and I can see what you mean about Dylan. He's a bright little guy."

"Sometimes too bright," Amanda laughed as they reached their cars next to the carriage house.

"No sign of Howard Hughes, though. When'll I get to meet him?"

"Maybe never," Amanda joked in an ominous voice as she opened her car door.

As they began to unload her belongings and carry them up the stairs to her new place, Amanda tried to stay positive and focused. She knew that she and Tom were probably being watched, and the fact that she was not totally welcome here by everyone, could be a bit unnerving if she let it get to her.

"What a neat place!" Tom eagerly took a look around at the small rooms. "It's really unique in a cool kind of way! Now I know you're going to be happy here."

"I certainly plan to be," she said as she laid a pile of clothing on the bed.

Tom turned her around and folded her into a hug. "I'll miss you at the old place, but now I can pretend I'm meeting you in a secret hideaway. Wait a minute! I *am* meeting you in a secret hideaway!"

She started to laugh just before his lips took hers in a long, tender kiss. She didn't want to offend him by pulling away too soon, but something in her was changing. Tom was still a wonderful guy – a perfect friend, but she had willingly gone along with him and now that he was unmistakably headed to the next level, she was suddenly mixed-up and ashamed for leading him on.

"Let's celebrate with the first pot of coffee in my new home," she quickly suggested.

"Well, I had other things in mind, but I guess that's one way to celebrate, for now." He followed her into the kitchen where he helped her fish through a box for the coffeemaker. When they had it set up he glanced at his watch. "Look, why don't I head back for another load while you start unpacking and then we'll see how much is left."

"Thanks – that's a great idea. I really appreciate all your help, Tom."

"Nothing could keep me away. You're stuck with me, now!" he grinned as he zipped his jacket. "Keep that coffee hot. It'll taste good when I get back."

She watched through the kitchen window as he clattered down the stairs and hopped back into his car. He was so enthused for her and it was wonderful having someone to share today with, yet the closer he drew, the more confused and uneasy she felt.

She turned from the window with a sigh and wandered into the living room, trying not to feel overwhelmed. She spotted her tape deck and a box of cassettes which had arrived with the first load of her belongings, and as the aroma of fresh brewed coffee began to fill her new home, she sifted through them and came across the tape version of the Marshall Stewart album she and Tom had discussed a few nights ago. The sounds were richer on tape than on the original album and although she couldn't remember the last time she'd played it, this drizzly, late Saturday morning in this new place seemed the perfect time.

She plugged in the player, arranged the speakers and put the music on, then curled into a chair as the first few guitar chords filled the room, as fresh and crisp as the splash of a waterfall. She glanced over at the stack of old records Tom had placed on the table next to the chair, and saw that the autographed Marshall Stewart album was on top. As the smooth, velvet voice surrounded her she was reminded of how much comfort it had always brought her. She needed a little comfort now as she gazed out the rain-speckled window at the grey morning. Leaning her head back and closing her eyes, she softly sang along:

If a tree falls in the forest, but no one's there to hear
Does it really make a sound? Doesn't someone know –
    somewhere?
If I love you but can't tell you – like that lonely, lonely tree
My aching heart keeps hoping soon you'll hear and come to
    me
I have loved you from a distance, I have wanted you so long
But our secret love's forbidden, so I'm sending you this
    song
If a tree falls in the forest, even though it isn't heard
Listen with your heart and you'll hear these tender words...

When the last few chords melted away, she reminisced a few moments longer, then sighed and got back to work as the next few songs played. She'd managed to unpack a couple more boxes when there was a banging sound on the outside stairs. Was Tom back already? She hurried to the door and pulled it open. "You're way too efficient —" Her greeting was cut short at the sight of Mark Sterner waiting on the doorstep.

The banging, obviously, had been his cane against the stairs and one look at him told her it must have been a difficult climb. The landing at the top was so small that she suddenly became aware of how awkwardly close they were standing. When she glanced up she was startled at how mellow his face seemed, contrasted against the striking dark curls damply scattered around his forehead. The deep, green foliage behind him cast an ethereal mood over the moment and she could hardly recall how unkind he'd been.

"Mind if I come in?" he finally asked.

"Oh, I'm sorry," she stammered, stepping aside. "Of course."

It wasn't until he maneuvered through the door that she saw the basket of flowers at his side.

"What's this?" she asked.

"My mother ordered these for you today, but they were delivered to us by mistake, and there was no living in that house until I brought them over to you."

So he had struggled up the stairs in the rain with his cane in one hand and the flowers in the other, she realized with newfound respect for him.

71

"They're beautiful!" She looked them over appreciatively as she took them. The kitchen table was covered with boxes, so she headed for the coffee table in the living room. "Let me take your wet jacket. You must be chilled."

"I'm fine."

"Well, I just made some coffee. Why don't you have some before you –"

"I'm not staying..." His voice trailed off and he took a few steps toward the living room.

***

This had to be another of the many nightmares that still brought him up from the bed, gasping in the dark – yet the music was real. How *could* it be?

"Are you sure you don't want to sit down for a minute?" He was vaguely aware of Amanda's voice as he glanced around to verify where the music was coming from. "Is something wrong?" he heard her asking.

He took another step into the living room and, noticing the stack of records on the end table, stared at the album cover on top. This was the worst nightmare yet, but he would gladly experience every moment of it to ensure that it was only a dream.

"You must be a Marshall Stewart fan, too," he heard Amanda say. "I even got his autograph at one of his concerts." She scooped up the record and handed it to him.

He gazed at the cover. The smiling, youthful face beneath the disarray of blond curls taunted him with regret. His signature, scrawled across the bottom under the words: "Forever yours" brought back a blur of backstage greetings by hundreds of screaming, young girls, exploding flashbulbs and the increasingly uneasy feeling that his life was not his own. And after one of those concerts, he must have briefly met a teenaged Amanda, her face barely discernible in the crush of people.

"No, I'm not a fan." He handed the cover back. He suddenly felt light-headed, his heart thundering in his chest, and he was barely aware that he had lowered himself onto the couch.

"Are you all right?" Amanda's voice sounded distant. "I'm getting you that cup of coffee." She went to the kitchen and was back momentarily.

"No – I'm fine," he heard himself say before she placed the cup in his hands. The steaming aroma startled his senses and he took a sip anyway.

"I hope that helps." Amanda seated herself across from him. "You were looking awfully pale."

He nodded slightly and took another sip. His music was still filling his head when he said, "Would you mind turning that off?"

"All right," she said reluctantly as she went over and clicked it off. In the silence she sat back down and he felt her studying his face. "So you really didn't like Marshall Stewart?"

"No." He drank more of the coffee as the shaking at his core began to subside.

"Any particular reason?" It was clear she wasn't going to let this go.

"No. He was just a fad and I never knew what the fuss was about."

Amanda let out an incredulous laugh. "*Fad?* Marshall Stewart influenced the whole world with his music and lyrics! He deeply affected me and I loved him – along with millions of others –"

As she continued to speak he took a long look at her, realizing that hers was the face of all those fans who'd awaited his return, gathering tearfully with candles to the backdrop of his recordings and declaring that their lives would never be the same without him. Besides re-living the accident that had taken Carrie, this had been among the worst of his nightmares and sleepless nights – to come face-to-face with a fan who could possibly recognize him and expose him to the world for who he really was.

The first part of the nightmare had come true. He *was* face-to-face with a fan, only he was surviving it. And for the first time he dared to believe that neither she nor anyone else would ever realize who he was because they had, however reluctantly, put Marshall Stewart to rest ten years ago and were not looking for him anymore. He let out a slow, involuntary sigh of relief.

"I'm sorry if I'm boring you." Amanda had obviously heard the sigh. "But how could you think he was only a fad?"

He dared to continue the conversation. "Because he was just a romantic idea in the heads of his fans." He took the last few sips of coffee and used his cane to get up. "I have to go."

"But if you weren't a fan, how could you claim to know anything about him at all?" Amanda followed him as he moved toward the door.

Keep moving, he told himself even as he turned to her. "And how do you come to know so much about him?"

There was that bold, upturned face again, green eyes and unknowingly enticing lips set for battle, much closer than they should be. "I read everything there was to read about him. I followed his entire career. He was a warm, genuine human being who would never deserve to be called a fad – especially by anyone who knew nothing about him."

Her poignant defense of her idol surprised and touched him deeply and he gave in to the unexpected temptation to brush the side of her cheek with his fingertips and cup them under her chin. As the color rose into her face he could see he had gotten to her and gently tilted her head back. "Marshall Stewart was fortunate to have your admiration, Amanda, but the man is long gone, so there really isn't anything to argue about, is there?"

She swallowed, for once lost for words, unable to do anything but gaze back at him. Just as he realized he'd gone too far, there were noises on the outside stairs and they barely had a chance to step apart before the door burst open.

"Time for that cup of coffee," Tom announced as he came in. "I got just about everything else and –" He stopped, his face registering surprise at not finding Amanda alone.

With the sensation of Mark's touch still warm on her skin, Amanda blurted, "Tom, this is Dylan's father, Mark Sterner."

Tom briefly looked from Mark back to her for some sign of what was going on. "Hi," he said without smiling, as he dutifully extended his hand.

"Hello," Mark answered with cool formality as he accepted Tom's handshake.

She jumped as Tom unexpectedly slipped his arm around her waist and kissed her cheek. "Amanda and I were just going to have some coffee. Care to join us?"

"He was just –" Amanda began to stammer.

"No, thanks. I was just leaving."

"Okay – nice meeting you," Tom said.

Mark went out the door and she could hear his cane as he took the steps one at a time.

"I'll get your coffee," she said to Tom as she busied herself at the counter.

He grabbed a doughnut as she poured him a cup. "Jesus, Amanda, forget about Howard Hughes, you're working for freaking Boris Karloff! What was he doing here?"

"He brought that basket." She gestured toward the living room.

Tom stopped chewing. "He brought you flowers?"

"No – Helen ordered them for me and they were accidentally delivered to the house." She tried not to stiffen as Tom put his arms around her.

"You seem all tense. Is everything okay? He wasn't bothering you, was he?"

"No, of course not." Out the window, she caught sight of Mark as he walked toward the house in the rain. Her mind was still reeling. What had just happened?

Tom turned her around to face him. "I'm serious, Amanda. Was he giving you a hard time?"

"No, he was not giving me a hard time," she replied evenly.

"Good, because you're mine, and we still haven't properly celebrated our secret hideaway," Tom murmured before he bent to kiss her.

This time Amanda could not feign a response and he drew back, searching her face. "I'm sorry," she said softly.

"What do you mean?"

"I mean, I can't do this."

Tom released her. "You're kidding, right?"

She closed her eyes and slowly shook her head. "I really care for you, Tom..."

"Oh, God. Not the "Dear John" speech, Amanda – not now –" Tom's tone had a sharp edge she hadn't heard before and she knew she'd struck a nerve.

"I've enjoyed having you for a friend and you've been so good to me," she began.

"I've been falling in love with you, Amanda, and all the signals I was getting from you told me you felt the same way – at least until the last couple of days."

"I thought I was ready." Her explanation sounded feeble, even to her. "But then things started to change for me –"

"When you met *him*?" There was a chill of suspicion in Tom's voice.

"What? No! How could you think that had anything to do with it?"

"Because I think it's too much of a coincidence that you and I were just starting to heat up when you took this job, and now you've gone cold on me, Amanda! Do you know how hard it's been to wait for you to come around? But I tried to be patient because you're everything I want and I knew you'd been through a tough time, so I gave you all the space I could."

"I'm sorry," was all she could say again. She knew Tom was staring but couldn't look at him.

"Amanda, tell me you're not attracted to that creep!"

"He's not a creep!" In the silence that followed, she knew her outburst had been too spontaneous and that Tom was still staring at her.

"I don't believe this," he finally said. "It's like a bad dream. I thought I knew you and we wanted the same things. I can't believe you'd go for something like that."

"Like what?"

"He's a little on the dark side, don't you think? I thought you said he was mean and miserable. Is that what turns you on?"

"How dare you! This has nothing to do with him!"

"The hell it doesn't! I've been a complete idiot. I'm not even sure I believe the flowers aren't from him!"

"Then don't! Believe whatever you want because I've had enough of this!" Her voice broke.

"Well, I guess that makes two of us, Amanda."

***

By the time he reached the house, even his good leg felt so weak it could barely support him. The drizzle had almost stopped but he was chilled and the trembling had started again as he cursed his situation. He should never have allowed himself to be drawn into that conversation with Amanda, much less touch her. But in that moment it was Marshall Stewart who had spontaneously reached out to her, who was reaching out to all of his fans, wishing he could say to each of them: "I'm sorry. I'm so sorry I betrayed your admiration and faith in me."

He peeled off his jacket and threw it over the coat rack in the vestibule, then with a shake of his wet hair, headed into the living room.

"My, you were gone a long time to deliver a basket of flowers," Helen's voice greeted him from the sunporch. She looked up from her knitting as he walked in. "Goodness, Marsh, you look all worked up."

"Where's Dylan?"

"Upstairs, playing in his room. He's been lost without Amanda today. How's the move going?"

He pulled the French doors closed. "Just great, Mother. She's all moved in."

"Well, that's good –"

"Oh, it's wonderful! And guess what? It turns out Amanda and I met years ago!"

Helen slowly lowered her knitting to the table in front of her. "When?"

"When I signed the album cover she showed me today while she was *playing my music*!" His cane banged the floor as he paced back and forth in an attempt to use up the nervous energy that was still making him tremble.

"She didn't –"

"Recognize me? No, not yet." He stopped and turned to face her. "I begged you not to hire anyone, Mother, and of all people, you had to hire *her*!"

Helen shrugged. "Well, Marsh, I'm sure there are a lot of people who still have your records or collect them. They're probably worth a lot of money by now."

"That's not the issue and you know it! Nobody's still playing my music except once in awhile on the oldies radio stations. Not in their living rooms! It looked like she had every record I ever made, along with cassette versions!" He continued to pace.

"She was moving, Marsh. She probably came across her collection and hadn't played them in years – maybe even forgot she had them –"

"Not a chance, Mother. She asked me if I was a fan. I didn't know what to say, so I said no and then she demanded to know why I wasn't. God, I couldn't believe it. She defended Marshall Stewart, wanted to argue about it, wouldn't let it go." He walked over to the windows. "If she's still that into it, how the hell do you expect her to live here without figuring it out?"

A distant flurry of movement across the yard attracted his attention and he saw Tom stomping down the carriage house stairs. He yanked his car door open, got in and took off, spraying gravel as he turned onto the road. It was certainly not the Tom he'd been introduced to a few minutes ago. He looked back at the apartment door and caught himself wondering if Amanda was okay, then pushed such a ridiculous concern from his mind.

"But you've got to remember, Marsh," his mother was saying, "you've been gone ten years. Nobody's looking for you anymore."

"I should never have moved back here. I should have stayed out of the country where I belong, and none of this would have happened."

"Not with Dylan, you weren't!" Helen's voice had lost its understanding tone. "That boy had been through enough with losing his mother and it was time that he had some comfort in a halfway normal home with his grandmother, since he wasn't getting any from you!" She picked up her knitting again and went at it determinedly.

"Mother, please don't start again. Yes, Dylan needs a stable home life and this is better for him. I'll even agree that he needs someone to help look after him, but not Amanda. Anyone but Amanda. She's got to leave."

"All right, you go ahead and fire her." Helen arched an eyebrow without looking up. "But you'd better hurry. I'm sure she's nearly all unpacked by now."

"*Me*? You're the one who insisted on hiring her!"

"That's right, and I want her to stay. If you have a problem with her being here, I'm afraid you'll have to tell her to leave yourself."

He sighed, running his hand through his hair. "You'll never stop finding ways to punish me, will you Mother?"

"You punish yourself, Marsh. You have to forgive yourself and start living again."

"Doesn't that sound lovely – and we'll all live happily ever after."

Helen threw down her knitting. "Now you listen to me. You're a thirty-six-year-old man with a child to raise, and you've felt sorry for yourself long enough. You haven't wanted to talk about this since you've come back, but that accident was not your fault. When Carrie grabbed that steering wheel from you, you've got to realize, she wanted to kill both of you. Thank God Dylan wasn't in the jeep, but

81

just the same, he could have been left an orphan!" Her voice dissolved into a rasp of emotion.

He stood quietly, head down for several moments. "She wasn't herself."

"She was drunk, as usual."

"You make it sound as though she drank because she wanted to. Mother, can't you see no matter how many times I tell you? The lie I was forcing her to live made her crazy. Can't you see that I drove her to it? She couldn't take the isolation anymore, even after we had Dylan."

"Well she had no problem going along with your stupid idea at the time. If I recall correctly, she even helped you plan it so you could change your identities and live in seclusion. It sounded like a grand idea at the time, didn't it? You were twenty-six years old and didn't like your life anymore. There was nothing original about that, Marshall, but you thought you were taking the easy way out. Well, there *is* no easy way out."

He sighed and gazed out the window wishing, as he so often did, that he'd had that wisdom ten years ago.

When Helen spoke again, he could still hear the pain in her voice. "You were so gifted and you worked so hard to get where you were, Marsh. Well, things aren't always what we think they'll be once we get there, but nothing's so bad that you have to do what you did. Neither you or Carrie really thought about what your actions would do to the rest of your lives or your families, never mind your fans." She knitted furiously as she added, "I didn't appreciate having to move and change my last name, either. I can tell you that."

He sat down beside her. "Would you at least give me credit for the forethought to put all my finances in that trust in your name before I disappeared?"

"Yes, I'll give you that much. At least those thieves who managed your affairs can't squander your millions or any future royalties, and you'll have enough to live on for the rest of your life, as you should for all your hard work."

"Mother, I know now that I could have done all of this differently if I'd only used my head. But I had a lot of pressure from all sides, including a manager and agent who were taking full advantage of my lack of business experience. I was burned out, ripped off, booked solid for the next several years and my life was out of control. I felt alone and had nowhere to turn. There was no relief from it."

Helen gently put her hand over his. "I know, dear. It broke my heart then and it still does. But you're where you are now for a reason. Dylan needs you," she gave his hand a squeeze, "and I need you."

He realized this was the first time he and his mother had finished a conversation without it ending in an argument since he and Dylan had arrived. It was the first time they'd been able to put some perspective on what had happened. But this had been an extraordinary morning in many ways. He'd been ambushed by a loyal fan who, thank God, didn't recognize him and he was beginning to taste the possibility of freedom from that terrible fear.

"I feel very strongly, Marsh, that we all need someone like Amanda right now," Helen said. "It's time to put Dylan first, and Lord knows I could use her help, as well."

He looked into her eyes and shook his head. "Amanda's the last thing I need right now, but I know you're right about Dylan and the help you need."

She patted his arm with a teasing smile. "I'm always right, dear."

"And what am I supposed to do about the chance Amanda could recognize me, since you have all the answers?"

"She's not going to recognize you, Marsh. She has her own problems to deal with, like everyone else, and she's only here to do her job. Trust me on this."

He gazed at her a moment, then leaned over and kissed her cheek. "You'd better be right this time, too, Mother." He gave her a quick hug before he got up. "I'll go check on Dylan."

"Tell him to wash up and we'll have lunch," Helen said as he headed out of the room.

When she heard him cross the living room and reach the stairs, she quietly opened the drawer of her sewing table and pulled out the two-page, stapled resume she had received in the mail from Amanda before she had interviewed her. On the second page under the heading "Hobbies and Interests" she re-read the delightful, self-revealing paragraph Amanda had written, concluding with: "I love long walks, good books and great music. I enjoy all kinds of music, but my favorite songs are the ballads of Marshall Stewart and I am still an incurable fan."

Chapter 5
Baseball and Other Games

It was only twelve-thirty in the afternoon, yet Amanda felt as though she'd already put in an eighteen-hour day. How could such a special morning she'd shared with Tom, have ended so badly? And now she sat alone in her new home, surrounded by boxes and piles of clothing, and it didn't feel like home at all. In fact, everything felt wrong as she drew her legs up into the easy chair and gazed out the living room window. The rain had subsided, leaving a grey, listless afternoon that pressed against her already discouraged spirit.

She sighed and leaned her head back. The break-up with Tom had been inevitable, and despite the guilt she felt at hurting someone so kind, there was also relief that it was over and she no longer would have to deal with the situation. But what had happened with Mark still haunted her.

Their conversation about Marshall Stewart had been so strange. If Mark didn't care about the singer, why would he be convinced that the fans had been somehow duped by a "romantic idea" in their heads? Why would he have given it any thought at all? But what she would never forget was the way he touched and held her face in his hand with a seductive gentleness that, until then, seemed completely out of character. As she replayed the moment in her mind, she recalled the look in his eyes, how it made her weak and speechless, and how it was as if he'd become someone else. It was over so suddenly that she wondered if she was making more of it now than had actually happened.

She looked at her watch. Twelve-forty. Time to take back the day. She reached for the phone and dialed the house. On the third ring, Helen answered.

"I've been wondering how you're doing. Are you all moved?"

"Most of the way – and thank you for the beautiful flowers. I love them."

"Just a little housewarming gift."

"They're lovely. Helen, I need to pick up a few groceries for myself tomorrow. Could I do some shopping for you while I'm out?"

"Oh, that would be wonderful, but it is your day off," Helen reminded her.

"I'll be happy to do it and then I'll be all set for my first official week of work. Do you think Dylan might want to come along? I've missed him today."

There was a bit of muffled conversation at the other end of the line before Helen got back on while Dylan cheered in the background.

Amanda laughed. "I'll take that as a yes."

"He's missed you too, but I'm keeping him out of your hair so you can finish what you need to do."

"Thanks – I'm just a little tired, but I'll stop over in the morning –"

"No, I'll save you the trip. I'll send Dylan over with my list and some money – say around ten o'clock?"

"That would be perfect, Helen. See you tomorrow." Amanda hung up, feeling better. Somewhat renewed, she put the radio on for company and tackled the unpacking.

Once she got busy it was suddenly five-thirty and she was hungry. She reached into the refrigerator for the only food she'd brought; a partially used carton of eggs, a quart of milk, a stick of butter and a loaf of bread. Scrambled eggs and toast sounded like a feast and she set about making supper. She found a box of tea bags she'd unpacked with the coffee supplies and made herself a soothing, hot cup of tea. It rejuvenated her for one more task she was dreading. She had to call her mother and let her know she had moved. If not for that, she would just as soon not bother until Christmas.

As usual, her mother answered the phone with a flat "Hello."

"Hi, Mom," Amanda got out in as pleasant a voice as she could manage.

"Well, if it isn't the prodigal daughter! Hey, cupcake, how ya doing?"

"I'm fine, thank you, Mom." Amanda could almost smell the cigarettes and booze in her mother's raspy voice. "And how are you and –"

"John."

"John? Is he the one I met when –"

"No, that was Dave, that worthless piece 'a –"

"Mom, I just called to let you know I've moved and to give you the new address."

"Why? Did you get a new job?"

"Well, yes."

"Doing what?"

"The same thing." It was much easier to lie than to have the energy sucked out of her while she tried to explain her change in occupation.

"Oh, so you're still some kind of hoity-toity Administrative Assistant?"

Amanda sighed. "Sort of. Anyway, I've only moved a few miles from where I was. I'm at 16 Meadowlark Lane. Same Zip Code." Amanda added her phone number.

"Hang on while I write all this down."

Amanda could see her mother balancing the receiver on her shoulder, cigarette dangling from the side of her mouth as she most likely scribbled on a nearby cocktail napkin.

"How's Jen?" Amanda dutifully inquired about her younger sister.

"She's doing great. She's dancin' at Dickie's Hideaway – makin' way better tips than at that other dive."

"So this is a better dive?"

"Well the clientele sure is higher class – all businessmen – like the ones you're working for, only you keep your clothes on and probably bring home less money."

"Okay, Mom. I've got to go."

"One more thing, cupcake. Guess who's been looking for you?"

"I'm afraid to ask."

"Your fiancé."

There was a pause while Amanda got over the shock. "You mean my ex-fiancé. What does Brad want?"

"He called here a few days ago and said he was trying to reach you, but your phone was disconnected. He asked me if I knew where you were. I think he's having second thoughts," her mother added smugly.

"He's already had second thoughts, and don't give him my new address or phone number. I don't want to see him."

"Are you sure about that? Let's face it. You're not getting any younger and you may not get another offer like this one."

"Like what?"

"Well look at the money this guy makes. So he hurt your feelings about the baby thing. Maybe he's willing to adopt, after all. Don't look a gift horse in the mouth. I'd definitely give him another chance."

"Yes, I'm sure you would, Mom, but I've moved on. No address or phone number. Period."

Her mother chuckled condescendingly. "Well, you may think you're too good for him now, but you're pricing yourself right out of the market, sweetie."

"Thanks for the advice, but since I'm not a piece of meat it really doesn't concern me."

This time her mother sighed. "I don't know where you get those uppity standards from."

"Don't worry, Mom. I'm sure they're not in the genes. I have to go now."

Amanda hung up, exhausted all over again, and poured herself a hot bubble bath. She pinned up her hair and lowered herself into the old-fashion bathtub, sighing with relief as the hot water slowly relaxed every muscle.

She lay back and closed her eyes, dizzy from all that had happened that day. Making the move, arguing with Tom, feeling Mark's unexpected touch, and now the news that Brad was looking for her. She let out a laugh at the absurdity of it all. She had gone from having no one in her life a few months ago, to a day in which she'd had to deal with three different men and three very different situations.

Yet the only one she saw every time she closed her eyes was Mark. She'd never met a man like him. No one had ever confused her senses the way he did. In the few days since she'd met him, she'd been certain she had him pegged. He was nothing but an egotistical tyrant who was bent on driving her away from this place.

She felt she could learn to deal with that over time, and was clear on where they stood with one another – at least until today when the feel of his hand on her face had completely disarmed her. What had it meant?

She sighed, her mind drifting in the comfort and peace of the bath. When she caught herself nodding off, she reluctantly climbed out, toweled off and shrugged into her bathrobe. She padded across the living room, turned out the lights and went into her new bedroom. It was painted a soft blue with white furniture and she loved it already. With a yawn she settled into the freshly made bed and drifted into a dream about a mysterious man who lived just across the yard.

***

The distant banging began somewhere in the haze of her sleep, then grew louder until she awoke with a start. She

90

blinked in the sunlight that streamed across the bed through unfamiliar windows and for a moment she felt totally lost. But as she slowly managed to focus her eyes on her surroundings she was reminded of the previous day's move and the fact that she was waking up in her new apartment.

The banging, now louder than ever, was at the outside door and she leapt out of bed, pulling on her bathrobe. Halfway across the living room she stopped. What if it was Mark? She couldn't answer the door dressed this way.

"Hey, Manda!" a little voice yelled urgently. "Let me in! It's me!"

Breathing a sigh of relief, Amanda unlocked and opened the door, then laughed at the sight of Dylan with his nose pressed against the screen. "Hi, you!" she greeted him as she let him in.

Dylan was out of breath and shaking. "I was bangin' and bangin' and I got scared that you left!"

He stood in her living room in a striped tee shirt, shorts and sneakers, looking up at her with large, liquid eyes.

"What do you mean, you got scared that I left?" Amanda crouched and swept him into a hug, kissing him hard on the cheek.

When she released him he gulped, anxiously prancing from one foot to the other. "I didn't know because nobody else who ever came here stayed and I thought maybe you left too!"

"I'm here to stay." Amanda opened her arms and they held each other again. "You're stuck with me," she murmured through his wispy curls. He squeezed her more tightly and she was amazed at the need in his grasp. He seemed so hungry for affection and reassurance. It verified her belief that she belonged here for however long she was needed. She drew back to look at him. "I missed you yesterday."

"Grandma wouldn't let me come over and I wanted to help but she said I could help more by staying in the house. I thought that was dumb!" He folded his arms.

"Not as dumb as you think." Amanda mussed his hair. "I wonder what time it is," she added with a yawn and a stretch. She glanced at the wall clock in the kitchen. "It's after ten o'clock, already?"

"Yeah! It's really late! I got up at seven-thirty!" When Amanda turned back to him he still had his arms folded and was staring at her with his most formidable expression. "Are you gonna do this all the time?" he asked with all the admonition of a dissatisfied employer.

Amanda laughed. "No, boss – it'll never happen again. Let me get dressed and we'll have some toast and go shopping."

"Neat!" Dylan was all child again.

"Did Grandma send her list?"

"Yep, and the money, too."

"Okay – I'll be right back."

He waited in the living room while she dressed. The late July morning was already quite warm and she put on a comfortable pair of white knit shorts, a matching pullover knit top and sneakers. She tied her hair up into a loose pony tail and dabbed some light color on her face.

Dylan was seated on the couch, swinging his legs and studying her Marshall Stewart album cover, still on the coffee table from the day before. "Hey, who's this?" he asked as though he'd been contemplating the picture.

Amanda opened her mouth to launch into an explanation, but a flashback of her encounter with Mark over the matter dampened her enthusiasm. "Never mind. Let's have some breakfast."

They shared toast and jam while Dylan chattered about more subjects than she could keep track of. Then they headed out to her car.

"Can we put the top down?" Dylan asked.

"I think we should."

***

Marsh walked between the French doors of the sunporch, coffee cup in hand.

Helen was reading the newspaper.

"It's too quiet around here. Where's Dylan?"

"Oh, he and Amanda are going shopping," Helen replied without looking up.

"Shopping? She's taking him out?"

"Well, that will be required if he's going with her."

"But –"

"But what, Marsh?"

The tinkling of distant laughter drifted on the breeze through the open window. He went over and looked out to see Amanda and Dylan by the carriage house, folding down the roof of her convertible. His eyes were unwillingly drawn to her appealing figure in her shorts outfit, then followed her shapely legs and the snap of her pony tail as she moved around the car, letting Dylan think he was helping her as they chatted and she showed him how to fasten down the canvas.

He heard Dylan's excited voice as she got him into the front seat and did up his seat belt before she went around and hopped in. As she started the car she pulled on a cap and a pair of sunglasses, then playfully revved the engine a couple of times, much to Dylan's delight before they headed down the driveway and turned onto the road.

For several moments he gazed at the empty driveway, trying to suppress an unexpected twinge of envy. He envied the two of them for the freedom they had to go out in public without a second thought. He envied Amanda for the ease with which she was developing a bond with his son, but most of all, he envied Dylan for having Amanda all to himself.

Helen watched her son from behind as he lingered at the window. "I don't imagine they'll be gone too long," she remarked.

"No – probably not," he said hastily as he headed from the room.

A knowing smile flitted across Helen's lips as she returned to her paper.

***

It was about an hour and a half later when Amanda and Dylan pulled up in front of the house and she'd barely parked before Dylan leapt out of the car wearing a new baseball cap and waving a vinyl catcher's mitt and plastic bat.

"Grandma!" he yelled as he raced inside. She heard his excited voice continue into the kitchen. "Look what Manda bought me and we're gonna play baseball!"

Amanda opened the trunk and took out the couple of bags of groceries Helen had asked for, then headed through the screen door and into the kitchen. "That wasn't on your list or mine –" she started to laugh before she caught a glimpse of Mark sitting at the table, looking at the bat and mitt Dylan had handed him. Despite her hopeful glance around the room, Helen was not around.

Without looking at Mark, Amanda went to the counter with the bags and began putting cans and boxes into the cupboards as Dylan's chatter filled the awkward space between them. She sensed him watching her as he responded now and then to Dylan's detailed discourse about their shopping trip

"And then we stopped at Manda's old apartment 'cause she had to pick up a couple more things, and we saw the man who helped her move here but she didn't want to talk to him so we left."

Amanda froze, still facing the cupboard, eyes closed.

"And what else did Amanda do that she wouldn't want you talking about?" Mark asked.

She knew by his tone that he was looking for a reaction from her and she went back to what she was doing as a flush rose into her cheeks.

"What's all this I heard about Dylan's new baseball career?" Helen asked as she wheeled herself from her room.

As Dylan began showing her what he had, Amanda turned, hoping the bright red had left her face. "Helen, I bought a chicken and I'd love to cook dinner tonight if you don't mind."

"Cool!" Dylan piped up. "Can we have mashed potatoes, too?"

"I'm sure we'd love chicken tonight, but this is still supposed to be your day off," Helen said.

"Yes, and I've been enjoying every minute of it. Cooking a nice Sunday dinner will be the perfect ending for me, if that's okay with you."

"Well, we're not going to argue about a home-cooked meal," Helen said, "are we, Mark?"

Amanda knew Mark had continued watching her, but when she looked at him now he quickly averted his eyes. "Whatever you want," he said as he took his cane and got up. "I'm not really hungry."

"Can we have mashed potatoes?" Dylan repeated as Mark made his way out of the room.

Amanda looked down at him with a little sigh. "Of course we can."

"But we hafta play baseball first," Dylan reminded her.

"Yes, we do. So just let me take my groceries to my place and I'll be back in a few minutes."

Dylan took off from the kitchen as Amanda reached into her pocket for her car keys.

"I'm hoping we'll get Mark to eat dinner with us one of these days," Helen said.

"You mean, he *never* has dinner with you and Dylan?"

Helen sighed. "Very seldom. Arguing about it hasn't helped, so I leave him alone. I suppose he will when he's ready." When Amanda shook her head, not understanding, Helen said softly, "He's still got a ways to come back, Amanda. But I'm hoping that, over time, he'll be all right."

"I hope so, too," Amanda said, "for Dylan's sake."

"Of course," Helen agreed, gazing back at her. "For Dylan's sake."

***

Marsh sat in the easy chair in his room, trying to read the newspaper. The warm breeze from the window beside him ruffled the pages. Irritated, he grabbed them, wrinkling them in his tight hand. He wasted a few more moments of staring at the newsprint without really seeing it, then tossed the paper aside. Leaning forward he rested his elbows on his knees and wearily rubbed his forehead, blinking his tired, sore eyes. He'd slept even less last night than he usually did, but this time there had been a different energy keeping him alert and uneasy.

Rather than the usual concerns about his situation and how he'd gotten here, he found himself savoring the thought of how Amanda's skin and lovely face had felt in his hand, how close he'd come to touching his lips to hers and how grateful he was for Tom's interruption. Between those thoughts, he'd spent the rest of the night acutely aware of her proximity, just across the yard, in and around his home during the day and the constant threat of her finding out who he really was.

Even with that concern he couldn't stop thinking about how fresh and gorgeous she'd looked in the sunshine that morning when she and Dylan had left on their shopping trip, and the unexpected jolt of jealousy he'd felt when Dylan's chatter had revealed that Amanda had run into Tom at her old apartment building. It appeared they'd broken up, but why? How permanent was it? For God's sake, what was wrong with him? This girl hadn't even been here a week, yet she was already in his head.

He realized the irony of it all. Until now, his worst fear had been to have a stranger come into his home, the only place on earth where he felt secure and safe from being discovered. It had never entered his mind that this person could at the same time be so good for Dylan and so appealing to him. The fact that Amanda always had been and still was a devoted Marshall Stewart fan added a new element of terror to his daily life.

When he had decided to disappear at such a young, foolish age, he had planned on sharing the rest of his life in seclusion with Carrie and a growing family. He never foresaw the possibility that she could eventually crack under the strain of such a cloistered existence and end up an alcoholic who hated him for what he'd done to both their lives. He never anticipated that she could be gone in an instant, with the remaining decades of his secretive life stretching before him in a void he would never be able to fill with anyone other than immediate family, where he would no longer thrive on his passion of writing and performing music, where the realization would come too late that, while he had enough money to buy a new life, he would never have enough to buy back his old one.

"Daddy!" There was a light knock at his door.

"What is it, Scoot?" he asked without moving.

"Manda and me are tryin' to play baseball, but she doesn't know how to pitch good and she said maybe she could be the catcher and you could pitch."

"Great," he muttered under his breath as he got up. He opened the door to find Dylan standing there alone, bat slung over his shoulder.

"Please, Daddy, could you come outside?"

He tried to keep the reluctance out of his voice. "Sure, Scoot. I'll be right there."

As Dylan ran off, he reached for his cane with the uneasy feeling that Amanda had engineered this scheme to get him out of his room to play with his son.

***

After a couple of practice swings and the hasty establishment of first, second and third bases at various trees and bushes, Dylan adjusted his cap with all the confidence of a pro. "Okay, Manda, let's try one more pitch before Daddy comes!" He lifted the bat, which seemed almost too large for him to manage.

"Wait a minute." Amanda walked over to him. "Let's try something." She took the bat, put it over her shoulder and squatted slightly, slowly moving it back and forth. "I think you're supposed to hold it this way."

Dylan took the bat and assumed the stance while Amanda moved back to attempt another pitch.

"Go team, go!" Helen cheered from her seat on the front porch.

Amanda tossed the ball and by sheer chance, Dylan's bat connected with it and sent it careening off into the bushes.

"Run!" Amanda yelled. She took her time retrieving the ball as Dylan ran as fast as he could to each of the make-shift bases and dramatically slid into home base just before she set down the ball.

As Helen clapped and whistled, Amanda scooped Dylan up into her arms. "You did it! Give me five!"

Dylan slapped his hand on hers and she spun him around, setting him back down when she saw Mark standing on the porch.

"Daddy, did you see me? I just hit a home run!"

"I saw you, Scoot, but I'm not so sure you're learning to play baseball."

As he made his way off the porch, Amanda folded her arms with a toss of her pony tail. "Well, maybe I'm no Babe Ruth, but someone has to teach him."

"You tell him, Amanda!" Helen crowed.

"The stands are closed, Mother," Mark said over his shoulder as he shot Amanda a warning glance. He leaned his cane against the bench under the tree and walked over to Dylan. "You can control the ball better if you hold the bat a little differently, Scoot."

Amanda stood a short distance away and watched as they conferred for several moments, then Mark stood behind him, his hands over Dylan's as they held the bat and practiced several make-believe swings. They were so absorbed in being father and son that she wished she could preserve the moment, until she remembered Mark's irrational reaction to her camera the other day.

When they separated, Mark walked over and reached for the ball. As she handed it to him, his fingers closed around hers and held them. She glanced up, startled.

"You may be very good at playing games, Amanda," he spoke so that only she could hear him, "but baseball isn't one of them." When he released her hand and walked away, she let out a breath, unaware that she'd been holding it.

"Remember what I showed you," Mark prompted Dylan.

"I remember! Put it right here, Daddy!"

Mark pitched and Dylan swung, then squealed when his bat made contact.

"Run!" Mark yelled as he reeled backward to catch the ball. Dylan dropped the bat and took off just as Mark lost his balance and his bad leg went out from under him.

Amanda watched helplessly as he fell before she could reach him.

"Daddy!" Dylan screeched, forgetting all about first base.

"Marsh!" Amanda thought she heard Helen cry out from the porch.

When Amanda got to him, he was clutching his leg and wincing with pain. "Here, let me help you up." She reached for his arm.

"I'm fine," he groaned without looking at her.

Dylan reached them. "Daddy, you're hurt!"

Mark got to his knees. "I'm okay, Dylan. Just go in the house."

"Wait – I'll get your cane," Amanda offered.

"Leave me alone, dammit!"

As Amanda and Dylan stood there, the only sound that remained was the faint drone of an airplane somewhere overhead. The spell was broken. Everything was back to the way it had been, as if the past few minutes had never happened.

"I'm sorry, Daddy!" Dylan put his dirty hands to a suddenly wet face. "I didn't mean to make you fall!"

Amanda waited for his father to reassure him, but when he didn't answer, a surge of anger came over her along with the overwhelming urge to straighten Mark Sterner out.

"It's not your fault, Dylan," she said, taking his hand. "We'll go inside and do something else now. This game isn't fun anymore and besides, Daddy's too busy feeling sorry for himself."

Mark sent her up a murderous glare as she collected the ball and bat and headed for the house with Dylan.

"Is he hurt, Amanda?" Helen asked anxiously as they reached the porch.

"I have no idea, but he wants to be left alone, so we'll give him his space."

"But he's obviously in pain. He needs help!"

"What he needs most is for us not to watch him," Amanda said. "Let's go inside."

Helen reluctantly let Amanda help her up and they went into the kitchen. Amanda helped her back into her wheelchair and bent to wipe the dirt from Dylan's cheeks as he continued to sob. "Why don't you go wash your face and I'll meet you on the sunporch in a minute." She kissed his forehead and he nodded and slowly headed for the bathroom.

Amanda sat down at the table as Helen pulled out a handkerchief and sniffled into it, shaking her head. "You're right about leaving him alone. He's so stubborn and difficult, but I'm still his mother and it hurts me to see him hurt. When your child needs help, you want to help him, no matter how old or obstinate he is."

Amanda gazed at her, trying to phrase what she wanted to say. "Mark does need help, Helen," she said softly, "but not just to get up off the ground."

"I know. Oh, Amanda, if only I could tell you everything..."

"Why can't you?" she dared to ask.

Helen took Amanda's hand and looked into her eyes. "I hope a day will come when I can, and then you'll understand all this. It's just too soon now, but at least you got him outside with Dylan today, and that's a start." She smiled gratefully, patting Amanda's arm.

"Yes." Amanda smiled back. "It's a start." She leaned forward to look out the window. Mark was limping over to the bench where he picked up his cane. "I think he's going to be okay," she assured Helen, breathing her own sigh of relief despite the anger she still felt over his behavior. "I don't want to see Mark hurt anymore than you do."

As Amanda got up to go and find Dylan, she caught the glow in the older woman's face as she said, "Yes, Amanda, I believe I do know."

Chapter 6
Please Don't Leave

Although the fall had hurt, Marsh could tell he hadn't done any more damage to his leg. By the time he had slowly drawn himself up off the ground, he'd resigned himself to the fact that the only thing that really smarted was his pride. What good was a father who couldn't even handle a simple game of baseball with his son? And after seeing the look on Dylan's face as he'd struggled to get up, he was convinced the only thing worse was earning the sympathy of a six-year-old.

But there had been no sympathy from Amanda. In fact, she'd eyed him with outright contempt when he refused her help. Worse yet, she had insulted him and made him look foolish in front of his son, and something had to be done about that. He probably shouldn't have been so gruff, he admitted to himself as he limped toward the house. But dammit, what did she know about pain – or the frustration of feeling a failure at parenthood?

As he entered the kitchen, he was instantly annoyed at the anxious expression on his mother's face and he braced himself for the inevitable questions.

"Marsh, are you okay?" she asked in a hushed voice. She cast a furtive glance over her shoulder, making sure they couldn't be overheard.

"I'm fine, Mother."

"But you took such a bad tumble. Are you sure?"

"I said I'm fine."

"Well, your son isn't. He thinks this was all his fault because he hit the ball and you fell trying to catch it and you never said a word to make him feel better."

"But that's ridiculous. It was an accident."

"Then you need to make sure he understands that. And while you're at it, you need to apologize to both Dylan and Amanda. They were only trying to help."

"Maybe one of them was," he muttered as he left the kitchen.

He wasn't sure if Dylan and Amanda were downstairs until he heard their voices on the sunporch. Neither of them noticed him as the sound of his approach was muted by the living room carpet and he used the opportunity to hold back behind the curtain on one of the French doors until he knew what to say.

Dylan lay on the braided rug with a bright array of crayons scattered around him as he worked diligently on a picture in his coloring book. Amanda was curled into one of the large wicker chairs paging through a magazine, her slender legs draped over the arm.

"So how come you don't have any kids?" Dylan was asking as he continued to color without looking up.

Amanda continued to turn pages.

"Well, for one thing, I'm not married."

"You don't hafta be married to have kids," Dylan pointed out matter-of-factly. "Daddy's got me, and he's not married."

Amanda glanced at him. "Yes, but he was – to your mother."

Dylan cocked his head thoughtfully, still studying his picture. "So, were you married before, too?"

"I almost was, once."

"What happened?"

"He changed his mind."

"Why, Manda?"

"Oh, I guess he just wasn't Mr. Right."

"Who's he?"

Marsh was torn between interrupting their conversation to spare Amanda any further explanations and letting them go on, to satisfy his own curiosity.

"Mr. Right is the man I'll marry someday, if I ever find him."

"Oh. And then will you have kids?"

She sighed and put down her magazine. "No."

Dylan sat up to stare at her. "Why not, Manda? Doncha want any?"

"Of course I do, but – well, this conversation is getting too grown-up for you, so let's –"

"No it's not! All I ever talk to is grown-ups!"

"I suppose you're right." Amanda studied him thoughtfully, then sat up straight, chin-in-hand. "You know who God is, right?"

Dylan nodded. "Pretty much. Grandma says Mommy went to live with him. I hope he's nice."

"He's very nice, and God decides everything, so he decided a long time ago that I wouldn't have any babies."

Dylan's eyes widened. "How can he be nice if he won't let you have babies? Aren't you mad at him?"

"I suppose I was for awhile." Amanda got out of her chair and went over to him. "But he's given me something else that's very special."

"What?"

She smiled as she bent to caress his head. "He's given me you to take care of," she said softly, "and I'm awfully glad he did."

With nothing more to say, Dylan grinned bashfully and went back to coloring.

Marsh felt an ache rise into his throat as he watched Amanda's hands lovingly stroke his son's hair. As he forgot himself and shifted his weight, a floorboard creaked. Startled, Amanda and Dylan turned at the same time and he was forced to own up to his presence in the doorway before he was ready.

***

When Mark stepped into the room, Amanda slowly rose to face him. She made no effort to hide her irritation. After the unpleasant scene in the yard, she didn't owe him any courtesies. It also annoyed her that she hadn't heard him coming and she wondered how long he'd been there.

"Daddy – are you okay?" The tremor in Dylan's voice made it clear he was still concerned about where he stood with his father.

"Yes, I'm okay." Mark looked at Amanda until she turned and busied herself, straightening the magazines on the table. "Come here," she heard him say to Dylan.

When she glanced over her shoulder, he was bending over, talking softly to his son as Dylan nodded. Amanda knew they were finished when Dylan asked, "Can I ride my bike now?"

"Go ahead."

She heard Dylan race from the room and turned to find Mark still standing there. Without acknowledgment, she knelt on the floor and began to pick up the crayons. She needed to keep moving to quell her anger.

"I've apologized," Mark said.

"Good." Amanda shoved the crayons into their box. "That's the least you can do."

"I'm sure it is, and I suppose I should apologize to you, too."

"Fine."

He had come closer and it only irked her more to have him standing over her as she gathered the last few crayons, still refusing to look up.

"It was my own fault. I should know my limitations by now."

She slammed the box of crayons onto the floor. "Well maybe you can't run the way you used to, and maybe there are a lot of other things you can't do the way you used to, but you don't have to take it out on your son."

"I've set that right with him," Mark's voice rose in frustration, "but you had no right to belittle me in front of him!"

"You belittled yourself by the way you behaved!"

She gasped as he grabbed her arm and pulled her up in front of him. The firmness in his grasp surprised her and his expression told her he was furious.

"I would appreciate it if you would stop judging me when you have no facts!" His words cut like jagged shards of glass.

Amanda's adrenaline kicked in, giving her a false sense of courage. "The facts are, you have a beautiful little boy, relatively good health and obviously enough money to live comfortably. What happened to you was terrible and I understand that you're still grieving –"

"You don't understand *anything*! And I'm getting tired of you interfering in my relationship with my son!" His hand was still around Amanda's arm, holding her close to him, as she tried not to lose her nerve.

She glanced up, then looked away. "One thing I know for sure is, Dylan needs you to be with him and to know that you love him. Anyone can see that." She could feel his glare penetrating her face and she knew she was visibly trembling. "You can let go of me now."

There was an eternity of a moment in which she thought he might not. Then, as quickly as he released her, there was a tug against her head and her hair tumbled around her shoulders. She lifted her hand reflexively to find that the ribbon in her pony tail was gone. Unable to move, she felt strangely vulnerable. When she dared to look up, his eyes were no longer angry, but were filled with an emotion she couldn't read.

"For the last time," he said slowly, "I never wanted you here, but since you're hell bent on staying, here's how it's going to be. You'll do the job you were hired to do and nothing more. You'll stop interfering in matters that are none of your business and we'll talk only when and if it's necessary to make decisions concerning Dylan. Do I make myself clear?" His tone chilled her before he lifted her hand, placed the ribbon there and closed her fingers around it.

She looked down through a wavy blur as her eyes began to sting. An unexpected, profound sadness had come over her.

"My goodness, Amanda," he said with a note of triumph, "You're not coming undone, are you?"

She drew her hand back and looked up at him, determinedly blinking back the tears. "You win."

"What?"

"You've proven to me that I'm doing more harm than good here, so I'll leave as soon as I can find another place to live. This was a mistake and I'm sorry I've wasted everyone's time." She glimpsed a look of shock on his face before she turned and walked out, across the living room and to the front door.

"Amanda? Is anything wrong?" Helen called from the kitchen.

"I'll call you later." Amanda let the screen door slam behind her.

***

110

Marsh stood staring at the floor, struggling with the panic that was rising into his chest. He turned to the windows. She was marching toward the carriage house, hair streaming behind her in the breeze, that damn ribbon clasped in her fist.

"Marsh!" Worse yet, his mother's voice was closer than the kitchen. She appeared in her wheelchair between the porch doors. "What happened? Why is Amanda upset?" When he didn't answer, Helen moved closer. "You didn't *dare* fire her!"

"No. She told me she wants to leave."

"And how, pray tell, could she have possibly reached *that* decision?"

He looked at the floor again. "I've been an ass."

"Well now we're getting somewhere! So you got what you wanted, Marsh! You're right back to nothing! No help with Dylan and – God forbid it would occur to you – no help for me! I hope you're happy!" Helen turned her wheelchair around and headed back toward the kitchen.

He sighed and shook his head. It would have been bad enough having one woman mad at him, but now there were two and he knew what he needed to do.

When he reached his room he shut the door, threw down his cane and collapsed into the chair. It had been his goal from the moment Amanda was hired, to drive her away, and as of a few minutes ago, he'd succeeded. He had chipped away at her, every chance he had, and she'd finally broken. In the short time he'd known her he could tell she was not one to cry easily. But what disturbed him even more was that he could tell she was a no-nonsense young woman who didn't make idle threats. If she was upset enough to say she was quitting, she would quit. Even with no new job prospect or place to live, even if it meant going hungry, he suspected she had that kind of determination. Even with her heart breaking over leaving Dylan.

Hadn't he heard her telling Dylan she couldn't have children and how much it meant to have him to care for? What kind of miserable person would not be happy for that, especially if it was a much-needed help to himself and his mother?

He sighed and gazed out the window as the cooling, late afternoon breeze rustled the leaves below. It had been a beautiful day – like so many others he'd barely noticed or appreciated. Amanda and Dylan had tried to enjoy it but he'd taken it away from them. And now he forced himself to face the fact that he had done it out of jealousy. Besides a jumble of other mixed-up feelings he'd felt since Amanda had arrived, his jealousy over her closeness to his son and her ability to shame him for his lack in that area had been a constant jab. He was angry that she could sweep in here and bond effortlessly with his son, angry at how her presence had only magnified his shortcomings as a parent, and afraid of an inevitable new phase in his life that could lead to demands he had no idea how to meet.

The only thing he was sure of was the undeniable certainty in his gut that he had to fix this. Pulling the ribbon out of her pony tail had been his desperate attempt to bully her, even to symbolically rough her up a bit, but the sight of her hair in disarray around her shoulders had aroused him as much as when he'd touched her the day before.

He mustn't let Amanda go. Instinct told him that if he let that happen, it would be the second most colossal mistake of his life.

***

Amanda sobbed hard, into her hands as she stood at her bedroom window watching Dylan teeter around on his bicycle in the distance. She wished, for his sake, that she'd never answered Helen's ad. She couldn't bear the thought of letting Dylan down, leaving his life as suddenly as she'd come into it, putting him through another abandonment. Yet, she could hardly face the thought of going back to the loneliness and lack of purpose she'd felt when her wedding was called off. How many times could she reinvent her life? When would it make the kind of sense she thought she'd found here?

Until now, her encounters with Mark had been tense, baffling at best. But what had just happened was different, as if a line had been crossed that changed everything. There had been a stone coldness in the way he treated her, even taunting her tears. Whatever part of him had tenderly touched her the day before was a mystery. She'd wanted to believe she had glimpsed the real Mark Sterner, but he had convinced her today that she was nothing more than an intruder in his home and a nuisance in his life and he would continue to make things as unpleasant for her as possible. The problem was, her inability to get along with Mark was also making things unpleasant for Dylan, and that was defeating her purpose.

She had just decided to calm herself with a cup of tea when the phone rang. She sighed. It had to be Helen, asking for an explanation, and although she wasn't up to talking, she knew Helen would be worried if she didn't answer

"Hello," she said wearily into the receiver. There was silence. "Hello?"

"Please don't leave." It was barely above a whisper but she knew it was him.

She held her breath, not knowing what to say.

"Amanda."

"Yes." Not ready to deal with him again so soon, she put her hand over her face.

"We need you to stay – all of us."

She gazed out the window with red, swollen eyes. Helen had probably given him an ultimatum and he would most likely do anything to restore the peace.

"Amanda?"

She sighed. "I don't think it would be good for Dylan if I stayed. It's not a healthy environment – for any of us."

"I know I've made it that way and I know I have to change."

"Well, I hope you can get the help you need –"

"I need *you*. I mean – I need you to stay." When she didn't reply he continued slowly, "After the accident, before you came, Dylan was sad and quiet. I didn't realize how much until I saw the way you drew him out. I didn't realize because I was only thinking of my own pain, and I knew it was wrong but I couldn't find my way out of it."

"How long ago was the accident?" Amanda dared to ask. Too much curiosity on her part could abruptly end this conversation.

There was a slight pause before he answered, "A year ago – next month. I tried to go it alone with Dylan for a few months but it wasn't working and my mother urged us to come here."

"You did the right thing," she said.

"That remains to be seen."

Amanda thought a moment. "I still don't know."

"I promise I'll stay out of your way, Amanda. I won't bother you and I'll let you take care of Dylan the way he needs to be cared for. I know that's the least I can do for him."

"And what about you?"

"What do you mean?"

"How will *you* heal?" She held her breath, knowing she'd entered risky territory.

"I'll – find my own way," he said quietly. "Will you stay?"

Amanda closed her eyes tightly. "I would like nothing more."

"Good. Thank you."

They hung up and she sat on the side of the bed, offering a silent prayer of her own thanks. She looked back out the window where Dylan had gone to the swing that hung from the giant back yard tree and was slowly turning, winding the chain before he spun wildly. She glanced at the clock. It was nearly three-thirty – time to head back and start the chicken dinner with the mashed potatoes she had promised.

She went into the bathroom and washed her face, then put some fresh color on her cheeks and lips. Gazing into the mirror she let out a shaky sigh of relief that always came after a cleansing cry. She couldn't wait to start her routine tomorrow. Looking after Dylan on a day-to-day basis, caring for Helen and making the lovely house they shared feel like more of a home, would also make her feel needed and worthwhile.

As for Mark, his manner in their phone conversation had shown yet another personality somewhere between the various moods and rants she'd encountered up to now. Who was this man, really? What else was he struggling to overcome besides the obvious tragedy he'd endured?

She thought back over the doomed baseball game and how livid he'd become when he fell. She recalled that she had distinctly heard Helen call him by a slightly different name -- something like "Marsh" – and wondered if it could be a childhood nickname that had slipped out in her expression of concern.

"Marsh". She turned it over in her mind. If that was what Helen had said, the only other time Amanda had heard anyone called that name was all those years ago when interviewers or fellow musicians who knew him well spoke to Marshall Stewart. She had video tapes that had been compiled and released after his disappearance, showing him working in the recording studio, on the road between concerts, composing his music in a quiet corner as he strummed his trademark twelve-string guitar. In those films, the people around him could be heard referring to him as "Marsh". It really was a rare nickname for a man, and she decided that she couldn't have heard Helen correctly. She convinced herself that "Marsh" was close enough to "Mark" to be misheard in certain situations.

She grabbed a large clip from the bathroom shelf and drew her hair up on top of her head, pinning it to keep it out of the way while she cooked dinner. Something told her she was done with pony tails and ribbons.

***

Helen was relieved and overjoyed when Amanda walked into the kitchen that afternoon and although it wasn't discussed, it was understood that Mark had straightened things out with her. They chatted non-stop as Amanda prepared dinner, and it was as if their friendship from years ago had picked up where it left off, effortlessly, with the added delight of getting to know each other better. Helen made her feel completely at ease, giving her free reign of the kitchen. "Just treat this place like your own, Amanda, and I know you'll take good care of it," she'd said in the first few days Amanda was there.

When dinner was ready, they called Dylan in from outside and the three of them shared their meal, as was becoming their habit. Dylan loved his mashed potatoes and as Amanda watched him eat, she offered another prayer of thanks that she would be here for him, after all.

When she cleaned up the kitchen and put away the leftovers, she fixed a plate, wrapped it up and placed it in the front of the refrigerator where Mark would see it later. It was a gesture of appreciation for his phone call. And although it was in their agreement that they would make a point of avoiding each other, she made a silent promise that she would find a way to get him to start having meals with his son again. It would be a vital first step in healing their relationship.

Chapter 7
The Way You Should Be Loved

July quickly passed into August and as Amanda went about her babysitting and household tasks over the next few weeks, Mark kept his word about staying out of her way and she only caught occasional glimpses of him.

She learned that it was his habit to take his morning coffee on the sunporch with Helen and to sit and read on the bench on the outside porch during some of the remaining August afternoons. She also found out that he liked gardening and tended to a small vegetable patch in the yard on the other side of the house along with Helen's assorted flowerbeds and bushes in the back. Sometimes when she was starting dinner he would bring in some fresh vegetables and leave them on the kitchen counter with a brief nod or hello, but he never lingered.

Although she pretended to go along with his distant manner, it excited her when he was near and she longed for another conversation with him. But if this was the only way her presence here would work, she was willing to invest the time in this phase with the hope of eventually developing an easier, more natural relationship.

Her relationship with Dylan, however, was flourishing. Each day she learned more about the thoughts and behavior of a six-year-old. Each day she sought to understand and fulfill his needs. The physical part was obvious and easy – make him balanced meals, make sure he had clean clothes, washed his face and hands and kept his bedtime routine, especially with school starting soon. He was an eager passenger any time she invited him, with Helen's permission, to accompany her on an errand or grocery shopping. But the emotional part of looking after Dylan was trickier and more involved. He was starved for reassurance and affection, and as much as his grandmother was able to give him, he looked for and found just as much from Amanda.

Amanda had discovered the local Library and from the first time she took Dylan, he was enthralled, and delighted in picking out storybooks she would read with him in the evening before his bedtime.

As thrilled as she was with the extra attention Amanda gave Dylan, Helen insisted that she take her well-earned time off for fear she might "burn out" and grow tired of the routine. During her mornings and evenings, Amanda got back into enjoying long walks and explored the area neighborhoods as well as catching up on some reading. She'd always loved biographies, especially stories of people who'd conquered and risen above difficulties in their lives. It had given her the courage to leave her dysfunctional home and make a decent life for herself. She'd always enjoyed sketching, but hadn't had much time for it since she'd taken art classes at the community college. On one of her mornings off she'd gone to the local art shop and treated herself to a large pad and box of pastels, getting back into the habit of picking it up whenever she felt inspired.

Toward the end of her first month with the Sterners, Amanda realized that, despite the bleak outlook in the beginning, she'd become very comfortable in this place. She loved working for these people and knew it was because Mark wanted her here and was willing to keep out of her way and let her do her job, to ensure that she would stay. Yet, she wondered how long this arrangement could realistically continue, since he had to be even more reclusive to avoid her. This still was not good for Dylan, and she hoped Mark would gradually feel more at ease and make his presence felt, for Dylan's sake.

Although August was quickly turning into September, there was a languid, hot spell that Amanda impatiently tolerated, given the promise of the cool Fall days she knew were coming soon. But she would remember that warm, humid Friday night of Labor Day weekend for everything but the weather.

That evening Amanda was in the kitchen, finishing her usual after dinner clean-up when there was a knock at the front screen door around seven-thirty. Helen had gone to her room for the night after not sleeping well the night before and Mark was upstairs. Dylan, who'd been playing on the sunporch, got to the door first and called, "Manda – there's a man who wants to see you!"

Wiping her hands on a dish towel, Amanda walked up behind Dylan. "Can I help you –" Her voice faded to silence.

"Hey, gorgeous." The muscular, roguishly handsome young man on the other side of the screen grinned and looked her over with a knowing smile.

The sight of the man she'd planned to marry, left her speechless.

"Wanna come in?" Dylan invited as he started to push on the door.

Amanda grabbed the handle. "Dylan, it's time to get ready for bed. Go upstairs and I'll be there in a few minutes."

"Okay," he said reluctantly as he headed up the staircase.

Amanda slipped out onto the porch, closing the door. "What are you doing here, Brad?"

"Your mom told me where you were. I've been trying to find you. Look at you, Mandy! You haven't changed a bit. You look amazing." He put his arms around her and kissed her before she could pull back.

"You're wrong," she said. "I've changed a lot."

***

Marsh turned off the evening news. It should be about time to say goodnight to Dylan, but he hadn't heard the usual sounds and conversation between Dylan and Amanda as she helped him get ready for bed. He listened for her all the time, now. Her voice and laughter, her quick footsteps, her rattling around in the kitchen as she cooked and did the dishes. Her presence warmed and energized the entire house. He could always tell when she'd left, after Dylan was in bed. The silence was palpable.

The only thing worse than her leaving was losing sight of her when she was here. Although he was determined to stay out of her way, he caught whatever glimpses he could and the more he saw of her, the more he struggled against a growing desire for her. The lovely shape of her body and the way she moved had attracted him from the beginning, but her inner strength, openness and tenderness piqued his interest to know more. She was real and seemed incapable of pretense. Reality and a sense of stability in his life was something he hadn't experienced in all of his adulthood. It was especially obvious to him on the couple of occasions he'd come out of his room a few minutes early to tuck Dylan in and had seen him with Amanda, through the slightly open door. They were curled up together on the bed, his head nodding on her breast as she read to him, and it had made Marsh long to be a part of that and to be closer to her.

He got up and went into the hall. The bathroom door was ajar and he heard water running. He glanced in to find Dylan standing on tip-toe on the small step in front of the sink, brushing his teeth.

"Hey, Scoot – you doing okay in there?" he called out.

"I'm fine, Daddy," he answered through foamy lips.

"Where's Amanda?"

Dylan spit out the last of the toothpaste and filled his plastic cup. "A man came to see her and they went on the porch. Manda told me to come up and said she'd be here soon."

"Did you hear the man's name?"

"Uh-uh. But she wouldn't let him come in."

"Come on. Let's get you into bed."

"But Manda and me didn't read our book yet and say our prayers."

122

"It sounds like she's busy and you might have to wait till tomorrow night."

Dylan made noises of disappointment as Marsh helped him into bed and kissed his forehead. "If you're still awake when Amanda's done, maybe she'll have time to come up," he offered, knowing he would be fast asleep by then.

Dylan squeezed his toy puppy. "Will she come up even if just Dogby's still awake?"

"We'll see," he said as he turned out the light.

"You gotta stay awake, Dogby," he heard Dylan murmur sleepily.

Marsh went downstairs into the fading light of the kitchen. Amanda and her visitor were still on the porch and he wondered if Tom had come back. He could tell by the tone of their voices that someone was giving her a hard time.

"I've had enough time to figure out that I didn't like who I was with you," Amanda was saying.

"What're you talking about – 'who you were'? What's that supposed to mean?"

"The very fact that you have to ask, says it all."

"Mandy, you're not making any sense. You never talked to me like this before."

"That's right, Brad, and that's just the way you liked it. You weren't interested in what I thought or what I really wanted."

"Look, Mandy, we can straighten all that out. If you want me to listen more, I'll listen. I'll do whatever it takes. I told you, I'm okay with not being able to have my own kids. We'll adopt. I just want you back. I made a mistake when I let you go."

"Actually, as it turned out, you did me a favor."

"You didn't act like it when we called off the wedding."

"*You* called off the wedding, Brad. You broke my heart and made me feel worthless for a long time. But I'm over it and I'm over you."

"Come on, Mandy. You know you still want me the way I want you. Just give me a few minutes. I know what you like. Come on."

"I want you to leave, Brad – right now, and don't come back."

"You don't mean it, baby. And your mom and I agree, you and I are meant to be together. Come on, tomorrow would've been our wedding day. Look – I still have your diamond ring. Let me put it back on your finger and we can set another date and still do this."

"Let go of me and leave! Now!"

Marsh set his cane inside the door and stepped out onto the porch. Amanda looked startled from her place next to Brad on the bench.

"I believe I heard the lady ask you to leave," he said.

Brad looked up. "Hey, man, we're having a private conversation here, do you mind?"

"As a matter of fact, I do. This is my porch and I want you to leave, too."

Brad looked at Amanda. "Who's he?"

"My boss," she said.

"You live with your boss?"

Marsh quickly replied, "Amanda rents a room here, from me – and my wife."

Amanda thanked him with her eyes and let out a visible sigh of relief.

Brad looked back at her. "What's going on here? Your mom said you had your own apartment and another office job. What do you do for *him*?"

"I'm done answering your questions and I'm done with you, Brad."

"You'll regret this, Mandy." He got up from the bench. "I was willing to make a huge sacrifice and give this another chance."

"I'm honored." Amanda's tone was bitter.

"Yeah, well good luck finding another guy who's okay with raising somebody else's kids."

Marsh felt a rush of anger and took another step before Brad turned and sauntered off the porch to his car. "You have a nice life, Mandy!" he called out before he got in and took off.

Marsh looked over at Amanda. She hadn't moved, but now sat with her hands over her face. His heart broke for her and he didn't know what to do. "Are you all right?" he asked.

She nodded without looking at him. "I would thank you for what you did for me, but you'd probably say you just wanted him off your porch."

"No. It was more than that." He was torn between leaving her alone and going to her, but turned and headed back to the door. He had just pulled it open when he looked over his shoulder. She was bent over, crying softly into her hands, finally letting herself react to what had happened.

He quietly closed the door and made his way to the bench, then slowly sat down beside her. A couple of minutes passed. It was getting dark and the only sounds were the soft whirring of insects and a light breeze rustling through the trees.

She lifted her head slightly. "Dylan – I forgot Dylan –"

"I put him to bed. He's fine."

"I'm so sorry. This never should have happened. I can't believe he had the nerve to show up here." She lowered her head again.

Marsh brought his arm up to the back of the bench, then lay his hand on her shoulder. "He had no right to hurt you that way," he found himself saying.

She shook her head with a slight laugh. "You know, it's the strangest thing. I really thought I loved him and wanted to spend my life with him, but I can see now what a terrible mistake that would have been. He didn't really love me."

Marsh gazed at her exquisite profile in the half-light. "Not the way you should be loved," he said softly as he drew her closer and her head rested on his shoulder. He felt the tension leave her and sensed her sudden awareness of how close they were before his lips touched her forehead.

The rich scent of her hair filled his head as he moved to the slender bridge of her nose. Her face lifted slightly and he kissed each cheek, tasting the salt of her tears and taking in the sweetness of her skin.

Don't do this, came from a shadowy place in his mind. *Don't open yourself to an impossible situation.*

But he'd already touched his lips to the rosebud mouth that had tempted him so many times. It was as soft and warm as he'd imagined. *Don't ruin another life with your lie.* His lips brushed hers a second time and lingered, then suddenly

126

she began to return his kiss, sparking his desire as her mouth moved against his.

She came willingly into his arms, lacing her fingers through his hair as her lips parted. Her response was that of a woman who'd been waiting for him, wanting him as much as he'd been wanting her. It surprised him to think she'd been feeling the same way, even terrified him a little. Aside from the occasional alcohol-inspired flings he'd had with the ever-present groupies when he toured, the only other meaningful relationship he'd known was the one that had started in high school with his wife. But now he found himself unexpectedly filled with a ravenous hunger for Amanda that he knew would not go away. They were entering a new territory that demanded to be explored. The discerning voice in his head had gone silent and he knew he wouldn't hear it again. He had to have her in his life.

When she drew back, he reluctantly gave up the kiss but couldn't take his eyes from hers.

"I'd better go," she whispered. As she stood, he took her hand and buried his lips into her palm before letting go. "I'll see you tomorrow," she said before she stepped from the porch and started across the yard to the carriage house.

"Goodnight," he said, barely making a sound. He watched her disappear into the rising moonlight and waited until he heard the distant thud of her apartment door closing. He couldn't recall the last time he had looked so forward to another day.

***

Amanda wasn't sure how she'd made it across the yard, much less off of the porch. She sank into her living room chair, still breathless. The man who had touched her face so tenderly the day she moved in, was back. His kisses cherished her, teased her, reached into her core and stirred a craving she'd never felt with anyone before. And when he had kissed the soft inside of her hand, she had felt his desire for more of her and it left her trembling.

Maybe it was because of her mother's obvious promiscuity as she was growing up, that Amanda had only had a couple of serious boyfriends. She'd made an unconscious vow to never live the way her mother had, in fact to never be anything like her mother. She knew there must be a man out there who was meant for her and she realized she'd been far too hasty in her willingness to settle for someone like Brad. But he had made her feel protected, would probably be a good provider and had led her to believe he could handle not having children of his own. At the time, that had seemed enough.

But since she'd been around Mark Sterner, Amanda had found a side of herself that Brad could never have fulfilled. What lovemaking she'd had with Brad had been uninspiring and mostly for his satisfaction. She was even willing to accept that aspect in the life she would have as his wife. She had never wanted Brad the way she had come to desire Mark, in fact could now see that she hadn't known what desire for a man was until now.

The question that had haunted her since she'd met Mark was becoming a quest. Who *was* he? What was he hiding and why was he so deeply conflicted? Despite those uncertainties, Amanda was positive she'd been destined to meet him and hoped she was meant to help him put his life back together and be a good father to Dylan.

When she went to bed, her kiss with Mark became a dream that she drifted in and out of all night, never wanting it to end.

***

Saturday was the beginning of the long Labor Day weekend and Dylan would be starting school the following Tuesday. He was excited about it and Amanda and Helen were relieved that he couldn't wait to go. Amanda had taken him shopping earlier in the week for school supplies and new shoes. He had already prepared his Spiderman backpack with the notebook, pencils and lunch sack they'd bought. He would be going to school all day and it made him feel grown-up.

Amanda got up that morning feeling a little lost. Weekends were supposed to be time off, but her presence here felt less and less like a job. Caring for Dylan wasn't a task, it was becoming a way of life she loved. Looking after the house and helping Helen came naturally to her and now, more than ever, she wanted to be close to Mark, needed to feel his kiss again. At the same time, she knew she should be cautious.

Had she finally met the Mark who wanted more of a relationship with her or would she find he'd gone cold again the next time she saw him? The thought was unbearable. Whatever he was struggling with, she wondered if it had left him permanently incapable of a close, loving relationship with anyone, including his son. One thing she was sure of was that her response to his kiss last night had taken him by surprise. For her it had been spontaneous, a loss of control that felt deliciously exhilarating yet a bit frightening.

The phone rang. *Please let it be him*, she thought as she picked it up on the second ring.

"Good morning." His voice filled her ear with a tone she knew was meant only for her.

"Good morning," she murmured with a smile.

There was a pause before he said, "I couldn't sleep last night."

"That's too bad," she sighed with a contented stretch. "I was busy dreaming about a wonderful kiss."

He laughed softly. "It seems we have a situation, Amanda."

"Yes, it does."

"How do you feel about it?"

"Truthfully?"

"Yes – I want the truth."

"I feel like I'd love to kiss you again."

"Your honesty knocks me out."

"You'll never get anything but the truth from me."

"I know. It's one of the many things I've come to admire about you. So I'm going to be honest and admit that I can't give you the whole truth – at least not for awhile."

"It's all right. I know enough for now."

"And what do you know?"

"That you're doing the best you can to heal from a terrible trauma and loss, and that you need someone to care for you."

"God, Amanda." He sighed. "I can't make any promises –"

"This was supposed to be my wedding day. I've had enough promises for awhile."

"You're a survivor," he said.

"So are you."

"I guess I never looked at it that way. Can we take it a day at a time, then?"

"That fits my schedule perfectly."

He laughed again and she basked in the warmth of it.

"I'll see you," he said softly.

As they hung up, she was profoundly grateful that she wasn't marrying Brad that day. Something that had been so heartbreaking at first had turned out to be an absolute blessing. Gazing out the living room windows at the mellowing leaves, she sipped her morning coffee, content in the certainty that she was where she belonged, with people who needed her and wanted her, and the newfound hope that she and Mark could grow in a relationship that might lead to a love they'd both been waiting for. This day and all the days to come were full of wonderful possibilities and she couldn't wait to get started.

She got dressed and headed out into the soft morning sunshine for a walk before it got too warm. She struck off on a new road in the nearby subdivision she'd been exploring on her previous walks and marveled at the lavish homes and perfectly manicured lawns along the route. About halfway down the road she'd gotten into her stride when she thought she heard someone call her name. When it came again, she turned and traced the voice to a yard on the other side of the street. A woman was waving frantically, as she got up from a flowerbed she'd been working on.

Amanda recognized the petite, round figure and short brown hair. "Angie?"

"Hey, kiddo! I can't believe it's you!" Angie called to her.

Amanda crossed the road and Angie met her at the sidewalk as they spontaneously embraced.

"When I didn't see you and Dylan at the pool again, I figured you didn't take the job with the Sterners after all," Angie said.

"No, I took the job. I've been there all along."

"Great!" Angie leaned toward her. "So how are things at Wuthering Heights?" she asked in an ominous voice.

Amanda laughed. "It's going better than expected."

"Wow – have you got time for a cup of coffee? I'm ready for a break and I'm dying to hear about this."

"I'd love some coffee."

Angie wrapped her arm around her and they walked across the lawn to a sprawling, stone mansion of a house. The inside was as beautiful as the outside, with huge, airy rooms and modern furnishings and art. Angie poured two cups of coffee in the large kitchen and they went through a sliding glass door to an elaborate, multi-tiered deck overlooking a wooded backyard.

They sat at an oval, glass umbrella table as Amanda continued to take it all in.

"This is so beautiful, Angie," she said. "You must be very happy here."

"Truthfully, I'd be happier in a smaller place if I could have my husband home more," Angie admitted. "David's a dentist. He's very successful and well-known, and no one would complain about that, but he has evening and Saturday hours and, along with his out-of-town conventions and community involvement – well, you get the picture."

"Yes, I guess I do. So how do you fill your time?"

"Oh, I have no problem with that. I do a lot of volunteer and charity work that I enjoy. I'm active at the school and I golf and lunch with my friends at the Country Club. Don't get me wrong, Amanda, I know I'm really fortunate." She sighed. "I guess I expected to have more of a family life. Conner's an only child, like Dylan, and that's a whole other thing. How is Dylan, by the way?"

"He's terrific. It's been an absolute joy for me to take care of him."

"He must be lonely," Angie said.

"He's used to playing by himself, but that doesn't make it right."

There were voices at the far corner of the yard and Amanda noticed the tree house and spotted Conner with a couple of other boys, moving around inside.

"Conner has some friends," Angie said, "but I'd rather see him play with someone like Dylan. These neighborhood kids are so spoiled. Conner really liked Dylan and asked me several times when he'd be back to the pool. Do you think Dylan's father would let him come over to play now and then?"

"That would be great." Amanda was already excited about the idea. "I'm hoping once school starts and Dylan's involved in more activities, Mark will get used to letting him go."

"So." Angie cupped her chin in her hand. "Tell me all about Mark."

Amanda shifted in her chair. "Well, there isn't much to tell, except that he's agreed to my being there and he leaves me alone to do my job."

Angie put her hands on her hips. "Is that all you've got?"

Amanda shrugged and smiled.

"You're holding out on me. I can tell."

"I'd better get going, anyway, Angie. Thanks for the coffee. I really enjoyed seeing you."

"I'm so glad you're just down the road, and we'll work on that Dylan-Conner thing."

"Definitely."

"Will you be bringing Dylan to school Tuesday?"

"Yes – I'll see you then!" Amanda resumed her walk as she began thinking up ways to convince Mark to let Dylan and Conner become good friends.

When she got back to the Sterners', she heard voices as she started up the carriage house steps and looked toward the house. She paused when she saw the distant figures of Mark and Dylan in the front yard. Mark was pitching and Dylan was brandishing his bat. The sight of Mark outside, fully engaged in being Dylan's dad, inspired an idea as she ran up the remaining steps to the apartment.

She grabbed her sketchpad and pencils and the folding lounge chair stashed behind the kitchen door, then headed back outside where she set up in the shade and began to draw. As she sketched the large house and trees, then the two figures, an inspiration came to her to do a series of four pastel drawings, one for each season, depicting the father and son playing baseball in summer, raking leaves in fall, making a snowman in winter and planting a garden in spring. Each drawing would have them in the same location in front of the house.

Unaware of how much time had passed while she was absorbed in her work, she looked up awhile later to see that Mark was gone and Dylan was headed toward her on his bicycle.

"Whatcha doin', Manda?" he asked as he reached her.

"Come and see," she said as he came around the chair.

He dutifully glanced at the drawing before launching into what was foremost in his mind. "I wanna water Grandma's flowers and bushes but she says I can only do it if you help me, cuz..."

"Because why?" Amanda reluctantly set down her pad.

"Cuz sometimes I put too much water on and forget to turn off the hose."

"Sometimes sounds like more than once."

He nodded. "Yeah, lots more."

"Okay, I'll help you, and maybe if you do it right, Grandma will let you do it alone next time."

***

Marsh was pulling weeds in his vegetable garden when Dylan ran around the corner of the house from the back yard. "I gotta turn on the water, Daddy! Manda and me are gonna water Grandma's plants!"

Marsh leaned around the corner and spotted Amanda over by the flowers and shrubs as she fiddled with the nozzle on the hose. He helped Dylan turn the faucet on and stood back, watching as she adjusted the spray and stood with her

135

arms around Dylan, holding his aim in the right direction. As he watched her from behind, Marsh lingered over the curve of her hips and the slender, graceful lines of her legs, uninterrupted by the flip-flops on her bare feet. Her hair was loosely pinned on top of her head with wispy, stray tendrils around her face and neck.

For a few minutes Dylan cooperated with Amanda's guidance and got the first couple of shrubs sufficiently watered, before he announced, "This is boring, Manda."

"That's because it's a job," Amanda explained patiently. "A job can't be fun all the time, but it still has to be done."

Dylan sighed and scratched his head. "How much more do we hafta do?"

"We have to do all the shrubs and flowers. You promised Grandma you would."

He shuffled his feet and sighed again. Another few moments passed. Then with a sudden giggle, he broke from Amanda's arms and turned the hose on her.

She shrieked, flailing her arms in the spray, then took off after him as he dropped it and ran.

"You get back here, Dylan Sterner!"

"Try to catch me, Manda!" he yelled before he disappeared at the far end of the house.

She stopped, gasping, shaking off the excess water before she went back and retrieved the nozzle. The soaked knit of her shorts and top etched every detail of her body as she pulled the clip from her hair and shook it out.

As Marsh watched, she went back to the watering. Still out of sight, he lightly tugged on the hose.

"Very funny, Dylan. Now come and finish your job," she called without looking up.

Marsh tugged again.

"I'm warning you," she scolded playfully. "If you don't come and finish this, I'm coming after you."

Her reply was a harder yank.

"That's it!" She spun and ran for the side of the house, rounded the corner ready to aim the hose, then screeched as Mark snatched her into his arms and pulled her, full-length, against him.

"I'm all wet!" she pretended to protest.

"I know," he teased with a lusty growl before he drew her into a deep kiss.

Wanting him as if last night had never ended, she dropped the hose and it snaked along the ground as she threw her arms around his neck and eagerly moved her mouth against his. "This 'day-at-a-time' stuff is working so far," she murmured between kisses.

Her willingness aroused him even more as he moved his warm hands up the cool hollow of her back, then around her sides until he found the soft mounds of her breasts, already breaking into goosebumps. She whimpered and held him tighter as her kiss grew more urgent.

"Where are you, Manda?"

They broke apart just as Dylan appeared at the far corner of the house.

"I'm here." She was still breathless as she quickly tried to smooth her clothes and hair.

"Wow – you sure musta been running fast. You're all messed up!" Dylan was obviously impressed. "Not only that! Wait till I tell Grandma *you* left the hose on, *too*!"

Chapter 8
Something About Him

From her seat near her bedroom window, Helen shook her head and laughed. She'd had a perfect vantage point, watching and listening through the screen as Dylan and Amanda had staged their unwitting comedy act. Their shrieking and yelling was a welcome sound. This place had been too somber for too long.

She hadn't realized Marsh was just out of view, tending to his garden, until Amanda had stumbled onto him and she'd heard the hushed voices and intimate sounds of a romantic interlude before Dylan interrupted them. She wondered when it had begun between them, but knew it had quite possibly started the night before, because Marsh had seemed different this morning. He'd been enthusiastic about the day and had been the one to suggest some baseball practice with Dylan.

Helen was delighted that Amanda's presence was having the effect she'd hoped for, and more. It was clear from the time of the interview that Amanda would be good with Dylan. They'd had a natural, easy rapport from the moment they met, assuring her that, besides being an excellent caretaker and babysitter, Amanda could provide the love and attention Dylan so badly needed. Helen had been impressed with Amanda's ability to also take care of the house, shopping and laundry, often doing more than the job description called for. She seemed to truly enjoy her work as though it had become a way of life, and now there was evidence of a bonus Helen could have only dreamed of.

Marsh and Amanda were attracted to each other and she hoped for a lasting relationship. She wanted more than anything to see Marsh find meaning and happiness in his life again and for Dylan to grow up with the care and influence of a mother figure. With what Helen knew about Amanda, she even dared to believe that Amanda was strong enough, compassionate enough, and could be committed enough to ultimately handle learning and accepting the truth about Marsh. It was a long shot, she knew.

A faithful Marshall Stewart fan would have every right to feel betrayed, made a fool of, enraged at her idol's decision to leave behind a grieving public and live out his life in guilty seclusion. But someone who already loved Marsh and his son before discovering the truth, might be able to separate the myth of Marshall Stewart from the human being who made an irretrievable mistake many years ago. While it might be too much to hope for, the events of the past ten years had taught her that anything was possible. After a brief career in which his super stardom took him away from her, followed by years of seclusion at a great distance from her, her son was home, with a beautiful grandson.

She heard Marsh, Amanda and Dylan, still outside the window, chatting about the garden and what to plant in the spring. Yes, she thought with another smile, anything was possible.

The phone rang and she reached for the receiver on the nightstand.

"How are you, Mother?" her daughter's voice greeted her.

"Jean – I'm fine. How's the mother of the bride holding up?"

Jean sighed. "Barely. I think Vicki's just thrown her third tantrum this week. She's such a control freak!"

"Hmm... I wonder where she gets *that* from?"

"Could you just humor me, Mother, and *pretend* you're siding with me?"

"I'm sorry, dear, but it *is* a bit of divine justice for me."

"I know I was an obsessive bride – the first time, anyway, but you've got to admit I was much better two years ago."

"Yes, the second wedding was a breeze."

"And I got a wonderful man this time."

"So it seems."

"Michael's a sweetheart and to have the kids like him too is positively sublime. So, have you decided about coming to the wedding? Vicki's asked about it every day this week. She's made it clear she'll be heartbroken if her grandmother isn't there next Saturday. We can have a family reunion while you're here. Is the new babysitter working out well enough that you feel you can leave for a week?"

"Amanda's absolutely wonderful. It's just Dylan I'm worried about. I haven't been away from him since he and Marsh got here."

"So who's going to miss who more?" Jean teased. "Besides, I assume Amanda is a reliable older woman with enough experience to handle Dylan and take care of the house for a week on her own."

Helen chewed her lip. "Yes, Amanda's very capable." She knew Marsh's older sister would not approve of such a young, attractive babysitter, for a variety of reasons.

"Come on, Mother. You've been tied to that house since Marsh got back. You need a change of scenery. Let me come and get you next Friday. It'll do you good to get away and it'll mean the world to Vicki."

"I know," Helen said.

"Besides, I've waited long enough to see my younger brother. I don't care whether he's up to it or not. I at least deserve a chance to meet my nephew and to re-introduce Marsh to *his* nephew as well. Jason was only four when Marsh took off and even then he'd only seen him once when he was a toddler. Vicki has some memory of a couple of backstage visits with Marsh and Carrie, but she wasn't old enough to understand what was going on, thank God. So, they've both grown up just thinking of him as Uncle Mark, the black sheep. But now that he's back, he needs to be part of the family again, however we have to do it."

"I'm glad to hear that, dear," Helen said. "You can't stay angry with him forever, even though I understand why you were."

"He abandoned us."

"He did what he had to do."

"He had choices."

"Yes, and he made some bad ones. He's the first to admit that. I was angry with him, too, Jean."

"Well, we're only four hours apart now, instead of on the other side of the world. I'm willing to try to put all that in the past and start over."

"I'm sure Marsh would like that, too and I want nothing more than to have us all back together again," Helen said. "Your brother's in a new phase of his life he hadn't planned on, but I'm so happy to have him and Dylan with me now. Anyway, let me talk to Amanda about the extra hours and Marsh and Dylan about the trip and I'll call you back tomorrow."

By the time they hung up, Helen already knew she would go. She didn't want to miss her granddaughter's wedding, and after overhearing Marsh and Amanda today, she couldn't pass up a well-timed opportunity to get out of the way and give their budding relationship some space.

Helen was in the kitchen when Amanda brought Dylan into the house to get cleaned up. "Are all my bushes watered?" she asked with a sideways wink at Amanda.

"I tried, Grandma, but then I got too tired," he said very seriously. "Then Manda got too tired from running and --"

"I'll finish the watering as soon as I'm done in here," Amanda quickly intervened.

"Don't bother, they didn't need it that badly today. But when you're done with Dylan, I have to talk to you."

Amanda felt a twinge of apprehension. "Okay – I'll be right back." She wondered if anything was wrong as she took

Dylan upstairs and helped him wash and change. She left him playing in his room as she returned to the kitchen.

"I have a chance to go away for a week to my granddaughter's wedding," Helen began.

Amanda was relieved as she lowered herself to the bench at the table. "That sounds wonderful."

"Well yes, I'm very excited about it. It would be the first time I've been away in ages. I couldn't even think of leaving until now, but I need to talk to you first, Amanda, because it would require more work on your part. Of course, I'll make sure you're well compensated."

Amanda smiled. "This isn't work, Helen. I love what I do and I love doing it for your family."

Helen measured her words carefully before she added, "Well, the other thing I want to be sure of is that I'm not putting you in an awkward situation with my son."

Amanda felt an unexpected blush of heat rise into her cheeks. "No" would sound too nonchalant and "yes" could squelch the trip. She looked up as Helen put her hand on her arm.

"It appears that you and Mark are getting along very well, and nothing could make me happier," she said softly.

As Amanda had surmised on the day she met Helen, nothing escaped her and it was obvious she knew there was something happening between her and Mark. "I'm comfortable with you being away if he is," she said.

"You're the best thing that could have happened to all of us, Amanda, and I'm so grateful I found you again – for many reasons."

"Me too." Amanda's words caught in her throat as she gave Helen a quick hug.

"I'll tell Mark and Dylan about the trip. And I have another idea, a little off the subject. How would you feel about a Labor Day cookout?"

"I think that would be a great idea."

"There's an old charcoal grill in the garage. It hasn't been used in years, but –"

"I'll clean it up and we can cook hot dogs and hamburgers."

"We'll need some things from the store..."

"Why don't you get a list ready and Dylan and I can go tomorrow," Amanda said. "The weather's supposed to be beautiful Monday and we'll have a nice picnic at the table in the yard."

Helen clapped her hands. "Oh, I can't wait! Now you take the rest of the day off. You'll be very busy over the next couple of weeks."

***

Marsh sipped his lemonade as he sat on the front porch reading the newspaper. The mid-afternoon heat was heavy but rain was forecast for Sunday, and Monday promised to be sunny and clear. He hadn't cared much about the weather until lately, but he'd enjoyed the outdoors more in the last few weeks, in fact was enjoying everything a little more and it was because of Amanda.

Helen had just talked to him about her trip to Jean's. He was happy that his mother had an opportunity to go to the wedding and reconnect with some of the family. He'd also been glad to hear Amanda didn't mind the extra hours and that, as Helen had told him, she was "comfortable" with the "situation" if he was. "Comfortable" didn't describe how he felt about the promise of time alone with Amanda. It was a gift he hadn't dared to hope for until now.

Out at the road the lawn service had just arrived and it would be noisy for the next thirty minutes as the two large mowing tractors raced around the property. He reached for his cane and got up off the bench to head into the relative quiet of the house when he glanced over and saw one of the workers talking to Amanda, who had just come down the carriage house steps with her purse, wearing her sunglasses. He appeared to be close to Amanda's age and was very attentive as they chatted and even shared a couple of laughs. Then she headed for her car, unaware that he was still standing there, watching her every move as she opened the door and sat down, tucking in those lovely legs before she took off.

It served as a blatant reminder to Marsh that there was a ten-year age difference between Amanda and himself, just as he'd realized when he'd seen her with Brad and Tom. What business did he have getting involved with someone so much younger? What business did he have getting involved with anyone at all? Did he actually think there was a chance that Amanda could learn the truth about him and still love him? Was it worth risking nothing but heartbreak for both of them?

Yet, she'd made it clear that she was attracted to him and it made him want to take her into his arms in a place where no one could find them and tame that mischievous spirit of hers into loving only him. He couldn't let that possibility slip away.

Another look at the handsome, self-assured lawn worker as he climbed onto his tractor and fired it up, convinced Marsh that he needed to make a move soon. This guy would be back a few more times before winter set in, and he'd be looking for Amanda again, no doubt. But if it wasn't him, it would be someone in the check-out line at the grocery store or the guy who pumped gas at the service station. Everywhere she went, someone would notice Amanda and would want to talk to her. Marsh realized that, if he wanted to have any kind of a life with her, he would not be able to do it sitting and waiting for her each time she went out into the world. At some point, somehow, his need to be with her would have to overcome his terror of being recognized and maybe then he could find some semblance of a normal life again.

Marsh went inside and made his way to his room. He closed the door and walked over to the picture of Carrie on his dresser. He was gradually coming to terms with what had happened between them and sometimes sensed that she was at peace and may have even forgiven him. He hoped it was true as he tried to envision himself moving on, imagining new possibilities in the life he had left. He needed to feel he had Carrie's blessing as he sought a new love, and taking her image into his hands, he sat down in the chair. "We have to talk," he murmured.

***

As Amanda spent the rest of her Saturday browsing at the Library, doing a little clothes shopping and working on her pastel sketches, the sensations of Mark's second kiss shimmered in the back of her mind and kept her longing for more. Despite any lingering uncertainties about his moods or anything he might be concealing, Amanda was sure that when he held her and kissed her so deeply, she was experiencing the essence of who he really was and what he really wanted. There was something about him that completely disarmed her self-control and nothing had ever excited her more.

After a restless night, she awoke early on Sunday and called the house around nine o'clock. Dylan was anxious to go shopping for their picnic supplies and Helen had a list ready.

They took off by nine-thirty, before the stores would get too busy, and easily found everything they needed. Dylan wanted to check the school supply aisle one more time before his first day, so they browsed through the same varieties of notebooks, pencils and pens they had the week before.

"Hey, kiddo!"

Amanda looked up to see Angie and Conner coming down the aisle.

The boys enthusiastically greeted each other as if they'd been together the day before, slapping their small hands into a high-five and chattering about what they had bought for their first day of school.

"We're a little behind on the back-to-school prep," Angie admitted. "You, too?"

"No, we're all set with that, but we decided to throw a picnic together for tomorrow, so we just came for a few last minute things."

"Great! Hope you have a nice holiday."

"What are you doing tomorrow?" Amanda asked.

"Oh, nothing really. David's out of town and most of the neighbors have taken off for the weekend."

"Why don't you and Conner come over and eat with us?" It was out of Amanda's mouth before she gave any thought to getting pre-approval for her invitation.

"Cool!" Conner and Dylan chirped at the same time.

"We'd love to, Amanda, but are you sure it's okay?"

"It'll be fine," Amanda said, trying to reassure herself as much as Angie.

"What can I bring?"

"Just yourselves. You can come around two. It'll be fun."

When they got back to the house, Dylan bailed out of the car and arrived in the kitchen with the news of their picnic guests before Amanda could get there. She was very relieved to see that it was only Helen receiving the news as she carried in the first couple of bags.

"Helen, I apologize," she hastily began. "It's just that Conner and his mom were going to be alone tomorrow and I thought it would be a great chance for Dylan and him to get to know each other better –"

"It's a wonderful idea," Helen commended her, "and long overdue."

Dylan had run back out to the car to grab the last bag as Amanda added, "I know I should have checked with Mark first –"

"Don't you worry about Mark. I'll tell him and I'm sure there won't be any problem. The most important thing is for Dylan to have a playmate."

***

Although it rained all Sunday afternoon as forecast, Amanda found the old charcoal grill in the garage and set it up in the open doorway under the overhang where she cleaned it out and scrubbed the racks. Dylan insisted on helping and Amanda gave him a small scrubbing pad, which he repeatedly rubbed on the same area as he chattered non-stop about anything that came into his mind. She enjoyed listening and commenting now and then, letting him bask in a sense of having a "grown-up" conversation.

When they went back into the house, Helen insisted Amanda take off and enjoy the rest of her day.

"Would you mind if I come back tonight and use the kitchen to make the potato salad for tomorrow?"

"Of course not. I just don't want you to work too hard today." Helen was always adamant about that.

Amanda assured her it would be fine and, after a few hours at her apartment, went back at around seven-thirty that evening to peel and boil the potatoes and chop up the other ingredients for her salad. Helen had gone to her room to watch television and because it was the weekend, Dylan was supposed to have gotten himself to bed with the usual tuck-in from Mark. She was disappointed she hadn't seen Mark all day, and found herself constantly looking for him. But just knowing he was nearby tantalized her with the possibility of running into him yet today.

By about eight she had put the marinade over the hot potatoes and was leaning on the kitchen counter, looking over dessert recipes in one of Helen's cookbooks.

"Manda?" Dylan's small voice came down the stairway.

"Yes, Dylan."

150

"What are you doing here now?"

"Making food for the picnic. Why aren't you in bed?"

"I was, but then I heard stuff and I didn't know you were here."

Amanda smiled to herself, knowing what the next question would be.

"Could you read me a story before you go, Manda?"

She closed the cookbook. "Of course I can."

When she went upstairs she saw Mark's door closed and heard the sounds of his television.

She sat on the bed with Dylan in her arms and read one of his favorite stories aloud as he recited along with her until his voice trailed off into a series of yawns. It was then that she noticed Mark leaning in the doorway and she smiled, wondering how long he'd been watching. He smiled back as she closed the book and began to gently move Dylan from her lap.

Mark made his way to the other side of the bed and kissed Dylan's head as he pulled the blanket up around him. "Goodnight, Scoot," he said.

"Night, Daddy. I can't wait till Conner comes over tomorrow for our picnic," he murmured as he curled up with his puppy and nodded off.

Amanda headed into the hallway as Mark followed, pulling the door closed. She turned to him, ready to steal a goodnight kiss.

"What picnic and who's Conner?"

"Your mother didn't tell you? She said she'd let you know."

Mark sighed. "I can't believe you haven't caught on to my mother yet. If she wants to do something without my input, she just makes it happen and leaves it for me to figure out later."

Suddenly faced with giving Mark an explanation, Amanda swallowed and began, "Dylan and I met Conner and his mom at the pool that day we were there, and the boys really hit it off. We ran into them at the grocery store this morning and found out they were going to be alone for the holiday, so – I invited them for a cookout."

The corners of his mouth twitched as though he had just heard one of Dylan's explanations. "That was very presumptive of you."

"I know – I should've checked with you first, but you probably would've said no and Dylan needs a friend when he goes back to school."

Amanda waited, feeling Mark's gaze on her, but not wanting to look back at him.

"So what's Conner's mother like?"

"Angie? Oh, she's very nice. We've become friends, ourselves. Her husband's a dentist but he's never home and – well, you need to meet her tomorrow because we'd like to arrange a couple of play dates for the boys and –"

"I don't want anyone upstairs in this house but you and Dylan," Mark said.

"But Dylan's room is up here and kids always want to play in each other's rooms –"

"This is not the place for strangers."

Amanda felt a wall going up between them, the same wall she encountered when she'd started her job. The difference was, she felt she knew Mark better by now. She gently touched his arm. "What are you afraid of?"

He pulled away. "Drop it, Amanda."

She could see the tension in him. "I just don't understand –"

"No – you don't, so stop asking. And don't ever invite anyone here without my permission again." He turned away from her.

"Mark, please –" Her answer was the closing of his door.

As she stood there in desolation, she gazed toward the door at the end of the hall. Over the past few weeks of coming and going in this hallway she had glanced at it now and then, wondering about its apparent significance. What was in that room that Mark was so intent on guarding? She was certain it held the answers to all her questions.

She remembered the day of her interview when Dylan showed her the forbidden door and tried the knob before Mark caught them. Dylan had told her he knew where his father kept the key in the drawer beside his bed and that someday, he would get it and unlock the door. Obviously, Mark had no idea Dylan had been in his bedroom, much less that he knew about the key and it assured her that it was just a matter of time before she would know the truth about Mark Sterner.

***

As the weatherman had promised, Labor Day was sunny and clear with a bright, blue sky. It energized Amanda as she set up the large picnic table in the yard, arranged benches and lawn chairs and worked in the kitchen making a snack tray and baked beans, putting the finishing touches on her salad and baking a batch of brownies to have with ice cream for dessert.

"Now I know why I've missed having picnics!" Helen cheered when she saw all the preparations. "This is such fun, Amanda!" With Amanda's help she had already settled into a lawn chair in the shade where she was ready to enjoy the day.

"It's going to be a lot of fun," Amanda said to convince herself, knowing she did not have Mark's approval.

At two o'clock sharp, Angie and Conner arrived amid enthusiastic greetings and slamming car doors. Angie had brought a couple of bottles of wine and a day's supply of chips and crackers. She was delighted to meet Helen and immediately struck up an easy conversation as she sat down beside her.

Before Dylan and Conner took off to explore the yard, Amanda gently informed them they could play anywhere except upstairs if they were in the house. Then she brought out the snack tray and wine glasses and the three women sat together, chatting and sipping Chardonnay.

***

Marsh stood behind the window blinds of the spare room overlooking the front yard, taking in the festivities below. Dylan and his new friend were catching frogs in the drainage ditch that ran along the edge of the property, while Amanda, Helen and Conner's mother laughed and waved their hands in animated conversation near the brightly covered picnic table.

Since Amanda had come, this place had felt more like a home than it had since he and Dylan had arrived, and it had certainly enriched Helen's life to have more activity and joy in the house. He watched Amanda as she sipped her wine and

154

enjoyed the girlish chatter she shared with Angie. Every time he looked at her she was more beautiful and desirable. He longed to be beside her, sharing in everything she did.

Although he regretted the tense conversation he'd had with her the night before, it had been necessary. He couldn't afford to have anyone intruding or prying upstairs. He was sure he'd successfully instilled the fear of God into Dylan about never entering his bedroom or going near the door to his private room at the end of the hall, but playmates could tempt mischief and the opportunity had to be avoided.

He looked at Angie again. She appeared to be around Amanda's age, the age of another possible Marshall Stewart fan. Somehow, he needed to work up the courage to walk out there and meet her face-to-face. He needed to do it for Amanda and to ensure that he could trust another person with his son's care if the boys were to be playmates.

He fidgeted with the pair of sunglasses he held in his hands. For now anyway, they would provide the buffer he needed as he took his first few steps back into the real world. It had come to his doorstep and it was time to venture out of his self-imposed refuge and face it.

***

Amanda and Angie were giggling at Dylan and Conner's antics when Angie suddenly choked on the chip she was munching and grabbed her wine glass, pointing toward the porch.

Amanda turned and felt a rush of excitement at the sight of Mark standing on the top step.

"Oh my God, Amanda!" Angie half whispered. "He's gorgeous! I never pictured him that way!"

Seeing Mark through someone else's eyes thrilled Amanda as she gazed at his tall, slender physique in khaki trousers and a beige, long-sleeved shirt that was open slightly at the collar. His dark curls rippled in the warm breeze. His full beard and sunglasses lent him an unwitting air of mysterious glamour.

A sense of pride came over Amanda and she stood up as Mark used his cane to make his way down the steps. Despite his displeasure with her last night about having this picnic and inviting strangers to his home, she realized he had listened to her and was honoring her request that he meet Angie and Conner. It touched her heart with an affirmation that he truly cared for her and wanted to please her. As he walked over to the picnic table, she knew his hidden eyes were on her.

"Mark, this is my friend, Angie Wilson," Amanda said as he reached them. "Angie, this is Dylan's father, Mark Sterner."

Angie stood up, wide-eyed.

"Hello, Angie," Mark said.

"N-nice to meet you," she stammered.

Amanda called the boys over. When they reached Mark, Conner shrank back and Amanda remembered the story Angie had told her about Conner and his friends coming over to ask if Dylan could play and how Dylan's father yelled at them and drove them away.

"Conner, say hello to Mr. Sterner," Angie said.

Mark bent slightly and held out his hand. "Hello, Conner."

156

The boy timidly moved closer and touched Mark's hand. "Hello," he barely got out before he quickly pulled back.

"Hey, Conner – wanna go on my swing?" Dylan asked.

Conner nodded and the two boys took off again.

"Sit down, Mark," Helen said. "Amanda's going to cook pretty soon."

Amanda realized that Angie was still unabashedly staring at Mark, and she could tell it was beginning to unnerve him as he adjusted his sunglasses.

"Maybe later. Have a good time," he said as he turned and made his way back to the house.

"Thanks for having us!" Angie called after him. She plopped back onto the bench and took another sip of her wine. "You know, Amanda, there's something about him," she said slowly. "Something about his voice, his manner – I don't know why, but I feel as though I've seen Mark before – maybe a long time ago…"

Helen coughed slightly and shifted in her chair. "I can't believe what a beautiful day it is after all that rain yesterday – can you, Amanda?"

Amanda glanced at her in surprise. "Yes – it's really beautiful today." She looked back to where Mark was crossing the porch to the door and suddenly the sunglasses took on a new significance. She'd never seen him wear sunglasses, yet he wore them to meet Angie and kept them on when it would have been more polite to remove them and make eye contact.

As Helen and Angie began to chat again, Amanda was left with a strange uneasiness. She'd known all along that Mark was keeping to himself because of the recent trauma in his life. The few times she'd actually asked herself who this man was, it was more a question of, what was he about? But this was the first time she'd seen anything to make her think he could actually be hiding his face from a stranger. Helen's obvious attempt to distract Angie from her observation made it all the more unsettling.

There was a sudden tug on her arm. "Manda, when are you gonna cook the hotdogs? We're hungry!" Dylan urged.

"Sure. We'll start cooking right now." Amanda got up and headed to the grill.

As she lit the fire and poked at the charcoal, her suspicions sharpened. Mark was indeed hiding something, but her instincts had just awakened to a new question: Could he be hiding his very identity?

Chapter 9
Opening the Door

With many thanks and compliments on Amanda's cooking, Angie and Conner left around six, heading home to prepare for tomorrow's school day.

"What a perfect afternoon, Amanda," Helen praised her as she began to clear the table. "Thank you for all your hard work."

"I enjoyed it."

"Your friends are very nice," Helen added.

"They are, and that's why I wanted Mark to meet them, so he might be willing to let Dylan go to Conner's house now and then."

"I think he will."

As Amanda helped Helen into the house, she resisted the urge to mention Angie's comments about Mark. She would play along with Helen and Mark and not press for answers. It was becoming clear that the truth was not far below the surface and now that she had another clue, she had a better idea of what she was looking for.

But as she finished cleaning up the kitchen, a new concern began to take hold. She was falling in love with Mark and longed for a future with him and Dylan. But if Mark Sterner was actually someone else, just whom was she falling in love with and how much of their relationship was real? Was his concealed identity hiding a dangerous person, or was he an innocent person who could be hiding from other dangerous people?

Her imagination took over, confusing and frightening her. She calmed herself with what she did know. Mark was striving to overcome a difficult situation that had changed his life, and he genuinely cared for her. Her instincts told her whatever his actual name was, this man's desire for her was real. It would have to be enough for now and she was not willing to jeopardize that.

It was nearing seven-thirty and Amanda went upstairs to make sure Dylan was getting ready for bed. He was still wound up, and she had to prod him to get into his pajamas and brush his teeth.

"The sooner you get into bed and sleep, the sooner I can get you up and take you to school," Amanda told him.

"And when I go to school tomorrow, I'm gonna see Conner again!" Dylan exclaimed.

"Yes, you'll see your new friend." Amanda stroked his hair and smiled, glad that he had so much to look forward to. She read him a story as he became sleepy. There was no sign of Mark and when Dylan nodded off she pulled up his blankets and went to the door, flipping the light switch off.

As she started down the stairs, she thought she heard Mark's bedroom door open. She hurried down the remaining steps and was out the front door before he could see her. She needed time to process what had happened that afternoon before she saw him again.

***

Although it should have been brighter at six-thirty the next morning, it was cloudy and dim as Amanda arrived in the kitchen, put the lights on and headed upstairs to wake Dylan. His bedroom light was already on and he was rummaging through his dresser drawer. "I got my underwear, Manda," he announced proudly.

"You're way ahead of me." She was relieved to see that the reality of his first day of school hadn't dampened his excitement.

She helped him dress and he grabbed his backpack as they went downstairs where she started a pot of coffee and put the tea kettle on to make oatmeal. Dylan chattered incessantly as he sat on the bench at the table, carefully checking the few contents of his backpack.

Amanda worked at the counter, making his lunch and trying to keep up with his questions while she intermittently glanced at the clock over the stove. By seven forty-five she had successfully gotten Dylan to eat most of his breakfast, had his lunch packed and got him to agree on which jacket to wear. She had just helped him put it on and was doing up the zipper when Mark came down the stairs.

"Daddy! I'm going to school now!"

"So I see," Mark said. "You look all grown-up."

"I am."

Amanda leaned down and whispered in his ear before he ran to his father, arms spread, and Mark bent over to catch his hug and wet kiss.

"Let's go, Manda!" Dylan urged as he headed out the door.

"Go get in the car and I'll be right there," she called after him. She turned to where Mark still stood, gazing appreciatively at her.

"Good morning," he said.

"Good morning."

"I missed you last night. I lost track of the time."

"No problem. I was tired and needed to go. Thank you for coming out yesterday to meet Angie and Conner."

"You were right. They seem like nice people."

"Well, Angie thought you were pretty nice, too. In fact, to quote her first impression of you, she thought you were 'gorgeous'."

He laughed self-consciously and while she had him off guard she added, "The sunglasses were an interesting touch, too."

"I – got up with a headache and didn't want it to get worse."

"I see," she nodded. "Well, I hope you're feeling better today."

"I'm fine. When will you be back?"

"When I pick Dylan up from school. I'll see you then." There was a moment in which she could sense Mark wanting to kiss her goodbye as much as she wanted to kiss him, but they knew Dylan could barge back in looking for her at any time. Instead, she smiled and gave him a little wave as she headed out the door.

**

Marsh heard Amanda's car door close and watched her headlights go by the window in the early grey light. Helen would not be up for at least another hour and the house felt huge and empty. The tiny wet spot from Dylan's kiss that still tickled his cheek had happened with gentle prompting from Amanda and he realized she loved him, even through his son.

He turned and, with his cane, slowly made his way back upstairs. Time and opportunity had finally aligned themselves and found him in the frame of mind he could only have imagined until now, the one where he could get the key from the night table beside his bed and go to the door at the end of the hall, ready to confront his past.

Dylan would not suddenly race around the corner, Amanda would not appear with a laundry basket and Helen would not hear him and want to talk about it.

He turned the key in the lock and as the door opened with a soft creak, he felt the cool, musty air against his face and saw the shapes of large boxes and draped objects in the light from the hall. He stepped inside and closed the door. Timid rays of sun were just beginning to play around the window blinds, laying pale stripes across the opposite wall. He leaned against the wall and closed his eyes, taking in the profound silence of an abandoned life and career.

He had not been in this room since he'd had his belongings shipped here just over ten years ago. When he hatched his escape-from-show-business plan, he and Carrie had packed up the things most important to them and had them shipped here, with Helen's approval, for safekeeping. True to his lack of planning, he'd had no idea how or when he and Carrie might return to claim their things. But coming back without her had not been an option. Yet here he was, back in his mother's home, without Carrie and with a child he'd been left to raise alone. He had learned the bitter lesson that came from trying to re-write his intended script; life would do as it pleased and living consisted of coping with it.

He set his cane aside and walked over to the row of windows, lifting the blinds on each one amid small billows of dust that floated in the sudden bursts of sunlight. He moved from one to the next until all were open and he turned to find the large, rectangular room flooded with daylight. The apprehension of facing what was here began to fade and he sensed he could begin to heal. Suddenly the objects around him seemed smaller, less ominous. He could only have come in here today because Amanda had come into his life. Her love for him was changing everything in ways he would not have believed possible.

He tentatively reached for the drape that covered a tall, triangular-shaped object. Carrie's spinning wheel. Ten years vanished as he ran his hand over the wood and fingered the remaining few wisps of cotton on the spool. He was touching her again, cherishing the good times he'd had with her. It was the first time he'd had a joyful thought of her since her death nearly a year ago and although his eyes filled momentarily, it was a tangible sign that some form of healing had begun.

He moved to the large, ornate armoire against the wall and peered into a couple of drawers. Some of Carrie's jewelry was there along with his assorted collection of cuff links and tiepins, designed to match his stage outfits. He slowly opened the wardrobe door and found the plastic clothing bag that contained his suits. The outside of the bag had yellowed somewhat over time, but when he unzipped it he found the jackets, shirts and memories as fresh as when he had packed them.

There was the grey Nehru jacket with the black trim he had worn on his wedding day, a look that had set a trend in men's wedding jackets for the next couple of years; the turquoise jacket with the white and turquoise beadwork on the yoke that he wore the night he accepted his Grammy award in 1974.

Carrie's mastery of crafts had included the exquisite beadwork she had applied to much of his clothing and accessories. Even that had, for a time, generated an interest in crafts among his young, female fans. He glanced at the remaining suits and closed the armoire, then moved to the large cabinet beside it and opened the double doors. The Grammy was on the top shelf, with his five gold records stacked beside it. On the second shelf were photo albums, among them his and Carrie's wedding album. With a little more time, he would be willing to open them and remember every detail of his past.

When he closed the cabinet doors and turned, he saw the two guitar cases and draped amplifiers in the corner, the only things that had not changed with time, the only part of his life that he could pick up and resume exactly where he left off.

He went to the slightly larger case and ran his hand along the shape of it before he laid it on the floor and undid the latches. As the lid popped open, he lifted it the rest of the way and gazed at the unchanged face of an old friend, his twelve-string Gibson; a faithful companion who had always understood him, comforted him, and helped him to express the deepest longings of his soul. As he took it from the case, the beautifully hand-beaded shoulder strap fell from behind it; another of Carrie's cherished touches. He pulled the strap over his head and it settled on his shoulders like the arm of an old buddy, greeting him after many years of missing each other.

He opened his right hand over the strings and ran his left hand down the elegant neck, recalling every variation on the textured fingerboard and along the frets. Taking a breath, he brushed the strings with his fingertips once, then again. The rich, warm tones filled the room and echoed in a place deep inside of him that had gone silent. The guitar was sorely in need of tuning, but he would take it back to his room and together, they would rediscover what had been missing all these years.

***

The drive to school in the morning traffic seemed to take forever and Amanda barely found a place to park amidst the chaos of slow moving school buses and parents dropping their children off. She walked Dylan the half block to the front door of the school.

"Amanda!" Angie was waving from a short ways down the street and caught up to them, with Conner in tow. Conner looked as though he'd been crying but at the sight of Dylan he broke into a smile.

"What a morning!" Angie hastily swiped at Conner's hair and straightened the shoulder straps on his backpack. "It's amazing how much drama you can cram into an hour and a half."

Amanda laughed. "I guess I got off easy this morning."

The young, female principal appeared in the school doorway and waved to them as she greeted many of the newly returning students by name.

"Well, this is where we peel off," Angie said as she let go of Conner.

"We don't walk them in?"

"No, the school prefers we don't, if the kids are okay."

Dylan grinned up at Amanda. "I'm okay! See ya after school!"

He broke away from her and joined Conner before she could say goodbye.

"Be good!" Angie called after them. "Oh my God – free at last. Got time for coffee? There's a little café down the street."

"I guess so," she said.

"You look so forsaken," Angie laughed. "Believe me, you'll really get to like this time of day."

They went to the café and ordered two cappuccinos while Angie raved about yesterday's picnic again.

Amanda sipped her coffee, absently taking part in the chatter until she'd worked up the nerve to casually ask, "So have you figured out who Mark reminds you of?"

Angie looked momentarily surprised before she said, "No, but I'm still working on it. He's got this quiet kind of charisma – well, you must be aware of it if you're around him all the time."

"I'm not around him that much," Amanda said, hoping for more information.

"Really?" Angie eyed her with mock suspicion. "Because I wouldn't want to let him out of my sight. I just couldn't have been more surprised when I saw him. All I'd ever heard was what a miserable grouch he was, so I assumed he had to be ugly, too."

They laughed.

"But, besides his actions, did you really think he looked like someone else?" Amanda persisted.

Angie gazed at her. "Yes, the whole package reminded me of – well, it had to be someone in the entertainment business or in the public eye. You don't just see people like that walking down the street. Like I said yesterday, there's just something about him –"

"You sure got a lot out of a two-minute meeting."

"Maybe too much," Angie admitted. "Because I'm alone most of the time, I read a lot of fiction and sometimes I have an over-active imagination. Just ask my husband. He accuses me of that all the time."

Amanda mentally added that to Mark's explanation of wearing the sunglasses to ease a headache on a bright day and decided maybe her own imagination had been a bit over-active. Maybe Helen had coughed because of something in her throat and hadn't really paid any attention to what Angie was saying. When she'd changed the subject, maybe she just felt like talking about something else.

Sitting in the coffee shop with Angie while the world bustled around her lifted Amanda's spirits and gave her a fresh perspective.

"Oh, before I forget, Conner's birthday is this Saturday and I've decided to take him and a couple of his friends for lunch and to the movies. Do you think Mark would let Dylan come? Another mom's coming along, so there'll be plenty of supervision."

"I'm sure Dylan would love that. What time do you have in mind?"

"Well, we could pick him up around two, and it's a bit of a drive to the Denny's, but it's right near the theater, the movie starts at four and runs till about six – I'd say we'd have him back by about seven."

"I'll ask Mark tonight, and I'll make sure he lets Dylan go."

"So you've learned how to get your way with him?" Angie teased.

Amanda rolled her eyes. "You really *do* read too much fiction."

***

By the time Amanda had finished her coffee with Angie, browsed at the Library and cleaned up her apartment, it was time to head back for Dylan's three o'clock pick up from school. She arrived a few minutes early to get a good parking spot and fixed her gaze on the front doors. She was anxious to see Dylan, to find out if he was okay and had a good first day. Any concerns were gone when the front doors opened and as the children began to pour out, there was Dylan. Just as she'd noticed at the pool that day when he was with the other children, he stood out with his curly blond hair, blue eyes and shining, eager face. Was he really that much more beautiful than the others or was it just her growing love for him?

She got out of the car and when he spotted her he came running, waving several huge pieces of paper. "How did you do today?" she asked as she bent down and scooped him up in a hug.

"I did good and I had fun!" he yelled, still wound up from the day's activity.

Amanda got him into the car and navigated traffic to his non-stop chatter as he tried to tell her everything at once.

"I drew five pictures!" He held up his hand with fingers spread as Amanda took a quick sideways look. "And I wrote some words and the teacher read a story and I ate all my lunch but I'm hungry again and I'm gonna be in a play!"

"A play?" Amanda reacted with appropriate surprise.

"Yeah, I'm gonna be a tree but it'll be windy so I can move around."

"I see, and when will this be?"

"A week from Friday."

"Well, that should give you plenty of time to learn your lines," Amanda said straight-faced.

"But – I don't hafta talk. I just hafta practice being a tree."

She resisted the urge to laugh at his seriousness. "Well that will be enough work, I'm sure."

He chattered the rest of the way home, then ran to find Helen on the sunporch and launched into the story of his day from the beginning again. Amanda smiled at Helen's distant grandmotherly oohs and ahs as she hung up Dylan's jacket and went to work putting in a load of laundry and starting dinner. She wondered how Mark's day had gone and hoped he would come down to hear about Dylan's.

By five o'clock, the laundry was done and folded, the meatloaf was out of the oven and Amanda was mashing the potatoes when she called to Helen and Dylan that dinner was ready. There had still been no sign of Mark and she was getting annoyed that he hadn't acknowledged his son was home from school – especially on the first day.

She served the food as Helen and Dylan settled around the table, then started to sit down when she saw Dylan pushing his peas around his plate.

"I know you don't care for vegetables, honey, but you need to have a little," Helen gently urged him.

"I don't mind the peas so much." Dylan replied, propping his head up with his hand. "I just wish Daddy would eat with us so I could tell him what I did today."

Amanda's eyes met Helen's and she slowly rose from the table, tossing down her napkin as if it were a gauntlet. "Eat your dinner before it gets cold and I'll be right back."

She trooped up the stairs, crossed the hallway and rapped sharply on Mark's door. The TV was on and she heard him get up before the door opened.

"Hi," he said, obviously glad to see her. "I guess I dozed off. What time is it?" She noticed that he seemed relaxed and happy.

"Dinner time," she replied, all business.

"Okay – I'll be down a little later."

"Your son is having dinner now."

His lips twitched at the determined look on her face. "Don't start with me, Amanda."

She folded her arms and leaned against the doorway. "Do you want to know what I think?"

"No, but I have a feeling I'm about to find out."

"I think enough time has passed that you've just gotten into the habit of not coming down for dinner, but you need to spend that time with your son."

Mark nodded, feigning solemn consideration. "Have you thought of charging for your psychiatric services?"

She smiled sweetly. "You know I'm right and besides, just making you uncomfortable is compensation enough."

"Come here, you!" He grabbed playfully at her as she danced away.

"I'm setting a place for you now," she called over her shoulder as she headed back downstairs.

"Daddy will be right down," she announced when she got back to the kitchen. Helen's eyes widened and she gave a thumbs-up as Amanda went to the cupboard and took out another dinner plate, then got the silverware and a napkin and put them on the table.

Mark came down the stairs.

"Daddy!" Dylan exclaimed. "I got lots to tell you!"

Mark sat down at the place Amanda had set and helped himself to the food as Dylan proudly gave his third account of the day's events. He listened and nodded as he ate, commenting with words of encouragement as Helen and

Amanda provided occasional reinforcement. When Dylan got to the part about being a tree in his class play, Mark asked when that would be and everyone realized it was set for the Friday evening before Helen would be back from her trip to Jean's.

"But can't you come home early to see it, Grandma?"

"Oh, I'm afraid I can't, honey." Helen was obviously disappointed. "Aunt Jean arranged a family reunion for that Saturday so I could see all the relatives before I come home."

"I'll be at your play," Amanda said, hoping to ease the look of desperation on Dylan's face.

"Daddy, could you come, too?" Dylan asked.

Mark stopped chewing and hesitated.

When the pause became awkward, Helen said, "I'm sure your father would love to see your play."

Mark cast his mother a withering glance.

"Great!" Amanda said brightly. "Daddy and I will both be there!"

Helen winked, grateful for the back-up.

Mark was looking at her and when she dared to look back, he couldn't suppress a slight grin as he shook his head.

"Can I get you some coffee?" she asked him as she got up to clear the plates.

"I think you'd better."

She poured his coffee, got some for Helen and herself and put a plate of leftover picnic brownies on the table.

"Daddy, wanna watch 'Star Trek' with me?" Dylan asked as he munched on a brownie. "It's on right after supper."

Mark glanced at his watch. "Well, the six o'clock news is coming on..."

This time Amanda turned her gaze directly on him.

"Sure, Scoot. Let's watch "Star Trek"."

"Cool!" Dylan drained the remaining milk in his glass and started to hop down, then straightened in his seat, remembering what Amanda had been teaching him.

"May I be excused?"

"Yes you may," Amanda smiled.

Dylan rushed out of the room as Mark moved to the end of the bench and reached for his cane. "How about me?" he asked.

"You're inexcusable," Amanda teased as Helen chuckled.

When Mark had made his way toward the living room, Helen leaned over. "Amanda, you're the charm. I never could have gotten him to do what you have."

Amanda shrugged. "Maybe with a little practice, it could get to be second nature for him."

"I think I'll get undressed and turn in." Helen moved her wheelchair from the table. "My favorite shows are on tonight. By the way, would you have a little time tomorrow to help me get some clothes ready for my trip?"

"Sure. I can come back after I take Dylan to school."

"Thank you, Amanda. See you then." Helen went to her room and closed the door as Amanda began cleaning up the kitchen.

At seven o'clock, she glanced around the corner into the living room. Mark sat on the couch with his arm around Dylan, who was leaning against him. Neither of them noticed her as they gazed at the TV, absorbed in the end of the program.

She wondered why Mark seemed different today. As she'd seen when she had gone to his room to get him for dinner, he radiated a contentment, a calm self-assuredness she hadn't seen in him before. What could have changed since she'd seen him early that morning? Whatever it was, he had graciously responded to her gentle prodding and had made more progress in his family life today than since she'd arrived.

Dylan looked over and saw her. "Do I hafta get ready for bed now?" he asked. "I wanna watch more TV with Daddy."

Mark glanced at her.

"It's up to Daddy, then." Amanda went back to the kitchen.

"No, Scoot," she heard Mark say. "This is your bedtime and you've got school tomorrow."

Amanda heard the sounds of Dylan's reluctance, followed by footsteps on the stairs. She went back to wiping up the cupboard, then jumped when Mark's arms encircled her from behind. "I thought you went back upstairs," she said, pretending not to notice his lips on the side of her neck. "Aren't you missing the rest of the news?"

"It's over with, no thanks to you, but I've found something better to do."

She noticed Helen's bedroom door was slightly ajar. "Your mother will hear us," she half whispered as he turned her around.

"Don't kid yourself. She knew about us before we did." He drew her into an intense kiss.

Her response was spontaneous as she felt the familiar twinge of desire begin to spread from her core to her limbs and back again, awakening every nerve ending. She felt the warmth of his hand as he slowly eased the side of her sleeveless knit top down, baring her shoulder, and her breathing dissolved into tiny gasps as his kisses became a shower of maddening tingles down the side of her neck and along the softness above her collar bone.

"I'm ready, Manda!" Dylan called from upstairs. "Can you read me my book?"

"I'll be right there," Amanda called back.

They sighed and straightened, facing each other.

"The privacy around here leaves something to be desired," Mark murmured. "But there *is* that out-of-town wedding coming up."

"Oh, I almost forgot – I saw Angie today and she wanted me to ask if she could take Dylan for awhile on Saturday. It's Conner's birthday and she's taking him and a couple of friends to lunch and a movie."

"What time?"

"Two. She said they'd be back by seven."

Mark gave it some thought. "Five hours is a long time."

"I know, but another mom is going along and the kids will have plenty of supervision."

Mark smiled. "And we won't." As Amanda's eyes widened, he nuzzled her neck again. "And that thing about me missing the news? Just making *you* uncomfortable is compensation enough."

Chapter 10
The Music Upstairs

By the time Amanda came back from taking Dylan to school the next morning, Helen was up and eager to start packing for her trip. They shared a light breakfast of English muffins and coffee, chatting about the upcoming wedding and some of the relatives Helen would be seeing for the first time in years. Amanda laughed at Helen's unflattering descriptions of certain cousins and in-laws. "But I can't wait for you to meet my daughter, Jean," she added.

Amanda was apprehensive about meeting Mark's older sister. Older sisters could be bossy and judgmental, but the possibility that Jean could also be just like Helen gave her some comfort.

When they'd finished breakfast, they went into Helen's room and started to pick out the clothing she would take. They ended up with enough mix-and-match variety for the week without over-packing, and Helen had a lovely, long sapphire blue dress she would wear for the wedding. They spent some time trying jewelry with it until they found the perfect necklace and earrings to compliment the outfit.

"You have such good taste!" Helen said as she gazed into her dressing table mirror while Amanda held the jewelry against the dress.

"I'm glad you think so."

Helen turned and took her hands. "And I *know* you have exquisite taste in men," she said with a reassuring squeeze.

Amanda's mouth opened. Helen's honesty always disarmed her.

"You don't have to answer if you don't want to, Amanda, but I just wondered, how do you feel about Mark?"

Amanda looked into Helen's candid blue eyes and sighed. "I think I'm falling in love with him."

"Then don't be afraid to show him, dear. I can already see what your love is doing for him and I can tell he cares very much for you. You don't know how I've prayed that he could find happiness again."

"I think I do know," Amanda smiled as they embraced.

"Well, I should probably freshen up some of these things that have been in my closet for awhile," Helen continued.

"We'll throw in some laundry. I'll check the upstairs hamper and we can do it all at once."

Amanda went to the basement and grabbed the laundry basket, then collected Helen's things before she headed upstairs. On the way to the second floor, she couldn't suppress a mischievous smirk. Mark didn't know she was here this morning and she would tap on his door and fling her arms around him with an unexpected kiss.

Halfway up the stairs she heard the mellow sounds of guitar music. The tones were so rich and deep that she thought Mark must have an amazing tape player she hadn't heard before. She reached the top step and started toward his door.

The music paused, then suddenly there were a few tentative chords. Amanda stopped. Another pause, a few more chords. She had to remind herself to take the next breath. Someone was softly singing, pausing, then singing again. Although she'd never heard anyone composing music before, it must sound like what she was hearing. There was another period of silence, a little longer this time. She didn't dare move for fear of the floor creaking.

Like the rush of a waterfall, the music suddenly launched again, engulfing her, sweeping her senses into a whirlpool of excitement as the multi-tone notes rapidly climbed, ebbed, then soared before the voice joined in. She'd never heard the song before, but she knew the distinctive sound of a twelve-string guitar and the voice singing the lyrics was smooth, easy, unexplainably familiar. It transported her back in time. She was a young teenager. She was drawing comfort and peace from the music. It was the unmistakable music of Marshall Stewart. Only that was not possible.

She would wake up now in her apartment and sit with her morning coffee, shaking her head at the preposterous dream she'd had. Yet she was still standing there, clutching the laundry basket, barely hearing the music above the wild thud of her heartbeat in her ears.

The music stopped abruptly again, followed by a few more practice chords.

"Amanda? Are you all right up there?" Helen's voice carried from the bottom of the stairs.

There was silence followed by footsteps in Mark's room and Amanda spun and raced down the stairs, nearly tripping in her panic. By the time she heard Mark's door open, she had breathlessly rounded the corner into the kitchen, almost running into Helen in her wheelchair.

"My goodness, dear! You look as if you've seen a ghost!"

"I – I decided to straighten the pillows on the sunporch, and I thought you needed me for something."

"No, I'm fine, but I should have known you'd be trying to do two things at once. You need to slow down, Amanda."

"I will." Amanda tried not to sound as though she was still out of breath. She heard Mark coming downstairs. "I'll go throw this load in the washer." She hurried through the basement door and closed it.

Her legs wobbled as she got herself down the stairs and tried to get to the laundry room. She could hear muffled voices as Mark and Helen spoke in the kitchen and she purposely made a lot of noise as she slammed cupboard doors while she got out the detergent and measuring cup, then loudly closed the lid of the wash machine before she turned it on. As the water began to gush at the start of the cycle, she sank onto the step stool in the corner and covered her face, allowing herself the chance to try to understand what she'd heard. No matter how many explanations she tried to invent, nothing made any sense.

This dark-haired man with this child, who was recovering from a car accident just a year ago that killed his wife, this man who had disparaged her praise of Marshall Stewart in a seemingly pointless argument – what was he doing composing music on a twelve-string guitar in his room when he thought he was alone? What was he doing sounding like Marshall Stewart, a blond-haired man who never had children, who had disappeared with his wife ten years ago? She brought her face up out of her hands.

"Are you all right, Amanda?" pierced the drone of the wash machine.

She jumped to her feet. How long had Mark been in the doorway? "I'm fine." She forced a nervous smile. "What are you doing here?"

"Mother sent me down to check on you. She was worried."

"Why?"

Mark leaned his cane against the wall and moved toward her. "She said you went upstairs to get some laundry and you were gone so long she got concerned."

"Actually, I never made it upstairs," Amanda said as he reached her.

"No?" He searched her face. "Because Mother said you came back upset and out of breath."

"Oh –" Amanda waved it off. "I got side-tracked and was straightening up the sunporch and when she called me, I thought she needed me and I moved too fast and tripped on the rug."

He touched the side of her face. "Did you hurt yourself?"

"No – no, I caught myself but I guess it shook me up a little." She tried not to lose her nerve as he drew her closer.

"There's something you need to know Amanda," he murmured through her hair.

She felt light-headed. "What?"

He nuzzled her neck. "Clumsy women turn me on."

She stood motionless until she felt him begin to shake. She stepped back to look at him. "Are you laughing?"

He nodded, snickering. "You should see your face, Amanda."

A wave of relief washed over her and she swatted at him. "You came all the way down here to make fun of me?"

"No, I'm going to make it worth my while." He folded her into a warm hug and began to kiss her.

It was the same, thrilling sensation she was growing accustomed to. Nothing had changed between them. Her confidence began to come back and she took his face in her hands and kissed him lovingly. His embrace tightened and she calmed down with the comfort of familiarity. Despite the uncertainties she couldn't yet explain, their love for each other was genuine and growing every day.

"So what are you up to?" she asked.

He shrugged. "Just catching up on a few things, that's all."

She gazed intently into his face.

"What're you looking at?"

"Your eyes. They're the most beautiful shade of blue."

"Nah – it's just the glow from the laundry room lights."

She gave him another quick kiss. "I'd better go back up. I promised your mother I'd help her pack."

"So that's what you're doing here."

"I work here, remember?"

"Yes, but I'm never sure when." He draped his arm around her as they headed upstairs.

"Then I'll just have to keep you guessing."

"Well, you're doing a good job." They reached the kitchen and he kissed her cheek. "See you later," he said before he continued to the second floor.

She stood alone in the kitchen, thinking about what she had found just now when she'd looked deep into his eyes. Even if she tried to be objective after coming to know him as she had, it was the first time she'd detected a hint of another familiarity that reached back in time...

"Amanda? I'm leaving Friday, you know," Helen teased from her room.

"I'm sorry! I'm on my way."

***

Over the next couple of hours the laundry was done, folded and a few pieces were ironed, then carefully packed into Helen's suitcases or placed on hangers in plastic bags. Although Helen had another day before she left, she was delighted to have things ready. Jean and her son would be coming around eleven o'clock on Friday and Amanda planned to make lunch for them before they started their four-hour drive back to Syracuse, New York with Helen.

"We'll work on lunch tomorrow," Helen said. "But now you go back and relax until you have to pick up Dylan."

Amanda headed back to the carriage house, grateful for a little time to think. She slowly sat down in her living room. The same fact had repeated itself in her mind all morning: No trace of Marshall Stewart or his wife was found after their disappearance. After the legal time limit had passed, they were declared dead.

She recalled the feeling, just a few years ago, when she'd heard it on the radio as part of the day's news. She was sitting at her desk at work when it was announced lightly and briefly, like one of those bits of trivia thrown in for interest. She'd paused, feeling a deep sadness that the world had stopped waiting for him to return and had moved on.

She remembered the fervent hope she and her friends at school had held out in the weeks and months after his disappearance. DJs and talk show hosts had enticed their audiences with various speculations about where Marshall Stewart could be, what he could be doing, or if he was alive at all. But despite the passage of time, Amanda had known she would always have a tiny ache, deep in her heart, for the man whose music had spoken to her during some of the most difficult times of her life.

In the midst of her reverie she spotted the autographed cover between the other albums in her small record cabinet. She went over and pulled it out, then sat again, studying the face, the laughing blue eyes, the infectious smile of Marshall Stewart. It had taken some time before she'd seen Mark's smile beneath that dark, full beard, but it got to her like no other smile... except the one in this picture.

Her gaze lingered again over the eyes in the photograph. They appeared eager, full of energy and kindness. Mark's eyes had gone from dull and lifeless the first few times she'd encountered him, to bright and engaging. It was as if a spark had been rekindled after a great loss. The increasing glimpses of his humor and the self-assured calm she'd begun to see in him were evolving right in front of her. She sensed that Mark was a man who was "coming back" from something much more than a recent tragic accident.

An unnerving, new question began to weave through her mind: How long had he really been gone and where had he actually been?

***

Marsh was certain Amanda hadn't heard him playing his guitar that morning. Her face would have shown it. He had no problem believing that she hadn't been where Helen thought, and she'd tripped on the sunporch rug. Her fumbling, embarrassed explanation had erased any doubt, but it had served as a warning that he couldn't count on Amanda's daily schedule to assure him of privacy at set times. He'd need to pay closer attention to where she was when he was composing.

He picked up the notebook on the table beside his chair. Since early yesterday he'd already filled several pages with scribbled, edited lyrics. From the moment he'd begun to play his guitar again, years of pent-up inspiration had fallen out. It was different this time. At the height of his career, he'd become blocked, immobilized by pressure from the record company to produce only what would sell. His manager had negotiated contracts that kept him awake at night and forced him to work at a frenetic pace to meet the demands placed on him. It wasn't long before he lost touch with his inner self, the one who wrote and played the music in his heart, not the one shackled by dollars and cents calculations.

He leaned back in his chair and closed his eyes. The courage to go into that locked room, the desire to pick up his guitar again, the words and music that were filling his head and spilling onto the paper, none of this would have been possible at this point in his life without Amanda. Her honesty and unabashed love nourished his soul and renewed his faith in himself as a worthwhile human being as well as a musician.

In the coming week he and Amanda would have the time and opportunity to take the next step into total and complete intimacy. There was so much he wanted to show her and give her, so many ways he wanted to love her. But there was something else that needed to happen in the course of that few days when Helen would be gone and Dylan would be at school. Somehow, Marsh needed to find a way to tell Amanda the truth about who he was, or at least who he used to be, and they would need the time and space to work it out.

While he had no guarantee how Amanda would react, he drew strength from the fact that she already loved him, minus his real name. He hoped she loved him enough to accept and forgive what he'd done to her and the world. And then, as if he wasn't asking enough of her already, he hoped she would be willing to commit to a long-term relationship with him.

He had to ask himself how he'd gotten to this impossible place in his life when, just two months ago, he was facing the abyss of several more decades in lonely seclusion with no one to love and the prospect of trying to raise Dylan on his own. Was he deluding himself? Could this relationship with Amanda end as unexpectedly as it had begun? The only thing he was sure of was that he loved and believed in her enough to risk everything to have her.

***

186

After picking up Dylan that afternoon Amanda kept busy with some light housework while she made dinner. Dylan crouched on his knees at the breakfast nook, drawing a picture and while she swept the kitchen floor she found herself stealing sideways glances at him, looking more closely at his blond curls and bright, blue eyes. Had Marshall Stewart had a son, he could have looked exactly like Dylan. But so could any other blond-haired, blue-eyed little boy, and the world had plenty of them.

After the previous night's prodding, Mark came downstairs at five o'clock without reminding, and the four of them enjoyed Amanda's spaghetti and meatballs.

Every time Amanda looked up during dinner, Mark's eyes met hers from across the table, signaling a desire that made her anxious for Dylan's bedtime. The more she was in the familiar comfort of Mark's arms, the less fear she had of the unknown.

"I've been practicing for the play!" Dylan piped up as Amanda cleared the plates and poured coffee for Mark and Helen. "Wanna see me be a tree?"

"Well, as long as you've been practicing," Mark said. "We don't want any amateur stuff."

"Any what?"

"Go ahead," Helen said.

They watched as Dylan stood in the middle of the kitchen. "Remember, it's windy, okay?"

"Okay," they answered in unison.

His face took on a look of serious concentration as he began to slowly sway and wave his arms in a spastic kind of hula. Mark covered his mouth and pretended he was coughing while Amanda managed to smile without her shoulders shaking and Helen clapped and whistled.

"I don't know who he takes after," Mark said in the hall after they'd tucked Dylan in for the night.

"You mean there's no show business in the genes?" Amanda teased, watching for his reaction.

Mark cleared his throat. "Well, none that we want to talk about, anyway."

It sounded enough like a joke, but still left her wondering.

"I'm glad you came down to dinner again tonight," she said.

"I found out what I was missing. Great food and a beautiful view."

Amanda took another close look into his face before they kissed. Each kiss they shared seemed more tender, more intimate and absolutely real. Whatever mysterious things were happening, she was in love with this man who clearly desired and loved her. She knew she needed to go where this took her because she also knew the truth was getting closer by the day.

***

After a sleepless night, Amanda was glad she had time to herself when she dropped Dylan at school on Thursday.

"Got time for coffee?" Angie asked when she saw her.

"I've got a miserable headache today," Amanda said. "Can we do it next week?"

"Sure. Hope you feel better. Oh, and if I don't see you tomorrow, remember we're picking up Dylan at two on Saturday."

"He'll be ready. See you then."

Amanda wasn't up to making small talk and with Angie's keen observation skills, she would never get away with pretending she was okay. She went home and spent the morning and early afternoon listlessly puttering at the apartment. Besides her nervousness over meeting Mark's sister the next day, she wondered about the coming week with Helen away and Dylan gone to school each day.

When Mark had teased her about Dylan being gone for so long on Saturday, the opportunity for uninterrupted lovemaking had tantalized and excited her. Although it still did, there was an undercurrent of uneasiness in her anticipation, now that she'd caught Mark playing his guitar. What other surprises would she have to deal with and how long could she keep pretending she was unaware?

That afternoon when she'd gotten Dylan home, Amanda prepared a salad and baked an apple pie for lunch the next day, hoping Jean and her son would enjoy it and they would have a good visit. All through dinner that evening, Mark and Dylan conspired, keeping up a banter of reasons why they needed to try out the pie before the company came and Amanda realized they were truly beginning to relate to each other, even if it was at her expense.

"You look tired," Helen said to her when the meal was over.

"I guess I am, a little." Amanda knew that was an understatement as she began to clear the table. She felt totally depleted, but didn't expect to sleep any better that night.

Mark put his hand over hers. It was the first time he touched Amanda in front of Helen. "I'll put Dylan to bed tonight. You have enough to do down here."

"Thank you," she said as their eyes exchanged a goodnight kiss.

He headed for the living room to join Dylan for what was becoming a ritual of watching their program together.

"I'd better turn in early for my trip tomorrow," Helen said.

"You have such a good time to look forward to," Amanda said as she rinsed the plates in the sink.

"I think we all do."

When Amanda turned, she was waiting with a knowing smile.

"Really, Helen!" she laughed. "You're so delightfully bad."

"I may be stuck in an old body, but I still think like I did at twenty-something."

"That's what I love about you. I hope I can be the same at your age."

"Well, at this stage of life any fun I have is in my mind. But you have the chance to enjoy the real thing. Don't pass it up."

Amanda went to her and kissed her cheek. "I wish you'd been *my* mother," she said.

Helen patted her arm. "No, dear, I need you right where you are."

***

After a second sleepless night, Amanda was raw and on edge. Although the idea was ludicrous, the evidence was

190

undeniable. She had distinctly heard Mark playing a guitar and sounding like Marshall Stewart. Mark was clearly hiding himself and, as she had more recently suspected, his identity. She had intermittently rolled and sprawled until her bed sheets had become a tangled mess, only to sit straight up at the recollection of Mark's fall during the baseball game when she'd thought she heard Helen call him "Marsh". What if her ears hadn't deceived her, after all? She got up, paced, made a cup of tea and paced some more.

After several hours of wild speculation she ended up distraught and wanting to cry out of frustration. Exhausted, she still vehemently rejected the idea that kept trying to penetrate her mind – that Mark was Marshall Stewart. It defied every shred of logic, changed the meaning of every moment she'd spent with him, and yet explained every uncertainty she'd had about him.

She looked at the clock through burning eyes. It was five-thirty. She had to get Dylan up for school in an hour and she had to pull herself together to serve lunch to Mark's sister and nephew, and then get through whatever the coming week would bring. She dragged herself into the shower and tried to put herself back together.

Helen was up early to have breakfast with Dylan and say goodbye. As awful as Amanda was feeling, she sensed Helen's apprehension at leaving Dylan and how much he would miss his grandmother while she was away.

"Have fun at the wedding, Grandma," he said quietly as he put his arms around her neck.

"I will, honey, and you be good for Amanda. I'll be back before you know it."

Amanda heard the tremor in Helen's voice and had to blink back her own tears. She didn't want Helen to go, either. She felt like a frightened child, facing something huge and scary by herself, and when they were alone in the kitchen she had to resist the urge to blurt out her suspicions about Mark in the hopes that Helen could resolve everything before she left.

The ride to school with Dylan was uncomfortably quiet. Amanda mustered as much fake enthusiasm as she could, but nothing seemed to help. She tried to put herself in his place, a child who'd lost his mother suddenly, was brought to a new place to live and hadn't been without his grandmother since he'd arrived several months ago.

You'd better pull yourself together, she told herself. *Dylan is still the only reason you're here at all.*

When they got out of the car, she hugged him tightly and kissed his forehead before he broke away and ran into school, and she trusted he would have enough distractions in his day to take his mind off of missing Helen.

When she arrived back at the house, she felt she was getting things into better perspective. She had coffee and toast with Helen and helped her with the last-minute packing, then vacuumed the living room and sunporch and put together a sandwich tray to complete her lunch preparations. As tired as she was, she was grateful to be too busy to do much thinking. She had just finished clearing the table on the sunporch, where Helen wanted to have coffee when Jean arrived, and was headed back through the French doors when Mark caught her from behind the sheers.

Before she could protest, he was kissing her and she felt all the tension melt away. His presence, his touch and his

192

hunger for her were real. That existed apart from anything else that was happening, and she held him tightly, kissing him with all the emotion she'd been keeping inside. It was a way of clinging to what she knew for sure, in the face of what she might soon discover.

"Amanda, it's such a beautiful day, let's have lunch at the picnic table outside!" Helen called from the kitchen.

"I'll set it up," Amanda called back. "I've got to keep moving," she said to Mark, "your sister will be here in less than an hour."

"Thanks for the warning." He reluctantly let her go.

"Are you saying I *should* be this nervous about her coming?"

"No – but I should be."

"Why do you say that?"

"No reason. You'll probably like her. She's just like my mother. Nothing escapes her and she takes no prisoners."

"Thanks – I feel much better now."

***

Amanda had smoothed the tablecloth and was arranging the plates and silverware on the picnic table when a white Nissan Pathfinder came slowly up the driveway and parked at the end of the walk.

A long-haired, gangly teenage boy got out of the passenger side and cast her a timid wave while a tall, blonde woman emerged from the driver's side. She was the picture of sophistication in her crisp, blue and white pants outfit with high-heeled sandals and her hair was swept up in a graceful twist that, Amanda could tell, wouldn't dare fall out of place.

She didn't notice Amanda until she shouldered her purse and closed the van door. "Hello, there," she smiled.

Amanda saw how much Jean resembled Helen as she summoned all her self-confidence and walked toward her. "Hi," she greeted them as they came up the walk. "I'm Amanda."

The woman looked surprised. "Dylan's babysitter?"

"Yes."

"Well, I'm Jean and I've heard a lot about you, but apparently not everything," she said, discreetly looking her over. "I thought you'd be older."

"Sorry!" Amanda replied lightly. She noticed Jean's son who seemed to be making his own, less discreet observation.

"This is my son, Jason," Jean said.

"Hello, dears!" Helen called from inside the front door where she waited in her wheelchair. "Come in – let me look at you!"

"Nice meeting you, Amanda. Brace yourself for a hug-fest," Jean warned Jason as they continued up the walk.

Chapter 11
Alive and Living in Rural Connecticut

Amanda took a deep breath and finished fussing with the table as Jean and Jason went inside. When she went in a couple of minutes later, the greetings were still going on just inside the front door. Mark had his arm around Jean as she dabbed at a few tears and they spoke softly and Helen was determined to not let go of an obviously uncomfortable Jason.

Amanda headed for the kitchen to get the coffee ready. She heard the conversation move across the living room and by the time she brought in the tray, everyone had found a seat on the sunporch. Mark sat next to his sister on the wicker sofa in front of the coffee table and Jason sat in the chair across from them, politely coping with his grandmother's chatter as she sat beside him, her hand over his.

Amanda felt Mark's appreciative gaze as she set down the tray, but was afraid to make eye contact because Jean was watching her.

"So you've both already met Amanda," Helen said with obvious pride.

"Yes, she's lovely," Jean replied, "and so young."

"I don't know what we'd do without her," Helen said. "She's so good with Dylan and such a help to me, and –"

Jean turned to Mark and raised her eyebrows. "And?"

"She's the best thing that could have happened to all of us," he said.

Amanda realized he hadn't stopped looking at her and she couldn't resist casting him a hint of a smile.

"Then you have my vote, too, Amanda," Jean concluded.

But Amanda sensed Jean's subtle scrutiny wasn't over.

"I'm honored," she replied, "but I think I'd feel better if you talked about me when I *wasn't* here."

Everyone laughed.

"Would you like some coffee, Jean?" Amanda asked.

"I'm dying for some, thank you."

Amanda held the cup and saucer a few inches above the tray and began to carefully pour.

"Uncle Mark," Jason piped up from behind her. "I'm starting a band with some friends and I'm taking guitar lessons."

"Good for you, Jason," Mark replied quickly.

"Mom says you play the twelve-string."

The cup and saucer Amanda was holding tilted without warning and rattled loudly as she barely got it to the tray before it splashed.

Jean drew her legs sideways, brushing at her white trousers.

"Oh my gosh! I'm so sorry!" Mortified, Amanda reached for a napkin.

"No harm done. Don't worry about it." Jean was mercifully gracious.

"My goodness, Amanda. I've never seen you spill a drop of anything," Helen said.

"Then you haven't been watching." Amanda tried to make light of it as she wiped up the mess.

"So Uncle Mark," Jason continued, "when we bring Grandma home next Sunday, could you show me some stuff on your guitar?"

Amanda raised her eyes to peer into Mark's face and she could tell he was thrown off by the request.

"I – really haven't played in years. I don't think I'd be a very good teacher."

"Oh, don't be so modest, little brother." Jean accepted a fresh cup of coffee from Amanda. "You were always considered one of the most accomplished –" She suddenly felt the sideways daggers Mark was sending her. "I mean, I'm sure you're still very good."

Helen cleared her throat.

"We'll see about it when you come back, Jason," Mark said as Amanda handed him a cup. He purposely didn't look at her as he took a sip.

"Amanda, please sit down and join us," Helen invited.

"Oh, no thanks – this is family time," Amanda said as she handed Jason a can of soda. "I'll finish getting lunch ready and I'll call you when it's on the table."

She was glad to get back to the kitchen and tried to steady her shaking hands as she put the ham and turkey sandwiches on a platter and poured a bag of chips into a bowl.

It was as if Jean had forgotten herself and had almost given away the very secret that Mark and Helen were struggling to protect, yet Jason seemed unaware of what was going on.

Adding the salad to the platter, she opened the screen door with her elbow and carried the food to the table. As she went back for the pie, she called out that lunch was ready. When everyone had gotten outside and was seated around the table, Helen and Jean insisted Amanda sit with them and eat. She sat beside Jean and nibbled on a sandwich while everyone complimented her on the food.

"Are you glad your daughter's wedding is almost here?" she asked Jean.

Jean cast her a wry smile. "I'm glad now and I'll be really glad when it's over."

They laughed. "Well, I hope it goes just as you planned," Amanda said.

Jean looked at her and was obviously forming a favorable opinion. "Why, thank you. That's very kind of you."

After more small talk the sandwiches and salad had all but disappeared.

"Let's wait a few minutes for the pie," Helen suggested.

"Mother says you had a garden this summer," Jean said to Mark. "Where is it?"

"At the side of the house. Come on and I'll show you." He grabbed his cane and the two made their way across the yard.

"I'll get some of these dishes inside." Amanda set the used plates and salad bowls onto the platter.

"Jason, would you go with Amanda and hold the door for her?" Helen asked. "Oh, and Amanda, would you be so kind as to get my brown sweater from my bedroom closet? It's a little cooler out here than I thought."

Jason went to the porch with Amanda and held the door. "Can I help you in here?" he asked.

"No, I'm fine," she said. "Why don't you keep your grandmother company?"

He rolled his eyes and grinned. "Okay."

Amanda got a few dishes rinsed and stacked beside the sink before she went into Helen's room. It took her a few moments to locate the sweater and she laid it on the bed while she double-checked Helen's suitcases, making sure nothing would be forgotten.

The screen door opened and closed.

"Come have another cup of coffee with me. I need a few minutes alone with you." Amanda heard Jean's voice and then footsteps coming into the kitchen.

She knew it had to be Mark with her and realized they were about to have a private conversation. As she heard someone around the coffee maker, she knew that with each passing second, she was losing her opportunity to come out of the bedroom.

"I'm glad you're back, Marsh, but for God's sake, you've been here for almost four months and haven't shown any interest in seeing or even talking to me. Do you have any idea how that feels?" Jean's words turned into a sob. "As if I wasn't hurt and angry enough over the last ten years, you've hurt me even more since you've been back."

"I didn't mean to, Jean. I was all wrapped up in myself and my own crazy life. I knew you and Mother were mad at me for what I did, but I always thought Carrie and I could come back at some point and reconnect. After the accident last year, I couldn't talk to anybody. I couldn't even look in the mirror. So I understand."

"No, you don't. You and I were so close growing up, but then I lost you when you made it big and started to tour. I hardly ever saw you but I accepted that because you were a superstar and that was part of the package."

Amanda's chest felt like it was squeezing her heart as she slowly lowered herself to the bed.

"But from the time you pulled that stunt without any regard for your family or even your fans –"

"For God's sake, it wasn't a stunt, Jean. I was desperate. I didn't do it to hurt anyone. I was only thinking of myself. I know now it was a terrible lapse of judgment that affected everyone involved, and I've spent the last few years wishing I could take it back, but I can't."

"So life as the former Marshall Stewart isn't all it was cracked up to be?"

Amanda exhaled sharply and put her hand over her mouth.

"Don't rub it in, okay?" Marsh sighed. "The truth is, it wasn't bad till I lost Carrie. Then it all fell apart."

"You *do* know you lost Carrie long before the accident, don't you?"

Marsh sighed again. "If I'd had any idea what life in seclusion would do to her, I never would have gone through

200

with it. But she was willing and anxious for us to try to have a normal life. She just didn't realize what it would be like."

"And you did?"

"Like I said, I was fine with it and if she'd been okay, I could have been happy that way for good. But I could see the unhappiness growing in her and I didn't know what to do. I thought when we had Dylan it would give her some stability and purpose, and it did at first. But then I think she felt even more lonely when she couldn't share him with family and friends."

"Is that when she started drinking?"

"Yeah, when Dylan was about two I started noticing. I knew what it was about and I tried to be patient, tried to work with her to overcome it, but it just got worse."

Amanda heard the sound of a spoon clinking against the side of a cup.

"I tried to get her some help," Marsh continued, "but by then she was getting nasty with me and threatened to blow our cover if I made her go for counseling. It just went downhill from there until she absolutely loathed me and blamed me for ruining our lives."

"Mother says you two were fighting the night of the accident. She told me a little, but why didn't I hear it from you?"

"I couldn't talk about it to anybody. I'd still rather not, but I guess I owe you that much."

"Don't bother if it's too much trouble." There was a sting in Jean's voice.

"Give me a break, all right? By then we were fighting all the time, but I suggested we leave Dylan with a sitter so we

201

could get away for a quiet dinner. I knew Carrie'd been drinking before we left, but I still thought getting out might do her some good. I told her we needed to talk and get some things straightened out and that's when she accused me of having someone else."

"She didn't have any reason to think that, did she?"

"Of course not. There was never anyone else. When she was sober she knew that, but the drinking made her paranoid and irrational. Anyway, she goaded me into an argument and in the middle of it she grabbed the steering wheel out of my hands without any warning."

"Oh, my God, Marsh."

Amanda waited, sensing his reluctance to continue before he spoke again, quietly.

"We rolled over and I was thrown out of the jeep. I came to in the ditch when the medics got there." Amanda closed her eyes as Marsh's voice grew hoarse. "She was still in the wreckage, but – I knew she was gone. I just couldn't believe it all ended that way."

There was a silence before Amanda heard Jean sniffle. "And what about your leg?"

"It was almost severed below the knee. I know I didn't get the care I should have at the time, but at least they kept it attached."

"Mother says you have a lot of pain."

"I do, at times. Nothing I can't handle, nothing I don't deserve."

"Marsh, stop. Listen, Michael knows about your injury."

"How much have you told him?"

"It's all right. All he knows is that you were involved in a terrible accident overseas and that you were left with a very serious leg injury. Mother may have told you he's an osteopathic surgeon and he'd like to have a look and see if more can be done for you."

"I don't know –"

"He'll be back with me next Sunday, so just think about it, okay? He can't wait to meet you and for now, anyway, he knows you as my brother, Mark. But that's another thing I wanted to talk to you about, Marsh. Now that you're back to stay, we need to be a family again. I can't wait to meet Dylan when we come back next week and I want him to grow up knowing his cousins and having the security of a happy family life."

"Dylan *is* the only reason I came back. I couldn't cope with losing Carrie and every time I looked at my son, the guilt was eating at me so bad I couldn't function. Mother insisted we come back and I knew it was the best thing for him."

"It was, Marsh. It's time you put *him* first. He needs some roots, and he needs to know he's loved."

"That's where Amanda's helped so much. They bonded immediately."

"Is that why you hired her?"

"Mother hired her."

"Hmmm – that's even more suspicious. And what else about Amanda?"

"What do you mean?"

"You know exactly what I mean, and besides whatever's already going on, you'll be alone with her all next week."

Amanda fidgeted in the pause.

203

"Come on, Marsh. You know Mother will have told me everything before we leave the driveway. Wouldn't you rather I hear it from you?"

"Okay, we're involved."

"How involved?"

"Jesus, Jean."

"Are you in love with her?"

Amanda put her fingers to her lips and waited.

"Head over heels," she heard Marsh say softly.

"And how is that supposed to play out in your situation?"

"I've decided to tell her the truth this week, while we have some time to work it out."

"My God – do you honestly think you can trust her, Marsh?"

"I wouldn't even consider such a thing if I didn't. All I know is, I want to see Dylan grow up with her influence and, if she'll have me, I want to be with her for the rest of my life."

"And if you're wrong about her?"

"Then you'll see me in handcuffs on the news."

"Why?"

"Because I left my manager and agent holding the bag with a multi-million dollar contract when I disappeared ten years ago. Not that they didn't deserve it for the way they took advantage of me, but I know they're both still around because I see their names occasionally in the entertainment news. If I'm ever exposed, they'll be the first in line to take a crack at me."

"God, Marsh, I hope you know what you're doing."

The screen door opened. "Have you seen Amanda?" Jason asked.

"No, why?" Jean said.

"She came in a half hour ago to get Grandma's sweater."

There was an excruciating pause, then the sudden shuffle of feet. Amanda launched herself from the bed into Helen's closet and had just drawn the folding door closed when Jean came into the room.

"Amanda?"

She watched through the louvers as Jean glanced around before taking the sweater from Helen's bed and going back into the kitchen.

"She's not around."

"Thank God," Marsh said. "She probably got side-tracked, as usual."

"We'd better go back outside," Jean continued. "We have to get going pretty soon."

Amanda heard more shuffling and the sound of the screen door closing as the footsteps continued across the porch. In the silence, she took deep breaths, feeling as though she hadn't breathed for several minutes. She eased out of the closet, straining to hear if anyone had stayed behind in the kitchen, then cautiously peered through the doorway. She was alone.

She looked at the basement door. If she could make it across the kitchen without anyone coming back, she could pretend she'd been down there the entire time. With one more glance around, she took off across the room, ripped open the basement door, and ran through, pulling it shut. Adrenaline still pumping, she grabbed the railing and scrambled down the stairs so quickly that her feet tangled. She stumbled down the last three steps and yelped, landing on her hands and knees on the thin carpet.

In the relative safety of the basement, she wheezed as her throat began to close. She couldn't move. Both wrists felt as though they were sprained and her knees were scraped. Marshall Stewart was alive and living in rural Connecticut. She'd been living with Marshall Stewart for the past several weeks. But she'd fallen in love with an entirely different man named Mark Sterner.

A wave of nausea suddenly overtook her and she forced herself up off the floor, running blindly toward the laundry room. She grasped the stationary tub and leaned over the side. Nothing happened but she'd never felt so sick.

There were footsteps in the kitchen again. Frantic, she grabbed a handful of towels, threw them into the dryer and punched the start button. She heard the basement door open.

"Amanda?" It was Jean.

"Yes!" she called above the noise of the dryer.

"We've been looking all over for you. What're you doing down there?"

"Oh – I remembered I had a load of laundry I needed to dry and fold."

"For heaven's sake, don't bother with that now. Mother wants you outside. We're having our pie and then we have to leave."

"I'll be right there!" Amanda called back.

The door closed and she sat on the stool, clutching her stomach. She couldn't stop shaking. All at once, there was an answer to every question she'd had since she'd arrived.

This complicated, mysterious man was the same man she'd idolized as a teenager, the same man who produced the music that had touched her and millions of others so deeply, the same man who had signed her album cover all those years ago. Only he seemed nothing like the Marshall Stewart she'd known then. But what Marshall Stewart *had* she known? The fact was, she'd only known him in her imagination.

Mark Sterner was a human being, with all his mistakes and doubts and fears. He was ten years older and wiser and full of regret and guilt for what he did, and he loved and needed her. She was ten years older, too. There were no stars in her eyes when she looked at him. What she saw now was real and the love she had for him was the same as it had been thirty minutes ago. But in the same thirty minutes she'd learned that, as Marshall Stewart, he had betrayed her and the rest of the world with his ill-conceived scheme. She wondered if she would ever be able to reconcile that conflict in her heart.

More footsteps in the kitchen. Someone was at the basement door again.

"Amanda, darlin', tell me you didn't trip and fall again!" It was *his* voice and she could not believe the irony of his calling her "darlin'" for the first time, when Marshall Stewart had used that term of endearment so frequently in his songs.

She gulped and tried to find her voice. "Very funny! I'm coming up now!"

She heard him head back outside as she made her way to the steps and clung to the railing to steady herself. *Get a grip! Get a grip!* her mind screamed. She took the steps slowly, giving her buckling knees a chance to hold her legs up. She tried to breathe more evenly to subdue the absolute panic that threatened to overtake her. Making her way from the basement door along the side of the staircase, she heard the sounds of chatter on the early afternoon breeze that stirred her hair through the screen door.

She paused, grateful for the chance to check her appearance in the hallway mirror. She smoothed her hair and hastily licked her fingertip to rub off the stray mascara that had streaked at the corners of her moist eyes. She straightened the ruffled neck of her blouse and smoothed the skirt she'd so carefully chosen to wear today. She pushed the door open and looked out at the small group sitting at the picnic table. Suddenly they were all strangers, these people who still thought they were keeping their secret from her. Only Jason seemed unaware of the truth about his "Uncle Mark".

She gazed at the man whose real name was "Marsh" and he looked happier than she'd ever seen him. From what she'd heard him tell Jean, she was the reason for his happiness and the hope for his future.

Suddenly Helen spotted her. "Amanda, we've missed you. We're almost ready to leave!"

"I'm sorry I took so long." She emerged from the house and started down the porch steps to the yard, determined to appear unaffected by what she'd just learned.

"Oh my goodness, dear, what did you do to your knees?"

At Helen's prompting, everyone turned to look at Amanda. Filled with dread, she dared to look down. Both knees were raw and there was a red smear where she'd bled slightly.

Marsh got up and came toward her. "What happened? Are you all right?"

Amanda's carefully honed alibi skills kicked in again and she forced a laugh. "I lost an earring in the laundry room and I got down to look for it. I guess I got a brush burn off the rug." She thanked God she'd put earrings on that morning as Marsh put his arm around her and studied her face.

"We thought you went to Mother's room to get her sweater," he said.

"I was headed there when I remembered the laundry and then I got busy looking for my earring. I'm sorry I got distracted."

He smiled. "What am I going to do with you?" he murmured into her ear.

His touch and nearness electrified her nerves. How long would she have to pretend she hadn't heard his and Jean's conversation? How long would it take him to level with her?

She was barely aware of the small-talk over the next few minutes as Jean complimented her on the pie, thanking her for the lunch, and Amanda wished her luck with the wedding.

As Helen gave her a long hug, Amanda hoped she couldn't detect that she was still shaking. "Take good care of Mark and Dylan for me," she said.

"I will," Amanda promised.

Jason went by with Helen's luggage. "I'll bring my guitar next Sunday, Uncle Mark, and maybe we can play together," he said on his way to the car.

"We'll see what we can do, Jason."

Within a few more minutes they were ready to go.

"See you next weekend!" Jean called out as she and Jason waved out the front windows and Helen blew a kiss from the back seat.

As Amanda watched them head down the driveway before turning onto the road, she became acutely aware that she and Marsh were now completely alone. She struggled with another wave of panic as she busied herself clearing the table.

"Stop working so hard." Marsh's voice was close to her ear as his arms encircled her from behind. "We're finally alone and Dylan's in school for two more hours."

The very situation Amanda had longed for was suddenly impossible for her to handle.

"You're shaking," he said as he turned her around. "What's wrong?"

"I don't know. I didn't sleep last night and I really haven't felt well all morning."

"You look exhausted," he said, taking her face in his hand. "You're not getting sick, are you?"

"I hope not. I probably just need a little rest and I'll be fine."

"Whatever it takes. Why don't you go in the house and lie down? I can finish cleaning up here."

"Thank you." She forced a nervous smile. "Mind if I just go back to my place for awhile?"

He looked disappointed, then smiled back. "No, wherever you can sleep is fine. And why don't you call Angie and see if she can pick up Dylan from school today."

"Really?" Amanda tried not to sound as relieved as she felt. "You wouldn't mind?"

"Not at all." He took her hand and kissed it. "I need you to be well. And besides, I've got plans for you."

Her mouth dropped open. The devilish grin, the direct, blue eyes – suddenly it all came together and she was looking across the years at Marshall Stewart. It was the first time he'd let his guard down so completely and it took all she had to keep her expression unchanged. "Thanks for understanding," she said. "I'll be back later to make Dylan's dinner."

When she reached her apartment she immediately called Angie, who was glad to help out and bring Dylan home from school.

"You haven't been feeling good for a couple of days now," she said. "I hope it's not the flu or anything."

"No, I'm just a little worn out."

"Hey, while you're on the phone, I wanted you to know that Conner's party tomorrow is turning into a sleep over. Do you think Dylan would want to stay?"

Amanda couldn't think at all. "I don't know – I don't think he's ever slept away from home."

"Should I check with Mark?"

"Maybe you should." Amanda gave her the number for the house. "And thanks again for covering for me this afternoon. You're a good friend, Angie."

"You'd do the same for me, kiddo. Just feel better. Besides, you'll owe me a drink after *this* gig."

Amanda pretended to laugh, then hung up and sat motionless. Her whole world had changed in one morning, yet she had to find a way to face it, cope with it and keep functioning by dinner time. Even in her craziest imaginings and worst fears combined, nothing could have prepared her for the truth she'd found out today. The old adage, "Watch what you wish for", came to mind and her lips formed a small, rueful smile. She'd always wished Marshall Stewart hadn't disappeared and, since she'd met Mark Sterner, she'd wished she could uncover his secret. Having both wishes granted in one astounding revelation could never have happened in her most bizarre dreams.

She went to the kitchen for a soda and spotted the unopened bottle of Merlot Angie had brought to the picnic on Labor Day. Although it was her habit to sip wine only on special occasions and she never bothered when she was alone, it suddenly invited her to open it and savor the consolation and perspective it promised. She took a wine goblet from the cupboard and filled it, taking an appreciative taste. The subtle but crisp purple bite down the back of her throat was reassuring.

She carried the glass and the bottle to the living room and set them on the coffee table, then opened the drawer of the record cabinet where her tapes were stored. There was the box with the Marshall Stewart documentary collection, a set of three video tapes that covered his entire career from his first performance in 1970 at the age of twenty-one, to his final concert tour in 1975 and the reports of his mysterious disappearance later that year at the age of twenty-six.

She was seventeen and still missing her idol when the tapes came out. She'd watched them again and again, as a way of being with him, keeping him close. But after awhile she'd put them away as a keepsake and had reluctantly moved on to adulthood. Now, as she put the first tape into the player and sat back on the couch with her glass, it was as though she was seeing it for the first time.

A slender, young man with those disheveled, long blond curls and a shy smile walked onto the stage of the Ed Sullivan Show, shouldered his ornate twelve-string guitar and gave a poignant performance of his first hit single, "If a Tree Falls". As he took his bow the applause thundered, the girls in the audience squealed and his career took off. The remainder of Tape One was a collage of larger and larger concert venues, backstage interviews and the first few glimpses of Carrie, who was then Marsh's fiancé.

Tape Two concentrated on Marsh's work in the recording studio as his music matured and took on more mainstream aspects, creating an even more diverse audience and broader popularity. He began to write and perform with orchestral back-up, which enhanced the nuance and appeal of his songs. There was thrilling footage of his concerts in Madison Square Garden and on stages in the capital cities of Europe and Asia. In each appearance he was gaining more confidence and ease as he opened his arms and waved to roaring crowds and seemed to truly enjoy what he was doing. At the end of Tape Two were pictures of his and Carrie's wedding. "She's my soul mate," he told reporters as the couple stood with their arms around each other.

Amanda's eyes filled with tears as she remembered what Marsh had told Jean about the disintegration of his marriage and how he'd lost Carrie, first to alcohol and then in the accident.

As the third tape began, she poured her third glass of wine, surprised at how much of it splashed onto the coffee table. She watched Marsh's Grammy Award acceptance speech and recognized the inflections in the speaking voice of the man she'd come to know. She watched his posture and the way he held his hands and saw what she'd been seeing every day. As a love-sick teenager, she'd had every characteristic memorized and would have recognized him anywhere. But ten years and the lost hope of ever seeing him again had dulled her perception, until now.

In the behind-the-scenes glimpses on the tape, his demeanor was changing. The public Marshall Stewart was still upbeat and seemed to be in charge, but the private one was beginning to show the strain and tension that would lead to his fateful decision. Although Amanda's mind was beginning to numb with the alcohol, she was suddenly overwhelmed by the realization that she was the only fan who knew the truth.

The next scene showed him waving and walking onto the set of the Tonight Show and as much as she tried to focus, there were two Marshall Stewarts on the screen being interviewed by two Johnny Carsons. The last thing she would remember was the arm of the couch hitting her in the face.

Chapter 12
Arrogant Bastard

Marsh dialed Amanda's number on the portable phone for the third time. Again, it rang repeatedly as he gazed out the sunporch window at the carriage house. Something had to be seriously wrong. It was nearly five-thirty and she'd said she would be back to make dinner. The first time he'd called to see if she was feeling better, he'd hung up on the third ring for fear of waking her. The second time, about an hour later, he'd let it ring longer and decided she must be in the shower. But it had been another hour and a half and her failure to answer this time was worrying him.

He walked into the living room where Dylan sat on the couch, clutching his toy puppy, eyes fixed on the television. Dylan was worrying him, too. He'd barely spoken since Angie dropped him off from school and the couple of times Marsh had asked him about his day or if he was feeling all right, he'd made it clear he wanted to be left alone.

"Hey, Scoot, I have to go over and talk to Amanda for a minute, okay?"

Dylan nodded sullenly without taking his eyes off the TV.

"I'll be right back." Marsh glanced at him once more, grabbed his cane and headed across the yard.

He hoped Amanda was okay and that she was feeling well enough to come back to the house because he sensed he was going to need extra help with Dylan tonight. He knew Dylan was missing his grandmother and he had no idea how to deal with it.

He made his way up the carriage house stairs, hoping his cane made enough noise on the wrought-iron steps to wake her up so he wouldn't startle her. He knocked on the door and cupped his eyes, peering through the glass. No movement. He knocked again and called out to her. Then he spotted her arm, draped off the seat of the couch. He grabbed the doorknob, found it unlocked and shoved the door open as he rushed through the kitchen and into the living room. "Amanda!"

She was on her side, hair over her face. As he dropped his cane and went to her, he kicked something behind the coffee table and looked down to see the wine bottle laying in a fresh, red stain on the rug, along with the cracked goblet that had fallen out of her hand. He noticed the remote on the coffee table in front of her, then saw the scattered tapes, each with his image on the box. He glanced at the blank but pulsing TV screen, picked up the remote and clicked it. Audience laughter filled the room and he saw himself at the age of twenty-five, responding to Johnny Carson's jokes about his female following.

"So do you ever get tired of being chased down by crazed women everywhere you go?" Johnny asked in his tongue-in-cheek manner.

"No, not really, would you?" Marshall quipped, straight-faced before he fluttered his eyebrows to the delight of the audience.

He clicked off the remote and tossed it onto the table as Amanda stirred. She opened her eyes slightly, then bolted up. "Oh, God – it's you!" She drew her bare legs up and huddled against the back of the couch, gasping and staring at him through bleary eyes and messy hair. The wide, ruffled neck of her blouse was down, revealing half of her bra. She suddenly noticed and tugged at it, self-consciously pulling it sideways, leaving her shoulder still bare. She seemed unaware that her skirt was bunched up around her hips.

He stood looking at her as her features melted into Carrie's and he re-lived the many times he'd found his wife in the same condition with only himself to blame. He could hear the vicious arguments and recalled how increasingly volatile they became until she sometimes came at him with fingernails and fists.

Amanda pushed her hair back. "What time is it?" she moaned.

"Going on six. What the hell are you doing, Amanda?"

"Oh, God." She put her hand to her forehead. "I'm sorry – I'll go and make Dylan's dinner right away." She struggled to get up but fell back. "Oh, my head –"

"Don't bother. I'll take care of it."

"No – I'll be right there –"

"Forget it, Amanda." He reached for his cane. "And when you get yourself straightened out, we need to talk."

She glared up at him. "Don't you dare talk to me like a boss." There was a bitter edge in her voice that he'd never heard before.

He headed for the door without looking back. He had to get out of there and away from whatever it was she expected of him.

As he crossed the yard again he realized he was shaking. She knew. She had to know. Somehow, she'd figured out the truth about him. Nothing else could explain the way he'd found her, drunk and watching the story of his life. And now that she owned the truth, what was she going to do with it? Was she the woman he'd come to believe he could trust and seek a deeper relationship with? Or was she someone who couldn't pass up an opportunity to expose an outrageous lie and pursue what would amount to fifteen minutes of fame and fortune?

Over the last few days he'd decided to rely on his instincts to guide him on when to tell her, most likely after they'd made love and were sharing their deepest secrets. But now that she knew, did she think he'd had no intention of telling her at all? And if she still loved him, could she ever trust him again?

***

Amanda shivered under the cool water of the shower. Her head pounded and she felt sick to her stomach, but somehow she had to get herself over to the house and take care of Dylan. She cursed herself for drinking so much, but she never meant for Marsh to know about it. He'd looked completely distraught at finding her that way and she sensed that, besides being shocked at her intoxication, he'd panicked at the sight of the tapes she'd been watching. Rather than tell her when he was ready to and in the way he wanted to present it, he'd had no control over how she found out.

She knew he must be terrified but his dismissive manner had hurt and enraged her. *"When you get yourself straightened out..."* He'd spoken to her as though she was a hapless employee who had stepped out of line and would require a talking to.

As her mind began to clear, she allowed herself to feel angry with him for holding out on her this long. He'd been the one who initiated their first kiss and encouraged her involvement with him, all the while keeping his secret. And although he'd told Jean he planned to tell her the truth in the coming week, would he have actually had the nerve to level with her even then?

It was around six-thirty when she arrived at the house, breathless from trying to hurry when she could barely function. It was quiet. Marsh was standing at the kitchen counter but didn't look up as she walked in.

"Where's Dylan?" she asked.

"Upstairs," he said as he made a couple of sandwiches.

She saw the pan of soup heating on the stove. "I came over to make dinner."

"I told you we could manage."

"I'm sorry for what happened."

He kept working without looking up. "What's going on with you, Amanda?"

His coolness brought her anger to the surface and she walked over to him. "I could ask *you* the same question, but – oh, that's right – I agreed *not* to!"

He dropped the butter knife and turned to her. "I don't need your sarcasm right now. If there's something you want to say, why don't you just say it?"

She reached for the counter, trying not to sway with the dull pain in her head. "Maybe you have something to say to me first."

"Yes! Go back to your place. We don't need you here tonight."

"How dare you dismiss me when I came to help!"

"You're in no condition to help anybody. I'm not even sure who you are."

Her mouth dropped open and she could tell he instantly regretted his choice of words. "*You* don't know who *I* am?" She took a step closer and looked up at him boldly. "Why don't we talk about who *you* are?"

"Amanda..." A look of anguish crossed his face and he reached for her.

She moved away. "This may come as a surprise, but it turns out I'm as good at acting as you are."

His jaw tensed. "What do you mean?"

"I *was* upstairs the other morning when you were playing your guitar, and I *was* in your mother's room this afternoon when you and Jean were in the kitchen. I *didn't* trip over the sunporch rug, forget the laundry or lose an earring. But you believed me because you thought you knew me. Sound familiar?"

"This isn't how I wanted it to be."

220

"Neither did I. But when were you going to tell me?"

"When the time was right."

"For who? You?"

He caught her arm. "Amanda, listen to me –"

"You arrogant bastard." She shook him off and headed out of the kitchen. She could hear him coming after her but when she got outside, she broke into a run as the yard fused into shapeless variations of green through her tears. When she'd almost reached the carriage house, she thought she heard him calling her name, but didn't look back.

***

Marsh grasped the porch railing and watched Amanda run up the steps before she disappeared into her apartment. He ached with the urge to follow her, but even if she would let him in, he couldn't leave Dylan alone for the interminable length of time it would take to try to make things right.

His throat swelled and he blinked back the sudden sting in his eyes. The only thing worse than an arrogant bastard was a *stupid*, arrogant bastard. He should have known it would come to this. Had he really thought she would rejoice at the news that her idol was alive and well? Right here? And they would live happily ever after? How delusional was he to think that, even if he found love again, any woman could accept what he'd done and be a willing accomplice to his lie?

He pushed off from the railing and walked back into the house. The loud, sizzling noise coming from the kitchen reminded him he'd left the soup heating on the stove. It was bubbling into the burner and before he could grab the pan, the smoke alarm began to taunt him with its piercing beep.

"Son of a bitch!" he yelled as he threw the soup into the sink.

He wanted to forget the whole thing and head for the solace of his room, but Dylan needed dinner and he needed to be a father. He opened the cupboard and took out another can of soup.

He couldn't believe he was continuing with such a mundane task after Amanda had confronted him with his lie and could be calling the media right now. She held his future in her hands. All his fears fluttered from out of the dark corners of his life to roost in this moment. It was too surreal to take in and his mind retreated into slow-motion as if to numb the shock.

When the soup was hot, Marsh poured it into the bowls on the table and set the plate of sandwiches between them. He went to the bottom of the stairs.

"Dylan! Come on and eat. It's ready!" he called.

"I'm not hungry," the small voice responded from Dylan's room.

"You gotta eat, Scoot. Come on, it's supper time."

"I don't want any." Dylan's voice was more insistent.

Marsh sighed. "Please come down, Dylan."

"No!"

"Get down here now!"

There were footsteps in the hallway and Dylan slowly descended the stairs, one hand on the railing and the other clutching his puppy. He'd obviously been crying. He climbed onto the bench at the table and Marsh sat down across from him.

"Where's Manda?" he asked, head down.

"She's not feeling well."

"'Cause you had a fight?"

"What are you talking about?" Marsh pushed the sandwich plate toward him.

"I heard you fighting."

"We weren't fighting. She didn't feel well and she left. Eat your soup. It's chicken noodle – your favorite."

"I hate chicken noodle." He started to cry.

"For God's sake, Dylan." Mark dropped his spoon onto the table and rubbed his face. "What's wrong?"

"I miss Grandma. When's she coming back?"

"We talked about this before she left, remember? She'll be home a week from Sunday."

"But how many days will that be?"

"That's eight days," Marsh said, trying to keep his voice even.

"When will Manda be back?"

"When she's feeling better."

"How many days will that be?"

"I don't know!"

Dylan sobbed harder. "I want Manda!"

Marsh gazed across the table at the little boy who was crying brokenheartedly, rubbing his eyes with his small fists. He looked around at the empty kitchen and felt the vast hollowness of the house. This was what it would be like without Amanda, without Helen, with no one to care for Dylan and himself. This was what he'd condemned himself to. But seeing his son suffer for it was more than he could bear.

***

Amanda cried on and off all evening. Part of her wanted to be with Marsh, to let him know she still loved him and wanted to work through this, yet she was furious at his attitude and his refusal to be honest with her when he had the opportunity. Even at that, she understood how frightened he must be, with everything on the line and her own unwitting display of bad behavior. Nothing could have prepared him for finding her sprawled on her couch, drunk. Yet, she'd had no idea how to cope with the truth.

Then there was Dylan. He was surely the one who'd suffered the most. She hadn't been there for him since she'd dropped him off at school that morning, knowing he was upset. How had his day gone? And how did he feel when she was not there after school, to bring him home and listen to whatever was on his mind and make his dinner?

She and Marsh had been selfishly involved in their own concerns and she felt she'd let Dylan down on the day his grandmother had gone away, the very day he'd needed her most. It made her cry even more. Mentally and physically exhausted, she went to bed early and fell into a restless sleep.

In the midst of a dream she would not recall, a phone rang. As it persisted, she rolled over, turned on the lamp and reached for the portable on her nightstand. The clock beside it read 12:35 and she wondered if she was answering a crank call. When she put the receiver to her ear there was unearthly crying and screaming in the background, so shrill it went through her and she held it away from her ear.

"Amanda."

She came fully alert, barely recognizing Marsh's jagged voice. "What's wrong?"

"I don't know. Dylan's inconsolable. He's been like this for the last hour and I don't know what to do."

"I'll be right there!" Amanda jumped out of bed, pulled her bathrobe on over her nightgown and stepped into her slippers, then ran down the carriage house steps and across the lawn. Her head was still aching but she was glad her stomach felt better or she never could have moved so quickly.

Marsh had put the outside lights on and was waiting at the door. As she ran up the porch steps, the sounds of Dylan's screams hit her like a wall. Marsh looked exhausted and frayed and as she entered the hallway, she saw Dylan standing in the living room in his pajamas, clutching his puppy with both hands as he wailed like a child possessed. The wild look in his eyes told her he was in such a dark place, he didn't even know she was there. Seeing him that way frightened her but she knew she was the only one who could calm him.

"Hey, sweetie," she soothed as she approached him. Red-faced and shuddering with sobs, Dylan suddenly seemed to focus on her and he reached out as she hoisted him into her arms. "My goodness you're heavy! Do you know how big you're getting?"

He hiccoughed and nodded, putting his arms tightly around her neck. "I thought you were gone," he said between gasps.

"I'm right here and I'm not going anywhere." Amanda looked at Marsh. His eyes were red and he ran a shaking hand through his hair. "Why don't you go relax and I'll see what I can do," she said.

He nodded and walked slowly to the sunporch where he sat on the wicker sofa just out of sight.

Amanda carried Dylan to the lounge rocker beside the fireplace and sat, holding him on her lap. His arms hadn't loosened from around her neck, but he was crying more softly and she could tell he was beginning to calm down.

"Why don't you tell me what's going on," she said as she smoothed his damp curls.

He shuddered for the last time. "Grandma went away and then I thought you did, too."

"I know, sweetie. It wasn't a good day. I'm sorry I couldn't pick you up from school."

"I miss Grandma," he murmured. "I want to talk to her."

"Well, I'm sure she's sleeping now, but we can call her in the morning – in fact, she's probably planning on calling you."

"Really?"

"I'm sure." She rocked him gently. "So is there anything else that's bothering you?"

Dylan sniffled. "I miss Mommy, too, but I can't tell Daddy."

"Why not?"

"'Cause I don't want to make him sad again."

Amanda kissed his forehead and stroked his hair. "Do you know what I think?"

He sniffled again. "What?"

"I think your Mommy's right here, watching over you all the time, even though you can't see her."

"You do?"

"Yes, and I think she loves you very much and she'll always watch over you, wherever you go and whatever you do."

"Is she watching over Daddy, too?"

"I'm sure she is."

As Amanda continued to rock, she could feel him relaxing as his head rested on her shoulder.

"Why were you and Daddy fighting tonight?" he asked.

Amanda closed her eyes. "Why did you think that? What did you hear?"

"I couldn't hear words, but I knew you were both yelling."

She let out a quiet sigh of relief. "We were just talking and we got upset. But it's okay, now."

"You're not mad at him?"

"No."

"Is he mad at you?"

"I hope not."

He picked up his head to look at her. "Do you love Daddy?"

Amanda found herself captive to his inquisitive blue eyes. "Well, what would you think if I did?"

Dylan cupped his chin in his hand. "I think he needs it."

She laughed softly. "I think he does, too."

He smiled and dropped his head back onto her shoulder. They rocked for a few more moments before Dylan said, "Conner's mom asked Daddy if I could stay over tomorrow night. Do you think I should?"

"Do you want to?"

"Yeah, I think so. I think I'd have fun."

"Well, just remember, if you don't like it you can call me and I'll come and get you."

"I know. Thank you for taking care of me, Manda. I really love you."

"I love you, too." The words caught in her throat and she squeezed him a little tighter. "And now I think you need some sleep so you can have fun tomorrow."

"Yeah – I'm sleepy now."

"Good. Then let's get you to bed."

He slid from her lap and she took his hand before they headed upstairs. "Dogby's tired, too," he said as he clutched his puppy.

"I think he's been sleeping all along," Amanda said.

"You do?"

"Well, I think I heard him snoring."

"No you didn't," Dylan giggled.

"I'm pretty sure I did."

***

As their voices faded into the upstairs hallway, Marsh took his hands from his face and gazed into the soft lamplight of the living room. All at once the house was warm, tranquil, filled with love. This was how it was with Amanda here. Everything seemed in place. Everything made sense.

He got up when he heard her coming back downstairs, and met her in the entrance hall. "Thank you for coming over. You're amazing with him."

"It's nothing you can't do, in time."

They stood face-to-face for a long moment. "I'm sorry," they said in unison.

"I've never been drunk before in my life," Amanda said.

"I wouldn't believe you if you weren't so bad at it," he gently chided her. "Would it be okay if we talked tomorrow, after Dylan gets picked up?"

She nodded. "What we both need now is sleep."

"Don't go all the way back. It's going on two a.m. Why don't you just get some sleep in the spare room?"

She smiled. "Even though we're being appropriate, do you really want Dylan telling Angie tomorrow that I slept over?"

He let out a laugh. "Good point."

"I'll be back to get Dylan his breakfast and get him ready to go."

"Thank you, Amanda." He longed to reach for her, but knew it was too soon. Instead, he settled for being grateful to still have her here. When she left, he watched her disappear into the darkness, listened for the closing of her door and was already waiting for her to come back.

Chapter 13
If It Would Lead Me to You

When Amanda went back to bed, her fatigue became a drug that put her into a sound sleep. She was glad, when she awoke with the alarm at eight o'clock, that she hadn't had a chance to think about anything for a few hours.

It was about eight-thirty when she got back to the house and when she went in, she heard Dylan's excited voice in the kitchen. He was sitting on the bench at the breakfast nook, legs swinging as he held the portable phone to his ear.

Marsh sat beside him, reading the morning paper. He looked up with a smile, the one she'd come to realize he gave to only her, along with that intimate look in his eyes. The one that made her feel more and more helplessly in love with him.

"Yeah, Grandma – Manda just got here. Okay, here she is." He held out the phone to her.

"Amanda! How's everything going there?" Helen's voice in her ear reassured her.

"Fine – are you having a good time?"

"Oh, the best. We had a beautiful rehearsal dinner last night but I was so tired after the trip, that I slept in this morning."

"That's good. I'm sure you have another busy day."

"Yes – I'm really looking forward to the wedding this afternoon. Tell me, is Dylan okay?"

"He's fine. He misses you, but he's busy today, too."

"So I heard. He's going on his first sleep over. I'm glad Mark agreed to it."

Amanda wished she could tell Helen it was okay to call her son Marsh, but that conversation would have to wait. "Would you like to talk to Dylan again?"

"Yes, put him on so I can say goodbye. I'll talk to you again soon, Amanda."

She handed the phone back to Dylan and went to the stove. Dylan finished his goodbyes and ran to the counter, putting the receiver back in its cradle. "Grandma called, just like you said, Manda!"

"I thought she might." Amanda took a pan out of the stove drawer. "Would anyone like pancakes?"

"Yay!" Dylan clapped. "Want some pancakes, Daddy?"

"Sounds good to me."

Amanda turned on the burner and put oil in the pan. "I need some things at the store after breakfast," she said to Dylan as she took the box of pancake mix from the cupboard. "Want to come with me?"

"Yeah! I'll get dressed now so I'll be ready!" Dylan took off and headed upstairs.

In the silence Amanda got a bowl and began to mix the batter.

"Did you get any sleep?" Marsh asked.

"I think I was too exhausted not to. How about you?"

"The same, I guess. Thanks for coming back so early today."

She put a couple of spoonfuls of batter into the pan. "Dylan needs to know I'm here. I feel terrible about what he went through yesterday. I abandoned him."

"It was a difficult day for all of us."

She flipped the pancakes without looking up. "There's more coffee. Would you like some?"

"I can get it. You're busy."

Amanda took the pot over and filled his cup. She was aware of him watching her every move, his eyes holding her in an embrace.

"So you *don't* hate me," he said.

She took the pot back and poured herself a cup.

"Of course I don't hate you." *'I love you,'* she wanted to say.

"Can you ever forgive me for what I did to you – and the rest of my fans?"

His fans? Marshall Stewart was sitting in front of her, asking her forgiveness for deceiving the world. The question was overwhelming so she calmly took the finished pancakes from the pan and added more batter. She knew the silence was lasting too long before she turned to face him. "I suppose you did what you had to do."

"I'm not so sure about that, but I did the only thing I *could* do at the time."

She gazed at him before she took a sip of her coffee. "Would you do it again?"

232

"Only if it would lead me to you." He hadn't taken his eyes off of her.

It took her breath away and she swallowed hard and lowered her cup, clutching it between her hands as she met his gaze. His words were as beautiful and powerful as the lyrics from one of his songs, but he'd said them to her, in his kitchen, without hesitation. He had just told her that all he'd been through in the last ten years was worthwhile because he'd found her.

"Manda, can you fix my shirt?" Dylan was back, looking down at his shorts outfit and the top was lopsided.

She set her cup down and bent to look. "Your buttons don't match up, that's all." She began to undo them and re-align them. The small buttons were difficult to do up with her trembling fingers. "Didn't you wear those blue socks yesterday?"

"Yeah."

"Then you need to put them in the laundry hamper and get a new pair from your drawer. You need to put on clean socks every day. You know that."

"I know – I was in a hurry, 'case you went shopping without me."

"I won't go without you. Besides, your pancakes are about ready and we have to eat first. Go change your socks."

"Okay." Dylan trekked from the room again and she returned to the stove, still shaken.

***

They didn't speak in the few moments Dylan was gone again. Marsh sensed that he needed to hold back until they were alone and could have a complete and open conversation.

233

He knew he'd inadvertently stunned her with what he said and she needed time to think about it.

Dylan provided enough lightness and background chatter to get them through breakfast and after Amanda cleared the table, the two of them headed to the store while Marsh went upstairs.

He picked up his guitar and strummed softly, letting the melodic chords calm his mind. He was profoundly thankful for a second chance with Amanda and the realization that her sweet and loving heart hadn't closed the door on him yet. Everything rested on tonight and although he'd looked forward to it in the hope of making love to her, he knew he would be fortunate if she would just give him the time to talk this out, even if it took all night.

About an hour and a half later he heard car doors and Dylan's laughter followed by the slam of the screen door. When he reached the kitchen, Amanda was putting groceries away and Dylan was waving something that glowed a bright red.

"Look, Daddy – Manda bought me a toothbrush that lights up when you use it!"

"That's very cool," Marsh remarked.

"Anything to make it more exciting," Amanda said over her shoulder as she opened the refrigerator.

She sounded so much like a mom, Marsh had to smile.

"And we got a birthday present for Conner! Wait'll you see it!" Dylan fumbled through one of the bags on the table.

"I have to take some things back to my place," Amanda said. "There's paper and ribbon in the bag with the gift – would you help Dylan wrap it?"

"Sure."

"I'll be back before Angie gets here."

"When's she coming?"

"Around two. It's twelve-thirty now, so I'll be back in an hour." Amanda headed out the door, gone like a whirlwind. He looked at the empty doorway, hoping for the day when she would live here and not have to go back to her place.

"Look what we got for Conner, Daddy!"

Marsh sat down at the table as Dylan held up a box with a window that displayed a black plastic hot rod with orange flames down the sides. "This is Conner's favorite kind of car – mine, too – and I can't wait to give it to him!"

Marsh gazed at his son. Gone was the frightened, hysterical little boy of last night. Amanda had chased the monsters away with a rocking chair and all the right words. And it touched Marsh to see Dylan's joy in giving his friend a gift he'd like for himself. It was one of Dylan's many qualities that would be nurtured and encouraged by Amanda's presence in his life.

"I'm sure Conner's going to like that. Let's get it wrapped."

Dylan ran to the utility drawer and pulled out scissors and tape and they set about measuring and cutting the paper.

"Manda told me a secret, Daddy, and I promised I wouldn't tell, but I think you need to know."

Marsh's stomach knotted. "What's that?"

"She bought some special stuff and when I asked what it was for, she said she's gonna make you a fancy dinner tonight, so you gotta act surprised, okay?"

Marsh exhaled. "Thanks for the tip, Scoot. Can you tear me off some tape?" As he folded the edges of the paper around the box, Dylan tore a large piece of tape from the roll. "Not so big. We're not wrapping a *real* car."

"Guess what else Manda bought."

"What?"

"She bought some wine and a whole bunch of candles, too."

"Really."

"Yep, but the candles are just for if the power goes off."

"How do you know that?"

"'Cause I asked her what they were for and that's what she told me."

"I see." Marsh let a smile play across his lips. "You shouldn't ask so many questions, Scoot. But keep up the good work."

***

Amanda had put away her groceries and was picking up and straightening the apartment when Angie called.

"How are you feeling, kiddo?"

"I'm fine, thanks. Are you ready for the onslaught?"

"I'm totally ticked off."

"Why?"

"Conner's other two friends backed out at the last minute and then I got wind that one of the other kids at school is having a party at Wonder World."

"Isn't that the amusement park?"

"Yeah. So they dumped Conner to go to that. Shame on their parents for letting them!"

"Oh, I'm sorry, Angie. Poor Conner."

"He was really upset, but we had a talk about how lucky he is to have Dylan for a friend and now he's all psyched about the fun they're going to have. Now that the other moms aren't coming, David's going to come along for the movie and dinner. So I guess it worked out."

"It'll be fine, Angie. Dylan's really looking forward to it."

"Great. So we'll still be there around two. I can't wait to see Helen again. She's quite a lady."

"Well, Helen's away at her granddaughter's wedding."

"Oh, okay. Then I'll see her tomorrow when we bring Dylan back."

Amanda braced herself. "Helen's staying with her daughter in Syracuse for the week. She'll be back next Sunday."

There was a speculative pause before Angie said, "Oh. Oh – you and Mark – are you–"

"Going to manage without Dylan? We'll be just fine. I'll see you at two."

"Okay – see you then."

Amanda could tell Angie's over-active imagination was in full gear as they hung up. She laughed with a shake of her head. "I might as well have slept in the spare room last night after all," she murmured to herself.

When she got back to the house around one-thirty, Dylan was sitting on the porch bench with his backpack and gift.

She sat down beside him. "Looks like you're all ready to go."

"Yep – I got everything, and I'm gonna have fun."

"Did you have any lunch?"

"Daddy let me fix a bowl of cereal with fruit."

"Good. There's something you should know before Conner and his mom come."

"What?"

"You know the other two boys he invited?"

"Yeah – Andrew and Sam."

"Well, they let Conner down. His mom told me they're going to another boy's party today instead."

"Oh, yeah – Tyler Manning's party at Wonder World."

"You know about that?"

"Yeah. My whole class got invited. It's 'cause Tyler's dad is rich and he always gets a big party and lots of cool stuff on his birthday. But I don't care 'cause Conner's my real friend and I just wanna be with him today."

Amanda reached out and stroked his hair. "I'm really proud of you, and you're right. Conner *is* your real friend, and you're being a very good friend to *him*. He needs you today."

Angie's car came up the driveway with Conner waving wildly out the front passenger window. "Happy Birthday, Conner!" Amanda called to him as they got out of the car.

The two boys ran to each other and exchanged a "high five". Angie opened her trunk as Amanda met her with Dylan's backpack and the gift.

"I bet they'll have even more fun with just the two of them," Angie said.

"I think you're right."

Marsh emerged onto the porch and waved to Angie.

"By the way –" Angie said to Amanda as she waved back, "I've finally figured out who Mark reminds me of."

238

Oh, God – was this *it?* Did Angie actually know who Marsh was? "Who?" she asked calmly, thankful that Marsh was out of earshot.

"That gorgeous actor with the dark, curly hair and beard – Ian – oh, what's his last name?"

Amanda took a breath. "I can't think of his last name, either, but I know who you mean," she was happy to concur.

"Mystery solved." Angie closed the trunk. "That about drove me crazy."

"Me, too." *You have no idea*, Amanda said to herself.

Angie looked back at Marsh as he stood with his hands in his pockets, talking to the boys. "Hope you don't mind me saying this, but if you didn't have anything going on with him, I'd be tempted – married or not."

Amanda smiled. "Well, maybe there's a *little* something."

Angie's eyes widened. "I *knew* I could get you to fess up! You've got to tell me all about it the next time we have coffee."

"We'll see."

"That's one thing the two of you definitely have in common," Angie said with obvious frustration. "You're both such private people."

"And you're a shameless matchmaker, but I'm really glad you're my friend."

Angie looked pleasantly surprised. "Me, too. Hey, guys – let's get this show on the road! We've got to stop back and pick up Dad!" She shook her head. "It takes David forever to get ready, but I'm glad he's coming with us. He needs more time with Conner."

Dylan gave Amanda a quick hug as he and Conner ran past to the car. "Have fun!" she called after him.

"Is about eleven tomorrow morning okay to bring Dylan back?" Angie called out to Marsh.

"Oh, you're bringing him back?   Yes, eleven's fine, Angie."

"Gorgeous *and* funny," she remarked as she opened her car door. "Have a nice night."   She gave Amanda a secret "thumbs-up" before she got in.

Amanda waved as the car backed up, then headed down the driveway. As the crunching of the gravel faded, all that remained was the gentle swish of leaves stirring in the trees.

She turned to where Marsh was still standing on the porch. "I think this will be really good for Dylan," she said.

"I think so, too."   As he gazed at her, she could tell he was unsure of what to do or say next.

"I'm making dinner at my place, if you'd like to come around six," she said, making it sound as casual as possible.

"I'd like that."

"See you then."   Amanda turned and headed back across the yard.

***

Marsh watched her go. It was two-thirty and six o'clock with the promise of wine and candles seemed ages away, but he reminded himself that, after yesterday's trauma, he was fortunate to be invited to her place at all.

He couldn't wait to be with her and to have as much time as they needed, to talk. So far, he and Amanda hadn't had a conversation that wasn't interrupted by Dylan's needs or Helen's proximity or even the late hour when Amanda had to go back to her place. Each chat – each kiss, had been stolen in a few moments, never allowed to last.

But tonight offered an endless, seamless gift of time to be together in any way they chose. No, he told himself, it would be the way Amanda chose. He was already there, waiting for her.

***

Amanda peered into her bedroom mirror as she put the finishing touches on her make-up and drew her hair up into a twist, pinning it with a decorative comb and fluffing the wispy tendrils around her face. The slender woman in the flowing, turquoise tunic and long skirt suddenly looked more mature, more sure of herself.

She gave her cheeks another dab of blush and etched her lips in the light coral shade of lipstick she'd just bought. The combination of colors made her eyes a deeper green. She stepped back and studied this new woman who was about to embark on an even newer life than she'd had for the past few weeks.

She looked around and tried to imagine what it would be like to have Marsh here tonight, just the two of them with all the time in the world. So much had happened since the day she moved in and he came to her door with Helen's flowers, clearly unhappy she'd taken this job. His odd reaction to her Marshall Stewart music that day made absolute sense, now. And his impulsive touch to the side of her face had only been a foreshadowing of their unlikely relationship.

She went to the kitchen, got a serving tray from the cupboard and the box of candles she'd bought, and brought them into the bedroom. She made a space on top of her dressing table in front of the mirror and arranged the eight, lavender scented votive candles on the tray. Her bed was reflected in the mirror behind them. She'd put on fresh sheets and pillowcases and had fluffed and smoothed the silken coverlet.

Opening a dresser drawer, she slowly took out a midnight blue, lace negligee and held it in her hands, gazing at it. Although she'd bought it for a honeymoon that wasn't to be, she could still wear it for the man she wanted to spend the rest of her life with. Despite the almost unbelievable revelation she'd discovered yesterday about Marshall Stewart, her hopes for tonight had not changed. She wanted to make love with Mark Sterner.

Chapter 14
The Man Standing in Front of Me

Around five-thirty, Marsh grabbed his garden clippers and cane and went outside where he carefully picked the best of Helen's flowers behind the house. The sky had gradually become overcast during the afternoon and now the clouds hung low, dark and groaning with muffled echoes of thunder. He put together a long-stemmed bouquet of asters, mums and sprays of goldenrod in colors of crimson, rust and gold, then headed back into the house as the first large splotches of rain began to hit the ground. In the kitchen he wrapped the stems in a large piece of foil.

By six o'clock it was raining steadily. He knew he didn't stand much chance of handling an umbrella with the flowers, his cane and the railing on the steps to Amanda's place, so he struck out toward the carriage house without the umbrella, moving as quickly as he could. Through the dim veil of rain, he saw the tiny flame of a candle in Amanda's kitchen window, flickering with an inviting warmth that told him she still loved him and had taken special care to show him.

By the time he'd crossed the yard and labored up the steps he was drenched, but Amanda had been watching for him and had the door open as he hurried inside.

"You're soaked!" she exclaimed as she closed the door.

"Well, it was either the umbrella or these." He handed her the flowers. "By the way, they're from me this time." He set his cane in the corner against the wall.

She laughed and her eyes shone as she took them. "You got wet so you could bring me flowers?"

"Anything for you."

"They're beautiful. Let me get you a towel."

"Something smells delicious." He noticed the small, round table by the kitchen window, covered in a white cloth and set with brightly colored dinner plates, two wine glasses and the candle he had seen from outside. "This is lovely," he said as she came back with the towel. "And you're lovely in that dress. That's one of my favorite colors, you know."

"I remember now – the color of your guitar strap."

It seemed strange to hear her refer to his other life so casually.

She helped him pat the rain from his hair and the feel of her fingers caressing his head through the towel made him want to skip dinner. Her face was close enough to kiss and, as though she sensed it, she drew away. It was clear that their relationship needed some healing.

"Dinner's ready – have a seat."

He sat down and looked out the window through the rain. "The house looks different from here," he said.

"It looks smaller," Amanda said. "Much like the carriage house looks from there."

"You're teasing me."

"No, I think you made a very scientific observation."

He couldn't suppress a grin as she brought a bottle of white wine to the table. He wanted to grab her around the waist and pull her into his lap.

"Would you like some Chablis?" she asked.

"Sounds good."

She pursed her lips as she poured it. "Strangely enough, red wine doesn't appeal to me much anymore."

"I love your humor, Amanda. You can laugh at yourself. You're very strong that way and I admire you for it."

"I'm strong in lots of ways," she said.

"So I'm finding out."

She sat and held up her glass. "Shall we toast?"

Marsh raised his glass. "To tonight." Then he added softly, "Whatever it brings."

They clinked glasses and let their eyes meet as they sipped. She served the salad, then placed a steaming dish of shrimp and sauce with angel hair pasta on the table.

"Thank you for all this, Amanda," he said. "No matter what you thought yesterday, I couldn't be more sorry for what I've put you through."

"And I couldn't be more sorry for what you've *been* through," she said as she placed some dinner on his plate. "Now that I've had time to think about it, I'm actually glad I found out the way I did because I heard the whole truth, in your own words, and I understand now."

"I wouldn't have blamed you if you didn't. I don't think most people would share your understanding and that's why no one else can ever know."

245

"I promise, no one else will ever know unless *you* choose to tell them. But what I don't think you realize is, you can still lead a happy, reasonably normal life under the radar. You don't need to be a prisoner in your home. You can go out and be around other people."

He shook his head. "I'm terrified of being recognized. You don't know what it took for me to meet Angie. I hadn't been around anyone but you since Dylan and I came back."

"And we know how well that went at first."

Marsh laughed, wiping his mouth with his napkin. "You were my worst nightmare."

Amanda put down her fork and folded her hands under her chin as she gazed at him. "But what I'm saying is, if I – an avid Marshall Stewart fan, could virtually live under the same roof with you and have no idea who you were, the average person walking down the street will never suspect a thing."

He nodded. "I suppose."

"You'll see for yourself when you come to Dylan's play next Friday."

"Oh, God. I forgot all about that."

"Well, he hasn't. He just mentioned it to me again the other day. We'll do it together and it'll be fine. I promise."

"You make me feel like I can do anything, as long as you're beside me, Amanda."

"You can." She smiled and went back to her dinner.

They ate in silence for a few moments before he said, "Obviously, you know almost everything about *my* past, but I don't know anything about yours."

"Except that my mother is a conniving trouble-maker?"

246

"I guess I picked up on that the night your ex-fiancé showed up."

"There isn't much more to know. I was forced to grow up in a dysfunctional family. My mother is a low-life alcoholic, my sister has a stellar career as a barroom dancer. My father, who I adored, couldn't take it anymore and left when I was fourteen. I begged him to take me with him, but he said I belonged with my mother and never contacted me again. My world was destroyed."

"How on earth did you manage to survive all that and turn out the way you did?"

Through the candle flame, he saw her eyes suddenly fill as she looked back at him. "There was this beautiful man who wrote songs that spoke to my heart and expressed my pain, and he set his lyrics to music that healed and sustained me when I was broken. And then he left suddenly, too, taking his music with him. At least I knew I wasn't alone with that terrible loss, but I never forgot him and never stopped missing his presence in the world or feeling his lasting influence in my life."

Marsh's eyes glinted with emotion. "You break my heart, Amanda, for all the fans I betrayed. But you mean so much more to me." He looked down at his plate. "When I lost Carrie's love, I thought no one would ever love me again. It was one of the darkest times of my life because I always thought I'd have her with me and our separation from the rest of the world didn't seem so bad. But by the time she died, she hated me and there was nothing between us anymore. It was like losing her twice and it was unbearable."

Amanda put her hand over his. "I can understand now, the way you were when I met you. You were dealing with so many more things than I could have known."

He put his other hand over hers. "The way you came into my life, Amanda – what were the odds of us ever meeting? I was doing all I could to not be found by anybody, yet you found me. It's as if your love brought you to me... as if all this was meant to be." He gazed at her as the steady rain outside beat gently on the roof.

She looked back at him before she rose from the table. "Would you like more dinner?"

"No – it was very good, thanks." He was disappointed that she had nothing to add to what he'd said.

"Why don't you have a little more wine and relax in the living room. I'll be right there."

"I'll help you clean up."

"No, I'm just going to rinse the plates for now. Go ahead."

Deciding he needed it, he poured another glass of wine and moved into the living room. Why had she seemed to shrug off what he'd just said from his heart? A feeling of dread gripped him. Was her coolness tonight more than a temporary show of displeasure? Had her feelings for him really changed with what had happened? It left him wondering what his next move should be. Whatever it was, it had to be the right one.

As he heard her cleaning up the kitchen, he noticed the easel at the end of the room and walked over to see a partially completed pastel drawing of the house. There was another sketch on the table beside it and then he noticed the figures of the man and boy in each drawing, in one playing catch and in the other raking leaves.

"How long have you been sketching?" he called out to her.

"Oh, on and off since I was in school," she answered over the sounds of running water and rattling pans.

"These are really good."

"It's you and Dylan in front of the house. I want to do one for each season."

She had two seasons to go – winter and spring. Marsh sipped his wine and continued to look at the drawings, reassuring himself that she would be here to complete them. There were a couple of art books on the table and he took his time paging through them. Several minutes had passed before he realized he didn't hear her in the kitchen anymore.

He turned around. "Amanda?" The kitchen was dark and he was alone in the living room.

"I'm in here."

Her voice had come from the bedroom and as he looked toward the doorway, he saw a faint, gently pulsing glow. He took another, deeper swallow of his wine and set down his glass, then walked over, unsure if what he'd heard was an invitation. Through the doorway he saw the candles on the dresser, their light dancing in the reflection of the mirror, filling the room with a mystical illumination and the subtle scent of lavender. He ventured another step and saw Amanda.

She stood facing the dim light of the window. The rain had tapered to a steady drizzle that sounded like a bubbling waterfall and the breeze lightly billowed the curtains. She took his breath away as she slowly turned in a short, blue, gossamer-like nightgown that moved with the breeze, clinging to the curves of her silhouette. She'd taken her hair down and it blew in wisps around her shoulders.

He wanted to speak but couldn't.

"You were right," she said. "Marshall Stewart *was* a romantic idea in my head. But I'm in love with the man standing in front of me."

He moved toward her. "I want you more than I've ever wanted anything, Amanda. But I need you to be absolutely sure of what you're doing. I want you with me for the rest of my life."

He had reached her and she put a finger to his lips. "I'm already yours," she murmured. "I know what you need for the rest of your life and I'm going to be here."

Before he could answer, she began to kiss him. His response was instantaneous and hungry. She felt his fingers untying the ribbon between her breasts and as the spaghetti straps began to fall away, his hands followed their descent, caressing her breasts as he kissed her with an intensity that spoke of how long he'd been waiting.

She unbuttoned the collar of his shirt, then the next few buttons until she could pull it down, baring his chest. There were the tell-tale, tawny tufts of hair that gave away his true identity. She ran her fingertips down the front of him and kissed his shoulder, inhaling the musky scent of his skin, suddenly overtaken with a desire for him that had been growing for weeks.

They held each other tightly, tasting each other's kisses as they moved toward the bed and as his hands moved further down and began to slowly lift and peel away the negligee, her heartbeat thudded in her ears, leaving her breathless at the awareness that they were completely alone with nothing to stop them. As they sat on the side of the bed, the negligee was suddenly off over her head and as it drifted to the floor she pulled down the coverlet and lay back on the cool expanse of the sheets. She watched through half-closed eyes as he slipped out of his clothes, then joined her, bringing the full-length of his nakedness against hers.

A delicious feeling of helplessness came over her and she thrilled to the alternate sensations of the tenderness of his lips and mild titillating scratch of his beard as he slowly, maddeningly began to claim each of her secrets. Again and again, each time a surprise, his lips teased her senses until he reached the place where he awoke a sweet ache that he coaxed until it surrendered into a lasting flutter of pleasure. She turned her head on the pillow, at first not recognizing the sounds of her own soft moans.

Crazy for more of him, she put her arms around his shoulders, grasping his back and drawing him tightly to her, then gasped as he effortlessly filled the hollow of her moist anticipation and began to move inside of her. As his raspy breathing filled her ear and his arousal became more urgent, a queasy craving deep in her core stirred, awoke and became ravenous, demanding to be satisfied. It began to scream inside of her, becoming unbearable until it focused to a pinpoint, then burst into an ecstasy that tingled every nerve ending as her back arched and she cried out. The orgasm possessed her for several more moments, before it gradually dissolved into lingering echoes that left her blissfully weak.

His breathing still heavy, he lowered his head to her breasts, his hair tickling her damp skin. "As much as I imagined being with you, Amanda, it was nothing like this," he murmured.

She entwined her fingers in his hair, stroking it lovingly. "This was all I imagined and more," she said. And as she lay in his arms, aware of the pulsating glimmer still deep inside of her, she realized she'd never once thought of Marshall Stewart.

***

Amanda opened her eyes to the intricate shadows of dancing leaves in the bright sunshine on her bedroom wall. A cool, clear breeze sighed through the window. It was a vibrant, early Fall day, and she couldn't wait to share it with Marsh. He was still asleep, breathing softly into her ear with his arm draped over her. She smiled and snuggled against him. She had never felt so loved.

He snored slightly and shifted, then rolled the other way, obviously in a deep sleep.

She looked at the clock. It was nearly eight and Dylan would be back at eleven. As much as she wanted to keep lying beside Marsh she decided to shower and make some breakfast so they could get back to the house. She slipped from the bed, pulling on her bathrobe as she looked over at him, certain that what he'd said at dinner last night was true. This was all meant to be. Nothing else in her life had ever felt so right.

The warm water of the shower felt wonderful and she'd just begun to shampoo her hair when the curtain opened.

"You've never looked so good in the morning," Marsh smiled.

"I've never had a night like last night."

"Well I've got news for you, darlin', it's still last night and intermission's over."

"So I see," she laughed as he joined her and they made love again, more playfully this time, savoring the unique pleasures of the warm, sudsy water. Being with Marsh this way felt so natural, as though the two of them were simply sharing physical expressions of desires they'd always been aware of.

"I think we should do this every morning," Marsh remarked as they sat across from each other having breakfast.

"All of it?"

"Well, we could skip the toast and coffee."

"What are we going to do about Dylan?" she asked as she poured them more coffee.

"Maybe Angie could keep him."

"You know what I mean."

"Yes, seriously, I do, but I'll trust your judgment on that. What do *you* think we should do?"

"I think he really doesn't need to know anything about this for awhile. His world's been disrupted enough lately. I don't think he needs to be dealing with another change right now."

"I couldn't agree more. But where does that leave us?"

"We'll keep doing what we've been doing. I'll stay here and come over to take care of Dylan and the house."

"And I'll come and visit you here."

"Only when Dylan's away or in school."

"For how long?"

She smiled. "Now you sound like Dylan."

He sighed and leaned back in his chair, taking her in through covetous eyes. "You belong in the house with us, like a family."

"Maybe we can set a time-line, for when we think it would be acceptable to Dylan."

"Three o'clock this afternoon works for me," Marsh said. As she cast him a wry glance he straightened. "I love that little guy more than I can say – so much that it scares me," he said before he took another sip of his coffee.

"I know," Amanda said. "I think it's complicated and you're just beginning to let yourself feel it and show it."

"It's because of you, Amanda. You bring me to my knees and make me look at myself for who and what I am. I can't escape myself when I'm with you. That's why I need you in my life – mine *and* Dylan's."

Amanda stirred cream into her coffee as they sat in silence for a few moments. "What if we start slowly with Dylan," she said.

"What do you mean?"

"We can gradually show affection for each other in front of him – just a word or gesture now and then, and see how he takes to it."

Marsh nodded. "I think that's a good idea."

"He already suspects we love each other, you know."

"I know. I couldn't believe what he came out with the other night – the part about 'do you love Daddy'." He gazed at her with admiration. "And you handled it so beautifully."

"But keep in mind, he thinks I love you the same way I love him. I guess that's where the gradual show of grown-up affection comes in."

Marsh finished his coffee, set his cup down and leaned toward her, taking her hand. "And when we feel we have Dylan on-board, will you marry me, Amanda?"

Even his question sounded perfectly natural, but it still took her breath away. "Of course I'll marry you," she said softly.

"You'll be Mrs. Mark Sterner, if that's okay with you."

"He's the one I fell in love with. He's the one I want to marry."

***

They headed back to the house before ten o'clock and Angie was on time with Dylan, pulling into the driveway at eleven. The car had barely stopped when the rear passenger door popped open and Dylan raced up the steps to the porch where Amanda and Marsh had been waiting. Conner was close behind as Angie and her husband got out of the car.

"I saw a transformer movie and I had popcorn and pizza and I got to stay up till midnight!" Dylan greeted them as he gave them each a hug. Conner fell in line and hugged each of them as well.

"Looks like it's back to prison life," Marsh remarked.

Angie's husband overheard and let out a hearty laugh. "Yep – we spoiled him and he's all yours again."

They came up onto the porch as Angie did the introductions. "Mark and Amanda, this is my husband, David."

David was a big, affable-looking man with a firm handshake and a ready gleam of humor in his eyes. "Nice to meet you both," he grinned.

Amanda liked him right away. He seemed a perfect match for Angie and a possible friend for Marsh. As the two men began to chat, Amanda and Angie went back to the car to get Dylan's things from the trunk. As Amanda stood beside the car, Angie pulled her around behind the raised trunk lid.

"You're absolutely glowing, Amanda!"

"No I'm not!" Amanda self-consciously put her hand to her face.

"You are! Did it happen?"

Amanda gave up her denial and nodded with widened eyes. "It happened, all right."

"Oh my God!" Angie squealed. Amanda shushed her and they lowered the trunk lid to find Marsh and David gazing in their direction. "Don't worry. I guarantee you, they're clueless," Angie assured her. "But I feel a coffee date coming on, and soon. How about tomorrow morning after we get the kids to school?"

"It's a date." They walked back to the porch.

"Would you two like to sit down and stay for awhile?" Amanda asked.

"We'd love to, but I've got a heavy schedule at the dental clinic tomorrow and I've got to go in this afternoon and get some things taken care of," David said. "How about another time? Mark and I were just getting into an interesting political debate."

"We'll have to get together again soon," Marsh said.

256

Amanda looked at him and smiled. He had just taken another small step into the outside world and she was proud of him.

"Okay –" Angie gave Amanda a quick hug. "I'll see you in the morning."

"Thanks for having Dylan," Marsh said. "I hope he behaved himself."

"It was a pleasure to have him around," David said. "He's a special little boy."

***

Amanda, Marsh and Dylan spent the remainder of the day in leisurely enjoyment of the sunshine, the pleasant breeze and the sense of being together. While Marsh read his Sunday papers on the porch, Amanda pushed Dylan on the swing as he chattered about every detail of his day with Conner. Later, as Dylan rode his bicycle, Amanda sat with Marsh as they exchanged soft kisses and began to plan their future.

When Helen called later in the afternoon, Amanda answered the phone in the kitchen where she was peeling potatoes for dinner.

After their greetings, Helen said, "I'm still enjoying the visit here, but I miss Dylan terribly. I waited to call to make sure he was back from his friend's house. Is he doing okay?"

"Well, I'll admit, his first night without you was a little rough, but the sleepover at Conner's came at a good time and he really enjoyed himself. I think he'll be fine now until you come home."

"Are you alone, Amanda?"

"Yes."

"How are you and Mark doing?"

"We're doing very well." Amanda chewed her lip a moment before she added, "And you can call him Marsh now."

There was a brief silence in which she could tell Helen was cautiously processing what she'd heard. "You mean – he told you?"

"Well, not exactly. I'd had some suspicions and then I overheard him and Jean talking in the kitchen on Friday and –"

"And how are you taking it, dear?"

"Not too well at first, but I'm adjusting and it hasn't changed my feelings for him."

"You don't know what a relief this is, Amanda. I knew he wanted to find a way to tell you this week, but I was very worried about how you might react."

Amanda laughed. "You had reason to be. I'm glad you weren't here for that, but I'm looking forward to you coming home. This place isn't the same without you."

Helen chuckled. "You mean without a meddling old woman around?"

"That's exactly what she means," Marsh joined in on the portable extension.

As both women protested his intrusion Amanda asked, "How long have you been on the line?"

"Long enough to get hungry. Is dinner ready yet?"

"I'll go get Dylan while you two talk," Amanda said. "See you soon, Helen."

When Amanda had hung up the kitchen extension Helen said, "How are *you* doing, Marsh?"

"Fantastic. So well that I'm afraid I'm going to wake up. She's accepted the truth, she's committed to me and a life here with us and I couldn't ask for more."

"It's all I've wished for you, Marsh. All I've wanted is for you to be happy again."

"I know, Mother, and I love you for it. Thank you for insisting that Amanda stay. You can even say 'I told you so'. It's changed all of our lives for the better."

"Hi, Grandma!" Dylan's voice suddenly permeated the line.

"There's my little man!"

"I'll let Dylan tell you all about his sleepover. Talk to you tomorrow." Marsh got off the portable from where he still sat on the front porch.

After a couple of minutes he heard Amanda in the kitchen again and went inside. Dylan's excited chatter with his grandmother came from the direction of the couch in the living room and Marsh took advantage of a moment alone with Amanda.

"I need a fix," he said as he turned her from the stove and folded her into a tight hug. "I can't think about anything but making love to you again."

"Neither can I," she whispered into his ear.

They lost themselves in a deep kiss that lasted several moments.

"No, they're busy kissing, Grandma. I don't think they need to talk to you again." They jumped apart as Dylan stood in the doorway with the phone still to his ear. "Okay – love you too – bye."

Marsh grabbed for the phone just before Dylan turned it off and handed it to him.

"Is dinner ready yet, Manda?"

"In a few minutes," she said.

"Okay!" he chirped before he ran upstairs.

Marsh sighed. "Looks like his 'adult education' is underway."

Chapter 15
Key to Betrayal

As the three of them sat at the dinner table, Amanda savored the new dimension in their relationship. They were beginning to feel like a family and she could tell by the way Marsh caught her eye and smiled, that he felt it, too. She was excited and eager to embark on her life as Amanda Sterner, wife and mother. She could hardly remember how lost she was feeling the day she came for the interview, wondering what her future would hold. This was unlike anything she could have imagined, and she knew Marsh shared her joy at the unexpected turn of events in his life.

Dylan seemed completely unaffected at having caught them in their passionate embrace as he chattered about school and the upcoming play on Friday.

"So we didn't exactly rock his world," Marsh remarked when dinner was over and Dylan had headed back upstairs.

"Apparently not," Amanda laughed as she took the dishes to the sink.

"It's cooled off a little, so I think I'll try to get the rest of that garden cleaned up tonight." Marsh gave her a squeeze and a kiss on the cheek. "I'll be outside for awhile."

Amanda finished cleaning up the kitchen, taking her time and humming softly. She felt wrapped in a blanket of contentment and basked in the sense of peace that everything was as it should be.

When she looked at the clock again, nearly an hour had passed and it was going on seven-thirty. Time to make sure Dylan was getting ready for bed and his school day tomorrow. She headed up the stairs. "What are you up to, sweetie?" she called out as she reached the hallway.

It was strangely silent. She looked through his bedroom doorway and didn't see or hear him moving around. "Dylan?" The bathroom door stood open. She became aware of a whisper of cool air and as she turned, she heard distant rustling sounds that drew her attention to the other end of the hall. She had to blink to be sure of what she was seeing. Then a dagger of panic stabbed her in the gut. The door to Marsh's private room was ajar.

"Dylan!" She rushed down the hall. The key was still in the lock and she grabbed it and stuck it into her pocket as she pushed through the door and flipped the light switch. "Dylan! Where are you?"

"I'm here, Manda." His voice came from the direction of an armoire that was open and she could see several of Marsh's stage costumes hanging inside. "Look what I found!"

She charged through the maze of draped objects and stacked boxes. "Dylan – what are you doing? You know you don't belong in here!"

He was sitting on the floor, looking through an array of scattered pictures he'd pulled from the large envelope beside him. They were publicity and stage photos of Marshall Stewart. "Who's this guy, Manda?"

She could see that he'd been there for awhile. The drawers of the armoire were open, revealing jewelry and accessories. It was then that she noticed the doors of the large cabinet beside it were open, and she saw the Grammy award and gold records on the top shelf, along with the picture albums on the lower shelves. She could clearly see what appeared to be Marsh and Carrie's wedding album. She paused, unable to keep from taking in all the tangible proof of Marshall Stewart's existence, before she dropped to her knees and began to frantically collect the pictures. "Dylan! We've got to pick these up and get out of here – now!"

"But I still hafta find Mommy," she thought she heard him say before he got up and wandered away.

"I don't know what you're talking about, Dylan." She decided she couldn't worry about what else he was doing. All she could think about was trying to put everything back exactly as it had been and getting the two of them out of there before they were discovered.

After several more moments she had most of the pictures picked up and turned on her knees to check behind her, when she spotted Marsh in the doorway.

"Amanda? Are you in here?"

She closed her eyes and sighed. "Yes," she answered as she slowly stood up.

He walked over to her, gazing at her in disbelief. "How did you get in here?"

She took the key from her pocket. "I –"

"You were in my room?" His insinuation stung.

"No, I –"

"I was going to bring you in here myself, Amanda."

Dylan emerged from behind a stack of boxes.

"You brought Dylan in here, too?" Marsh's voice had a wounded tone.

"No –"

"I'm sorry, Daddy – I didn't mean it!" Dylan began to cry.

Marsh looked from one to the other. "What on earth is going on?"

Amanda fell silent, too hurt by his suspicions to want to respond.

"I got the key from your room, Daddy," Dylan blurted.

"How did you know where it was?"

"'Cause I was bad and I looked before, and I found it in your drawer by your bed, but I never took it till today – honest!"

"Why did you take it, Dylan?"

"'Cause I needed to come in here and look for Mommy."

Marsh looked at Amanda for help, but she lowered her eyes. She no longer felt like his partner.

"Why would you look for Mommy in here?"

"'Cause when I missed her and I was crying, Manda told me that Mommy's right here and even though I can't see her, she's watching over me all the time. So I thought if I couldn't see her, she must be in this room. So I got the key and I came in here, but I can't find Mommy – just a lot of stuff that belongs to somebody else."

Marsh looked at Amanda again, but she didn't react. Dylan began to cry harder and Marsh picked him up. "It's okay, Scoot. Mommy's not in this room. There's nothing in here for you and you don't need to come back again, okay?"

Dylan nodded as he rubbed his eyes. "Okay," he sniffled before he put his arms around his father's neck.

Despite her hurt feelings, Amanda was grateful for the way Marsh was handling Dylan.

"Now it's past your bedtime, so Amanda and I will help you get ready."

He cast her a smile but she couldn't smile back. He hadn't trusted her just now and the pain of that revelation was still smarting.

"Are you all right?" he asked.

"I'm just tired," she replied to avoid an argument in front of Dylan. "I'll let you two have some time alone."

"Okay," he said, "but wait for me. I won't be long."

She watched him carry Dylan down the hall. She would have been rejoicing that he'd risen to this opportunity to be a good father if he hadn't betrayed her in the process.

She looked around, suddenly alone, surrounded by the reality of Marshall Stewart. Until now, he had still seemed a separate entity from the man she'd come to love. But in this room the two seemed to merge and she walked around slowly, taking in the silent, almost eerie vestiges of a past life.

When she reached the armoire she couldn't resist looking through the clothes on the hangers, feeling the fabric of the jackets and shirts she'd seen her idol wearing in pictures and on film. Even though she'd heard him talking to Jean and knew for a fact that Mark Sterner was Marshall Stewart, it was not the same as standing amidst the physical proof of his belongings.

At the end of the clothes rack, tucked behind the other door, she found Carrie's wedding gown. Oh, how she and her friends at school had envied Carrie when she had become Mrs. Marshall Stewart.

"Maybe it won't work out and he'll still marry *me* someday," one of them had pined. Along with the others, Amanda had giggled at such a preposterous idea. Now the memory of those girlish voices faded into the sound of her own heartbeat as she ran her hand along the lacy sleeve and down the length of the dress. The wreath of flowers with the long ribbons that Carrie had worn on her head was on the shelf above. The flowers were dried and brittle and she didn't dare touch them but she gently ran the ribbons through her fingers as she remembered seeing them stirring in the breeze during the brief interview Marsh had allowed the press on their wedding day. Amanda had watched Carrie's expression on the film footage, wondering what she was thinking, what it was like to stand beside Marsh with her whole life ahead of her as his wife.

As she looked down at the ribbons and continued to let them sift through her hand, a sense of Carrie's emotions began to seep into Amanda's consciousness. Suddenly it was clear that in her forced seclusion and ultimate alienation from the world, Carrie had felt like a caged bird. She had given up everything to follow Marsh's wild scheme and, over time, alcohol had become her friend and her only comfort as she faced the rest of her life in hopeless confinement. The truth whispered to Amanda. Carrie wasn't selfish or thoughtless. Carrie had no way out. Like Amanda, Carrie, too, had been just twenty-six when she'd made the choice to live the rest of her life with the consequences of Marsh's actions.

An unexpected wave of apprehension passed through her as she released the ribbon and took a step back. Was she any different from Carrie? This was the first time she'd doubted herself. How could she find herself in a dilemma over a man with whom she'd made rapturous love just last night and to whom she'd promised herself today?

But being in this room had changed her perspective, and apparently, Marsh's as well. His assumption that she could even consider exposing Dylan to the contents of this room, much less sneak in here herself, was an insult when he should know by now that her only concern was for Dylan's well-being. If Marsh didn't really believe that, she would never be able to prove it to him. And if she could never prove it to him, she could not be with him at all. The question forming in her mind frightened her: would a life with Marsh be as beautiful and fulfilling as she'd thought, or could it turn into something terrible and filled with regret?

A sudden storm of confusion began to swirl through her head. She had to get out of there.

***

Marsh tucked Dylan in and went to kiss his forehead before he popped up again. "Daddy, who was that man with blond hair in those pictures?"

There it was – the back side of the nightmare Marsh thought he had a few more years to prepare for. "Just somebody I used to know," he said. "Get back under the covers, Dylan."

"Where is he now?"

Marsh gazed at him a moment. "He went away."

"Do you miss him?"

"No, not anymore." He hesitated before he asked, "What *else* did you see in there?"

"I don't know – just a bunch of boring stuff."

Marsh was relieved. "You're right. It *is* boring stuff. Now settle down and go to sleep."

"Isn't Manda gonna say goodnight to me?"

Marsh went to the window to lower the blinds. "No, she –" He paused. There was a pair of red taillights at the end of the driveway. Although it was nearly dark, he could tell it was Amanda's car that turned onto the road and disappeared.

***

All Amanda wanted to do was drive and as she started down the road she was surprised by an odd sense of freedom. It was as if she was escaping a situation that suddenly felt repressive. Where had that feeling come from?

She thought she understood and had accepted what being with Marsh would mean, but her dreamy, fairy tale idea of being his wife had overlooked many realities she would face in her everyday life as Amanda Sterner – the secrecy, the limitations and now the disturbing discovery that he didn't fully trust her yet. Would he always have that sliver of doubt about her loyalty? Would he never be absolutely certain she would guard his privacy at all cost? How could she live with someone who doubted her character? How could she love someone who didn't truly know her heart?

I'm twenty-six years old, the thought kept repeating itself. While she considered herself mature enough to know what she wanted, marrying thirty-six-year-old Marsh and closing the door on the option to change her mind or pursue another path in life seemed frighteningly final. Yet there was Dylan, separate from her relationship with Marsh. She had all of Dylan's trust and knew his needs, even better than Marsh did at this point, and Dylan couldn't bear another abandonment.

It all felt so different, from the outside looking in. Amanda was unprepared for the perplexity of it. Which perspective was real? The one she'd had up to today, or the one that had been scaring her since she'd walked into that room?

Trying not to panic, she reached out and tapped the radio button, hoping for a mild distraction. A commercial jingle was just winding down. "And welcome back to our Oldies Classics Sunday night Tribute," a dee jay's smooth voice announced. "Tonight, if you're just joining us, we're remembering Marshall Stewart, the young balladeer who inspired a generation with his lyrics and music and left us all too soon."

Amanda spotted the entrance to a shopping mall, slammed the brakes and pulled off the road. She came to a jarring halt on the outer fringe of the dark, nearly empty parking lot.

"You loyal fans of his will remember that he mysteriously disappeared after one of his concerts on October 12th, 1975. Despite much speculation and many theories over the years, it seems fairly safe to say, we'll never know what happened to Marshall Stewart or what more he could have accomplished had he remained with us, and so in commemoration of the upcoming ten-year anniversary of his disappearance, we invite you to sit back and enjoy the memories as we continue with the timeless music of Marshall Stewart."

Marsh's comments at dinner last night about how it seemed as though all this was meant to be, came back to her. And now it was as if she'd been meant to turn on the radio to this station at this exact time.

A series of rich, poignant guitar chords filled the car and her spine tingled as Marsh's low, velvet voice engulfed her. She crossed her arms on the steering wheel, and leaned forward, letting the tears come.

You know I love you – always will
The love we made is with me still
Don't leave me, now – no, please don't go
Before our love has time to grow

The words and music she'd listened to years ago on the record player in her room at home, were speaking to her again, but with an intimacy she never could have imagined. She was transported back into his arms and the heat of their lovemaking flashed through her body again. She had never been so profoundly in love – hadn't even known such passion existed until she'd found it with him. She lost track of time as she clung to the steering wheel and let the music go through her.

A sudden rap on her partially open window startled her and she looked up as a uniformed security guard shone his flashlight into the car.

"Are you okay, Miss?"

She quickly blotted her tears with her fingers. "Yes, I'm fine."

"Are you sure? Do you need me to call someone for you?"

His genuine concern touched her and she sniffled and managed a smile. "No, I'm fine, thanks."

"Okay – but you'd better not sit here too much longer. The mall's closed and I'm going off duty. You shouldn't be out here alone." He heard the song on her radio, paused a moment and grinned. "I like your choice of music," he said before he walked off, humming the tune.

Amanda heaved a shaky sigh and finished wiping her wet cheeks. Her thoughts were becoming more rational. The clock on the dashboard told her she'd been gone for over an hour. Marsh must be looking for her, but she wasn't ready to go back yet. She needed to be sure of why she was going back, needed to know without a doubt that when she got there, she would stay.

She put the car into gear and headed back onto the main street, which was all but deserted by now. She needed a soothing, hot cup of coffee and a lot more thought before she went home. As Marsh's voice continued to surround her, she began to softly sing along with him as she headed down the road.

***

By ten-thirty Marsh had reached for the phone more times than he could remember. Where was she? Was she okay? How much longer should he wait? He had taken up an anxious vigil through the sunporch windows and had spent most of the first hour willing her headlights to reappear in the driveway, telling himself she'd be back any moment. But it had been two and a half hours. The rationale that she'd gone for a ride to unwind or was browsing through a store had worn thin. It was Sunday night. Most stores were closed by now and the thought of her driving around alone worried him. But he still preferred that scenario to the unthinkable – that she might not come back at all.

When he had finished putting Dylan to bed, he'd gone to the other end of the hall to turn off the light and lock the room. Leaving Amanda alone in there meant she'd had time to look around. He went over to close the armoire and noticed the ribbons from Carrie's headpiece dangling from the upper shelf, an impossible place for Dylan to reach. Amanda had been there, looking at Carrie's wedding gown, fingering the headpiece and thinking – what?

He'd also had time to realize that his hasty appraisal of the situation when he'd found her in there with Dylan had offended her. She'd suddenly fallen silent and he'd been too preoccupied with Dylan's explanation to acknowledge that something was wrong between them. But something obviously was wrong. Had she had left out of hurt? Anger? Maybe even fear?

He should never have asked her this morning to marry him and then allowed her to respond so quickly. He did want to marry her – would have married her today, if it was possible, but he had rushed to ask her because of his own selfish need to assure himself that she would commit to staying with him, to guarantee she'd be his forever. Well, there were no guarantees, only hopes that things would work out and that she would be happy enough to stay with him. No wedding ring could ensure contentment or a deeper love. Those were things he could only try to lead her to by being the best husband he could. He could start by allowing himself to fully trust her, not just in word, but in reality. It was another step he had to take to conquer the effects of the constant vigilance and paranoia he'd been living with over the past ten years.

He looked down at the slip of paper in his hand. The only person he could call was Angie. He'd gotten her number out of the kitchen address book where Amanda had written it, but if Amanda wasn't with her, he loathed the idea of having to admit he needed help finding her. The less Angie or anyone else knew, the better. But if Amanda *was* with her, he would at least know she was safe. He wouldn't even worry that she might have shared too much information with Angie. He wasn't going to think that way anymore.

Ten forty-five. He would surely be disturbing Angie this late if Amanda wasn't there, but he forced himself to pick up the phone and dial her number.

She answered on the second ring. "Mark?" she asked when she heard his voice.

"Sorry to bother you so late, Angie, but is Amanda with you by any chance?"

There was a pause. "No. I haven't seen her – why?"

Marsh sighed. "I don't know where she is and I'm getting worried."

"Why – Did something happen?" There was immediate concern in Angie's voice.

"We – had a misunderstanding earlier tonight. It was all my fault. Anyway, she took off around eight and I know it's not that late, but it's not like her to stay out this long – especially on a Sunday night."

"Well, she can't have gone far. She probably went to the mall or something, but you're right – she should still be back by now. Listen, David's here to watch Conner. I'll take a quick ride downtown and see if I spot her car."

"I don't want to put you out, Angie."

"Amanda's my friend, Mark. I want to make sure she's okay, too. I'll call you."

Marsh hung up and leaned back on the wicker sofa, closing his burning eyes. Images and sensations of his lovemaking with Amanda filled his head again and he prayed she would be back in his arms tonight.

Chapter 16
No Going Back

Amanda sat in the booth at the coffee shop where she and Angie often went when they dropped the boys off at school. Although she'd never paid attention before, she was relieved to find it was open twenty-four hours and she felt safe and comfortable sitting there, gazing out the window at the darkened, empty street. Across the room, four high-school age kids sat at another booth. The two girls and two boys appeared to be on a double date and were on their best behavior.

Except for the soft background music, Amanda appreciated the quiet, but sitting there alone made her miss Angie. She should have been able to call her and tell her about what had happened and how it made her feel. What good was a girlfriend if she couldn't confide in Angie for the very help she needed the most? One more reality of a life with Marsh. She could never share the most basic day-to-day problems with anyone else. Could she really live that way for the rest of her life? She stared into her coffee cup, letting her mind wander with the curls of steam that rose from it.

"Hey, kiddo." Angie's voice abruptly brought her back.

Amanda looked up, stunned. "I was just thinking about you. What are you doing here?"

The waitress appeared and Angie ordered a cup of decaf as she slid into the other side of the booth.

"You first," she replied softly.

Amanda opened her mouth, then lowered her head as the tears returned.

Angie reached over and put her hand on Amanda's arm. "Mark called. He's worried sick about you."

Amanda nodded.

The waitress brought Angie's coffee and she stirred in cream and sugar. "He said the two of you had a misunderstanding and that it was all his fault. Why didn't you call me? You don't have to be alone when you're hurting."

Amanda sighed. "I *needed* to be alone for awhile, but I'm really glad you're here now."

Angie waited for more before she asked, "What happened? Can you talk about it?"

"Some of it. That's the problem, Angie. I need you and want you as a friend forever, but..."

"But what?"

"As you said yesterday, Mark and I are very private people. There will always be things I can share with you, but there will also be things I can't."

"Why not?"

"This is where it'll be unfair to you." Amanda gazed at her, looking for a flicker of understanding as she continued, "If you still want to be my friend, I'll have to ask for your acceptance that I'll never be able to completely level with you about everything, but on the things that I can, I'll always want your confidence and advice."

As Angie stared at her, Amanda saw the wheels of imagination begin to turn. "Is he in some kind of trouble?"

"No."

"Is he in the Witness Protection Program?"

"No." And as Angie looked perplexed, Amanda said, "This is the part where I need your unconditional acceptance, Angie. It means no questions, no guessing – and I know how unfair it is to ask that of you, but I have no choice."

Angie sighed and tucked her hands into her jacket pockets. "So does this mean you can't tell me what happened tonight?"

Amanda looked back into her coffee cup. "He displayed a lack of trust in me."

"Why? Did he think you stole something?"

"He thought I'd taken a liberty I didn't take and would never have taken, and although Dylan confessed to causing the problem, I can't get past it."

"It must have been pretty serious to make you leave. It sounded as though the two of you had such an amazing night together, I'm surprised something like this could happen."

"Last night was magical. That's what makes tonight so painful. I can't marry him if –"

"Marry him? Oh my God – he asked you to marry him?" Angie blurted too loudly.

Amanda covered her face as all eyes in the coffee shop rested on them for an excruciating moment.

"I'm sorry," Angie said under her breath, "but when did this happen?"

"Only this morning."

"That must have really been some night. And what did you say?"

"I said yes, but –"

"Wasn't it awfully soon for him to ask, Amanda? Everything's been moving so fast for you. Is that why you left – are you reconsidering because of tonight?"

"I need to consider a lot of things. I know I love him and want to be with him, but I guess I'm just trying to make sure that I fully understand what marrying him will mean."

Angie raised an eyebrow. "Is that –"

"Yes – one of the things I can't really discuss. I'm sorry, Angie. You don't deserve this."

"Well, I at least deserve the right to be mad at him for hurting you."

Amanda shook her head slowly. "No. Now that I've calmed down a little, I know he didn't mean to. It was a reflex, and I understand where it came from."

"If you know him well enough to know that, you've already forgiven him."

Amanda smiled and nodded.

"But I think he still owes you a long, groveling apology."

Amanda let out a laugh. "That's why I need you to be my friend. I need your perspective." She gazed appreciatively at Angie. "I'm so sorry to have bothered you tonight, but you've made me feel much better. Thank you for coming to find me. You're a real friend."

Angie squeezed her hand. "I'll be your friend forever – no questions asked. Besides, we're going to need each other when Conner and Dylan hit adolescence. I'm not going through *that* without you."

Amanda got a sudden thrill at the thought of raising Dylan to be a young man. And the thought of doing it with Marsh excited her all over again.

***

The shrill ring of the phone jolted Marsh out of a restless doze and he grabbed it off the table beside him.

"Mark? It's Dave Wilson. Angie just called me from the phone booth at Reese's coffee shop down by the school. She found Amanda there."

"Thank God. Is she alright?"

"She's fine and she's on her way home."

Marsh heaved a shaky sigh. "Thanks, Dave. I owe you and Angie."

"Any time, buddy. We're just glad Amanda's okay. Anything else you need?"

Marsh rubbed his face. "Yeah. I need to keep my foot out of my mouth."

Dave let out a hoot. "I've been a dentist for almost ten years now, but I've never learned how to do *that* extraction."

Marsh managed a weary laugh. "Let me know if you do."

"Sure thing. See ya."

Marsh hung up with the feeling he'd just talked to a good friend. It seemed like forever since he'd felt that way. He looked at his watch. It was nearly midnight. He reached for his cane and got up. As stiff and sore as his leg was, it didn't bother him. Amanda was on her way home.

***

Amanda turned into the driveway just as the last chords of the Marshall Stewart tribute faded on the radio at midnight. She parked next to the carriage house and sat taking in the main house, its downstairs windows glowing with a mellow warmth. It welcomed her, beckoned her with the unmistakable sense that she was home. Her heart inhabited those rooms and nothing seemed more right than being there with Marsh and Dylan.

As she got out of the car, the porch light went on and she saw Marsh come out the front door and head down the steps. Her reaction was instantaneous. The sight of him sent a fresh glimmer of desire through her, as though she hadn't seen him in days. He turned into a silhouette, moving across the lawn toward her. If he hadn't come out so quickly, she would have gone straight up to her apartment, fine with waiting until she'd had some sleep before they talked. But she knew he had waited anxiously for her, had eventually called Angie, which she was sure he would have preferred not to do. And now he wanted to see her and she owed him that much, however late it was, however worn out she was. He had to be tired, too.

She started to walk, slowly, then felt a magnetic pull that grew stronger until she found herself running. Before she could reach him it was as though he grabbed her out of the air, holding her tightly as she melted into the familiar solace of his arms and the reassurance of his mouth against hers.

For several moments they communicated only through the intensity of their kiss until it ebbed into gentle, teasing sensations that left them breathless.

"Thank God you're safe. I didn't know where you were and I was so worried," he murmured against the side of her face. "Please forgive me, Amanda. I was too stupid to think that Dylan would be bold enough to do that and I couldn't believe you would, either."

"It didn't add up, I know," Amanda said. "It took us both by surprise."

"Surprised or not, there was no excuse for what I said. It was thoughtless and I had no reason to doubt you. I promise, it'll never happen again."

"Dylan only went in there because he thought his mother was there, and that's my fault for what I told him."

"No." Marsh held her tighter. "No, Amanda. What you told him was beautiful and comforting and you gave him a gift he'll keep with him for the rest of his life. He's just too young to grasp the whole concept right now, but we can talk to him some more about that."

She loved the sound of "we" and drew back to look into his face. "I want to be here to watch Dylan grow up, and I want to be with you. It's just that – when I was in that room tonight, it hit me hard. It was all there, who you really are and – what it must have been like for Carrie. And then in the car, I turned on the radio and there you were – on the Sunday night classics."

"Looks like you couldn't get away from me."

"Looks like I wasn't meant to."

They turned, arms wrapped around each other, and slowly headed for the porch.

"You know how much I want you here with me, but I was selfish to ask you to marry me so soon. I haven't given you any time to be sure of what you want." They reached the porch and he kept his arm around her as they sat on the bench.

"I know what I want, and I told you I was sure last night before we made love," Amanda said. "But there are things I have to get straight in my mind about what it will mean when I marry you."

"We're not going to rush this, Amanda. You'll call all the shots and it won't happen until you're ready." He sighed. "The hard part for me is knowing you won't move into the house until then."

"We can't let Dylan see us together until he's seen us get married. It may seem old fashioned, but –"

"No, I'm with you on that. He needs a secure home life and that's an important part of it, and I love you even more for insisting on it."

"And we both know your mother will heartily agree."

Marsh laughed. "Yes she will. No one loves a wedding more than my mother."

They sat in silence for a few moments before Marsh said, "I'm sorry it bothered you to be in that room tonight, but I was looking forward to taking you in there and sharing everything with you when Dylan wasn't around. I never meant for you to see it that way, but we'll go back, Amanda, and we can –"

"I don't want to go back," she said. "I don't need to. It's like you told Dylan, there's nothing in there for me, either." She looked at him. "Is there anything in there for you anymore, Marsh?"

He gazed out onto the lawn. "Carrie and I packed those things and had them shipped here when we went away. I had just bought this place for Mother and I had my things moved in with hers so it wouldn't look suspicious. At the time, I guess we actually thought we could come back someday, until reality set in. Losing Carrie the way I did was so unexpected and, along with the situation I'd created for myself, I was sure my life was over. When Dylan and I came here, I was broken and had no hope. So I guess before I met you, I needed the things in that room, to remind me of who I was, or at least who I used to be. Otherwise, it was as if I didn't exist. But meeting and falling in love with you, and having you love me back, is a new beginning I never thought could happen to me." He looked at her. "No. There's nothing in that room for me anymore, either. I'm not that person anymore. But I took out the Gibson when I went in for the first time the other day. That's all that matters to me now."

"When did you go in?"

"When you and Dylan left for school and Mother wasn't up yet."

"What made you decide to do it?"

"Your love. I might never have gone back in if it weren't for you. You gave me the courage to face it and kind of say goodbye, let it rest in peace, I guess."

"Carrie, too?" she wasn't afraid to ask.

"Yes. Carrie, too. It was the first time since her death that I had some happy memories of us."

Amanda looked at her hands. "I guess that's when you know you're beginning to heal," she suggested softly.

His arm tightened around her. "I knew I was beginning to heal the first time I kissed you, right here on this bench, and you stunned me when you kissed me back."

"Well in that case, let me stun you again." She put her hand on the side of his face and drew him to her lips.

She felt the increasing desire in his kiss until he reluctantly drew back. "Now that I know what I'm missing, I want to take you to bed with me tonight and every night."

"Hmmm... looks like I've got some collateral in this marriage proposal."

He smiled, then grew more serious as he looked into her eyes. "I can't promise you this is going to be easy, Amanda. I wish I could, but the truth is, you're the only one who'll be making a sacrifice by staying with us. Dylan and I have everything to gain, but you have some things to lose. Carrie didn't know the direction our lives would take when she married me. Neither of us knew that was going to happen. But you have the advantage of already knowing exactly what this is and that it can't change. This is what our lives will be."

"I still believe your life can be more normal than you think."

"With you beside me, I can believe that's possible, too."

Amanda sighed. "One thing I've learned since I've been here is, anything's possible."

"Absolutely anything," Marsh whispered before they kissed goodnight.

***

In the few hours before she had to get Dylan ready for school, Amanda slept soundly. When she awoke, she knew she was where she belonged and she would not doubt it again. The feeling was exhilarating and filled her with an eagerness to get on with the new life that lay ahead of her.

"Don't forget, Manda, you and Daddy hafta come to my play on Friday," Dylan reminded her between mouthfuls of cereal while she made his lunch.

"We won't forget," she assured him. "Have you been practicing?" Her heartbeat quickened at the sound of Marsh coming down the stairs.

"Yeah. Conner and me practiced at his house 'cause he's gonna be the wind that blows on me."

"How's he going to do that?" Amanda asked as Marsh came into the kitchen. He went to her, slipped his arm around her waist and kissed her cheek. "Good morning," he murmured in her ear. They looked at Dylan but he was still absorbed in his breakfast.

"He's gonna run around and wave a cloth so people can tell he's the wind," he answered without looking up.

"Sounds like Academy Award material to me," Marsh remarked as he poured a cup of coffee and sat down at the breakfast nook.

"Like what?" Dylan asked, finally looking up.

Marsh reached over and roughed up his hair. "Morning, Scoot."

"Do you want some breakfast?" Amanda asked Marsh.

"Let's have it together, when you get back," he said, his eyes suggesting much more.

A flush of anticipation rose into her cheeks and they shared a smile as she finished preparing Dylan's backpack.

On the way to school, Dylan kept up his usual chatter while Amanda managed a few words of response now and then as she navigated traffic. Over time she had mastered the art of tuning out the distraction while appearing to be listening.

"Then Daddy told me that man with the blond hair in those pictures I found – he went away."

Those words pierced Amanda's consciousness and she looked over at Dylan. He was riding along, looking out the window as matter-of-factly as if he'd commented on the weather.

"Did he tell you anything else?" she asked.

"Nope – just that he was somebody Daddy used to know. But he doesn't miss him or anything."

"That's good," she said, admiring the way Marsh had handled it. Dylan obviously had no further curiosity on the matter.

When she parked at the school and got out of the car, Angie and Conner were coming down the walk. "How are things today?" Angie asked her while the boys greeted each other.

"Much better, thank you."

They walked the boys a little farther, then waved goodbye as they joined the noisy herd of kids heading into the school.

"So everything was okay when you went back last night?"

"It was better than okay," Amanda said. "We're going to be fine. But we both want to thank you and David for being such good friends to us. I think Marsh really likes David."

"Marsh?"

Amanda resisted the urge to stammer. She had prepared herself for the inevitable slip. "I'm sorry – it's a nickname his mother and sister had for him when he was younger and I guess I've picked up on it."

"Marsh," Angie repeated. "That's kinda cute."

***

When Amanda got to the house, Marsh wasn't in the kitchen. A glance onto the sunporch told her he wasn't downstairs at all.

"I'm back!" she called out. "Where are you?" Then she heard his guitar. The kaleidoscope of sounds drew her up the stairs and when she reached the open doorway of his room, she saw him in the chair by the window, eyes closed, rocking slightly back and forth, lost in the music as he played with an intensity that went through her. If only the world could know that Marshall Stewart was alive and well and still composing songs that could touch people's lives. But this concert was hers alone. She slipped into the room, folded her arms and leaned back against the wall. Through half-closed eyes she watched him and let the music surround her. She could have listened forever.

The sudden silence roused her and she straightened to see him grinning broadly at her.

"Please don't stop," she said. "I can't get enough, it's so beautiful."

"Maybe later," he said as he set down his guitar and stood up. "But something better just walked in."

She lowered her head and smiled as he moved toward her. "What makes you think I feel sexy at *this* hour of the morning?" she teased as he reached her.

"You leave that to me," he said before he took her face in his hands and began to kiss her.

Her legs went weak as his lips enticed her, his embrace slowly guiding her backwards across the hall and through the doorway of the spare room. "Are you sure we should be in here?" she asked.

"This is going to be *our* bedroom," he said as he lowered her to the bed. "It's time we practiced."

Chapter 17
Proposals

They made love each morning that week, after Amanda had taken Dylan to school, and then enjoyed a leisurely breakfast before they got on with the day's tasks. They knew that Helen's return on Sunday would change their routine, at which time, as Marsh put it, they would have to resort to stolen trysts at the "honeymoon cottage".

Afternoons and evenings were spent helping Dylan with his small homework assignments, sharing lively dinners with his incessant account of what happened at school that day along with the progress of his play rehearsals. After dinner, the three of them watched TV on the living room couch, with Dylan usually draped over both their laps.

When Amanda could steal an occasional glance at Marsh and Dylan together, she marveled at how far they'd come. Marsh no longer spent time in his room when Dylan was around, and they were settling into an easy, more natural relationship.

Amanda had thrilled to a couple more of Marsh's impromptu concerts and had heard him composing as she'd gone about her housework. Later in the week when they were sharing scrambled eggs and pancakes one morning, she looked across the table at him as he browsed through the newspaper and said, "You should record your new music."

He glanced up at her. "What?"

"You should record your new music," she repeated with more conviction.

He set down the paper and gazed at her. "So that *is* what I heard you say."

She nodded, knowing there were tears forming in her eyes.

He reached over and took her hand. "Why would I bother with that now? Who would ever hear it?"

"Dylan, your grandchildren –"

"Grandchildren? I've barely started to raise Dylan."

"Who knows what the future holds? All I know is, what you're doing can't be lost. You need to record it, to have something tangible to show for all your work."

"And how would I go about recording it at this stage of the game?"

"Well, I've been thinking about that, too."

"Not while I'm making love to you, I hope," he teased.

"Don't be silly." She stroked the side of his face. "What about putting some recording equipment in the room at the end of the hall? It's certainly big enough, and you could put in a sound booth or something – whatever you'd need. It wouldn't have to be elaborate."

"What you're suggesting is already elaborate. It would take lot of money and expertise, and I'm still not convinced it's even worthwhile."

"I know. But would you at least think about it?"

He laughed softly and shook his head. "Why not? You've gotten me thinking about lots of other things I never thought I would."

As he returned to his newspaper, Amanda was overtaken by a mischievous impulse and slipped her foot out of her sandal, running her toes up the inside of his pant leg. "Well now I've given you something new to think about."

He dropped the paper and grinned. "Okay – what was that first thing?"

***

On Friday, Amanda picked up Dylan from school at the usual time, but he would have to be back at five-thirty, to be ready for the play at seven. Since Angie and David were involved with the backstage preparations, they offered to pick up Dylan so Amanda and Marsh could go later.

Amanda tried to give Dylan a light supper, but he was too nervous and excited to eat much. Helen called to wish him luck and after a quick round of hugs and kisses he was out the door and gone with Angie, Conner and David. Amanda had changed into a skirt and blouse earlier, and Marsh went upstairs when Dylan left, to put on a clean shirt and a pair of dress pants. When he was gone for awhile, Amanda went upstairs and found him standing in front of his bedroom mirror, dressed except for his unbuttoned shirt.

"What are you doing?" she asked from the doorway.

"Nothing. I guess I'm just nervous, too," he said without looking at her.

"I'm sure he'll do fine," Amanda said before she fully realized what he meant. She went to him and put her arms around him. "And you'll be fine, too." She gently began to do up his buttons.

"I know I have to start going out like this now and then, but I haven't been around a crowd of people in a long time, and –"

"What better place to start than in a group of parents at a school play? Believe me, they'll only have eyes for their kids."

"I suppose you're right."

"And Dylan will shine, especially with you there."

"I know." He looked down at her as she finished doing up the last button and smoothed his shirt. Then he took her hands into his and kissed them. "Thank you for being here, Amanda."

"You can do this." She kissed his lips. "Let's go."

***

The school was bustling with the grown-up activity of an evening program. In the weeks Amanda had been bringing Dylan to school she had briefly been in the hallway on a rainy morning, when she'd met his teacher, Mrs. Crandall.

"I'm not sure where the auditorium is," she said to Marsh as they went in

He had decided not to bring his cane and they were arm-in-arm. She felt his grip tighten as they started down the hallway, into the surge of people headed in the same direction.

292

Amanda spotted Mrs. Crandall where she stood greeting parents and directing them around a corner. "Hello, Mr. and Mrs. Sterner – I'm so glad you could come," she smiled, holding her hand out to Amanda.

Sparing them all an awkward explanation, Amanda said, "This is Dylan's father, Mark."

"How nice to meet you, Mark," she enthused as she shook his hand.

"Nice to meet you," he replied.

"We'll have Parent Teacher conferences in a couple of weeks, but I can't wait that long to tell you what an exceptional little boy Dylan is."

Marsh beamed with pride. "Thank you."

"I can tell he has a very nurturing environment at home."

Marsh looked at Amanda. "I owe it all to her," he said.

"Well, Dylan shows a lot of promise and I won't be surprised if he does great things. The auditorium is down this hall to the right, and I'll see you both again soon."

"Right this way, Mrs. Sterner," Marsh teased as they moved along.

When they entered the auditorium, his heart began to thump. He resisted the urge to hold back as he and Amanda made their way down the aisle to within a few rows of the stage. Some of the mothers recognized Amanda and called out or waved to her. Marsh sensed they were sizing him up, and the thought of being scrutinized unnerved him.

"See? This isn't so hard," Amanda said as they sat down.

"I know it's crazy, but it feels like people are staring at me."

"Well, some of them *have* heard the legend of mean Mr. Sterner who wouldn't let their kids play in his yard."

"Really?"

"Oh, from what I've heard, you're the Village Ogre."

He detected the smirk on her lips and wanted to kiss her right there. He looked down at her blue satin blouse, grey skirt and black high heels at the end of those exquisitely shaped legs, smug in the knowledge that she was all his.

He settled into his seat and began to relax. Being recognized as the Village Ogre wasn't so bad, given the alternative. He dared to look around and meet other people's gazes. Amanda was right. There would be places he could go, things he could do. He really could have a more normal life than he ever would have thought, but it was only because of Amanda. He put his hand around hers. With Amanda, he could accomplish anything.

After a few more minutes of mayhem, the lights began to dim and people made the final scramble for their seats. Mrs. Crandall appeared on the stage in front of the curtain and welcomed everyone, thanking them for coming. She spoke proudly about the play which, she said, the children had helped her write, and praised them for their hard work over the past few weeks. The sounds of scrambling feet and frantic whispers could be heard behind her as she introduced the play and stepped aside.

When the curtain went up, there were several little trees on the edge of the stage. The trunks consisted of brown cloth, wrapped and pinned around small bodies. A silky, green fabric mounted on a series of long, flexible wires which were in constant motion, was worn over their heads and arms.

"How can we tell which one is Dylan?" Marsh whispered.

"He's the second one from the left. Those are his sneakers."

A grown-up looking little girl walked onto the center of the stage and seemed very much at home in the limelight as she began a narrative about Mother Nature and the forest. The entire stage came to life as other children in various animal costumes moved around her, each one pausing in front of her as she described what role that particular animal played in nature.

Marsh smiled as he watched Dylan's sneakers shuffling with characteristic impatience. When the little girl introduced the trees, they began to gently sway in unison. Conner galloped onto the stage waving two large, blue silk streamers. He had almost reached the trees when he stubbed his toe. A collective sound of concern went up from the audience before he recovered and danced around them as they responded, rustling furiously.

There was a smattering of applause and Marsh couldn't resist letting out a whistle. When Amanda turned to look at him he shrugged and smiled. "My boy's up there," he said.

The performance lasted about an hour. After a second encore and a raucous standing ovation, the children were reunited with their parents in the cafeteria where coffee, cookies and punch were served.

"You were amazing!" Amanda greeted Dylan as they hugged. "I'm so proud of you."

"How did I do, Daddy?" Dylan asked as Marsh hugged him. "You were the best tree I've ever seen," Marsh replied.

The shine in Dylan's eyes told him what it meant to have his father there and Marsh promised himself that, from tonight on he would always be there.

Conner appeared with his father and after everyone praised his performance as well, the two boys set off for the cookie table.

"Hey, buddy!" David greeted Marsh with a handshake. "Mi'Lady," he added as he gave Amanda a peck on the cheek. "Angie'll be along in a minute. She's still cleaning up backstage. Were those kids great or what?"

"Conner did a great job," Amanda said.

"Yeah – of not falling off the stage," David chuckled. "Angie thought if he got involved in the play it would give him some confidence and help him with his klutziness, but I guess the jury's still out on that."

They laughed and as David and Marsh settled into a conversation, Amanda watched, happy to see that a friendship was developing between them. It was something Marsh needed and she was excited about the prospect.

Coffee cup in hand she moved around the room, taking in the commotion of people chatting and kids running around. After a couple of greetings she drifted into the hallway and walked around in the relative quiet, looking at the artwork posted by the various grades along the wall. She had reached the far end when, lost in thought, she switched sides and began to work her way back, sipping her coffee and looking at the names and ages on the bottom of each drawing.

"Hello, Amanda."

She turned, surprised, to find a robust, sandy haired man with a familiar face, gazing at her in obvious admiration.

"Tom!" she put her hand on his shoulder as he leaned toward her and kissed her cheek. "What are you doing here?"

"My niece was in the play tonight."

"Really? Which one was she?"

"The narrator, the little ham."

"Oh, she was good. Wasn't it adorable?"

"Yeah, it was good."

The awkward pause arrived.

"You look beautiful, Amanda," he said.

"You look great, yourself." It seemed like a lifetime since she'd seen him.

"I've missed you," he said. "I'm sorry I was such a jerk that day."

"I'm sorry I was so on edge."

"Are you still with the Sterners?"

"Yes. I'm here for Dylan. He was one of the trees."

"Oh, a non-speaking part," Tom joked.

"Well, not to hear him at home," she laughed. "He's quite a character."

Tom thrust his hands into his pockets and paused as though he was carefully composing his next few words. "So, are you and Mark Sterner – together?"

"Yes, just since August." Amanda couldn't resist the chance to finally clarify that.

"Are you saying I shot myself in the foot by leaving that day when you weren't involved with him yet?"

She smiled. "Something like that. But if it's any comfort, it turned out that our relationship was inevitable. It was just a matter of time."

Tom didn't hide his disappointment. "So you and I weren't meant to be, after all. But are you happy? Is he treating you okay?"

"Yes, I'm very happy and he's a wonderful man."

"Then I guess I can leave with some closure."

"Leave?"

"Yeah, I'm moving to San Diego at the end of the month. Most of my family's there, and my brother-in-law has a very successful accounting firm. His partner just passed away and he's asked me to take his place."

"What a great opportunity! I'm really happy for you."

***

"I wonder what's keeping Angie," David said, glancing at his watch. "I'd better see if she needs a hand."

"Sure," Marsh agreed.

"I'll be right back."

Dave headed out of the cafeteria while Marsh took a sip of his coffee and looked around for Amanda. He'd lost track of her over the last fifteen minutes or so while he and David had talked. He spotted Dylan and Conner sitting at a table with a few other boys, but there was no sign of Amanda anywhere.

He made his way through the noisy groups of grown-ups and children, returning a couple of perfunctory nods, and went to the cafeteria doors where he glanced both ways. He noticed what looked like a couple chatting at the far end of the hall and suddenly recognized Amanda's blue and gray outfit. The man she was with was standing close to her as though they were having a private conversation. As he

298

watched them, the man looked more familiar until it hit him that it was Tom.

Marsh drew back inside the doorway. What the hell was Tom doing here? Could he have a child who attended the same school as Dylan? Was it possible that he and Amanda saw each other here all the time? He tried to keep his curiosity from igniting into jealousy. Instead, he wrestled with the frustration of not having that diamond on Amanda's finger yet.

He glanced back down the hall. They weren't in any hurry and it was time to break up the party. Marsh's leg was sore from being without his cane for so long, but he barely noticed as he started toward them.

***

Amanda and Tom glanced up as they heard someone coming and when she saw it was Marsh, Amanda knew from his expression that he wasn't happy. Unconcerned, she held out her hand. "Come say hello to Tom."

Marsh reached them and took her hand, but his wary eyes were on Tom. "I wondered where you were." He didn't try to keep the impatience out of his voice.

"Hi, Mark." Tom extended his hand.

"Hello, Tom." Marsh returned the handshake.

"I was just browsing along here and ran into him," Amanda casually explained. "Tom's niece was the narrator in the play."

She could feel some of the tension leaving Marsh. "We thought she was good," he said, slipping his arm around her waist. "Didn't we, darlin'?"

Amanda had to suppress a smile. "Yes, terrific. By the way, Tom just told me he's moving to San Diego."

"San Diego?" Marsh's face took on the glow of a man who had just won the lottery.

"Yes, I'm joining my brother-in-law in his accounting firm," Tom said.

"Good for you!" Marsh pumped his hand again. "Best of luck."

"Thanks." Tom looked back at Amanda. "I'm glad I saw you before I left," he said.

"Me, too."

"And good luck to the two of you." They exchanged goodbyes and as he headed down the hall, Amanda sensed his regret for what might have been.

"He still misses you," Marsh said as they watched him.

"I suppose, but he won't have any trouble finding someone else."

"There *is* no one else for me, you know."

She looked up at him. "Or for me. I told him that."

"I admit, Amanda, when I saw you with him..."

She touched a finger to his lips. "I know. I couldn't bear to see you with anyone else, either."

"Oh, there you are!" Angie, David and both boys appeared. "I'm finally done," Angie said. "What a mess to clean up! Hey we didn't have time for dinner tonight and we're starving. How about we all go out for pizza?"

Dylan and Conner clamored at the idea and Amanda looked at Marsh, relieved when he didn't hesitate.

"Sure," he said. "Let's go."

When they had reached the restaurant, Amanda looked across the table at Marsh as he and David began another lively conversation. Unexpectedly seeing Tom tonight had made her acutely aware of how timing and circumstance had brought her and Marsh together, how mundane her life would have been with anyone else. Tom would have made a loving husband and a great father, but it was Marsh who took her breath away every time he looked at her and made her want more every time he touched her. It was Marsh who was opening up before her eyes, just beginning to embrace fatherhood, new friends and a new life with her.

Best of all, Amanda could tell he wasn't nervous anymore about his first time out in public. He barely noticed the people at the other tables or the waitress who came to take their orders. He was too busy enjoying himself.

"I'm exhausted," Angie announced from beside her.

"I'll bet you are, but it all turned out," Amanda said.

"What did you think of the play, Marsh?" Angie called to him across the table.

He paused and turned to look at her and Amanda.

"Marsh?" David repeated.

"That's Daddy's nickname," Dylan piped up, proud to supply the information. "Grandma calls him that and now Manda does, too."

"Marsh." David mulled it over with a grin. "I like it."

"Only the people closest to him call him that," Amanda said as she cast him a benign look of reassurance.

"Well, in that case, I'd be honored to call you Marsh, if it's okay with you, buddy."

Amanda thought she detected a flicker of relief in Marsh's eyes before he replied, "I'd like that."

The pizza came as the chatter around the table continued. About halfway through the meal, Dylan announced, "Me and Conner got something to say."

"You mean 'Conner and I'," Amanda gently reminded him.

Dylan looked at Conner. "Did you tell Manda already?"

The adults chuckled.

"No, honey, I'm sorry," Amanda said when he looked perplexed. "We'll worry about proper English another time. Go ahead."

Dylan and Conner smirked at each other before they chirped in unison, "You two hafta get married!"

There was a momentary hush at the tables around them. "Conner!" Angie tried to reprimand him before she let out a giggle and David snorted and shook his head.

Unruffled, Marsh winked at a stunned Amanda. "What makes you think that, Scoot?"

"'Cause everybody at school thinks you are!"

"Well, maybe we'll have to do something about that. What do *you* think, Amanda?"

Amanda realized Marsh was using the opportunity to get Dylan "on board" with their plans, as he'd put it the other day. She shrugged and smiled. "I suppose it could be arranged."

Dylan and Conner cheered and clapped. "Okay, now you hafta give her a ring."

"I think I can take it from here, Scoot."

"And *I* think we've just witnessed a proposal," David said. He clasped Marsh's shoulder. "Congratulations, buddy."

Angie put her arm around Amanda. "Maybe it's not too soon after all."

Amanda met Marsh's waiting eyes. "Maybe not."

***

Saturday was spent preparing for Helen's return on Sunday. Amanda and Dylan went grocery shopping in the morning while Marsh tended to his mother's flowerbeds and trimmed the bushes and hedges around the yard.

Jean, her husband Michael and Jason would bring Helen home in the afternoon and stay the night before heading back. Amanda cleaned and prepared the spare room, vacuumed and dusted through the downstairs and worked on the dinner menu for Sunday. She'd finished putting together a pan of lasagna and was working on a lemon meringue pie when Dylan wandered into the kitchen.

"I'm bored, Manda," he said. "It's taking Grandma forever to get here."

"I know, sweetie. Not much longer. Is your room cleaned up for you and Jason?"

"Pretty much."

"Well, why don't you see if Daddy needs help picking up all the trimmings he did?"

"Okay!"

She watched out the window as Dylan went to his father in the yard and Marsh stopped a moment and showed him what to do. Not too long ago, Dylan would have most likely hesitated at the idea of approaching his father. When she'd

303

arrived here, it had deeply disturbed her to see how Dylan and Marsh seemed to deliberately avoid each other. But now, each day found them a little closer.

Chapter 18
Michael

Sunday was breezy and cool with bright sunshine and Dylan played outside, constantly looking toward the road. When the white Nissan came up the driveway, he yelled his grandmother's arrival to Marsh and Amanda and by the time they came out onto the porch, he was already hugging Helen through the open car door.

Jean got out of the passenger side and scooped up the unsuspecting little boy from behind. "Oh, my goodness you're beautiful, Dylan! I'm your Aunt Jean!"

Jason jumped out of the back seat waving his guitar while an elegant-looking man of about fifty climbed out of the driver's side. At first glance, he seemed the perfect match for Jean.

Helen was helped out and eagerly hugged Amanda and Marsh. "I had a wonderful time, but it's so good to be home again!"

"It's good to have you back," Amanda greeted her.

Marsh hugged Helen warmly. "Welcome home, Mother."

"Everybody, I want you to meet my husband, Michael." There was obvious pride in Jean's voice.

"Nice to meet you, Michael," Marsh said as they shook hands.

"I've heard a lot about you, Marsh. Nice to finally meet *you*." Michael was handsome and trim with what appeared to be an eternal tan and a distinguished hint of gray at the temples of his dark hair.

"And this is Amanda," Jean continued.

Michael turned his full attention to Amanda with his intense, dark eyes. "And I've heard a lot about you, too, Amanda," he said, taking her hand into both of his.

"Nice to meet you," she said. She caught a whiff of his cologne and, as his hold lasted longer than necessary, she withdrew her hand. A reflexive queasiness came over her as she was instantly transported back to the age of seventeen and the lingering touch of one of her mother's boyfriends. She tried to shake it off as a mistaken first impression as she helped Helen walk to the porch steps.

The van was unloaded and as everyone settled into the house, Amanda offered the coffee she'd made and helped Helen unpack in her room.

"In some ways it feels as though I've been gone for a month," Helen said. "So much has happened. Vicki's wedding, the family reunion – I've done more socializing in a week than I've done in a long time."

"And you got to spend time with Jean," Amanda said as she put some clothes into a drawer.

306

"Yes, that part was nice, but – just between you and me, Amanda, I'm a little worried about Jean."

"Really? Why?"

Helen glanced through the bedroom doorway into the empty kitchen before she said in a hushed tone, "I don't know about that new husband of hers."

Amanda sat on the edge of the bed. "Why? Has anything happened?"

"Nothing specific, but – there's just something about him I don't trust."

"Like what?"

"Well, he's so overly nice to me that he seems insincere. And then there's that night prowling."

"Night prowling?"

"Yes – he's usually up half the night, wandering around the house or outside, like he's restless. He jokes that he's just a night owl, but I've heard him go out in the car at odd hours, too."

"What does Jean say about it?"

"When I mentioned it to her, she told me his job is very high-pressure and she's fine with whatever he has to do to unwind. She's so in awe of him, Amanda, that I don't think she wants to see any flaws."

"How long have they been married?"

"Only a couple of years. It was a whirlwind romance. He's a nationally renowned surgeon who makes an obscene amount of money and travels in the highest of social circles. He seemed taken with Jean from the moment they met and she never hesitated. It was such a change from her life with her first husband." Helen shook her head. "He was a useless lout."

A series of melodic chords came from the direction of the sunporch as Marsh and Jason began tuning their guitars.

"Oh, it's good to hear that again," Helen smiled as though she was glad to change the subject. She patted Amanda's knee. "I had a long talk with Marsh on the phone last night. He told me about your plans. He's never been happier, Amanda."

"Neither have I. I know I'm where I belong, Helen. Thank you for making me feel so welcome."

"It's as if you've always been here, dear."

When they'd finished unpacking, Amanda pushed Helen's wheelchair to the sunporch where Marsh and Jason were sitting side-by-side on the wicker sofa strumming a duet of one of the pop songs Jason had been learning. They would pause now and then as Marsh guided him on his hand position or a certain series of notes, then they would return to the exciting sound of the two guitars playing in unison. Jean sat across from them, listening proudly and determined to hold onto an antsy Dylan. Michael sat in the other chair and Amanda was immediately aware of his groping stare as she got Helen settled and pulled up a chair for herself.

So her first instinct had been correct, she thought. There *was* something about Michael that needed watching, and knowing he would be here until tomorrow made her uneasy.

As Marsh and Jason continued their jam session, Dylan finally succeeded in wrestling from Jean's grasp, only to be caught by his grandmother and smothered with kisses before

308

he could head for the doorway. "This is boring, Manda," he said into her ear. "Can I go out and ride my bicycle?"

"For a little while," she said. "But we're going to have dinner pretty soon."

She watched him go and sensed that his apparent lack of interest in what his father and Jason were doing, might be due to a tinge of jealousy. Marsh was clearly preoccupied with Jason and the music and was thoroughly enjoying himself.

Ignoring Michael's intrusive presence, Amanda soaked up the energy in the room and thrilled to the rich sounds that filled the house. It was obvious Jason had done a lot of practicing on his own. He was anxious to show his uncle what he'd learned and seemed quite impressed with what Marsh already knew. Time passed quickly and when Amanda noticed it was after four-thirty she decided to start getting things ready for dinner.

As she got up Jean said, "Amanda, can I help you in the kitchen?"

Before Amanda could answer, Michael got up and put his hand on Jean's shoulder. "No, hon, you just relax and enjoy the music. I'll help Amanda."

"I really don't need –" Amanda began.

"Michael's a gourmet cook," Jean boasted as she put her hand over his and looked up at him adoringly. "It's one of his many talents."

"But I got almost everything ready ahead of time and there's really nothing to do."

"Come, come Amanda," Michael said. "I'm sure there's *something* you and I can do in the kitchen."

Michael's soothing voice and the touch of his hand on her arm sent a shudder through her. She looked over at Marsh but he didn't notice she was leaving. Helen just rolled her eyes sympathetically.

"What a charming kitchen," Michael said as he looked around the room.

Amanda took the large pan of lasagna out of the refrigerator and turned on the oven. She decided the best way to handle Michael would be to not let him think he was bothering her.

"That looks delicious, Amanda."

"Thank you. I may not be a gourmet, but lasagna's one of my specialties."

He chuckled softly. "Well, Jean's a little prejudiced, I'm afraid."

She took out the large salad she'd made and began to slice a loaf of Italian bread.

"Here, I'll do that for you."

He was suddenly too close behind her and she stepped aside. "Thanks," she said. "While you're doing that, I'll set the dining room table."

She began to take the plates out of the cupboard.

"You know, Amanda, I think I might be able to help Marsh with that leg injury."

"I've heard you're a very good surgeon," she remarked as she rummaged through the silverware drawer.

"I'm actually considered the best osteopathic surgeon in North America." He paused to watch her reaction but she continued to count out the knives, forks and spoons.

"Well that's good to know. We want Marsh to have the best care possible."

"I'd like to talk to him about making an appointment soon and coming in for an evaluation."

"Sounds like good idea," she said, already unsure whether she would want Marsh in the hands of someone like Michael.

She went through the archway into the dining room where she reached into the drawer of the china cabinet for the linen tablecloth. As she turned to spread it over the table, Michael was there, grabbing the other end of it.

"That must have been a terrible accident Marsh and his wife were in," he remarked as he smoothed his end of the cloth.

"It was." Amanda headed back into the kitchen and reached for the plates. Michael took the salad bowls and silverware and followed her back into the dining room.

"It makes you wonder what kind of rage would cause a person to grab a steering wheel out of someone's hands and risk killing both of them," Michael said

Amanda did not reply as she set the plates around the table.

"From what Jean's told me, Marsh and his wife were having some pretty serious marital problems when that happened."

Amanda folded the napkins and began to place the silverware. The increasingly personal nature of Michael's comments told her that he had more of an agenda than fixing Marsh's leg. She finished in the dining room and he followed her back into the kitchen.

She slid the lasagna into the oven and as she got a tray ready with the Parmesan cheese and salad dressings, she sensed him close behind her again.

"You know, Amanda, from what I hear, we're going to be in-laws soon." He spoke in an intimate tone as his hands came down on the cupboard on either side of her. "Don't you think we ought to get to know each other better?"

She took a deep breath, spun around and surprised him into taking a step back. "Truthfully, Michael, I think I already know you about as well as I care to, so as long as you back off, we'll get along fine."

"How's dinner coming?" Marsh asked as he came in with Jason behind him.

Amanda didn't shy from Michael's momentary glare. "It's just heating, so probably about thirty minutes," she replied as she turned and put the pan with the extra sauce onto a burner. She immediately felt at ease with Marsh there.

"Great. We need a cold drink," Marsh said over his shoulder as he reached into the refrigerator. He handed Jason a soda and took one for himself.

"You two sounded so good, you should start a band," Michael said. "You've obviously had extensive musical training, Marsh."

Marsh took a sip of his soda and leaned back against the counter beside Amanda. "No, actually, I'm a hundred percent self-taught."

Michael folded his arms and leaned on the opposite counter. "Really? Well, then you've certainly had a lot of experience. Have you played professionally?"

There was another one of his probing questions and Amanda shot Marsh a sideways glance as she fussed over the bread basket.

"No, I never got that lucky," Marsh said. "It's just been a hobby."

"Mom says you were the best around," Jason piped up, anxious to flatter his uncle.

"Yeah, around town." Marsh laughed it off. He turned and slipped his arm around Amanda. "That lasagna smells terrific."

"Yes, I was disappointed that Amanda didn't need my help in the kitchen," Michael said.

She looked directly at him. "No, not at all."

Everyone raved about Amanda's dinner and with Jason going back for a third helping there were barely any leftovers. Amanda had a chance to observe the interaction between Jean and Michael and realized that Jean was not the mature, self-confident woman she appeared to be – at least not with him. She was like a smitten school girl around Michael and he seemed to feed off of it, reveling in the spotlight she placed on him.

Marsh and Jason were still chatting about the latest trends in the music business while Dylan sat next to his grandmother, head in hand, pushing his food around his plate.

"What's the matter, aren't you hungry?" Amanda heard Helen ask him.

"Not too much," he murmured.

Amanda leaned toward Helen. "I think there's a bit of jealousy going on," she whispered with a nod toward Jason.

Helen's lips formed an "oh" of understanding.

Jason seemed to sense what was going on. "Hey, Dylan," he said. "Could I see your transformers after dinner?"

Dylan perked up. "Yeah – I got lots of 'em!"

"Why don't you eat a little more and then you can be excused," Amanda said.

Dylan brandished his fork and shoveled in a few more mouthfuls while Marsh shook his head from beside her. "How do you do that?"

"Sheer bribery," she replied as everyone caught on and laughed. Everyone, that was, except Michael. Although she didn't give him the satisfaction, she was aware of his gaze.

She knew she needed to talk to Marsh about Michael, yet couldn't bear the thought of causing Jean any embarrassment, should she find out. This was a family situation and Amanda was the newcomer. Yet Marsh would be upset if she didn't alert him to what was going on. The only good thing was that Jean and Michael would go home tomorrow. But the problem would come back with them at some point and Marsh would have to be told about it before then.

As soon as dinner was over, Dylan and Jason went upstairs and everyone grabbed a few dishes to bring into the kitchen.

"I'll help you clean up, Amanda," Jean offered.

"There's not much to do," she said. "I'm just going to load the dishwasher. It's such a beautiful night, you might enjoy sitting on the front porch for awhile."

"You're really spoiling me, Amanda, and your dinner was delicious." Jean grabbed Michael's hand. "Let's get Mother and sit outside."

Within a few moments the house was more quiet than it had been for several hours and Amanda finally found herself alone with Marsh.

"Come here. I've missed you." He pulled her into a hug.

"No you haven't. You've been too busy enjoying yourself."

He laughed. "It *has* been fun, seeing Jason's enthusiasm. It reminds me of myself at that age. Nothing mattered but music."

"Well, he's lucky to have you for a mentor."

"I think he's got what it takes if he's willing to work hard. And speaking of working hard, thank you for all you've done today. You make this place run like a top."

"It was my pleasure."

"And speaking of pleasure..." He drew her closer.

She eagerly threw her arms around his neck and they began to share a tender kiss until Marsh suddenly pulled back and she saw Michael standing in the kitchen doorway. She felt uncomfortable not knowing how long he'd been there.

"Sorry to interrupt you two lovebirds, but it just occurred to me, Marsh, we're leaving tomorrow morning and I still haven't had a chance to talk to you about what we can do for that leg."

"Oh, that's right," Marsh said.

"Have you got a little time now?"

Marsh glanced down at Amanda. "Remember where we left off."

"I won't forget. Go ahead."

Marsh went into the living room with Michael while she finished cleaning up and joined Helen and Jean on the porch.

They talked and laughed about how well Vicki's wedding went despite all the behind-the-scenes glitches.

"And I hear we have another wedding to look forward to," Jean said.

Amanda nodded and smiled. "In a few months, probably."

Jean studied her for a moment before she said, "It's as if you were delivered to my brother on a platter, Amanda. You're the very thing he needed."

"I guess it was all about timing," Amanda said. "He's the very thing I needed, too."

"It was all meant to be," Helen said. "What happened in Marsh's life the last few years seemed so wrong and you came along and made everything right again."

"I agree," Jean said. "There were times after Carrie died that we didn't know if he was going to pull through. He wasn't Marsh anymore, but you're bringing him back." Jean's words were kind but her tone didn't hide her envy that Amanda had won over her brother so quickly.

"He's pulled me through a tough time, too," Amanda said. "I invested a few years and rearranged my life for a man who, it turned out, didn't really love me."

The way Jean continued to look at her told Amanda she had something more on her mind. "I don't doubt any of what's been said, Amanda, but I have to ask – are you absolutely sure of what you're doing? Have you given it enough thought? Life with my brother won't necessarily be a piece of cake."

"Jean!" Helen reproached.

"No, I don't mind your question," Amanda replied. "Marsh has asked me that more than once himself. He doesn't want me to feel any pressure to marry him until I'm ready, so we're going to take our time."

"A bit of advice you could have followed yourself, Jean," Helen said.

Jean rolled her eyes. "Mother felt I jumped into marriage with Michael too soon, but when you find the perfect man, you'd better grab him before someone else does – especially at my age." Jean sat back and folded her hands with a satisfied smile. "Sometimes you've got to follow your instinct, and I just knew he was the one for me. I've never been happier."

It was Amanda's turn to study Jean for few moments. Did she really not know about Michael's other side? What instinct was she talking about?

Marsh and Michael had talked for about an hour before they appeared on the porch. "I think we have a possible treatment plan," Michael announced. "We'll know more after we run a few tests, but I'm sure we can do something to get that leg working better."

The women responded with sounds of approval but Amanda had a strange feeling the surgery might not take place. After a little more conversation Helen began to yawn and Jean and Amanda helped her into the house.

"I think I'm ready for bed," Jean said as she returned to the porch. "Are you ready, Michael?"

"In a few minutes," he replied as he and Marsh chatted.

Jean said goodnight and went back inside while Amanda sat down next to Marsh, anxious for Michael to leave so they could talk. But Michael wasn't going anywhere. It was as though he made a point of intruding on any opportunity for privacy they might have.

After another thirty minutes or so, Amanda gave up. "I guess I'll turn in," she said, trying not to sound as defeated as she felt.

"Night, darlin". Marsh kissed her cheek. "Sleep tight."

"Good night, Amanda," Michael said.

"Good night," she said over her shoulder as she headed down the porch steps.

"Where are you going?" Michael asked.

"Oh, Amanda's over at the carriage house," Marsh said. "We're leaving it that way until the wedding, for Dylan's sake."

"How quaint," Amanda heard Michael remark as she made her way across the lawn.

She would have asked Marsh to walk her back if she hadn't expected Michael to tag along. It only represented another lost opportunity to tell Marsh her concerns. But as she went into the apartment and locked the door, she reassured herself that Michael would be leaving tomorrow and she would have some time and perspective on what to tell Marsh about his brother-in-law.

Chapter 19
Pen Techniques

Amanda opened her eyes out of a sound sleep to the creak of her apartment door opening. She glanced at the clock beside the bed and saw that it was going on one o'clock. Someone was moving around in the kitchen, and through the bedroom doorway she saw a shadow momentarily block the night light that spilled across the living room.

She tucked both elbows under her back and rose slightly, as a smile played over her lips. Marsh had sneaked out of the house to visit her. It was deliciously exciting.

"You must really miss me," she called out in a teasing tone. She awaited his answer, but there was only silence. "Marsh?" She climbed out of bed. "You can't surprise me. I know you're there." She stepped through the bedroom doorway. "What are you doing?"

The hands that gripped her shoulders and shoved her against the wall were unfamiliar and she cried out as a surge of panic jolted through her.

"I couldn't sleep, Amanda, so I thought it was a good time to pay you a visit." The scent of Michael's cologne made her stomach wrench just before she recognized his face in the eerie glow of the night light. "Besides, *'darlin'*, we have some unfinished business."

He bore no resemblance to the impeccably groomed doctor she'd met earlier. Instead he wore a tank top and a pair of jogging pants. His perfect hair was mussed and the hint of a dark stubble outlined his face. He did not look at all like the Michael Jean had bragged about.

"How the hell did you get in here?" she breathed through clenched teeth.

"Well, you wouldn't let me help you with dinner, so I had lots of time to look around the kitchen and I saw a few keys hanging on the wall by the phone. I was curious about the one labeled "carriage house" until I found out you live here."

When Amanda began to struggle, he shoved her harder against the wall and brought himself full length against her as his grip tightened around the tops of her arms. This was much more than an edgy flirtation, she told herself. She could sense the current of violence in him.

"Let me finish my story, Amanda," he said close to her ear.

She nodded as she fought to swallow her terror.

"So when I couldn't sleep I thought, what better time to stop by, when we could have the place all to ourselves and get to know each other better."

"What makes you think you can get away with this?" She refused to sound intimidated, but tensed as his hand stroked her hair with deceiving gentleness.

"Well, actually Amanda, I've given that a lot of thought, too, and you're the only one who can answer that question. You see, you just have one simple decision to make." His fingers moved down her throat and across the bare skin above the neckline of her nightgown, coming to rest in the hollow between her breasts. As she turned her head to the side he leaned in closer. "Just how badly do you want to keep Marsh's little secret?"

Her eyes widened as the breath went out of her. He knew? Oh, God, how could he know? Jean would never have told him, would she? She was as adamant about protecting Marsh as Helen was. Amanda's eyes slowly began to narrow. If Michael was as deceptive about everything else as he appeared to be, maybe he only wanted her to think he knew about Marsh. Maybe he suspected something but had no facts.

"I don't know about Marsh," she said as calmly as she could manage, "But you seem to have a few secrets of your own, Michael."

She gasped as he grabbed the hair at the nape of her neck and pulled her head back, forcing her to look into his eyes. "Yes, and you're about to become one of them."

"How can you do this to Jean?"

"I'm not doing anything to Jean. She's an entirely different issue. You see, Jean's a very good wife. No complaints there. I'm a lucky man to have found her. But some men need a little something else now and then. You know what I mean, Amanda."

There was a wildness in his eyes, as if he had completely crossed over to the real Michael, the one few people saw.

How far would he go? She knew instinctively that she would need to cooperate or make him think she was if she wanted to come out of this intact. But she also needed to find a way to protect herself. Her right leg was against the end table at the side of the couch. She kept a pen there for jotting down grocery lists and doing crossword puzzles.

"I'm sure you're under a lot of stress with your occupation." She used her most understanding tone as she touched the tabletop with her fingertips. "People don't realize how lonely it can get when you're at the top of your profession."

He slowly shook his head, his face relaxing somewhat. "I *am* at the top of my profession, but nobody seems to get it. I'm an osteopathic surgeon, for Christ's sake, one of the best in the world."

She splayed her fingers and felt around for the pen. "People need to recognize how accomplished you really are," she said as she felt his hand slowly loosen on her hair.

"That's right, Amanda. People need to understand the constant pressure I'm under and give me my space. But since nobody wants to do that, I make my own space and find other ways to decompress."

Her hand closed around the stick pen. She never bothered to put the cap back on and she thanked herself as her index finger moved over the tip. She attempted again to slide from his grasp but he made it clear he wasn't ready to let her go. She carefully turned the pen around and folded it into her fist, dagger style, as she sent a silent prayer to Marsh to wake up, to sense something was wrong.

"So I had an idea," Michael continued as he cupped her breast with his hand and gazed into her eyes. "I got to thinking, how could Amanda help me relax, and then it came to me. This is the perfect opportunity for some sexual blackmail. It'll be fun. No muss, no fuss, and best of all, no paper trail. And you never know – over time as our families get closer and we visit more, you may even get to like it." His finger traced the outer edges of her lips. "That way, we can keep Marsh's secret indefinitely, and we both get what we want."

Amanda deliberately breathed slowly, trying to calm herself. Instinct began to override fear and the highlights of the self-defense course she'd taken a couple of years ago flashed into her mind with absolute clarity. She had excelled at pen techniques. Her instructor had said so.

***

Marsh rolled over and realized this was the third time he'd heard someone pass by his bedroom door. He sat up, pulled on his jeans and went into the dim hallway to find his sister standing at the top of the stairs in her bathrobe, peering down into the living room.

"What's going on, Jean? Is everything okay?"

"Oh." She straightened and turned to him. "I'm sorry if I woke you, Marsh. I was just looking for Michael."

"Why? Where did he go?"

"Well, he can't be far, but he tends to roam at night and he's been gone for some time."

"Roam?" Marsh repeated. "What do you mean?"

"He doesn't sleep well most nights – I'm sure he has a lot on his mind – and he sometimes wanders around the house or the yard. I was hoping he wouldn't do it here, but he must be restless tonight, too."

Marsh wasn't sure he liked the idea of anyone roaming around his place at one-thirty in the morning, restless or not. "Go on back to bed, Jean. I'll see where he is."

As Jean went back into the spare room, Marsh grabbed a tee-shirt and glanced into Dylan's room. He and Jason hadn't stirred and he softly closed their door before he headed downstairs. The house was silent. He paused to look through the sunporch windows at the darkened carriage house and imagined Amanda asleep, wishing he was holding her in his arms. He knew she was safe because she always locked her door. They had discussed how her distance from the main house and close proximity to the road dictated that she keep her door locked at all times.

He turned on the outside lights and went onto the porch, half expecting to find Michael sitting there, then looked around the yard for any sign of movement. He waited, wondering if he might emerge from behind the house on a late night stroll, but several minutes passed. Marsh decided to get a cold drink and sit on the porch awhile longer.

In the dim light from the stove, he opened a can of ginger ale and leaned against the counter as he took a drink. He absent-mindedly gazed around the kitchen, wondering where Michael could be, when he passed over something that didn't look right. He looked at the wall phone and the small wooden plaque beside it that held the various keys to the household. There were five of them, each with its own hook and label above it. Only right now there were only four. He walked

324

over and looked at the space where the fifth key should be. The label above it said "Carriage House".

***

Amanda had managed to stall Michael with ego-stroking small talk for a few more minutes but she was running out of ideas and he was testing her nerve, nuzzling her neck and slowly licking the side of her face. She closed her eyes, willing herself not to show the disgust she felt, careful not to anger him.

"Come on, Amanda. Have you made up your mind or do you need some persuasion?" His muscular arms encircled her waist and she stumbled as he moved her backwards through the bedroom doorway.

She tried to keep a space between them but he bumped her repeatedly, an eager smile forming across his lips. She gripped the pen slightly behind her back. When to strike? The time had to be right because if it didn't temporarily disable him so she could get away, it would simply guarantee more violence.

"You haven't told me what this secret of Marsh's is that you know so much about," she challenged him.

"And you haven't denied it."

"No, because I don't know what you're talking about."

"So you want to play a game, Amanda?" He shoved her backwards onto the bed. "Good. I like games. And we can get as rough as you want."

As he launched himself on top of her she thrust her arm up and stabbed the tiny pen point into the soft flesh below his jaw. He yelped and put his hand to the puncture. When it came away bloody she felt the rage overtake him and her

325

throat closed in panic. "You bitch!" He drew back and slapped her so hard that it knocked her sideways before she came back and slashed the side of his face.

"Jesus Christ!" He jumped away from her, bloodied and stunned.

She shoved him aside and leapt from the bed as he grabbed for her. Her kitchen door crashed open and she only heard a couple of Marsh's running steps before he burst through her bedroom doorway, flipped the light switch on and frantically looked around, trying to catch his breath. Michael backed up to the closet door and slid down it, hands over his face as the blood started to ooze between his fingers. Amanda's legs gave out and she sank back onto the bed, squinting in the harsh brightness.

"My God, Amanda – my God – you're bleeding!" Marsh rasped.

Amanda glanced down at the vivid flecks of red on the front of her nightgown. "No, it's *his* blood." She could barely move her lips.

Marsh took her face into his hands and she felt a wet sting as his thumb brushed the corner of her mouth. "Not all of it," he growled before he turned on Michael. "Get up, you son of a bitch!"

When Michael didn't respond, Marsh charged him, grabbed him by the arm and hauled him up. Michael opened his mouth to speak but Marsh slugged him in the jaw and his head thudded against the closet door before he slid down again.

"I'm bleeding like a goddamn stuck pig," he muttered through his hands.

326

"I'll get a towel." Amanda found enough strength to get off the bed and get one from the bathroom.

Marsh shoved it at Michael before he took Amanda into the living room and sat down with her on the couch. Her right hand was still a fist, clutching the bloodied pen and he gently pried it from her grip.

"Are you all right?" he asked again and again as he slowly rocked her. His chest heaved with exhausted emotion.

"I'm okay," she said, glad to feel the warmth of his arms.

"He didn't –"

"No. I'm okay."

"What the hell was he doing here?"

Amanda kept her voice down. "He claimed to know about you and threatened to expose you if I didn't –"

Just then they became aware of Jean standing in the kitchen doorway, in her bathrobe. "He's here, isn't he?" She saw the blood on Amanda and covered her mouth. "Oh my God, Amanda –"

There were sounds from the bedroom and Marsh got up and went to the doorway.

"I need to take care of this," Michael groaned.

Amanda and Jean looked in. Michael was standing and the small towel he held to his face was saturated with blood. "She damn near killed me," he muttered.

"What're you gonna do about it? Call the cops?" Marsh taunted him.

"No! Nobody needs to call the cops. Nothing happened." He saw Jean. "I didn't mean anything by this, hon. Amanda invited me here and –"

Marsh stalked over and slammed him against the closet door. "So you're a cheater *and* a liar! I should have you arrested, you sick bastard!"

Michael sighed. "Look, I'll do anything you want, just don't call the cops," he said grudgingly.

"That's all you have to say?" Jean stared at him with large, liquid eyes. "What about me, Michael? What about Amanda? I've just met Amanda and I already know her well enough to know she didn't "invite" you here, but I've been married to you for two years and obviously, I don't know you at all."

Michael lowered his eyes in sullen silence.

"Tell me," Marsh said. "What's this big secret you were holding over Amanda's head? Tell me the truth or *I will* call the cops."

Amanda knew Marsh was bluffing. He would never willingly call the police to his home.

There was a pause while Michael seemed to consider something. "I don't know," he finally said.

"I don't believe you." Marsh went to the phone on the bedstand. "You really *are* sick if you're willing to throw your reputation away like this."

Amanda marveled at Marsh's nerve, but they all needed to be sure of what Michael actually knew. Marsh lifted the receiver.

"No! I mean it. I don't know anything about you. I've only heard Jean talking quietly to her mother on the phone now and then and when she told me about your leg and I asked a few questions, I could tell she was holding back and not telling me everything about you or your accident. It was

328

all speculation. I was just having a little fun with it, that's all."

Amanda saw Marsh's fists double at his sides. "Well nobody's laughing, and I'm calling a cab to take your sorry ass to the airport right now. You've got fifteen minutes to pack your stuff and get the hell out of here and if you try to cause any more trouble for my sister or us, I *will* have you arrested and prosecuted and your career will be over."

"All right, all right," Michael grunted. He moved slowly, painfully toward the bedroom door, then paused in front of Marsh. "I'll leave and that's the end of it. Unless, of course, I *do* find out your secret."

"The only secret is why I didn't kill you tonight. Now get out," Marsh said.

Michael made his way to the kitchen door and left.

Jean covered her face for a moment, then said, "I'll get Jason up and we'll drive back tonight."

"Are you crazy?" Marsh demanded. "You're not going anywhere tonight. You shouldn't go back at all until you've got an order of protection against that monster."

Jean opened her mouth to protest, then dissolved into tears. "This is such a nightmare. I don't know what to do."

Amanda put her arms around her. "You don't have to do anything right now. You need to take your time and stay here where you'll be safe."

"I'm going back to the house to keep an eye on Michael till he's gone," Marsh said. "Grab a few things, Amanda, and come back with Jean."

"But —"

"Never mind protocol. You're not staying here alone tonight and that's that."

Chapter 20
Deliverance

Marsh made his way toward the house as quickly as he could without stumbling in the darkness. In his frantic run to the carriage house without his cane, he had tripped and fallen twice, then struggled up and kept running. Adrenaline had numbed the pain that was catching up to him now.

Was he dreaming? Had all this really happened? It had to be real because he was still deeply shaken at the thought of what Amanda had gone through and what could have happened had he not realized where Michael was.

The closer he got to the house with the porch light on, the easier it was to see the ground and he began to move faster, anxious to make sure Michael was getting ready to leave. The front door opened and Michael ran down the porch steps carrying his overnight bag. He ripped open the car door and jumped in as the engine revved to life and the headlights came on.

Marsh paused, then moved into the shadows as the car jerked backwards, turned and roared down the driveway. In the faint light he saw a flash of Michael's face as the car passed a few yards away. He was looking straight ahead and when he turned onto the road he took off, tires screaming into the distance.

"Marsh! Are you all right?" He heard Amanda's cry from near the carriage house.

He stepped back into the light. "I'm fine."

Amanda and Jean ran to him.

"I was so afraid he might try to run you down." Amanda threw her arms around him.

"I'm okay. He didn't see me." She was shaking and Marsh hugged her close.

As well as she'd handled all that had happened so far tonight, he could tell she was spent. Jean was crying and he put his other arm around her. "Come on, ladies. That's enough trauma for one night. Besides, my leg's had it and I could use some support."

Both women tucked their shoulders under his arms and the three of them slowly made their way to the house.

"I can't believe he took the car," Amanda said.

"At least he's gone, and good riddance," Jean said bitterly.

"Do you think he woke everybody up?" Amanda asked.

"I hope not," Marsh said. "I don't feel like explaining any of this tonight."

They went in quietly and paused in the hallway, listening. In the silence they breathed a collective sigh of relief.

Marsh locked and dead bolted the door. "I'm sure he's headed for home and won't be back, but we're not taking any chances. We should get some rest and we'll try to sort this out in the morning." He draped his arm around Amanda and they headed for the stairs.

"I think I'll stay up for awhile," Jean said.

Amanda paused. "I'll sit with you, if you like."

Jean was obviously touched by the offer. "No, thanks, Amanda. I'll be fine. You get some rest. We can talk later."

"You sure, sis?" Marsh asked.

"Yes. I just need some time alone."

"Okay. Call us if you need us," Marsh said over his shoulder as he and Amanda headed upstairs.

* * *

Amanda could not imagine what Jean must be going through, alone with the terrible truth about her husband, but it made her realize that she was becoming part of a family that needed healing on many levels. Marsh led her to his bedroom and as he closed the door, she was aware that they were in the most intimate place they could be. This was where he'd spent his darkest days after arriving here and now it was a special place where he dreamed and composed his music. The twelve-string Gibson on its stand beside Marsh's chair emitted a presence as palpable as if another person were in the room.

"Come here." He guided her into the adjoining bathroom and dampened a washcloth in the sink while she got a good look at herself in the mirror. The corner of her mouth had bled slightly and there was redness around her cheekbone.

"I wanted to kill him," Marsh said as he held her chin and dabbed the cool cloth on her face.

"But I damn near *did*."

333

He paused and looked at her as her lips twitched. "Sometimes you scare me, Amanda. How did you know what to do with that pen?"

"Oh, I've had to fend off lots of men. It's second nature now."

"Oh, yeah?" He pulled her into an embrace. "Well your "fending" days are over. You belong to me now. But I'll watch my step, just the same."

"You'd better."

He drew back and his expression changed. She looked down. Her robe had opened and she'd forgotten about the blood on her nightgown.

"We've got to get you out of that," Marsh said. He brought her back into the bedroom, went to his closet and took out a long-sleeved shirt. As he helped her slowly draw the soiled nightgown off over her head, his gaze caressed her nakedness and he kissed her tenderly as he helped her into the shirt. "Do you want it buttoned?" he asked.

"Not really," she said, folding it around her.

He smiled. "Me neither."

They went to the bed and she was glad to lie down as he gently covered her. He settled in on the other side and curled up behind her, taking her into his arms.

"I feel safe," she murmured.

"You are." She felt his lips touch the back of her neck. "I know it's late, Amanda, but I need to know everything that happened."

In a few sleepy sentences she told him about Michael's inappropriate attention and prying questions before dinner, then his behavior at her apartment before Marsh got there.

"Why didn't you tell me he was bothering you in the kitchen? Maybe none of this would have happened."

"I *told* him to stay away from me. He knew I wanted nothing to do with him. And I wanted to tell you before I went back to the apartment, but I couldn't get near you yesterday and the couple of times I did, Michael was always there, as if he planned it. Besides, I didn't want to start any family trouble. I'm the newcomer. I was afraid Jean wouldn't believe me."

"You shouldn't have had to go through that, Amanda, but you handled it the only way you could and I'm proud of you."

Amanda sighed and settled deeper into his arms.

"I never want to let you go," he said into her ear.

"Don't you dare," she murmured before she drifted asleep.

***

Marsh jumped and opened his eyes in the dark. The doorbell had awakened him. He sat up to the sound of pounding and turned on the lamp beside the bed, squinting at the clock. It was nearly five-thirty. Now there was silence. Had he really heard anything?

Amanda stirred beside him. "What is it?"

The pounding resumed and Marsh threw off the covers and reached for his jeans. "Someone's at the door," he said.

Amanda bolted up. "Oh God – do you think it's *him* again?"

"I hope not." Marsh got up and reached for his cane.

The doorbell rang again.

"You can't go down there alone." Amanda got up and grabbed her robe.

Marsh headed for the door. "You stay upstairs and make sure everyone else does until we know what's going on."

He crossed the hallway and as he started down the stairs, he heard the crackling of a police radio above the sound of an idling engine and stopped, every nerve in his body suddenly awake.

"Marsh – what is it?" Jean called down.

As he looked up, Amanda appeared beside her. "We need to wait here. Let's check on the kids."

As he reached the bottom of the stairs and turned the hall light on, he passed the oval mirror and glanced at the frightened-looking man in the reflection. It was Marshall Stewart in disguise and if he wanted it to work, he'd better calm down and look like any other surprised homeowner being awakened at this hour. He turned on the porch light.

A uniformed officer peered through the glass panel beside the door and saw Marsh. "State Police," he called out. "We need to talk to you."

As Marsh opened the door, the loudness of the radio and car engine hit him with the cool air and he took a deep breath.

There were two of them on the other side of the screen. One touched the brim of his Stetson. "Sorry to disturb you at this hour, Sir. Are you Mark Sterner?"

Marsh tried to swallow but his throat suddenly seemed full of cotton. "Yes."

"I'm Trooper Allen and this is Trooper Weller. Is there a Jean Farling at this address?"

"That's my sister," Marsh replied. "Yes, she's here."

"We need to speak with her. It's urgent."

Marsh turned to see that Jean was already coming slowly down the stairs. Jason and Dylan were with Amanda in the upstairs hallway and as Jason started to follow his mother, Amanda gently drew him aside and guided both boys back into Dylan's room.

"Come in," Marsh said to the officers.

They removed their hats and stood in the hallway as Jean reached them.

"Jean Farling?"

"Yes," she said, taking hold of Marsh's arm.

"Are you the wife of Dr. Michael Farling?"

She looked at Marsh, then each of the officers. "Yes I am."

Marsh felt her squeeze his arm and he put his hand over hers.

"Mrs. Farling, were you aware of your husband's whereabouts tonight?"

"Yes," Jean said. Marsh held his breath as she paused. "He had to leave. He – said he'd gotten a call – from his office, and he was on his way back to Syracuse."

Marsh exhaled in quiet relief.

"And he was operating the 1985 Nissan that's registered to him?"

"Yes."

"Mrs. Farling, we're here to regretfully inform you that, about three hours ago, your husband was involved in a fatal automobile accident."

Jean suddenly grew heavy on Marsh's arm and he helped her to the hallway bench beside the door.

337

"We're sorry it took us so long to notify you, but when we ran the plate we saw that he lived in Syracuse, New York and the phone number we were given turned out to be his office answering service. They told us you and your husband had been visiting at this address."

"What happened?" Marsh asked.

"Around two a.m. a motorist approaching from the other direction saw Dr. Farling's vehicle swerve to avoid a large deer. He apparently lost control, then went off the road and hit a utility pole."

Jean covered her mouth and closed her eyes.

Marsh wanted to know more, but didn't want to upset Jean any further.

Amanda came down the stairs dressed in jeans and a sweater.

"Again, Mrs. Farling, we extend our deepest sympathy. If you're up to it, we just have a few brief questions so we can finish our report and be on our way."

Jean didn't seem to hear and Marsh said, "Please come in." As they moved into the living room, he went to Amanda. "Michael's been killed in an accident," he said quietly

Her eyes widened.

"Marsh?" Helen called from her room. "What's going on? Is everything all right?"

"Go help Jean," Amanda said. "I'll take care of your mother."

***

Everything suddenly seemed in slow motion as Amanda went to Helen's room. She was sitting up in the lamplight.

"Who's here, Amanda? What's happened?"

338

"It's the police. Michael was involved in a car crash."

"Where is he? Is he okay?"

"They're talking to Jean right now. Let me help you up."

Michael was dead, Amanda told herself as she helped Helen into her robe and moved her to her wheelchair, yet none of this seemed real. When she went back to the kitchen, Jason was coming down the stairs. He saw the police sitting with his mother and looked frightened. Dylan, close behind him, started to cry. She guided them away from the living room.

"I couldn't stay up there anymore, Aunt Amanda. What's going on? Is my mom okay?"

"She's fine. They came to tell her Michael's had an accident." Dylan tugged on her sweater and she picked him up.

"Did Uncle Michael get dead, Manda?"

She shushed him and kissed his cheek. "We don't know what happened yet." Jason had more questions as Helen emerged from her room. "We'll know more when your mom and Uncle Marsh are done talking to the police," Amanda said. "How about some hot chocolate while we wait?"

Jason reluctantly agreed and settled into the breakfast nook with Dylan while Amanda prepared the hot chocolate and put on a pot of coffee. No one would be going back to bed.

***

About twenty minutes later the police had completed their paperwork over a gratefully accepted cup of coffee. As they left, Marsh followed them onto the porch.

"I didn't want to ask in front of my sister, but can you give me any more information about what happened?"

The officer sighed. "Well, it happened about fifty miles from here. A heavy rain had passed through the area a short time before the accident, so there was some ponding on the road, but we know Dr. Farling must have been traveling at an excessive rate of speed to have hit the pole as hard as he did. The car was cut in two and, due to the severity of his injuries, it appears that he died on impact."

Marsh lowered his eyes and nodded.

"Again, we're very sorry for the loss to you and your family, Sir."

They exchanged handshakes and Marsh watched them leave as he tried to process all that had happened. What he was left with was that his family had been visited by an unexpected evil that had been destroyed, all in the space of a few hours.

The screen door strained behind him and he turned as Jean came slowly onto the porch. She shivered in the morning chill and pulled her robe tighter. "What just happened?" she asked. "I can't believe this. I don't even know how I should feel."

Marsh put his arm around her as Amanda peeked through the door, then came out. "I can't hold Jason and your mother off much longer," she said. She stroked Jean's arm. "Are you okay?"

Jean nodded. "I'll be all right."

Marsh took a closer look at Amanda's face. The cut at the corner of her mouth and the bruise under her eye were indiscernible. He knew she had touched them up with make-up to avoid any questions from Helen or the boys and he loved her for it and for all the other ways she showed concern for his family.

"I suppose we'd better go inside," Jean said wearily.

"What are we going to tell them?" Marsh asked.

Jean paused, slowly shaking her head.

Amanda thought of something. "Does anybody besides us have to know what *really* happened tonight?"

The three looked at each other.

Jean drew a breath. "What happened was, we had a nice evening, went to bed and Michael got a call from his office and had to leave." She kept looking at Marsh and Amanda.

"That's all I know," Amanda said.

Marsh slipped his arm around her. "Me, too. Let's go."

Chapter 21
Christmas it Is

"I can't believe it," Helen said. She held a restless Dylan on her lap as the six of them sat at the breakfast nook. "The only good thing you can say about such a tragic accident is that Michael was on his way to help someone else."

Jean's gaze flickered over Marsh's and Amanda's faces. "I have to call Michael's relatives," she said, "and then Jason and I will head back to make the funeral arrangements."

"You seem so calm, Jean," Helen said. "I suppose it hasn't hit you yet."

"I suppose not."

Dylan yawned and stretched, having processed the news of Michael's death as much as a six-year-old could. "Grandma, can I go watch cartoons now?"

"It's almost eight," Amanda said. "Let's get you dressed first."

"I'll give him a hand." Marsh got up and Amanda sensed he was glad for the diversion. "Come on, Scoot." He lifted Dylan from Helen's lap. "I'll take care of this trouble-maker," he growled. Dylan began to giggle as he threw him over his shoulder and carried him toward the stairs.

"Why don't you go ahead and get dressed too?" Jean said to Jason. "I'm fine," she added when he looked at her with concern.

"Okay," he said quietly as he got up and followed Marsh.

"How do you think Jason's taking this?" Helen asked. "Was he close to Michael?"

"He admired and respected him," Jean said. "Michael treated him well."

"And I trust he always treated *you* well." Helen's voice held a mother's need to be sure.

Jean looked at her. "Yes, he treated me well. I had no complaints." There was a robotic tone in her response and Amanda cringed as Michael's words came back to her: *Jean's a very good wife. No complaints there.* How could someone who cared about his wife even think of doing what he'd intended to do to Amanda? Where did such evil in a person come from? If she wanted to get over this, she needed to let go of the lingering questions. The answers, if there were any, had died with Michael in the same way he had intended to take her – suddenly, violently.

"I guess I'll go get ready for the day," Helen said as she turned her wheelchair from the table. "Lord knows, it's already started without me." She went into her room, closing the door.

The kitchen was quiet as Jean and Amanda were left at the table.

Amanda touched Jean's arm. "How are you doing?"

343

Jean's tired, red eyes filled with tears. "I should be asking *you* that question. I'm so sorry for what happened, Amanda – for what could have happened – and I'm sorry for myself for being such a fool." Her voice broke. "And I feel guilty because I can't feel any grief yet for losing Michael."

"You're in shock."

"No, actually I'm surprised at how logically I'm thinking. It's as if my head is clear for the first time in a couple of years. Why didn't I see who Michael really was?"

Amanda chose her words carefully. "Maybe he had issues that kept you from really knowing him."

Jean nodded. "I can see that now. I was swept off my feet because I wanted to be. I decided it was my turn to be happy and fulfilled. I had a handsome, successful man who found me attractive and came complete with a six-figure income and the country club membership I'd always dreamed of. Only I hardly ever saw him and I was never comfortable at the country club, and Jason hated his new school and all the snobby kids. But I was determined to make it work because I deserved it. You're a lot younger than me, Amanda, but have you ever felt that way? Like you deserved something good in your life for a change?"

"Sure. That's why I took this job. When my engagement was broken, all my plans fell through. I had to start over and find out who I really was, and Dylan set me straight on that pretty quick."

They laughed.

"I'm glad your change turned out well and that you and Marsh found each other." Jean's expression became wistful as she looked out the window. "Marsh and I were very close growing up. We didn't have a father – Mother raised us on her own."

"I remember reading about that many years ago. Your father died in the Korean War?"

"Yes, before Marsh was a year old. We were always there for each other, but I never imagined he'd become a superstar and almost disappear from my life the way he did. I've been missing my brother for a long time and part of me is still angry with him. Do you know, besides a couple of backstage visits when he was still performing, I only saw him once in the years he and Carrie were in hiding – and I'd never met Dylan until yesterday. His fans praised him for his kindness and sensitivity but as far as I was concerned, his fame only made him selfish and thoughtless and he was never around for his family."

"But he's here now," Amanda said gently. "And I know he wishes he could change his past, but he's finally accepting that he can't and I think he's beginning to forgive himself. Maybe someday you can forgive him, too."

Fresh tears rolled down Jean's cheeks as she looked at her hands. "I've already forgiven him and I know he cares by the way he's handled this." She sniffled and looked at Amanda. "The same way I can tell *you* care. I had my doubts about Marsh thinking he could trust anyone with his secret, but you've already been through the ultimate test." Jean lightly touched the hidden bruise under Amanda's eye. "You're even willing to cover your pain to protect all of us. I'm not so sure I could do that. I'm really glad he's found you. You're a godsend to all of us and I already know I'm gaining a great sister-in-law."

Amanda smiled. "What a coincidence! So am I."

***

It was around ten o'clock that morning when Amanda got back to her apartment. Jean had contacted Michael's relatives and had booked a flight home for her and Jason that afternoon. Amanda had offered to drive them to the airport, but Jean had insisted on calling a cab. "You've been through enough," she said. "I want you to get some rest."

Although there wasn't much out of place, the apartment felt different. She straightened the couch pillows and noticed the bloodied pen on the coffee table where Marsh had taken it from her. She took a few more steps and braved her bedroom doorway. In the daylight, the mussed bed covers and rumpled throw rugs looked harmless enough. Then she noticed the flecks of dried blood that began in a couple of spots on the bed cover and ended in a small, dark stain at her closet door. There was relatively little of it considering the struggle that had taken place here just hours ago. It was the blood of a man who no longer existed, the residue of a nightmare that would not return.

That was why she'd suggested to Jean that no one else needed to know about what had happened here last night. What good would it do to upset Helen about an incident that was over and would never happen again? Jason had no use for such information about his stepfather and Michael's trusting patients and fellow physicians had known only the best part of him – the skilled, highly esteemed surgeon he'd been.

The sunlight played across the floor and cast a carefree brightness over everything that had been violated. Refusing to let the feeling last any longer, she moved into the room and gathered the soiled bedspread into her arms. She carried it into the living room where she picked up the pen and let it fall into the random folds, then took the bundle out the kitchen door, down the outside stairs and stuffed it into the trash can, jamming the lid on. Filled with a sense of triumph, she went back inside and grabbed a bucket of hot, soapy water and a cloth to wash away any lingering traces of the evil that had visited her. Now it was her room again. She wouldn't let it be anything but a peaceful, beautiful place where she and Marsh had made love for the first time.

The phone rang and she picked up the extension on her bedstand. "I'm fine," she said, expecting to hear Marsh's voice.

"Amanda?" It was Angie. "What do you mean you're fine – are you okay?"

"Hi, Angie. It's so good to hear your voice," Amanda said. "I just thought you might be Marsh."

"But is anything wrong? Is your company still there?"

"Jean and Jason are leaving this afternoon," Amanda said. She took a breath. "Michael was killed in an accident last night."

"What? Oh my God – how awful! What happened?"

"He told Jean he'd had a call from his office and had to leave. I guess that was around one-thirty this morning. Then the Troopers came here around five-thirty to give Jean the news."

"Was another car involved?"

"No – he went off the road and hit a pole."

"That's unbelievable! Everyone must be devastated!"

"I don't think it's set in yet, but Jean's going to be okay."

"This makes the reason for my call seem silly, now."

"Why? What's up?"

"Well, it's probably not a good time, but since Dylan wasn't going to be in school today, Conner wanted to know if we could pick him up and bring him over to work on their class project and have supper with us tonight, but Marsh will probably want him to stay home, with what's going on."

"Not necessarily," Amanda said. "We'd arranged for Dylan to stay home from school today so he'd have a little more time with the company before they left, but there's been so much disruption with what's happened, it might be good for him to get away for awhile."

"Could you check with Marsh and let me know? We can come by around three-thirty, after I pick up Conner from school."

"Sounds like a good idea," Amanda said. "I'll call you back."

When she dialed the house, Marsh answered. "You slipped out on me," he teased softly so no one else could hear him. "I miss you."

"Miss you, too. I'm just doing a little cleaning up here."

"I should be helping you."

"No, it's okay. I needed to be alone with this sooner or later, but Angie called." Amanda told him about Angie's offer.

"He's been kind of anxious today with all this strange stuff going on," Marsh said, "and he's not too happy about Jason leaving, so it might be a good idea for him to go to

Conner's for awhile. When are you coming back to the house?"

Amanda smiled at the wistfulness in his voice. "I just have a little more to do here and I'll be back before Jean leaves."

"It doesn't seem natural for you to be over there anymore, Amanda."

"I'll be back shortly." Amanda hung up the phone, aware that she felt the same way. It was becoming difficult to justify their reasons for living apart.

***

"Conner – did you know my Uncle Michael got dead in an accident?"

"Yeah – my mom told me!"

Dylan and Conner's voices were accompanied by the slamming of doors as they got into the back seat of Angie's car.

She turned to Marsh and Amanda where they stood on the porch. "I'm so sorry for what happened," she said.

"We'll get through it," Marsh replied. "Thanks for taking Dylan for awhile. He could use a distraction."

"I'm sure you all could. How's your sister doing?"

"She's coping. She left about an hour ago."

Angie shook her head. "What a shame. David feels bad about this, too. Let us know if you need anything, okay?"

"Your taking Dylan for awhile is a big help," Marsh said. "Thanks, Angie."

"I'll have him back by around seven," Angie said as she headed to the car. "See you then."

Dylan was too busy chattering to notice Marsh and Amanda's waves as the car headed down the driveway.

Marsh draped his arm around Amanda's shoulders as they went back inside. The house was quiet. "Where's Mother?" he asked.

"She went to her room for a nap a few minutes ago," Amanda said. "She told me it would be a long one because she's really tired from all that's happened."

Marsh folded her into a hug. "So let's take stock of the current situation," he said, looking serious.

"What do you mean?"

"Well, let's see – Jean and Jason are on their way home, Angie just drove away with Dylan and Mother's taking a nap – a long one, right?"

Amanda looked up to catch his smirk. "Maybe *I* need a nap, too –" she teased before his kiss ended her sentence.

"Come upstairs with me," he whispered, his warm lips moist against her ear.

They gave in to breathless kisses as they reached the top of the stairs and crossed the upstairs hallway. They had barely reached Marsh's room before their fingers began to frantically undo buttons, a belt buckle, a bra clasp, as Amanda was consumed by an urgent desire and anticipation that carried her outside of herself and into a blissful realm where each ravenous need would find perfect satisfaction.

She could feel Marsh's body reacting to her hunger for him as he kissed and stroked her into helpless surrender. For the first time, their lovemaking took on a demanding edge that crossed any physical boundaries left between them. Something had turned their new love into a unique bond that left no room for inhibition or uncertainty. Another man had threatened to not only rob them of their oneness as a couple, but had he known the truth about Marsh, he could have revealed his identity and destroyed the security of their lives as a family. The awareness of this in her subconscious spurred Amanda's desire to give herself completely to Marsh and she sensed the same need in him. It was an affirmation that they were safe, their life together intact.

Afterwards, they lay under the sheet in each other's arms, their gasps quieting into deep inhalations of savored ecstasy.

"Is it my imagination?" Marsh murmured, "or are we getting better at this?"

"Much better," Amanda moaned softly.

He sighed through her hair and kissed her shoulder. "I've been thinking."

"About what?"

"About how Dylan seems to be okay with us getting married and about how winter's coming."

"What's winter got to do with it?"

"Well, I don't want you to think I'm trying to rush things, but those conjugal visits at the carriage house could get rough with three feet of snow on the ground."

"Conjugal visits?" Amanda smiled and bit her lip. "Well I've been thinking that a June wedding would be nice."

"June?"

"Yes – outside in the yard."

There was a pause in which she knew Marsh was struggling to find some enthusiasm. "Sure, if that's what you want."

"But then, I suppose a Christmas wedding in front of the fireplace would be just as nice."

Marsh brightened. "Christmas? That's a great idea!"

She laughed. "I thought you might like that."

"Then Christmas it is. I don't want us to live apart any longer than we have to."

"Neither do I."

"You belong here, Amanda. I've never felt so sure of anything."

She caressed the side of his face. "I've never been so in love – except maybe with that one other guy."

"What other guy?"

"The one with the guitar."

"Oh, him. He's not so hot."

"Well, he was okay till you came along, but you play the guitar very well, too."

"I'm the real deal."

"You're the whole package. Everything I ever wanted."

"Okay, darlin', hold onto that thought." Marsh sat up and leaned toward the bedstand. Amanda heard the drawer open. She pulled herself up, holding the sheet against her as he turned back to her. "I've had this for awhile, but I was waiting for the right time. I know I should be doing this over dinner at a fancy restaurant or something, but I hope you'll think now's the right time."

Amanda's heartbeat quickened as she saw the small, black velvet box in his hand. He gently lifted the lid with his thumb and she opened her mouth in speechless surprise at the sight of the exquisitely delicate diamond ring.

"Amanda Morgan – will you marry me – at Christmas?"

She laughed through tears of joy. "So it comes with conditions?"

He took it from the box and held her hand as he slid it onto her finger. "The only condition is that you let me love you and care for you the rest of your life."

She gazed at the gem as it shimmered in the gold, late afternoon light. "I have a condition of my own."

"What's that?"

"That you never keep your music inside of you again."

"You *are* my music now. But I promise to get it all down on paper."

"*And* that you'll still take me to that fancy restaurant?"

"You're quite the haggler, aren't you? Okay, fancy restaurant included."

"Then yes, I'll marry you – at Christmas."

He grinned. "*This* Christmas?"

"Oh, was it *this* Christmas?" She giggled as he pushed her back onto the pillow.

"Looks like we have a few more conditions to work out."

Chapter 22
Dance With Me

Mid-December, 1985

"You look like a princess, Amanda." Helen's voice was filled with a myriad of emotions.

"Marsh's princess," Angie said as she swept Amanda's hair over her ear and carefully fastened it with a delicate, pearl comb.

"Oh, that's perfect!" Jean took Amanda's shoulders and turned her toward the mirror. "Just look at you!"

"It's lovely. Thank you," Amanda said, joining the assessment of her reflection with the three admiring faces around her.

"Simple and sooo elegant!" Jean remarked as the others agreed. "I wish Vicki could have been here, but she and Will had to be at his mom's seventieth birthday bash today. They want to come and meet you after the holidays."

"I'll look forward to it." Amanda smoothed the low-cut, draped neckline and touched the pearl cameo necklace at her throat that had been a wedding gift from Marsh along with her matching pearl earrings. She stood up from Helen's dressing table bench and turned slightly as the cream-colored silk gown fell around her. Form-fitting, it draped her figure gracefully and a discreet slit opened to just above her right knee. She had chosen something unpretentious and comfortable, wanting to look and feel as natural on her wedding day as was her relationship with Marsh.

There was a flash as she took the bouquet of red roses trimmed with white poinsettias from Angie, and David grinned around the door. "Gotcha!" He came in holding his camera as a look of reverence replaced his teasing smile. "You look beautiful, Mi'Lady," he said, using the nickname he'd given her from the time they'd met. "Marsh is one lucky guy."

"He's lucky to have you as his friend and his Best Man," Amanda said as he kissed her cheek. "How's he doing, by the way?"

"Well, he already spilled some coffee on his shirt, but his jacket should cover it okay."

"Don't tell us that stuff now!" Angie rebuked him. "Now go upstairs and make sure Marsh's door is closed so we can bring Amanda up there."

"I still think this is silly," Amanda said.

"No it's not!" Jean was adamant. "You have to come down the stairs when Marsh sees you. It's required bridal etiquette."

"Yeah, kiddo – you have to make your entrance!" Angie agreed.

"Oh, can't I just walk in?" Amanda asked.

Jean sighed. "Mother?"

Amanda looked to Helen for the final word.

"Go with the entrance," Helen said. "I know it will please Marsh very much. And thank you for getting ready in my room, Amanda. I couldn't have made it upstairs and I would have hated to miss it."

"Never." Amanda gave her a quick hug. "Besides, you started all this, you know."

"Yes, and I knew what I was doing," Helen said proudly. "I just hope you two will be able to get away tonight."

As a wedding gift, Helen had booked a luxury suite at an historical inn a couple of hours away. It was to be a two-night stay, as they didn't want to be away from Dylan for too long. The weather forecast over the past couple of days had worsened from a few inches of snow to a winter storm warning, and the snow and wind had increased from early that morning to blizzard conditions in the afternoon, expected to continue overnight.

With Marsh and Amanda's four o'clock wedding less than an hour away it was already growing dark outside and the minister had not arrived. The plowing service had cleared the driveway in the late morning, but it was rapidly filling in again.

After making sure they wouldn't be seen, the girls guided Amanda through the kitchen toward the stairway. As they passed the dining room archway, Amanda could see the large table set with Helen's Royal Albert china, the small, elegant three-tier wedding cake and the bottles of champagne and wine chilling in the silver ice bucket.

When they reached the bottom of the stairs, Jason looked up from where he sat in the living room practicing on his guitar. With a little help from his Uncle Mark, he had written a special song for the wedding. He stood up. "Wow – you look beautiful, Aunt Amanda," he said.

"And you look very handsome, Jason. I can't wait to hear your song." Amanda took a moment to gaze around the living room that glowed with the warmth of the Christmas season. Fresh pine boughs woven with red velvet bows and tiny white lights graced the mantle while bright orange flames danced in the fireplace. The stairway banister was decorated with the same fragrant garland and lights.

She looked through the sunporch doorway at the tall, dazzling Christmas tree she had joyfully decorated with Dylan and Marsh under Helen's fussy supervision a couple of days earlier. It shone like a jewel, reflecting off the small, snow-laced window panes and clearly visible from the road. She breathed in the awareness that this was now her home and these people were her new family and friends, the things she had always longed for, growing up. And the man of her dreams, ironically past and present, was waiting upstairs to become her husband. No fantasy could have matched the reality that surrounded her now.

"Come on, Amanda – let's go."

She let Angie and Jean whisk her upstairs to wait in the guest room.

***

Dylan and Conner tussled on the bed as Dave straightened Marsh's bow tie in front of the mirror. "Hey, knock it off, guys. We've only got twenty minutes till the ceremony. Don't mess up your suits now or we'll all be in trouble." He finished with the tie and frowned at Marsh. "Anything wrong? You're awfully quiet all of a sudden."

Marsh turned and looked into the mirror. "I don't expect you to understand this..."

"Try me."

Marsh shook his head slowly. "I know it sounds crazy, but I'm afraid I'll wake up any time now, and none of this will be true."

Dave clapped him on the shoulder. "Listen, I don't know a lot of details about what's happened to you so far, but I know it's been real hard for you and Dylan. If you ask me, you're due for some happiness and you deserve all the good things that are happening today."

Marsh looked at Dave's reflection beside him and grinned. "That's why I keep you around."

There was a tap at the door and Jean looked in. "Reverend Simmons just got here and he says the roads are almost impassable. He's heading back as soon as the ceremony's over."

"It doesn't sound good for your trip tonight, buddy," Dave said.

"No problem. Amanda and I have our own honeymoon suite just across the yard if we need it."

Dave winked and turned to the boys who were sitting side-by-side on the bed but still poking each other and giggling. "Okay, Dylan, remember how you carry the pillow with the rings and you hold Amanda's hand?"

Dylan nodded. "Manda says I'm giving her away to Daddy."

358

"That's right, Scoot," Marsh said as he reached for his white tuxedo jacket. "But we both get to keep her."

Jean went to Marsh and put her arms around him. "You look very handsome. Good luck, little brother."

"Thanks, sis – love you."

"Is Conner ready to usher me downstairs?"

Dave looked at Conner. "Okay, big boy, now's your chance to shine. Remember to hang onto the railing and for God's sake don't trip."

Conner nodded solemnly and took Jean's outstretched hand as they went into the hallway.

"Such a tragedy, what happened to her husband," Dave said. "Do you think she's doing okay?"

"She's doing well. She's got the house in Syracuse up for sale and she's planning to move here when Jason's school year is over. She'd like to get a place nearby."

"That makes sense."

"She never liked Syracuse and neither did Jason. They'd rather be with us."

"And what about that surgery on your leg?"

"Jean's got me set up to see one of Michael's associates in February. Michael had told them about me and they want to take a look and see what they can do. I wasn't sure I wanted to pursue it, but Amanda insists I give it a chance."

Angie appeared next. "We need Dylan and the rings in the other room," she said as she walked over to Marsh. "A kiss for good luck," she added as he bent for her to kiss his cheek.

"How's Amanda doing?" he asked.

"You know Amanda. The rest of us are more nervous than she is. We're all ready so you two need to head downstairs."

***

As Angie guided Dylan through the door, his eyes widened when he saw Amanda. Afraid of being overwhelmed by her feelings, she'd willed herself to not cry until after the ceremony but nothing could have prepared her for the sight of the little blond boy in the miniature white tuxedo, holding the pillow with the wedding rings.

She lowered herself and opened her arms. "Come here, sweetie."

When he saw her tears, Dylan suddenly looked shy as he moved toward her. "Why are you sad, Manda?" he asked as she hugged him tightly.

"I'm not sad. I've never been happier." She held him in front of her and smiled. "Is it okay if I marry Daddy today?"

He stepped back. "Why did you wait so long?"

Angie laughed.

"We're not waiting anymore," Amanda said. "Are you ready to take me to him?"

"Yeah, but I'm hungry, Manda."

"We'll eat in a few minutes after the ceremony. We have lots of good food for our party." Amanda took his hand and they moved into the hallway as the sound of Jason's guitar wafted up the stairs. Marsh's bedroom door stood open. The time was here and he was waiting for her downstairs.

"Good luck," Angie said as she kissed her cheek. "Thanks for asking me to be your Matron of Honor."

"No one else would do," Amanda said.

Angie was pretty in her burgundy gown, and her small bouquet with white roses and red poinsettias in contrast to Amanda's. She took one more look before she slowly started down the stairs to the soft, poignant tune Jason played.

***

From his place in front of the mantle between the minister and David, Marsh watched Angie until she'd almost reached the bottom of the stairs. A rustle of silk drew his gaze back to the top where he caught a glimpse of Amanda's white sequined high heels and the flash of her slender leg through the slit of her dress as she started down the stairs. At the sight of Dylan beside her, holding her hand and clutching the heart-shaped pillow with the rings, Marsh's throat ached. His son and the woman he loved were coming to him, to stand in front of this minister, so they could become a family.

When they reached the living room and Dylan saw his father, he beamed with the look of a boy proudly performing his first manly duty.

Marsh bent and shook his hand, then hugged him. "You did good, Scoot." He straightened, then took Amanda's hands and drew her to him. Her tear-filled eyes reflected his love and held the promise of no more loneliness or pain. As Jason's song faded into silence, the muted sounds of his mother's sniffles brought him back to the moment.

Reverend Simmons, tall and silver-haired in his long robe, looked into each of their faces and smiled. He pulled off his glasses and looked around at the small gathering. "This is truly a joyful occasion," he said. "And the fact that Amanda and Mark have chosen the Christmas season to take their wedding vows makes it all the more memorable. Mark's mother has been a parishioner of mine for many years, but over the past couple of months she's been coming each Sunday with Mark, her grandson Dylan and Mark's lovely fiancé, Amanda. I couldn't be more delighted that they've chosen to become a family in the eyes of God. I don't yet know Mark and Amanda as well as I hope to in the future, but I do know they've been brought together by fate, they're grateful for that and, with Dylan, they will make a strong, loving family. So let us begin."

As Marsh and Amanda looked into each other's eyes and exchanged their vows and rings the only other sounds were the wind outside and the occasional crackle of the fire. At the words, "I now pronounce you man and wife," they embraced and shared a lingering kiss to everyone's applause.

Dylan tugged at them before Marsh swept him up between them. "Can we eat now?" he asked.

"There's a kid who's got his priorities in order," Dave said as everyone laughed.

After hugs and handshakes, Reverend Simmons asked for his coat.

Helen urged him to stay and eat, but although he didn't have far to go, he was anxious to get home in the storm. While Jean packed some food for him to take before he said his goodbyes, Jason and Dave went outside to clean off his car and make sure he got out of the driveway.

"Now I *know* you two aren't going anywhere tonight," Dave announced a few minutes later as he and Jason came back looking like snowmen. "I'm not even sure *we're* going anywhere and we're only ten minutes away."

"We've got lots of room for everyone," Helen said, always glad for a houseful.

The champagne was poured and Dave toasted Marsh and Amanda before they nibbled on hors d'oeuvres, then sat at the table for a delicious meal of beef stroganoff that Jean had simmered in the crockpot all day. Dylan and Conner were just as happy chomping on the cheeseburgers Angie had made for them.

After a leisurely, laughter-filled dinner Amanda and Marsh were urged to cut their wedding cake amid more of David's camera flashes. By the time dessert had been served it was going on nine o'clock.

"Jason and me are going over to shovel the carriage house steps," Dave told Marsh. "Then I'll drive you and Amanda over."

"Thanks for everything, Dave." Marsh gave him a quick hug. "You're a good friend."

***

It was after ten o'clock when Dave slowly drove the newlyweds down the snow-drifted driveway to the carriage house and got out to help them up the slippery steps.

"You two better not have a fight tonight because you're stuck here," he teased as they reached the apartment door. When he was sure they were safely inside, he headed back to the house.

As Amanda and Marsh closed the door they pulled off their coats, still shivering, before melting into the warmth of each other's arms. "Are you disappointed that we couldn't get away?" he asked between kisses.

"Not at all. I'd rather be here tonight. Of course, if Dylan had his way, he'd be here with us."

"What was it he said?" Marsh tried to remember.

"He asked if he and Conner could come to our sleepover so we could all have popcorn and pizza."

They laughed.

"It's all so simple for him," Marsh said. "To be that innocent again. I hope he's okay when we leave tomorrow."

"I've talked to him about it and with Jason and Jean staying until we get back, I think he'll be okay. Your mother was really glad we were able to change the reservations." Amanda shivered again.

"It's pretty cold in here. We'd better turn up the heat," Marsh said as they made their way to the living room.

Amanda turned on a lamp and the room took on a soft glow as Marsh went to the thermostat. "I just thought of something we can do," she said, going to the cabinet that held her tape collection.

"I've been thinking about *that* all day," Marsh teased, still absorbed in adjusting the temperature.

She found the Marshall Stewart tape and put it into the player. The first few chords of "If a Tree Falls" filled the room and Marsh turned in surprise.

Amanda held out her arms. "Dance with me?"

He gave her look of mock reproach. "Are you still listening to that guy?"

"I love him. Both of him," she said as Marsh put his arms around her and they began to gently sway to the music.

"Well one of you is all *I* need."

"You mean all you can handle."

He began to sing softly into her ear and she closed her eyes and basked in the voices of her idol and her husband, blended into one sound, carrying her heart on a journey that culminated here in this moment.

"That's a lovely dress, Mrs. Sterner," he murmured during the instrumental, "but it's served its purpose, don't you think?"

She felt his fingers on the zipper at the back of her gown. "Just keep dancing, Mr. Sterner. I'm all yours when the song is over."

"Don't tell me you're still in love with that guy."

She took his face in her hands and kissed him tenderly. "Haven't you heard? I'm an incurable fan."

Epilogue

October, 2012

Veteran newsman Don Prentice adjusted the tiny microphone on his lapel, shuffled his notes one more time and looked over at the young man sitting across from him. "Are you ready?"

Dylan Sterner checked his microphone, uncrossed his legs and gripped the arms of his chair as though he was on a plane, taxiing down a runway. "Ready as I'll ever be, but go easy on me, okay?"

At thirty-three, Dylan was a tall, slender reflection of his father. He had Marsh's bright, blue eyes and curly blond hair which he wore close-cropped, never able to tame the stray curls around his forehead. He had the fine-boned facial structure that had been hidden under his father's dyed hair and beard, and he had Marshall Stewart's speaking voice, which until now had been lost on an unsuspecting audience as he reported the day's news.

But that was where the similarities ended. Where Marsh had been a quiet, soft-spoken man, Dylan, true to his childhood chattiness, was lively and boisterous. Where Marsh had never been comfortable in the limelight, Dylan enjoyed being "out there" and was in his element addressing millions of people on national television. Where Marsh had best expressed himself through music, Dylan had found his outlet in the written and spoken word. Yet Marsh could not have been more proud or amazed that he could watch his son on his favorite evening news program.

The countdown to air-time began and on cue, Don turned to the camera.

"Good evening. For the past eight years, we here at NBC News and you in our audience, have known Dylan Sterner as an award-winning reporter, covering high-profile stories from the wars in Afghanistan and Iraq to the big issues here at home. After gaining attention for his reporting skills at his local newspaper while pursuing his degree in Broadcast Journalism, he started out at our affiliate station in Hartford, Connecticut at the age of twenty-five and it seemed there was no holding him back.

"All of us who've had the pleasure of knowing Dylan have found him to be a hard-working, loyal friend, a family man devoted to his wife and three children and passionate about finding and reporting the truth in every story he covers. Yes, we thought we knew Dylan Sterner well. But unless you've been living under a rock these past few weeks, you were as stunned as we were to discover that Dylan Sterner has lived his own sensational story, which he has chronicled in his recently published book entitled, "My Father's Song." Ladies and Gentlemen, let me introduce to you, Dylan Sterner, son of music icon Marshall Stewart."

Don turned back to the subject of his interview. "This must be a bitter-sweet experience for you, Dylan, with the death of your father this past June and then the release and huge success of this book you've written about him."

Dylan crossed his legs again as he began to relax now that the interview was underway. "Yes, it's all a little surreal with everyone talking about him now and in many ways, it's as if he's still here."

"So, Dylan, you must know how this book has not only shocked the world, but shaken a lot of people, some of them your closest friends, who never suspected you were anyone but the Dylan Sterner we've all come to know."

"Yes, I've had some interesting reactions, mostly good. But the fact is, I was brought up with the name Sterner. My parents had their names legally changed when my father made the decision in 1975 to go into hiding. At that time, they went overseas and my grandmother changed her name and moved to a new place, as well."

"You've explained everything in the book, but for those who haven't read it yet, when did you first become aware of the fact that your father was someone else?"

"I was pretty clueless for most of my childhood, and in retrospect, I suppose there were a few red flags. But it wasn't until I was a teenager and started paying attention to music that I had questions. I discovered an oldies radio station that played some of the Marshall Stewart classics and would give little biographical tidbits about him. By then I'd started to notice some similarities, especially when I heard Dad playing his guitar. He didn't play much when I was around, and always shrugged it off as a hobby, but I knew he was much more into it than that. So I started going on-line and delving further and I figured it out."

"And you confronted him with it?"

"Yeah. I was about sixteen by then and finally one day I got up the nerve to just come out with it at the dinner table like, 'Are you Marshall Stewart?'"

"I know it's all in the book, but give us a sense of what happened."

"He looked me in the eye, man-to-man and said, 'Yes I am, and I'm sorry, Dylan.'"

"Just like that?"

"Just like that and I could tell he'd been expecting it all along and he was prepared for it."

"And what was your reaction? Were you angry?"

"Yeah. I didn't speak to him for a couple of weeks. I guess I was more hurt than angry, because he'd kept it from me all that time. It was that typical teenage '*I'll* show *you*' crap, and he gave me my space to work it out, but then my step-mother took me aside and talked to me."

"Ah – the lovely Amanda you so eloquently describe in the book."

"Yes. If it weren't for her, I don't think my Dad or I would have made it. Anyway, she and I had a long talk when Dad wasn't around and she put it all into perspective. She said he'd planned to tell me when he thought I could handle it and she made me realize that I'd had no use for that information until then. She explained why they needed to trust me with the truth, and said she had faith in me and knew I wouldn't let my father down. What I was left with was nothing but gratitude that my Dad had protected me from a lot of baggage I didn't need when I was growing up. Thanks to him and Amanda, I had a normal childhood and a solid home life."

"You describe a great childhood, once you and your father returned to the States and he married Amanda. They took an active part in your schooling, your interest in sports, and you talk about how much you enjoyed the family camping trips where you saw a lot of the country."

"Yes, I had a best friend who was also an only child and my parents were friends with his parents, so we kind of grew up like brothers and our families did lots of things together. It was great."

"You also tell the beautiful love story that developed between your father and Amanda when your grandmother hired her to look after you. You were only six years old at the time."

"Yes – my father wanted no part of having anyone around who might recognize him, but my grandmother was adamant about having someone to look after me, because he was still grieving and withdrawn."

"And you tell about what a matchmaker your grandmother was."

Dylan laughed. "Yeah, after she passed away, my dad found Amanda's job resume, and she stated right on it that she was an incurable Marshall Stewart fan. That's when we knew Grandma had a plan."

"And when did you gain insight into your father's reasons for disappearing and the tragic death of your mother?"

"The older I got, the more questions I had and once I knew the truth about who he was, Dad was more willing to open up about his past. Then, about a year ago, he was diagnosed with a rare form of liver cancer."

"And how old was he by then?"

"He was sixty-two. He turned sixty-three this past January. When he got sick, he felt an urgent need to get everything straight with his past, and that included apologizing to his fans and offering an explanation for what he'd done. That had always eaten at him, the idea that he'd let a lot of people down. So he asked if I would write his story. He knew it would drastically change my life if I did, and said he'd understand if I didn't want to take it on."

"What did you think?"

"As overwhelming as the idea was, I knew I was the only person he could trust and that he needed to have his story told to validate his life. I knew that was the only thing that would give him closure and peace."

"Did he get to see the book?"

"Yes, he got to see the final draft before it was published and it gave him a great sense of relief. He died peacefully and I think it was because, as I explain in the book, he'd felt so much guilt over the death of my mother that he never expected a second chance at love or happiness and he had twenty-seven years with Amanda and grew in his relationship with me."

"So would it be accurate to say that, despite the circumstances, your father died a happy man?"

"Absolutely. Happy and fulfilled."

"When you say 'fulfilled', a big part of that was because of his music, wasn't it?"

"Yes."

"Tell us about that."

"Well, when my parents went into hiding, my father left his music behind. Then when things got bad between him and my mother, he blamed himself and told me later he'd had times he wished he'd never picked up a guitar."

"But that was just the guilt talking, wasn't it?"

"Definitely, because ten years later when he fell in love with Amanda, he said it was like opening the floodgates and he couldn't write the music fast enough."

"So he was composing and playing his guitar again."

"All the time. And that's when Amanda encouraged him to record it."

"And how was that possible?"

"My father had a small recording studio built into one of the rooms at home."

"Did you find that unusual?"

"No too much. I was still a kid and most of that stuff went on when I was at school."

"That must have cost a fortune."

"It did, and as much as he loved recording again, he questioned whether it was worthwhile."

"But he kept at it?"

"Yes, Amanda insisted and he valued her judgment. Then when he was diagnosed with the cancer, he realized it was possible to have his work released after he was gone."

"And he had a special purpose for that, didn't he?"

"Yes, the set of four CD's will be out before Christmas and, as with the book, all proceeds will go to a fund he established for wounded war veterans."

"And what made him decide to do that?"

"My grandfather died in the Korean War when my dad was just ten months old, so he had first-hand experience with what families of soldiers go through in war times. He was deeply affected when soldiers came home from Iraq and Afghanistan, coping with injuries that would have killed them in the past, and he was appalled at what little help was available to them and their families. He decided to offer the new music he'd recorded and donate the proceeds as a way of helping others."

"And, as you say in the book, he had a sense of his life coming full circle."

"Yes, he felt he was able to give something back by doing what he loved, and he was comfortable with it going for a specific cause and not being about him."

"Well, Dylan, the world is still reeling with the unprecedented headlines that Marshall Stewart, who spent all those years hiding 'in plain sight', has just passed away and has left us an entire collection of new music. Your book, 'My Father's Song', is already headed to the top of the Best Sellers list and you're in great demand on the talk show circuit these days. Thanks for giving us your first interview. Where will you go from here?"

Dylan grinned broadly. "Home. Meghan and the kids and I are going for a few days to see Manda."

"You say in the book that you still call her Manda, as you did in your childhood."

"That's my name for her. No one else can call her that."
Dylan winked toward the camera. "Love you, Manda."

***

Curled up on the living room couch, Amanda blew a kiss
to Dylan's image on the TV screen.

From beside her, Angie squeezed her hand. "You did
good with that kid of yours."

"And now he's a beautiful man," Amanda said.

"Just like his dad," Dave added from the chair across
from them. "Marsh would be proud."

Amanda sighed. "I'm proud enough for both of us." At
fifty-three, she was a thinner, sharper-featured version of the
girl Marsh had fallen in love with. There were light crinkles
at the corners of her eyes from years of laughter and lines in
her forehead to attest to equal parts of worry. Her auburn hair
was lighter, tinged with hints of impending gray, but worn in
a short, jaunty cut that surrounded her face with youthful
appeal.

Dave shook his head. "I still can't believe I was Marsh's
best buddy all those years and never knew who he really was.
When he told me a month before he died, I thought I was
dreaming. Then he asked me to forgive him." Dave's voice
broke. "I told him there was nothing to forgive. I loved the
guy like a brother."

"And I finally found out why you couldn't tell me
everything about your life with Marsh," Angie added to
Amanda. "He was lucky to find someone as loyal as you."

Amanda wrapped her arms around herself and looked
over at the shiny, twelve-string Gibson with the intricately
beaded strap, mounted on a stand beside the fireplace. On the

374

mantel above, were the Grammy and gold record for "If a Tree Falls".

"No, I was the lucky one," she said softly, gazing at the instrument that had been the voice of Marsh's soul. "I was there when he found his music again."

About the Author

I've dreamed of being an author since I was ten years old. Born with the urge to express my ideas before I had words, I would fold a piece of paper into eight squares and draw a story. One way or another, I had to get it down. With the publication of my first novel, ***If a Tree Falls***, I admit to being a "late bloomer" but allow that, at times, life got in the way.

In my adolescence, I wrote "Beatle stories", in which I made up fictionalized romantic adventures for the music idols of my time. I always had an audience of a few friends at lunch time in the school cafeteria who wanted to hear the latest saga of the "Fab Four". Although it may have seemed a waste of time to not devote my energy to writing "serious fiction", I was still learning about characterization, plot and dialogue.

I took all the creative writing and literature courses I could, and after graduating from community college, I worked as a copy setter for a local newspaper and was given my own column, "Speaking of the Arts", in which I reviewed movies, entertainment and interviewed area artists and musicians.

While marriage, work, and managing my husband's photography studio kept me busy, at age thirty-two, a diagnosis of breast cancer changed everything. With the realization that my life would never be the same, I lost interest in both reading and writing fiction. I only wanted the truth. A grateful survivor after four recurrences and many surgeries, I co-facilitate the Mt. St. Mary's Hospital Breast Cancer Support Group. But I'm also a member of the Lewiston Writers Group, where I've found encouragement and inspiration and have rediscovered my passion.

If a Tree Falls is a modern day fairy tale that I had inside of me for years, and when I finally found the opportunity, writing it was an absolute joy. I'm presently working on my next novel and I look forward to writing many more.

***

Kathy Kifer lives in Lewiston, New York with her husband Al, and her beloved cats, Alex, Smokey, Millie and Amadeus.